CROWNS AND CURSES

The Paranormals of Ahl Book 3

ML CONKLIN

A Note from the Author

Hello, Reader.

Thanks again for reading this series. Crowns and Curses is the book three in the Paranormals of Ahl series. If you haven't read the first three books in the series (Book 2.5 is from Lily's perspective), I suggest you start there, or some things might not make sense.

Trigger warnings and heads-up:

1. A heavy reference to past child abuse.

2. References to torture.

3. Violence and death throughout the book.

4. Profanity.

5. A romantic theme between a dragon shifter and a mage.

6. I'm not a spicy writer. The love scene(s) end abruptly.

7. The romance has an age gap (I know some people don't like that).

CHAPTER ONE

WHENEVER I BELIEVED I was making progress in solving our problems, something new popped up, and everything shifted. In this case, there were two things. The first was the realization that Quin's new granddaughter was related to me. The second was Mat's strange behavior. I texted him as soon as Ara led the hybrids toward an antique sitting room, and he didn't answer. He hadn't replied to my messages since the battle, except for occasional single-word answers.

I slipped my phone into a pocket and focused on the vampires.

Tracy motioned toward the group. "I don't need to be part of this. I'm going to check on my dad's progress."

"Sure. See you at home later."

"Text if you need me."

I nodded, then trailed the group into Ara's mansion.

Quin didn't take his eyes off his new granddaughter, but kept his expression neutral. Ara's eyes glittered with excitement. The lack of boredom on her face made her look like a different person. I couldn't help but stare.

I took a chair and examined the pair of hybrid siblings. The mage-vampire hybrid tried to hide her nerves behind her puffed-out chest and attitude, but her clenched fists and rigid posture betrayed her.

A couple of inches shorter than me, we shared an unmistakable family resemblance. Even if I ignored the one gold and one red streak running down each side of her chestnut-colored hair. The shape of her eyes was the same as mine, and her cheekbones were like Mat's.

As far as her vampire side, her nose was Quin's, and her coloring resembled Jedediah's. My mother was so awful that it shouldn't have shocked me to learn she might have had a secret child. But it did. The question was how? Paranormals could only have children with their match. As far as I knew, my mother's match was my father. Not Jedediah.

I tore my gaze from the woman when the mage-shifter hybrid shifted in his seat. His brown hair was a mess, and his clothes were wrinkled. Intelligent amber eyes lazily examined us as if he wasn't even a little intimidated. I didn't need the staring contest to determine he was a dominant shifter. The power emanating from him made my nose itch.

"May we call you Liliana?" Quin asked.

"I hate that name. I'm Lily." The woman's eyes closed, and her face relaxed when his power ramped up. "Your magic feels amazing."

It had to be a vampire thing, because Quin's magic made me uneasy until I got used to it. Ara's made my skin crawl.

Ara's face lit up. "Thank you, dear. I am Ara, and this gentleman is my Consort, Tarquin. You may call me Meemaw."

Lily let out a strangled sound. She caught herself and waved a hand. "Okay. Should I call him Gramps?"

"You may call me—"

"Gramps is perfect!" Ara clasped her hands.

I bit back a laugh.

The hybrid, Lily, didn't bother hiding her smirk.

The shifter hybrid elbowed her in the ribs. "Stop it."

Lily's eyes locked on mine while I attempted to hide my amusement. "Feel free to call me Jenella or Jen. Either is fine."

She pointed to the shifter hybrid. "This is my adopted brother, Alex."

My phone buzzed with a text from Mat saying he was at the gate. I glanced at Ara and she gave a slight nod. A vampire zipped out the door.

I resisted the impulse to run outside and demand he tell me what was wrong. Not that he'd talk. Every time I asked, he insisted he was fine. It ate at me, so I wouldn't let it go until I knew.

Mat strode in and stopped beside an empty chair. His face remained neutral as his eyes scanned the two hybrids. "Lily. It's good to see you again."

"Hello, Prince Mathias. Sorry about all of this." she waved a hand.

"Wait. You two know each other?" I couldn't keep the bitterness out of my voice. He couldn't have failed to notice the family resemblance the first time they met.

"We met before the battle. The palace guard misread her magic as Bellicose. She's the adopted daughter of Jonas the First and an honorary member of the House of Roman."

That explained why he kept it to himself. He didn't want to cause friction with Jonas and Ann Marie. And Ara's brother, Roman, was rumored to be insane. The magic I sensed made me positive Ara was right, and she'd inherited Lilith's power. What I didn't expect was the touch of my ruling magic. The two blended seamlessly to create a unique power that felt both dark and light.

Ara crossed her legs. "Interesting. Tell me, Lily, how did that come to be?"

"Which part? Because both stories are long and complicated."

I wanted to hear that, too, so I leaned forward. "Start from the beginning."

She rubbed her face. "I spent the first twelve years of my life on the run with my biological mother. In hindsight, she was an awful person. I didn't know it at the time because when you're a kid, you don't know what's normal. She was a mage who insisted on shoving supernatural politics and laws down my throat." She pointed at me. "I think she was trying to turn me into you, though it took years of therapy for me to realize that."

My stomach soured, and I started doing the math in my head.

"We'd move every few weeks because she claimed people were chasing her, though I never saw nor sensed anyone. We stayed in slums, but she carried herself as if she was better than everyone else. Other people never appreciated that. It was not a good time. Around the time I turned twelve, she dumped me off with good old Jed."

I gasped. She was definitely talking about my mother. And she knew it. She knew she was our sister. I was sure of it.

Mat leaned forward. "On your twelfth birthday?"

She shook her head. "I don't know when my birthday is, but it was around that time."

He leaned back. "Go on."

The story about how Jedediah treated her made my heart ache. It was heart-wrenching, and her childhood was awful. When the vampire we met in Ferine told us about her, I had doubts. But her account was identical, only more detailed.

When she was done, Mat's face turned hard. "Tell me more about your biological mother."

"You'd know more about her than me. I once asked her why she ran away from others if she was so important. She went on a tirade about how useless children were and told me she'd make sure I was the exception." Lily shivered. "That woman didn't love or have any empathy. She told people what to do and expected them to follow her orders." She closed her eyes for a long minute. "I can't think of anything right now."

Ara patted her arm. "It's okay, dear. We will move along. What has Roman told you about your vampire heritage?"

"That I don't have one. He thinks Jed turned me when I was a baby, and my mage abilities developed over the vampire virus."

Quin leaned forward. "Show me your fangs."

"Why?"

"Because they will tell us a lot about what type of vampire you are," Ara answered.

I leaned forward to see better. Yep. Like Ara and Quin, she had four fangs. Though Quin wasn't a natural born vampire, so I assumed he got his fangs from the experiments Lilith did on him.

Quin leaned back and rubbed his chin. "Interesting."

She retracted her fangs. "Not much of a conversationalist, eh, Gramps?"

"No."

I tried not to smile as the two heritage mages entered the room. I bet Lily would be great for Quin. She wasn't even a little scared of him. If anything, she looked pleased.

The mages bowed to me. "Your Grace." Then, toward Ara. "Mistress. How can we assist you?"

Ara squared her shoulders. "I want you to test this woman's magic patterns and DNA against ours."

I raised my hand, realized how dumb it looked, and lowered it. "Test her against us, too."

Lily rubbed her temples. "I already know we share a mother. She made a big deal about how awful you were and how I needed to replace you." She raised a hand, and I wondered if she was mocking me. "Which isn't something I'd do. I just want to go home, save people, and find a new toxic workplace."

I gave her my kindest smile. "Let's get the tests, then we can talk about Anitta's plans."

"She's dead," Mat's gravelly voice sounded bitter. "She was the one responsible for the damage to the castle and Dragon Headquarters."

That last sentence held such a note of triumph that I couldn't help but shoot him a look. What the hell was going on with him?

"Good. I'll tick that task off my list." Lily's voice was as hard as dragon glass.

Mat didn't take his eyes off her. Nor did his expression change. "You hate her as much as I do, then."

"Everyone smart enough to see past her public persona hates her." Her focus shifted toward the heritage mages. "Those guys gonna be a problem?"

Ara's tinkering laugh rang through the room. "No, dear. They're under contract."

"Great. Let's get this done. I have things to do."

"Wonderful. Let's get started." I could almost feel Ara's excitement. It mirrored mine. I couldn't picture having a sister. It wasn't anything I'd ever thought about. But with her sitting across from me, I fought to contain my excitement.

We moved to the covered back patio to wait for the heritage mages' results. We kept the conversations casual while we waited. I tried to pretend I didn't sense the anxiety rolling off Lily. Her brother, Alex, tried to read my thoughts twice in the short time we made small talk. Drake's magic locked my mind tight, and he flinched both times.

Lily set down her glass and turned her attention to me. "Why is your magic ballooning out of control?"

I frowned. "I don't know what you mean."

She pointed at my chest. "You should probably release some before it explodes. I took out a good chunk of Jed's property when I let mine build up, and you're far more powerful than me. You could take out the whole pocket."

My heart leaped into my throat, and my eyes snapped to Mat.

He shook his head.

"Ah. So you don't know how." Lily turned her attention to Ara. "How long will this take? Because Alex and I will be going home. I don't want to be anywhere near this wretched pocket when she explodes."

I jumped out of my chair. "Wait. You know how to use this magic?"

"Yeah. My magic is different than yours. Darker. But if yours is anything like the bitch that birthed us, it's the same basic technique."

If that were the case, I wouldn't need the god to pop in and save me. I bet if she could show me the basics, I'd be able to learn the rest. "Show me."

She dragged me to the middle of the lawn. "This is how mother guided me. Keep in mind that my magic is dark. It manifests dark, bloody things. Yours is cleaner and you have a lot more."

I could feel the darkness of her magic, but some light, too. That was what I needed to focus on. "Got it."

A tingle in my chest extended down my arm as we connected. I threw my senses wide open to help her. She didn't even flinch. "Wow. You pack a punch. Pay attention to how I do this."

Lily tried to reject her darker magic and only used the light as she formed a shield. She guided me through it and formed little anchors at the bottom and top. Something I never considered possible. But then, I always believed I was a mage with Mat's magic. So, it made sense that I missed a lot of nuances. I paid close attention to those anchors and her intent. My new magic reached out and tasted her dark stuff so I could tell the difference.

She dropped my hand.

Twelve-inch bloody arrows exploded from her shield, sailed across the lawn, and lodged into the back wall. A spray of what looked like an acid burst from them and killed the grass below. The vampires on the wall looked at it with respect. I shifted my attention toward Lily.

Her mouth hung open in horror as she waved an arm. "Sorry!" She turned to me. "The bloody poisoned spikes are the part that you shouldn't have, in case you were wondering."

Oh, my fates. What a gift this dark little hybrid was. My face lit up. "I like the bloody spikes. They're you."

She recovered from her horror. "Give it a try."

I didn't need to fight my dark side like her, so I copied her method, trying to remember how I only had to will it instead of pulling power from my core. The tickle on my skin told me when it stirred, so I released and used it as I kind of emanated the magic. The anchors were a struggle for a few seconds, but it seemed so simple once I did it. "That's really easy."

"Yeah." Lily didn't even try to hide her skepticism. "No offense, but how in the hell do you plan to keep the coalition together when you can't even use your magic?"

I had no idea. But I'd done okay during the battle. And Cavil would teach me more now that I knew one small way to use it. "When I was a kid, assassins chased us for almost a year. I learned how to hide my magic, but screwed it up in the process. It's fixed now, but different."

Lily rubbed her face. "You're supposed to be the one who swoops in and saves us. The new queen to unite and rule us all. The chosen one. Yet you have no confidence." She leaned in. "What are you so passionate about that you will kill or die for?" She gestured toward her brother. "For me, it's my adopted family and the hybrids. But I don't sense that you give a shit about much. Because if you did, you would have figured this out by now."

"Hey! I have things!" I screeched. Mat took a couple of casual steps in our direction. I threw one of my new magical walls around him, noting how much easier the anchors were. I suspected they'd become automatic once I had time to practice. "Stay out of this, Mat."

Lily folded her arms and stared at the back wall. "Okay. You're a quick study and have a buttload of magic. I'll show you the three...no, four things that I do to release mine. You need to practice them until the pressure in your chest eases. Preferably before you explode. I have a friend who can help teach you more. It's up to you to decide if you give a shit enough to learn."

I had enough of her insults. "I told you I give a shit. Am I conflicted? Yes. But I'm figuring it out." I needed to think, so I paced. "I've been doing magic my whole life, so I'm sure I can learn it fast. But here's the thing. You can't tell anyone about my...shortcomings. Very few people know, and I can't have it getting out."

"I can keep a secret. And I'll help you because it's what my family does. We rescue people. Though, I've never met someone who needed rescuing from herself before. Besides, if someone doesn't do something, we're all screwed."

The weight of the world settled on my shoulders at her words. "I am aware. Who is your friend?"

She grinned. "Cavil." Lily pointed to the back wall. "He's a god. He said the First Drake already asked him to help you."

I knew Cavil was trying to establish himself, but was unaware he'd already moved to Allure. It was another thing I should have known that slipped through the cracks. We needed to get better at intelligence. "He showed up in the battle for a minute to help, but I haven't seen him since."

I liked Lily. She showed me a few other ways to use my magic, but they all used the same basic techniques. I could work with that.

The mages interrupted our training when one of Ara's vampires led the heritage mages onto the back porch. The female mage clasped her hands behind her back. "I've confirmed that Liliana First is the biological granddaughter of Mistress Ara and Consort Tarquin. She is a full sister to her grace, Jenella, and two-thirds sister to his majesty, Mathias. Liliana's magic is unique. She is a high-level mage of Ahl, with a touch of the ruling magic of Lissa."

"Ruling magic?" I asked.

The mage nodded. "Only a touch. Her levels are on par with Prince Mathias's. She is also a natural-born vampire. However, she's much more powerful than Master Jedediah or Mistress Vesna, considering her age. We've determined her power boost comes from ruling magic consistent with Lilith's bloodline."

"Unique, indeed." I'd never seen Ara so happy. It made the hair on the back of my neck stand up.

The mage nodded. "As with all hybrids, these magics have blended. Liliana is the most unique hybrid I have ever tested."

"What do you mean by blended?" I found heritage fascinating and knew little about what made hybrids so unique.

"Many paranormals have a recent belief that hybrids are weaker than those with a single magic type. But that is incorrect. It is often the opposite. They inherit a full dose of both magics. For example, if a shifter and a witch have a child, fate grants that child the full ability to weave spells and shift. As they grow, those magics blend and form a unique and powerful type of magic. It is rare to find a low, or even mid-powered, hybrid."

"How can I be a two-thirds sister?" Lily's voice quivered.

The mage examined her. "I have only seen it twice over my long life. It is always when one parent is a possessor. Possessors can merge their bodies with that of another. Our tests show Prince Mathias and Liliana First each have three biological parents. Liliana's parents include the second queen as one-half of her heritage, with the other half split between the Second Consort and Prince Jedediah. Prince Mathias's second father is an unknown mage. Queen Jenella has only two parents, the Second Queen and her consort. Magically speaking, the vampire virus and the magic of Lissa are both dominant. So, any gifts Liliana may have inherited from the consort are null, but the DNA is consistent. Prince Mathias inherited magic from all three parents."

Lily let out a wheezing sound and bent over, then sat up and wheezed again. Before anyone could say anything, she went fluid and vomited on the lawn.

I understood that kind of dread, so I flashed to her and rested a hand on her back. "It'll be okay, Lily. We'll figure this out."

"Sorry. This is lame." She stood up. "I always knew. But hearing it." She drew in a deep breath. "I had myself convinced that I could just live my life and not have to face any of this. Any of you. No offense. This whole situation sucks."

I dug out one of Tracy's potions and handed it to her. "This will clean out your mouth and make you feel better. My friend Tracy is an excellent alchemist, so it's safe."

She gulped it down. "Is that the gorgeous witch that was with you?"

"Yeah."

CHAPTER TWO

LILY SAID SHE NEEDED time to process the revelations, and Ara dragged her away. That was fine with me. I knew where she was staying and wanted to touch bases with Deva about her and Alex.

Mat trailed me through the gate. "Let's wait for Lily."

"And Alex."

He stopped, his golden eyes unfocused. "I was unaware Mother had another child."

"There was no way to know."

"Perhaps. But if I'd known, I could have saved her before she landed in Jedediah's grasp."

"No, you couldn't. You were too busy trying to save us." I tapped my chin. "Are you sure Father died when Jaques did?"

"Yes."

"So she was pregnant with Lily when..." I trailed off. I couldn't say it.

"It explains why it took her a year to catch up to and threaten us."

"Yeah."

The gate opened, and Lily, Alex, and one of Ara's trusted vampires, Elsie, spilled out. "Let's check out her situation, then I'll go see Deva."

We escorted them to the Dragon Hotel and exchanged numbers. Then, I headed across the street to Dragon Headquarters. As I walked, I craned my neck to examine the top of the tower. They'd made significant progress in replacing the dragon glass, but it wasn't quite finished.

Deva and Bastien had moved to the sixth floor, right across the street from Lily and Alex's rooms. I appreciated the extra protection. Especially since I found out she's not only Quin's granddaughter but also my sister. Excitement bubbled in my stomach at the thought, and I pushed it to the back of my mind to process later.

Deva's eyes seemed haunted every time I saw her since the battle. It was understandable. Drake said she took the loss of her dragons personally. And she'd lost a few when Anitta escaped, though I was afraid to ask about them.

Her eyes scanned Mat, who trailed me. He hadn't spoken since we left Lily and Alex's room. Deva's sad bronze eyes landed on me. "Jenella."

I settled into a chair opposite her makeshift desk. "Hey, Deva. How are you?"

Those sad eyes narrowed. "I'm fine. What do you want?"

"Nothing. Were you aware Jonas's daughter is our sister?"

She leaned back. "I suspected. If Ann Marie kept her from you, she had her reasons."

"Agreed." Mat sank into a chair next to me.

I threw up my hands. "I'm not holding anything against Jonas and Ann Marie. With our family history, I don't blame them. And I like Lily and Alex."

Deva tapped her desk. "My dragons are very fond of them, as well. Especially Glacintial. I would like to mentor the mental mage. His magic is unlike any other I've encountered."

"Alex," I said. "He's also a shifter. I can see why the Bellicose wants him. I wonder if Ann Marie sent them here because they knew about the blood connection."

"Of course she did. That old sorceress saw their trouble and used the situation to her advantage. It's what she does. I assume she considered every angle first."

Mat stood. "It doesn't matter. You two agreed to protect them, so that's what we'll do." He met Deva's eyes. "Be careful when dealing with the hybrids. The woman has Lilith's power."

"I am aware."

We flashed to the new family entrance at the palace. The old one was destroyed when that part of the castle collapsed. The entrance still looked the same, but my feet itching with the urge to run as far away as possible was new.

I fought that urge as I examined the upgrades. The biggest changes were to the kitchen, my office area, our unfinished apartments, and the visitor's entrance. Emine and Tracy worked with George to increase security. It included a wall that blocked off the main part of the castle from random visitors. I liked using the front stairs without everyone gawking at me. Or bowing.

Verity, my assistant, and Charlotte, Drake's assistant, sat at the gigantic half-moon desk that guarded the entrance to our offices. Before the castle got destroyed, Drake's office was across the hall. During the rebuild, I moved it next to mine and gave him an adjoining door. Verity came up with the idea of the half-moon desk with two workstations. It made working together easier for her and Charlotte, and more workstations could be added later. Or something. I let her run the office, so I was only vaguely aware of her reasoning.

She sat in her area, her chin resting on her hands. "Hey, Jen. How did the pocket-making go?"

My forehead scrunched as I examined her. I'd never seen Verity sad or depressed. But the eyes that examined me as she waited for an answer were flat-out painful to look at.

With everything that happened, I forgot we saw the wards get recharged. "Fine. Come on in. I have a lot to tell you."

Verity tucked her hair behind an ear when I finished explaining everything to her. "Well, you always keep things interesting, don't you?"

"I wish I didn't." I clutched the arms of my chair to keep from getting up and leaving. "Will you call the god Cavil and ask him to meet me for magic training?" I'd never had the urge to flee my office before. Sure, I hated being caged in it sometimes, but the feeling was somehow different. It was why I'd spent the duration of the reconstruction working out of the tiny office at the home Tracy and I shared. To learn my magic, I needed to be comfortable. And, though I couldn't explain why, the palace wasn't. "Maybe at Dragon Headquarters?"

"Sure. What about Jonas and Ann Marie?"

"I haven't processed having a sister yet and wouldn't know what to say."

She stood. "Your apartment here will be ready tomorrow sometime. Charlotte already told Drake."

"Great. Thanks. Hey, Verity?"

She stopped with her hand on the doorknob. "Yes?"

"Are you okay?"

"I'm as fine as I can be." She dropped her hand and turned toward me. "I've never seen people die. It's taking its toll."

Relief and concern flooded me. The relief because of the perfectly logical explanation. And concern because I hated she had to see death. "I'm sorry. I hoped by giving you a job here, you never would."

"The supernatural way of life has been a big adjustment, and then that happened." She shook her head. "It's a lot, but I don't hold it against you."

I moved to her and gave her a hug. "I'm still sorry. And if you need time off, take it. Please."

Verity stepped back. "Like I said, I'll be fine." She shut the door in my face.

Drake was in his office, so I popped my head in. He sat in his oversized executive chair, his back to me as he faced the bank of windows that looked out over the side lawn and the forest beyond. Double doors to the left of his desk opened to a massive balcony so he could come and go without using the entrances.

The office already smelled like him, and my muscles relaxed as I breathed in his scent. "Hey, Drake."

He swiveled toward me. His green eyes flashed. "I'm busy," he snapped.

My muscles stiffened, and I fought to relax them. Drake never talked to me like that. Or anyone else, for that matter. I slammed my hands on my hips. "Excuse me?"

"You heard me. I'm talking to my contacts in the field. Leave."

"Yeah. I heard you loud and clear. Want to rethink that statement? And tone?"

The glow from his eyes dimmed, and he blinked. "My apologies."

I tiptoed toward him and rested a hip against the desk. "What was that about?"

"I'm unsure why I'm angry." He swung back toward the window. "I am trying to fulfill my purpose."

"Yeah, well. I have no room to talk when it comes to being an asshole, but you're supposed to be the calm and reasonable one."

"I am not feeling calm and reasonable."

It seemed like everyone was acting strange. I couldn't allow my patient, wonderful dragon to fall into whatever funk everyone else was in. Everyone besides me. I wondered if it was because I compartmentalized all the trauma from the battle, and they hadn't. I probed the bond but got nothing. "Why do you suppose that is?"

"I don't know." He stood. "Nor do I have time for your nonsense. I'm going to the human city to check on some things."

"While you're there, see if you can find your manners," I said in a clipped tone as I made my way back to my office.

The door slammed with a thud behind me, and I had to lock my knees to keep from giving into the urge to flee. I spun around, my heart pounding. What the hell was going on? Grabbing my stuff, I raced downstairs to find Helen.

The griffin matriarch stood beside the magichef, barking orders at one of her kids or grandkids. It was hard to tell because their family was so big. "Hey, Helen. Are you okay?"

"I've got a castle opening coming up and a whole lot of pressure to make it perfect." She sighed. "My patience is running on low, that's all. How may we help you?"

"I don't need anything." She was off, too. Helen was caring and nurturing by nature. In all the years I'd known her, she'd never once yelled at her kids. I moved toward the back door. "I'll leave you to it."

After I stepped into the family flashing circle, I glanced back. The urge to leave was stronger than it had ever been. Sure, I didn't like being cooped up, but I also never had the compulsion to run away. Or did I? Maybe I was reading too much into it, I thought as I flashed away.

Booming laughter rang from the little house in the mixed magic neighborhood as I made my way through the wards and up the back stairs. Calvin and Tracy were seated at the kitchen table.

Tracy's head turned when I entered the room. "Hey, Jen. How did it go?"

Relief flooded me when she acted normal. "Fine, I guess." I headed toward the magichef and ordered some food. When it appeared, I gathered my plate and slumped into the chair across from Calvin. "Is Bastien acting strange?"

Tracy's eyebrows drew together. "No. Why?"

"Something's off at the palace, and I noticed Deva was a little down, so I wondered how Bas was doing."

"Oh. I've been working with my dad and haven't spent much time with him, but he was fine yesterday."

I dropped the subject and added it to the growing list of things I needed to deal with later. I gestured towards the two vials on the table. "New potions?"

Calvin nodded. "Yes. Ann Marie found a recipe for an immunity potion to counteract most demon-based spells. She said I should show it to you."

"Sure." I picked up the vial and tried to analyze it. Potions were tricky without a deep understanding of plants and alchemy, which I didn't have. The key ingredient was some kind of herb, but I couldn't tell you which one. "Can you recreate it?"

"We're working on it. Ann Marie is spreading the knowledge to the hybrids. I suggest we do the same in the pockets."

Of course she was. Ann Marie was a great ally, and I hoped the little tiff with her kids didn't alienate her. As the last sorceress, she was as brilliant as she was powerful. And her dedication to the hybrids was admirable. "I suppose I could send out a bulletin to the leaders. Who should they contact?"

"I am still working to gain the trust of the witches and eliminate the magic they spread through the shifter community. Many covens support me, but others are unhappy with how you treated the former president."

"I didn't treat her any different from the other traitors."

His eyes widened. "What's the matter with you?"

My spine snapped straight. "Am I acting different, too?"

"No." Tracy reached for my hand. "Your anger toward the former president is justified. I mean, if it were up to me, she would have died when she attacked you the first time."

I rubbed my constantly aching chest. "Can you check for spells on me?"

Tracy held out her hand. "With your magic, you'd know if someone tried to spell you, but I'll check."

"Thanks."

With a wave of her fingers, the detection spell settled over me. "All I feel is your weird magic."

My muscles relaxed, releasing the tension that had been knotting them since we discovered Lily. "Can you check Dragon Headquarters and the palace?"

"I've been to both places a few times, and nothing was off. What's going on, Jen?"

"It might be me, but...Drake snapped at me a little while ago. And Helen berated one of her kids. Verity is sad and droopy. And Mat doesn't answer my texts." I pushed my plate away, no longer hungry. "And I have an overwhelming urge to flee when I'm there."

"Would you like me to take a look?" Calvin asked.

I shook my head. "It's possible I'm reading something into the situation that isn't there." The string of betrayals I'd uncovered was making me paranoid. It was also possible my sanity was slipping like my mother's did. I didn't want Calvin, a member of the Leadership Council, to see it, though. "I'll give you a call if I need your help."

"Very well." He stood and squeezed Tracy's shoulder. "I will see myself out."

Tracy went with him, then came back in and propped herself against the kitchen island. "What's really going on?"

"Mat's been acting weird. Then Drake snapped at me, and he's never done that before."

"I hate to tell you this, but everyone wants to snap at you. I mean, I'm surprised he held out this long."

"True. All the betrayals might have made me paranoid." I put my dishes in the magiclean. "No. Something's wrong. I can feel it."

"Okay. What do you want to do about it?"

"Will you keep an eye on Bastien and Deva? See if you notice more?"

"Yeah. I'll see what I can find out."

"Thanks. I'll do the same at the palace."

"Sure."

I checked the bond as I slid into bed. Drake wasn't in the valley but in downtown Allure, probably at Dragon Headquarters. It wasn't unusual for him to visit his aunt, so I was a little more reassured. It could be I was overthinking the whole thing.

Or was I?

His behavior since the battle was normal for the first couple of days. Though he hadn't shared my bed since that first night. He said he wanted to take a step back and seduce me slowly and do things right. Court me.

My stomach erupted in butterflies, and I threw a pillow over my head. Nope. Wasn't going there. Besides, he hadn't lifted a finger to do either of those things. If anything, he avoided me.

I thought about the events of the day. I had a sister. A kickass sister who rightfully pointed out that I lacked confidence and wasn't strong enough. Or didn't care enough. Between that and everyone acting so strange, I felt like I was in an alternate reality. Or fell into a rut where my mind questioned everything while it whirled in circles.

I pulled my phone off the nightstand to make a new list and then put it back.

Stop thinking so hard and go to sleep. Drake's voice interrupted my pondering.

Where are you?

Downtown helping my aunt.

His voice filled me with warmth. He often divided his time between finding Bellicose and helping Deva. Drake dove into his purpose like no one I'd ever seen. As a result, he was everywhere at once. Everywhere except with me. I blinked back tears. No use feeling sorry for myself. I got myself into the situation, so I'd have to pull myself out. *Good night, Drake.*

Good night, Jenella.

CHAPTER THREE

I DRAGGED MYSELF TO the castle the next day and watched for signs of weirdness as I headed to my office. The family quarters were done, and everyone expected me to move in. I didn't intend to until I figured out what my senses were screaming about. Or at least until I could shake the overwhelming urge to flee that settled over me the moment I crossed the threshold. The grand opening was in a few days, so I didn't have much time to figure it out before people started questioning my absence.

I rubbed the knotted ball of acid in my stomach and reached out with my senses, searching for any hint of magic. The whole place felt off to me, though it could be the new, stronger wards. I wasn't used to them. I collected myself and continued toward my office.

Quin sat in the sitting area at the far end, staring out the window. I moved behind my desk and took a seat. "Hey, Quin. Have you noticed people acting strange lately?"

"Not a single day has passed in thousands of years where I did not ponder the strange actions of other paranormals." He had to be confused about finding Lily, but he didn't show it.

"That doesn't answer my question."

"No."

"No, you haven't noticed, or no, you're not answering my question?"

"I have not noticed."

So, it *was* just me.

Mat came through the door, his shoulders slumped. "Jenella."

Or not. "What's up?"

His dull eyes swept the room and landed on Quin. "Ann Marie and Jonas are here to see you."

I held his gaze for a few extra seconds, the dullness of his eyes making my heart ache. I wondered if killing our mother made him so sad. "Okay."

Verity led them in. The human makeup she often wore was absent, her puffy eyes and dark circles on full display.

I kept a blank expression on my face as I directed them to the new seating area. They took positions on each end of a new cream-colored sofa. Mat perched on a chair beside me. Quin stayed beside the window.

They didn't seem any different, but their calm demeanors set me on edge.

Mat didn't even greet them. "Explain."

Jonas leaned forward. "Explain what?"

I rubbed my eyes. "You knew Lily was our sister and Ara's granddaughter for years, yet you said nothing."

"Correct."

"You were protecting her," Mat said. "From us."

"Correct again."

An awkward silence followed.

Ann Marie shifted in her chair. "We left the decision to contact you up to her. She chose not to. Anitta planted some interesting thoughts about you in her head."

"Yet you manipulated Jenella into taking her in without warning Alex or Lily about the arrangement." Mat tapped the arm of his chair. "Why?"

"Because Alex needed a safe place to stay while we fight the Bellicose in the city." A smile ghosted across Ann Marie's face. "Lily chose to ignore her biological family's existence, which was fine with us. But she's also become stagnant in her skills and emotional growth. She thinks she can live her life pretending to be human. It isn't sustainable. Her power will only grow as she ages, and it will eventually draw attention. She needs a support network outside of what we can provide. When I realized Jen was the polar opposite of Anitta, I asked her to help."

"Yet Lily is the vampire heir," Quin said without inflection. "And you did not tell her."

"Because we weren't sure. Her magic isn't exactly like Lilith's. But even then, she refuses to use power beyond a few basic vampire abilities. It hinders her."

Jonas leaned forward, resting his elbows on his knees. "She doesn't like drawing attention to herself. Using her magic draws potential blood sources, which she claims are unbalanced humans."

"And Alex?" I asked, remembering Deva's interest in him.

"Alex can read anyone at any time without them noticing. If he stays stagnant, his mind will become addled. I've seen it before with powerful mental mages who can't control their abilities. The only creatures who can help balance that type of power are dragons. We knew you were close to Drake and Deva and desperate to keep our kids out of the clutches of the Bellicose. So, Ann Marie vetted you and put them in your care. It wasn't an impulsive decision. We love them and want what's best for their futures."

"Yet you didn't tell anyone, not your kids and not us." When he opened his mouth to answer, I continued. "I understand. Our family doesn't exactly have a stellar reputation when it comes to taking care of each other. So, what now?"

Ann Marie's eyebrows drew together. "That's entirely up to them. And you. Though I should warn you that Lily and Alex are inseparable."

"I like Alex and will gladly welcome him into the family. Quin?"

"My love does not wish to cause Lily any further duress, nor do I."

I pressed my lips together to hold back a smile.

"I'm pleased that's settled. Now, tell us about the Bellicose taking over your territory."

My head swung toward my brother at his abrupt change of subject. He was rough around the edges, sure. But he wasn't usually rude. Or I hadn't ever noticed. It was possible, especially if my sanity was slipping.

Jonas's eyes flared. "They are not taking over my city."

"Except they are," I said. "Dragons and vampires are keeping an eye on them. Drake says they're bringing demons in through several locations, and the hybrid leadership doesn't seem to care."

A small smile touched Ann Marie's lips. "You've come a long way in a short time." She focused on Mat. "What's the matter with you?"

I held my breath, hoping he'd realize he had a problem and answer her.

His spine straightened, and his menacing power surged. "Nothing."

I exhaled. Ann Marie noticed something was wrong. So it wasn't just my imagination.

"The other hybrid leaders don't see the Bellicose as a threat. One is considering joining them," Jonas said as if the exchange hadn't taken place.

I wondered if the hybrid leaders fell for Jonas's unassuming demeanor. If so, they were idiots. It was dumb to underestimate a First. "So, how can we help?"

"We'll send you the information Lily and Roman took from multiple Bellicose offices. Once you look it over, call me." Jonas directed the statement toward Mat.

He inclined his head. "How long would you like us to keep Lily and Alex here?"

"For as long as you can." Ann Marie stood. "And if you could help them better develop their magic, we'd appreciate it."

When they left, I spun toward my brother. "Ann Marie raised a valid point. Something is off about your behavior. Did someone put a spell on you?"

He stood and stomped toward the door. "Let it go, Jen."

I watched him leave. "Did you see that?"

"Yes." Quin glided toward the door at a human pace.

"What do you suppose is wrong with him?"

"I do not know, nor do I care." He disappeared.

The PISD, or Private Investigation Supernatural Division, was downtown near Dragon Headquarters and housed the licensing bureau for the independently contracted detectives. The first time I went inside, I had stars in my eyes and a plan to be free from my title for as long as possible.

Standing at the bottom of the stairs, I realized how stupid and naïve I was back then. At the time, I believed it would solve all my problems and was ready to throw myself into a new life. I supposed I accomplished that, though not in the way I expected.

I ignored the people who stopped and bowed as I rested against the railing halfway up the stairs and looked up at the sky. My stomach fluttered as Drake made his way towards me.

A sixty-foot dragon descended toward the narrow street. His green and black scales shimmered like crushed emeralds on velvet where the sun caught them. I took two steps toward him before my brain engaged.

Paranormals scrambled to avoid him, though they didn't need to. He morphed into his human form when he was still several feet off the ground. He landed on his feet and took the stairs two at a time. A blinding smile spread across his rugged face. "Hello, Jenella."

I unclenched my fists and tried to sound casual. "Hey, Drake."

"What are you doing here?"

The heat in his gaze lit my entire body on fire. "I need to find out if Travis is still fit to be the Director of the PISD." My former best friend, Travis, was the son of the Shifter Alphas who betrayed us. We were still working on untangling their sabotage.

His green eyes grew hard. "Is that so?"

"If you're going to snap at me again or tell me I shouldn't have come alone, don't waste your breath."

"I apologized for that. I have no idea what I was thinking and have no plans to stop you."

"But you were considering it."

His gaze swept over my body. "Among other things."

My face flushed as I turned and started up the stairs. "Are you coming with me, or would you like to wait here?"

He caught up to me in two strides. "I want to read his mind."

I hoped Travis wasn't part of the sabotage, but understood it was a possibility. It was a pattern in our relationship. I always wanted to see the best in him, and he never cared about anyone but himself.

A few detectives loitered in the main hall, but most made themselves scarce when we came through the door. The former alphas hired many of them to track down the missing shifters, even though they already knew what happened to them. It made my brain hurt to ponder the complicated web of lies they built.

Travis's office was on the top floor. I'd been there twice. The first time was to pitch my idea of becoming a detective and ask for his help. The second time, Quin and I got called in by the former director. He turned out to be working for the Bellicose and later kidnapped me. It was one of the last mistakes he'd make because he took me to where they kept Deva. She killed him as I rescued her from their magic siphoning devices.

I'd appointed Travis to the director position as one of my first acts as queen.

The outer offices looked the same right down to the short, squat brownie with a cap of bright red hair. She looked up as we approached. Her eyes grew wide as she sprang to her feet and bowed. "Your Grace, Sir First. How can I help you?"

"Is Travis around?"

She swallowed. "Um. Yes. But he's in a meeting."

"We'll wait." I stayed at her desk and folded my arms.

Drake wandered toward the windows and peered out, his presence somehow imposing without effort. I needed to learn how to do that.

The Director's door opened, and a woman scurried out. Her eyes widened when she saw me, and she picked up the pace. At least she didn't bow.

Travis appeared at the door. "Hey, Jen. Come on in."

The office had changed since the last time I'd seen it. The trinkets were gone, replaced by books, and the overall feel was much more professional. I lowered myself into the same chair I sat in when the last director tried to remove Quin as my mentor and folded my hands in my lap. "You know why we're here, right?"

"I'm not stupid." He slid into his chair. "My parents didn't trust my power level, so I wasn't part of their plan."

Being the fifth child of the former shifter alphas, he was the youngest and weakest shifter in his family. Magic favored threes, so the third and sixth were more powerful than the first, second, fourth, and fifth, etc. He wasn't weak, though. He had enough power where he could run a pack.

"Tell me everything you've dug up about their involvement."

He swept a hand through his hair, and his eyes shifted to Drake. "I'm sure the First already read me."

"I have," Drake said in a calm, even tone. "They were the ones who gave the Bellicose the location of Jenella's transport after her coronation?"

"Among other things." He shrugged. "It's all hindsight."

"Hindsight? What else did you learn?" I asked.

Travis shook his head. "You won't like it."

"I don't like a lot of things these days, so go ahead."

"They set you up to test you more than once." Travis picked up a rock containing a spell. "After the castle got destroyed, I knew you'd suspect my involvement, so I hired a detective to help me dig up information on them." He activated the spell, and holograms formed between us.

I gasped. The spell showed a timeline of events, starting with my first case. "Colonel Ballard was a plant?"

"Not necessarily. But we found a witness who said my dad sent the Colonel to the area where the dragon picked you and Prince Jedediah up. They were after Jedediah because he broke a contract with your mother."

I bet that had something to do with Lily. "And the shifters in Ferine who got infected?"

"Volunteers. My parents wanted to see how you'd handle it. Any case you worked on involving shifters was them testing to see how you'd respond. They knew something was wrong with your magic, but not what."

My eyes stayed glued to the hologram while I struggled to remember every interaction I'd had with a shifter over the last couple of years. Colonel Ballard said he was tracking black magic users. The raccoon shifters down the street from my house made excellent spies. I assumed Mat planted them. But what if he didn't? And then, out of the blue, Colonel Ballard hands me a case that involves more shifters.

I would have failed the test if I hadn't had Tracy with me. She was the one who figured out how to deal with the bug magic. I wondered if the former alphas knew about her abilities.

I swallowed the white-hot ball of anger that always lurked beneath the surface. "Why? They were friends with Mat for years. Why would they need to test me?"

"Mat never confided in them. It's why they encouraged me to befriend you. And why they tried to portray the caring auntie and uncle who gave the poor, lonely girl a place to socialize."

The pain of my childhood tried to resurface, and I flinched as I shoved it back down. "But Bastien saw right through them and removed me when he became my guard."

He shrugged. "I doubt Prince Bastien would have kept that information to himself."

True. "Drake?"

"Travis is not involved. He gathered this information to save himself from your scrutiny. He hasn't heard from his parents since the attack."

I searched Drake's face for a few beats too long, wondering why his tone was so icy, before turning my attention back to Travis. "Keep digging. Send anything you find to my office."

"I will. And Jen, I'm sorry my family did this to you."

I stood. "It's not me you should worry about. It's Mat. They made a contract with him and broke it. He'll kill them for it even after magic extracts its price." I walked out without looking back.

Drake was silent as we made our way toward the flashing circle. "What's on your mind?"

"We need a new Shifter Alpha and Jonas is busy with the hybrids. Will he be able to test potential candidates?"

"He is already working on it."

"Great. I have to learn my magic fast. I asked Verity to set up a session with the God Cavil at Dragon Headquarters, if that's okay."

"Deva would do anything for you. She'll see it as an opportunity to make amends for letting Anitta escape."

"It's unnecessary to make amends. She made a mistake and lost some of her people in the process. That kind of pain is worse than anything I'd ever wish on her. What have you learned about Lily and Alex?"

"Not much. I met them briefly at Jonas's house. Glacintial has been following them for a while and would know more. Do you want me to look into it?"

"No. Especially if Deva has someone watching them." It didn't surprise me. She would never pass up the opportunity to monitor a mental mage.

Drake wrapped an arm around me. "You can trust the dragons, Jenella. We won't betray you. And Jonas only cares about saving the people he feels responsible for. He's honorable for a First."

So was Drake. I turned, rested my forehead on his chest, and closed my eyes. His warmth wrapped around me like a blanket. "Something's wrong with everyone, including us."

He trailed a hand down my back. "Oh?"

"You lashed out at me yesterday for no reason and have been avoiding me. Verity's depressed. And Mat's not taking care of things like he usually does. On the surface, he seems fine. But he's not."

"I've been busy."

"Busy avoiding me. And Deva is off, too, if you haven't noticed."

"Have you tried talking to people you perceive as acting strange?"

"I tried to bring it up with Mat, and he shut me down like you're about to do." I tapped his chest. "Don't bother. I'll figure it out."

Drake released me and stepped back, taking his warmth with him. "I wasn't going to shut you down."

Everyone on the street had paused to stare, so I continued to walk. "Sure, you weren't."

Anger flashed through the bond. "I wasn't."

I didn't want to argue, so I changed the subject. "What are your plans for the day?"

"I need to check in with the dragons stationed in the valley. The Bellicose still have a small presence in Allure, as well. We need to eliminate them."

"We've already proven we suck at finding them. Even when they're operating right under our noses."

"I'll find them."

I stopped outside the circle and met his eyes. They were distant, as if he were only half with me. I reached up and traced his scar, my heart cracking in two when he didn't react. "I believe you."

Mat sat at his desk staring into space, his eyes still dull. He knew I was there, but ignored me. Everyone knew where I was since my magic upgrade. It still irritated me.

I locked my knees to keep from fleeing as I leaned against the doorframe at the entrance of his office and folded my arms. "What's going on with you?"

He blinked. "Nothing."

I dropped my arms. "Liar." I moved further into the office and shut the door. "Talk to me, Mat."

His lips twitched. "You sound like me."

I nodded. "I'm becoming my parent."

He didn't smile like I hoped he would. His face turned to stone, and he leaned forward. "The last thing you want to be is me."

"Untrue. I've always wanted to be more like you."

"Don't use me as your role model. Be more like Helen or George. They are as kind and caring as they are deadly. That fits you better."

He misunderstood. I didn't want to become deadly and feared like him, but I wanted to tackle problems without my past trauma haunting me. "You haven't been the same since the battle."

"Correct."

"Why?"

"Because I failed you."

"Bullshit."

His dull eyes focused on a spot on his desk. "My mission was to keep you safe. To stand between you and those who would harm you. And I befriended the enemy."

"I'm still here."

"And Gabe and Linda are still alive."

"Sure. But they're no match for us."

He ran both hands down his face. "What would you do if Tracy turned out to be Bellicose?"

"She isn't. And she'd never betray me."

"That's what I thought, too."

My stomach soured. I didn't realize how close Mat and Gabe were. How had I missed that? Gabe and Linda were always around when I was a kid. But for some reason the closeness of their friendship never registered. "I'm sorry. What can I do to help?"

When his eyes met mine, the remorse and grief in them were enough to bring me to my knees. "Nothing. I'll have my revenge.

The hair on the back of my neck stood up with his intimidating magic. "Don't do anything stupid."

"I don't plan to."

He lied. Though it bothered me, it seemed more of a lie he told himself rather than me, so I changed the subject. "I'm going to train with the god in the morning at Dragon Headquarters. Do you want to go?"

"Yes. Emine would like to attend as well."

CHAPTER FOUR

THE PRACTICE GYM AT Dragon Headquarters was as amazing as it was huge, with its tall ceilings, raised benches on one end, and tables on the far wall. Mat and Emine stood by the tables, the tension so thick I could cut it with a knife. Emine crossed her arms as they stared each other down.

I strode in their direction. "What's up?"

Emine shook her head. "My match has his head up his ass, and I can't dislodge it."

"Yeah. I tried to talk to him yesterday."

"You'd assume someone in this family would be rational, but no."

Mat shook his head. "It doesn't matter what's going on with me. We're here for Jen."

I pointed at him. "You're wrong. You matter, and we don't like to see you struggling."

Emine threw her hands out. "See? We need you to get your shit together and be the rational one. Otherwise, Jen and I will run amok."

She was acting like her usual crazy self. It should have put me on edge, but I was relieved. It confirmed I read too much into the strange behavior of the others. Especially since they had rational explanations. I hoped so. But it also meant I needed to do some soul-searching and figure out why I had the urge to run away from the palace.

Lily's dark magic filled the room before she entered. No, not dark, I decided. More like a starry night on a hot summer day. The blonde god stepped into the room and scanned it. Lily scooted around him, spotted us, and headed in our direction. Alex and Ara's elite vampire, Elsie, trailed behind her. Their arms were loaded with trays, the rich scent of coffee coming from them.

Lily's chest puffed out as she reached us. "Hey, Jen, Mat. This is Cavil. The friend I told you about. Do you guys want coffee?"

Cavil bowed. "Your Grace."

I wiped my sweaty hands on my pants. "Hello, Cavil. You can call me Jen or Jenella. Either's fine. And no bowing, please."

Mat cleared his throat, his face all business.

Lily shoved a coffee into his hand, then turned to Emine. "I'm Lily. This is my brother, Alex, and my new buddy, Elsie. Do you want some coffee?"

A cunning gleam flickered in Emine's eyes. "I'm Emine. The sane one of the family. Oh boy. These two will not know what to do with you, will they?"

Great. I didn't know why Lily and Alex came with Cavil, but I knew it would be disastrous if she teamed up with Emine. Lily seemed like a button-pusher, and Emine's crazy would rub off on her. I was sure of it.

"No one ever does." Lily jiggled the coffee.

Emine plucked it out of her hand and took a swig. "Hey, Jen. How long will it take you to drag Lily into a stupid situation? I want to see what she's made of."

I rolled my eyes. "Stop it, Emine."

Alex set down his trays of coffee and slunk toward the seating area. The knowing look in his eye made me nervous.

The door opened, and Deva strode in. She glanced at me, then headed straight toward Alex. She once told me she liked to toy with mental mages. I sent her a warning look to mind her manners. The last thing we needed was to get on Jonas and Ann Marie's bad side because Deva manipulated their son into doing her bidding.

Bastien and Tracy came through next.

My stomach flipped when Drake appeared behind them, and his eyes landed on me. He made his way over and kissed my temple. "We will have a picnic later as a part of our courtship."

I couldn't help the sloppy smile that spread across my face. His declaration was more evidence that I'd imagined the strange behavior. Or rather, I read too much into it because of my newfound paranoia.

I wanted to build a relationship with Lily, so I picked up a coffee and sat beside her.

She turned to me as soon as my butt hit the chair. "So, you and Drake, eh?"

My whole body lit up at the mention of his name. "Yes. We're newly bonded, but it's been building for a while. He's amazing."

She fell silent.

Great. I'd barely met my sister and already said something that made her so uncomfortable she didn't want to talk to me. It was further evidence that I sucked at being normal. Not wanting to make her even more uncomfortable, I focused on my coffee. I sniffed it, then took a big gulp.

"I never thought I'd get to say my sister's banging my dad's oldest friend. Nice."

Coffee spewed from my mouth, and I coughed.

She patted my back.

Tracy waved a hand, and a cleaning spell took care of the mess.

"Why do you always gotta do that?" her brother asked, exasperation in his voice.

A sly look rolled across her face. "What? It's true. Don't you find it hilarious?"

"Not really, no. And it's not your business."

Bastien, who stood behind me with Tracy, snorted.

I didn't blame him. It *was* funny. At that moment, I realized Lily and I would get along just fine.

The god fought to hide a smile as he approached us. "I would like to start with creation magic. Remember that it is only a small part of what you can do. It is also the one you have in common with Lily. I'd like you both to participate so you can learn from each other."

I liked the idea of practicing with someone, so I let him pull me to the center of the room. He held out a tennis ball. "Make this as realistic as possible."

Lily already showed me creation magic, so I ran my senses through it to feel for the weave. I realized as I copied it that creations had a slight zing to them where regular objects didn't. Cavil watched me and then showed us how to make tiny anchors. Neat. I wondered if the magical feeling faded. Yes, I decided. Or, at least Rayar's architectural magic faded rapidly as the object became rooted. I bet mine would, too, even though it was a bit different.

Lily hesitated, then sighed when Cavil turned his attention toward her. She created a perfect ball. It held its form for a couple of seconds, then turned blood red. She dissipated it.

Cavil rubbed his chin. "I still believe your intentions matter. Though your power is night magic, it should not do that unless you want it to. Let's try a plant."

I loved peonies. How they started as a small, shy ball and bloomed into a glorious large flower amazed me. And their sweet floral scent made me stop and inhale every time I saw one in full bloom. So, I created a pink one. A smile formed as I brought it to my nose and sniffed. The floral scent was close to the real thing.

Lily chose a cactus with two-inch thorns and red flowers that oozed blood. Or maybe she didn't choose it. It reminded me of when my ruling magic did what it wanted. Though she could control hers and knew what she was doing, where the ruling magic didn't like being restrained and lashed out. I wondered if her subconscious was creating the problem or if it was how Lilith's magic worked. I suspected the former.

Emine shuffled over, her crazy eyes focused on the cactus. "That's way more handy than the smell-good thing Jen made."

Lily nodded.

"Try to concentrate on intent, Lily. You're trying too hard to not hurt anyone, so your thoughts of how you imagine your magic will respond are incorporated into the results," Cavil explained. "Stop thinking your magic is dangerous. Make a chair, and we'll move on to more complicated lessons."

I remembered a chair I'd seen at Castle Mahri and pushed the intent to the floor in front of me. A deep purple chair with ornate wooden legs and arms appeared. It wasn't an exact match, but it was close.

Lily created a puffy black chair that looked like it belonged in a shifter compound. My eyes drifted toward Alex, and I wondered if she had done that for her brother.

When she was done, Drake leaned over it, and a tug in my chest told me he used my magic to assess the thing.

"You might want to stand back," Lily warned.

He inclined his head as he moved beside me. "I recognize that magic."

Lily held up a hand. "I don't want to know." She turned to Cavil. "I'm slowing Jen's progress down. She needs to...."

Gurgle.

Blurp.

We all swung back toward her chair. The outer part of the beanbag changed. Blotches formed on the surface and spread as if it were bleeding. It scooted toward Lily.

Terror filled her eyes. "Uh, Cavil?"

His brow furrowed. "I can't eliminate it."

"What do you mean, you can't eliminate it? This was your idea." She shoved me into Drake. "Get her out of here."

He wrapped his arms around me, and I elbowed him in the stomach. "What the hell, Lily. I'm not helpless here." I used the previous lesson and created a barrier around the blob. The thing crushed my wall and didn't stop as it rolled toward me.

The room whirled by. When it stopped spinning, Lily's panicked eyes examined me.

I tried not to laugh because it was an obvious sore spot with her. So I turned my attention back to the deadly chair as it zipped toward us.

Tracy threw a spell. It bounced off and crashed into the wall.

Lily and I tumbled one way while Cavil went the other.

"Sorry," Lily croaked.

The blob switched directions and chased Tracy.

Bastien picked her up and ran toward the other side of the room.

Ara's vampire, Elsie, appeared next to Lily. "Fix this before you start a war."

After running from the blob for a few minutes, I stopped and threw my hands on my hips. "This is as stupid as my magic used to be, but more deadly. How did you make that thing?"

Lily grabbed my hand and dragged me toward Alex, who had changed into the biggest lion I'd ever seen. "I was trying to think of something that wouldn't wipe out two royal families."

"Which is why I told you not to think those thoughts," Cavil said.

"Stop this madness and get behind me," Deva ordered.

Lily latched onto my arm, and the room spun again as she ducked behind the three dragons. Before I got my bearings, she used her vampire strength to wrestle me to the ground.

The three dragons blew a stream of white-hot fire at the blob.

When the fire died, it was ash.

Lily let me go and stood. "I'm out." Her voice was two octaves higher than usual. "I'm going to kill someone if we keep doing this."

Drake stared her down as he helped me off the floor. "Has Jonas seen your magic?"

"Yeah. Lots of times. Why?" She examined me from head to toe.

His eyes flicked toward Deva. "I am surprised he has not recognized your power."

She held up a hand. "Nope."

Deva stepped forward. "Are you sure? It feels different."

"Because of the poor execution."

"Nope. We're not going there. I'm already on learning things about my origins overload. This training is about Jen. You know, the woman with so much pent-up magic she's about to explode?"

Drake's lips twitched. "Very well. I'll wait until you are more emotionally stable to discuss it with you."

"I'm not...it's not...never mind. The point is, Jen is good at creation magic, but she has a long way to go before she releases enough."

"Agreed." Cavil handed the human version of Alex some clothes and focused on me. "One facet of your magic is creation. As the ruling class, your other strength is to mimic. Conjure a small sample, please."

I held out a silver ball with faded strands of a thousand colors running through it.

Lily leaned forward. "That is so cool."

Cavil rested a hand on her shoulder. "You have already absorbed magic from Drake and Lily." He pointed to the green and red lines running through the silver ball. "And I suspect you have been mimicking Mathias's magic most of your life." He indicated a thick gold line.

"How is that possible?"

"I don't know. The point is, you can assimilate any magic you come in contact with."

My head spun and my heart raced. I thought back to when the uncontrolled ruling magic tried to drain the former witch president before my coronation. "How?"

"That is the question. How did you connect to Lily's magic?" He pointed to the deep red line.

"I didn't. She connected with me."

"Do you remember how that felt?"

"Yes."

"Try to use that feeling and connect to Elsie. Do not connect to any other hybrids, including your witch friend, until you know what you're doing. Hybrid magic is individualized and will not serve your immediate purpose."

"Tracy's not a hybrid."

"She is," Drake said. "She's not considered one by the haters because alchemy and spell weaving are both witch magics."

My eye twitched. "Haters?" A puzzled look crossed Lily's face, so I clarified. "He's obsessed with human clichés."

She shrugged.

"Every time you connect, the respective color will deepen," Cavil continued. "Once the color is vivid, you can mimic it. Elsie is a good start for vampires."

"So I can turn into a vampire or shift into a dragon?"

"I don't know how magic operates in this realm. I advise you to use caution until you understand your capabilities."

My hands were shaky because I didn't want to hurt her, so I balled them into fists. "This is insane. Ready, Elsie?"

"Sure."

I attached to her magic, imagined mine as a straw, and took a swig.

She gasped.

Cavil pointed to a new black line that streaked through the silvery ball. "You connected far too deep. You need a small sip rather than a gulp."

"How do you know this?" Mat asked.

"I have spent the last hundred years guarding a Crown Princess in my realm. Jen's magic is identical."

I didn't care where he learned it. I needed to learn fast.

"Right. So, I'll just get out of here so you can practice without killer blobs chasing you around." Lily turned to Alex. "I need to go see my new meemaw. You coming?"

"I'll stay here. Deva said she'd help me perfect my mental magic."

"Okay. But don't go anywhere alone."

Alex rolled his eyes. "Yes, Mother."

The fastest way to absorb new magic was to hit the streets. Drake and Bastien stayed at Dragon Headquarters to work with Alex. I didn't understand the dragons' obsession with the hybrid, but I had to admit his mental magic was special.

Emine and Mat left to take care of some Bellicose Lily spotted, so Tracy and I headed out to test my new skill. As we strolled down the street, I took a tiny sip of power from anyone who bowed. It helped ease the frustration.

Cavil caught up as we turned toward the main square. He watched an ogre who stopped in front of us. "Is bowing to you a requirement?"

I shook my head. "No. My mother made it up. I hate it."

"Then why allow it to continue?"

When my eyes landed on him, he held up his hands. "No offense. I only want to understand the customs in this realm."

A deep sigh escaped. "I hoped if people got used to me wondering around, they'd stop."

Tracy snorted. "How's that working for you? I mean, it seems like it's irritating people more than anything."

I took a sip of magic from the ogre and watched him for a reaction. He didn't even flinch. Instead, he straightened and pulled an envelope out of his pocket. "Your Grace. My queens wished me to deliver this to you."

Tracy took it from him and tucked it away.

"Thank you," I said, as the ogre trotted away. "They need to stop bowing."

"Are you not their queen?" Cavil asked.

"Sort of. I oversee the coalition. Each faction has their own leaders and follows their own laws. I oversee the leaders, and as an extension, I'm responsible for their people."

"So, yes."

"Like I said, sort of."

"I don't understand."

Tracy waved a hand. "Don't bother. Jen is the queen. She just doesn't like it."

Cavil examined me for a few seconds, and his face lit with a blinding smile. By blinding, I mean literally. The street somehow became brighter. "How do you do that?"

"Do what?"

"Make the light brighter when you smile."

"I can create and spread light. It leaks through, depending on my mood."

"Does it have the same benefits as sunshine?"

His eyes narrowed. "Yes."

"Can you injure a vampire who can't tolerate daylight?"

"Yes. But my power lies with my followers, so it is not at full strength yet. Should I gain followers, I can light up the night as if it is daytime."

Tracy leaned in. "Have you tested it on demon magic?"

His eyes bounced from her to me. "Some demons can withstand the daylight. If my magic becomes powerful enough, it can somewhat disable them."

I grinned. "So you're the polar opposite of Lily. She can spread night while you spread daylight. It's cute."

"I am a god. Nothing about me is cute. And I don't want to be involved in your war."

"Fair enough. I appreciate the magic lessons, though." I started walking again. "So I can create magic, dissipate it, and absorb powers. What else?"

"Once you collect enough power, you can manage others with their own magic."

I waved a hand. "Not interested."

Cavil's eyes swept over me. "You're a very odd queen."

"No, I'm not. I just don't want to control people."

"Like I said, odd. I have not found a realm where the ruler did not wish for more power and influence."

"I hope to lead without it." My mother led with control, and it didn't turn out well for anyone.

"I don't want to offend you, but you may change your mind once you learn your magic."

"Which is why we're here."

He smiled again, but the street didn't light up. "Once you absorb enough power from a faction, you can use it."

I considered Mage Mountain and how the rules were enforced. If a flying paranormal tried to take off, the magic from the mountain grounded them. I bet anything my grandmother was sleeping inside that mountain and used the magic she'd absorbed to enforce those rules. "Other than control, how will this help me rule?"

"Your abilities help you rule without effort on your part. You don't need to activate it. Other than control, I am unsure what purpose absorbing magic holds. All rulers in my realm absorb the magic of others."

"Do you have the urge to follow me, Tracy?"

She shook her head. "No, but you're like a beacon. It helps me find you."

I swung my head toward Cavil and raised an eyebrow.

"Perhaps you must will it, but it exists."

We meandered through the main square, where paranormals gathered, and I took sips of magic from as many types as possible. Every once in a while, I checked the colors running through the silver. "So, should I take a sip every time I pass someone? When is it enough?"

Cavil tapped his chin. "It depends on the expectations in this realm. In mine, the rulers spend five years after being christened as the next ruler absorbing powers. It takes even longer to achieve proficiency."

Five years was too long. "And you're sure my grandmother was from your realm?"

"Your dragon mate is sure."

That was good enough for me. Drake knew where all the Firsts came from. "So, what else can I do?"

He pointed to the flashing circle. "You don't need those. Gods don't leave a trail when moving from one place to another. You can appear anywhere and not collide with other paranormals."

"What about running into objects when I reappear?"

"It is a risk. It's best to study the terrain of the landing area, but your magic will not let you crash."

"Huh. What about my energy?"

His eyebrows drew together. "Should you have enough followers, which, based on your title and the bowing, I assume you do, then your energy is not as much of a factor."

I frowned, trying to remember if I'd read that in my grandmother's diaries. "Energy is the price for magic."

"Yes. And our followers rejuvenate us."

If that were the case, why did my mother look so dull when we captured her? She had the Bellicose behind her, so she should have been strong. "So, if I have the entire coalition behind me, I won't run out of energy?"

"Correct."

"Will I sap the energy from others as I replenish?"

"No. It is the belief in you that gives you energy."

"And why did you come to this realm again?"

"Because I wanted to. I am a god. Therefore, I go where I wish. I did not expect to run into other gods in this realm."

"I'm not a god."

Tracy grabbed my arm and dragged me toward the flashing circle. "Doesn't matter. Let's go to witch territory. I mean, you already know a bunch of spells. If you can absorb enough of their magic, you can use them."

Cavil eyed the circle. "I must return to my home. Use the phone device if you need more training."

"I will. Thanks, Cavil."

We spent the rest of the morning going from district to district. My eyes drooped as I ate a quick lunch. Apparently, I didn't have enough followers to replenish my energy. When we finally returned to our house, I dragged myself up the stairs and fell face-first on my bed.

The wards buzzed, and my eyes flew open. I forgot where I was for a minute. In my own bed, I realized. I dragged myself out of it and down the stairs. I wasn't much of a drinker because my body ejected alcohol like it was poison. But by the pounding headache and dry mouth, I had one. I wondered if the hangover was why the gods spent five years absorbing magic.

I didn't sense Tracy in the house, so I stumbled downstairs and opened the back door. Mat stood at the wards, his arms crossed. An unfamiliar dragon perched on the neighbor's house. I glanced in her direction, then dragged my brother through the wards. "Hey."

"Where have you been?" He asked as he followed me through the back door.

I showed him a ball of silvery magic with several colors of different intensities running through it. "I spent the morning absorbing magic. It wiped me out."

He poked at the silvery ball. "I see."

"Are you here to tell me what's wrong?" I blurted.

"Besides the fact that we are at war and the queen is missing?"

I let the magic go and jerked a thumb toward myself. "I'm right here. You want something to drink?"

He moved toward the kitchen table and lowered himself into a chair. "No."

I pulled up the menu on the magichef. A sloppy smile formed when I saw Drake had changed it. I ordered two sodas and put one in front of Mat. "Talk to me."

"Yes, let's talk. Let's begin by discussing the number of decisions we must make before the castle opens."

I rolled my eyes. "That's not what I meant."

He rubbed his hands over his face. "I've lost my sense of self."

His defeated tone caused a pang of sadness in my heart. Mat had always been my rock. The one person who always knew what to do. But so much happened over the last few months. Like me showing up and taking the throne, our mother's death, and Drake taking over some of his duties. It never occurred to me how it would cause him to have an identity crisis. "I'm sorry."

"It doesn't matter.

I touched his scarred hand. "It matters. And it's my fault. I'm sorry."

He retracted his hand. "You're simply doing what you are destined to do. My destiny is to protect you, and I no longer need to. It's...difficult."

That wasn't what was bothering him, but I let it go. "I'm going to visit the Conservatory to learn how to make a small pocket. The Dwarven Prince, Leebol, is smart and has studied their construction for years. Maybe he and Cavil can work together to teach me."

"That will help the hybrids, but not until we find our traitors and the Bellicose leadership."

"I agree. Though if Quin couldn't find their king, no one can." I took a gulp of soda to clear my fuzzy head. "Jonas and Ann Marie can't take on the ones in the valley alone. Especially if the other hybrid leaders choose to ignore the problem."

"Correct. Many of their people aren't enthusiastic about joining the coalition and refuse to acknowledge or work with us."

"It doesn't matter. They still deserve our protection." I sighed. "Drake's been spending a lot of time in the valley, so he might have some ideas."

"Then talk to him. Find out what he knows, and let's develop a strategy so we can move forward."

"Sure." I glanced toward the front door. "Did you plant the raccoon shifters in the neighborhood?"

"Yes."

I wanted to feel relief, but couldn't until I knew for sure they weren't working for the Bellicose. I didn't think so, but then, we didn't know Gabe and Linda were, either. "Where did they disappear to?" Penelope had a bunch of kids, and I hadn't heard them screaming since the battle.

"Many shifters are in hiding."

True. There were millions of shifters all over the world. Most wanted nothing to do with politics. Especially after Jonas's son, Morten, ripped them apart under his rule. I suspected it was even worse now that Gabe and Linda betrayed the coalition. "What are the odds that two alphas in a row would tear the shifters apart?"

"Low," Mat said as he stood. "And I've considered they were working together and ruled it out. Ann Marie put a tracker spell on Morten, and he hasn't left his home in years."

"Okay, but I still want to keep an eye on him."

"Noted. Now, let's make some decisions about the reopening."

CHAPTER FIVE

As Mat and I strode through the castle, my stomach tied into knots. I pondered the shifter dilemma and the complicated magic on the pyramid Quin and I got sucked into. If the spell caster was a powerful hybrid, he or she had a mixture of magic I wouldn't recognize. If Jonas and Ann Marie were sure Morten hadn't left his home in India, their other two biological kids and several other powerful hybrids needed to be investigated. I hated it.

Verity turned her dull eyes toward us as we approached. "What the hell happened to your hair?"

I patted my head. I didn't brush it after my nap. "It's not bad."

"If you say so."

Charlotte's eyes swept over me. "The First Drake is in his office."

I'd sensed him inside but nodded and skirted around Verity. Mat followed me and moved toward the windows. "What happened to the protesting witches?"

"Calvin and the gargoyles did something that scared them away. I haven't got the Gargoyle King to talk to me yet, and I'm not asking Calvin what they did. They're gone, so we can check it off our list."

"Perhaps you should change your communication strategy."

"Sure." The door to Drake's office was cracked open, so I cautiously stuck my head in and waited for him to acknowledge my presence. I didn't want to risk another snapping incident. When his eyes met mine, the usual spark at seeing me was absent. I forced a smile. "Do you have a minute?"

"I need to finish what I'm doing." He turned his attention back to his desk.

I'd half convinced myself that everyone's strange mood was all in my head. But Mat wasn't the broody type, and Drake wasn't cold and calculated. Even Verity and Charlotte seemed off. I shut the door and swung toward my brother. "What the hell is going on? Why is everyone acting so strange?"

He cocked his head but didn't turn from the window. "What do you mean?"

"No one in this place is acting right. What's going on?"

"Nothing."

I yanked my phone out of my pocket and texted Ann Marie. "Fine. Don't tell me. I'll figure it out myself."

"Your time is best spent on other matters."

The door to Drake's office opened, and his eyes bore into me. "Why do you insist everyone is acting strange?"

I pointed at him. "You were fine at the PISD and Dragon Headquarters, but you snapped at me yesterday, and today you're cold." I pointed at Mat. "He's lost his confidence and is moping around instead of getting things done. Verity's depressed, and Charlotte isn't stammering when she talks to me. Even Helen acted strange the other day."

He strode to the other side of the room, stopping beside Mat, and looked out the window. "The only thing wrong is your incompetence at disbursing the gargoyles."

"Correct," Mat said. "It makes you look weak."

That was true, but a little harsh. Realizing they wouldn't acknowledge the strange behavior, I let it go. "Any news about the Bellicose King?"

"None," Drake said. "Though we found two more offices. Tracking down their leaders will take time. Even if patience isn't one of your strongest virtues."

"Like I said, you're not acting like yourself." Drake had told me I needed to learn patience before. He was nicer about it, though.

I started pacing, so I wouldn't give in to the urge to run away. What if they had some kind of invisible bug magic on them that even I couldn't see? No, that didn't make sense. If I couldn't see dark magic, I'd feel it. And I sensed nothing strange besides the impulse to leave the palace.

Their abnormal behavior made me want to scream, especially since they refused to see it. But I'd never take down the Bellicose without them. I stopped pacing and rubbed my eyes. "Okay. Then, figure out who and where he is. How about our efforts to build rapport with the hybrid community in the city?"

Drake's eyes flashed, and he slammed the bond shut. "I am not incompetent."

"I didn't say you were. What I mean is we need to build stronger bridges with them. All of us. And we need to figure out how to mobilize fast if they're attacked."

Mat shook his head. "I forgot how bad you are at strategy. We cannot fill the human city with paranormals and fight in the streets. We should pull our people back and regroup."

Talk about poor strategy. The hybrids were strong, but I'd promised to help and planned to follow through. Until that moment, Drake and Mat had agreed. Especially Drake. I waved a hand. "No need to change anything right now. Keep doing what you're doing."

"Very well," Drake turned back toward the window.

My phone pinged with a text from Tracy saying Bastien was acting normal. "I don't care what strategy you use." I did, but wasn't about to say so since they were acting so weird.

Mat stood and moved toward the door. "I will develop a better plan and send it to you."

When the door closed, Drake turned from the window and crossed his arms. "You lied."

"Yes."

"Why?"

"Because something is wrong with the two of you."

"If something is wrong with everyone around you, then perhaps you are the problem."

"I usually am," I mumbled.

He nodded and strode toward his office. "I will touch bases with Jonas."

"Sure." I watched the door close and rubbed my chest to ease the ache. Tracy, Bastien and Quin were fine, but Verity, Mat, and Drake weren't. I wasn't sure about Deva. The question was, why? I thought about everything that had happened since the battle. Emine and Mat stayed in the guest wing of the palace because it was still intact. Verity oversaw the rebuild. The apartment she and Titus shared was also on the guest side. And Drake? He stayed with me one night and split his time between the human world, the palace, and Dragon Headquarters.

Tracy spent a lot of time with her dad. And I worked out of our house most of the time. I needed to figure out what was wrong fast. I swiped my phone off the desk and headed out to find answers.

The family entrance still spilled into a mudroom, but it was bigger than before. Helen, the griffin matriarch, stood in the doorway, her hands on her hips. "Where are you off to?"

"Dragon Headquarters, and then I want to see how Razazia is settling in." I examined her from head to toe, but didn't see anything wrong with her on the surface.

"Ah. Skirting your responsibilities again, I see." She swatted at her grandson as he set the table. "Not like that, you idiot. The flowers go between the second chair and the third. Can't anyone do anything right?"

Yeah, something was off. Helen never treated her family like that. "I better go."

She snorted. "As if you'll ever accomplish anything."

I hightailed it out the door and almost sprinted toward the flashing circle.

And smashed face-first into Emine.

"Ow, ya dummy. Where are you going so fast?" She rubbed her shoulder.

"Sorry." I stepped back and eyed her. She looked fine until I met her eyes. The crazy that normally reflected in them was absent, replaced with cold calculation. "What are you doing here?"

"Your job. Mat needs my help." Her eyes trailed over me. "You're no fun anymore."

I shook my head. "I don't think it's me this time."

"Of course it's you."

The flashing circle was a few feet away, so I skirted around her and scurried toward it. "Right." I flashed away.

I tried to hide my shaking as I made my way toward Dragon Headquarters to check on Deva. The yellow dragon who acted as the doorman at the hotel wasn't paying attention to me, so I took the stairs two at a time. I didn't want to act like prey in the dragon district, but I needed to hurry if I wanted to help the people I loved.

"Why are you scurrying around like a mouse?"

"Gah! Damnit, Quin. Not now." I swung the doors open and strode toward the purple dragon who manned the security desk, then stopped in my tracks when a thought hit me. "You know how I asked you about the people in the palace?"

"Yes."

"How much time have you spent there lately?"

"None. I now have other concerns."

"You mean Lily." When he didn't answer, I continued. "What kind of magic is undetectable but makes people grumpy or depressed?"

"Irritating personality and brain chemistry make the blood taste bitter."

I rolled my eyes. "Aside from that."

"Curses and hexes, though they do not work on vampires."

"You mean like magic doesn't work on you?"

"One cannot curse the cursed."

"Right." I wasn't going to get any answers from him, so I continued toward the security desk.

Quin followed without further comment.

Deva was in her makeshift office on the sixth floor with the hybrid, Alex, and Bastien. "Hey, Deva," I said as I entered, Quin on my heels. "Can I ask you a question?"

"Of course, love. Do you need privacy?"

I met her eyes. The sadness that plagued her was still present, but she hid it well. "Do you feel a little off since the battle?"

"What do you mean?" Bastien asked.

I shook my head. "Have either of you had unusual thoughts, or has anyone questioned your behavior?"

Deva's eyes narrowed. "Why?"

"Something's wrong with Mat and Drake, but I can't put my finger on what, and they insist they're fine and that I'm the problem. I wanted to make sure you guys were okay."

She waved a hand. "We're fine." Her tone left no room for argument.

"Sure." I rubbed my arms as I backed toward the door. And ran into an unmovable Quin. "Now that I see you're okay, I'll be on my way." I needed to remove Alex before he went crazy, too. Jonas would never forgive me if whatever was wrong with Deva spread to him. "Hey, Alex. Where's Lily?"

"At the hotel. Why?"

I formed mental images of mind-controlled dragons and used Drake's magic to send them to him. "Just wondering. Come on, Quin." I fled. When we spilled out of the building, I stopped and scanned the street while I caught my breath. "Are you following Lily?"

He eyed me from head to toe. "She is my granddaughter."

So, yes. I looked for signs of hostility as he answered. My muscles relaxed when I realized he looked as bored as ever. "Something's wrong, so stay away from the palace until I figure out what's going on."

"Perhaps you should attempt to use your senses for once."

I didn't use my senses around dense populations because it overwhelmed me. "Sure. I'll work on that."

"I do not believe you." He disappeared.

I pondered where to go next. The only sane person I knew well was Tracy. And she was busy trying to save the world. I glanced at the hotel one more time as an idea formed.

The First Razazia perched on a thick vine laced between two trees. "Had I known what a pain in the ass you were, I would have stayed in your mother's sleep stupor."

"I understand. If I'd known how difficult you'd be, I wouldn't have gone out of my way to find and wake you." I lowered myself to a stump and folded my hands in my lap. "But it doesn't change the fact that people are acting strange."

"A problem that is not mine."

"I hoped you'd seen something like it before."

She rolled her eyes. "Of course I have. Doesn't mean I want to be involved. I'm happy here with my elves."

I'd be happy living in their sanctuary, too. The elves had created an oasis on the outskirts of the city. A wide stone path ran through the center of the lush greenery, protected by a canopy of trees where they made their homes. Small resting spots dotted the area where narrow paths led deeper into the woods. Some even had creeks bubbling past them. Homes and businesses were built into the massive trees, half camouflaged by thick, colorful foliage. The place was as relaxing as it was unique.

I tore my eyes away from the scenery. "Either it's a new experimental magic, a hex, or a curse. I've never encountered a hex or curse, but I'd see magic."

She leaned forward. "Are you telling me you allowed a First and the Dragon Queen to be cursed?"

"I didn't *allow* it, no. But they're acting strange."

"Because they're cursed."

I shrugged. "Like I said, I don't know for sure. But it's the only explanation I can think of."

She stood. "Again, not my problem. Nor can I help you. Perhaps you should find a curse breaker."

"Okay." I stood and moved toward the stone path. "Thank you for your time."

As I started down the trail, she caught up with me. "Could another explanation exist?"

"Sure. And if it was one person acting strange, I wouldn't be here. But it's everyone. Drake acted normal for a couple of days when he wasn't at the palace. He also seemed okay at Dragon Headquarters. But at the palace, he acted cold and a little mean. Twice. Mat, Emine, the griffins, and even Verity are acting strange. I'm worried."

"And you can't feel anything through your bond?"

"No. He's keeping it closed." Drake also promised me a picnic that didn't happen. Which was unlike him.

"If it is a curse, it hasn't taken hold yet. One must be exposed to even a potent curse for quite some time for it to sink in."

My stomach soured. Mat had been at the palace nonstop since the battle. "How long?"

"It depends on the curse. If it's intended for you, then it would need to be strong. Even then, it's not guaranteed to work. Lissa was immune. However, if it is more general, then the time for it to sink in will vary by person."

"I'm not immune. It hits me different, though. Which is why I'm not so sure that's what it is."

Her forehead crinkled. "How and why?"

"Why what?"

She rolled her eyes. "How does it affect you?"

"It makes me want to run away."

She tapped her chin. "Then the question is, why are you not immune when your grandmother was?"

"My grandmother was a first-generation god. I'm not." And I didn't want to stay uncursed if everyone I cared about was a shell of themselves. "How many people can create a powerful curse?"

We came to a stop at the edge of elven territory. "You should be immune. The power of Lissa that runs through you eclipses the meager magic you inherited from your parents. Many can generate curses, but none awake who can hide them from you. But if it's intended to rip your safety net away, then it's working."

My heart jumped into my throat. She was right. Everyone I loved was acting strange. Everyone except Quin and Tracy. But Quin said he couldn't be cursed, and Tracy hadn't been at the palace or Dragon Headquarters much. "Thanks, Razazia. I appreciate the help."

Her hand landed on my arm. "Be careful, Jenella." Her eyes swept over me one last time, and she melted into the vines that protected their territory.

I stopped at the Conservatory on my way out. Mat didn't think it was a priority, but I disagreed. I needed to figure out how to make a pocket. If I could do that, then I might unlock the secret of using the magic I absorbed. Besides, I couldn't trust his advice.

Leebol, one of the many dwarven princes, raced down the stairs when I stepped through the door. "Your Grace! Welcome back."

I pasted a smile on my face. "Hello, Prince Leebol. I wondered if you could help me with something."

"Of course. Have you had time to think about the ward replenishment?"

"Yes. That's what I wanted to ask you about. Will you help me learn more about pocket creation?"

"Of course. Please, follow me." He led me to the back of the building and into a cavernous library with high ceilings and books as far as the eye could see. "I have a teaching workshop back here that may be of use to you."

My mouth dropped open when he opened the door to what used to be a dining room. Counters lined the walls, with bookshelves stretching to the ceiling above them. One contained several square models with what looked like miniature climates inside. Each one emanated different combinations of power.

I stepped to the one in the middle. "May I?"

"Of course. The ones on the right are where we started. The one on the left is our latest creation. Feel free to explore them, but please don't change anything."

"Okay." I went to the first one, then methodically moved down the line, noting the changes and the composition. When I got to the last one, I dug deeper because it seemed different. "You used Razazia's magic on this one?"

"Yes. She insisted."

They were on the right track but were missing some key ingredients. When my mother created the pockets, she insisted no one else could. Not only because she was selfish but also because she was the only one in the world with enough power to do it. I bet she even bragged and gloated about it. By the looks of the samples Leebol and his team created, she was wrong. Working together, they were able to replicate her efforts.

Throwing the thought out of my head, I studied each type of magic one by one. I recognized elven, witch, climate mage, tech mage, dwarven, pixie, and even a little minotaur power. "Why the minotaur magic?"

"We hoped it would solidify the walls."

It wouldn't, though it was a brilliant idea. Minotaurs were created when some rogue gods moved to the realm and tried to rule over a group of humans. They hand-picked some humans to become minotaurs. Not many survived after the gods abandoned them. My grandmother brought them into the coalition. They still had a bit of god magic, but nothing like Cavil's or mine. "Do you mind if I try to make a model?"

"Please do." Leebol rubbed his hands together.

My lips twitched as I moved to a blank spot and closed my eyes. Back when I used Mat's magic, I learned to reverse spells by examining the threads and then puzzling through a reversal. I'd absorbed magic from so many paranormals that I figured if I applied those principles, I might be successful. If I could access the different magics.

Creation magic wasn't any different from what I'd practiced my whole life. The trick to it was the anchors and how I accessed it. Instead of drawing it from my core, I had to imagine, in detail, what I wanted and will it. The process was more like piercing a well-placed hole in a dam instead of siphoning and spraying the water over the top.

I didn't grasp the concept until Lily showed me. If I tried to force it instead of letting it flow, it no longer worked. Cavil said I needed to tell it what to do, and it would comply. Easier said than done, but I kind of understood.

I started by creating a box, then 'told' my magic what to inject. I didn't anchor until each element was in place. Heart in my throat, I opened my eyes. And gasped.

Leebol moved closer and lifted his wide eyes. "What did you do?"

"I tried to copy your last creation." I leaned forward. It wasn't a pocket. Nor was it like the sample I tried to copy. No, I'd created a two-foot wide by four-foot long terrarium, complete with miniature trees and hills. The colors were off, though, and I didn't know how to create the climate. The grass was more blue than green, and the tiny trees had sand-colored bark. Everything was the same color of green, with no variation. The exact color of Drake's eyes. I threw the thought out of my head. It wasn't perfect or even great, but it wasn't awful. "What do you think?"

He took his time answering. "It's unusual, but closer than anything we've done." He waved a hand toward the other models. "You need practice and access to my team in real-time. If you can direct their magic instead of using guesswork, you might make a proper pocket."

I didn't like his calculating look. I squared my shoulders. "Great idea. But right now, I need to go." I moved toward the door. "Call my assistant, Verity, and set up a couple of practice sessions."

He tore his eyes from my experiment, and a wide grin formed on his face. "It will be my honor."

CHAPTER SIX

IF SOMEONE CURSED THE castle, I needed to learn how to break it before it soaked into everyone inside. Or, to save time, find someone else who could help. I headed toward the flashing circle and paused. One of my theories about the Bellicose King was a First woke up and wanted to bring my family down.

Two Firsts specialized in curses, though I didn't remember the details because, when I learned about the Firsts, I never dreamed I'd actually meet them. The palace library had books about their abilities, but I didn't want to spend more time than necessary inside until I figured out what was wrong.

No, what I needed was someone who could sense and break curses. I knew some ogres could. The trick was to find one and have them analyze it without drawing suspicion. And that was going to be a problem. Drake and Mat would figure out what I was doing before I even made it to the gates.

I sighed. If Razazia was right, I had at least some immunity. The following day was the public reopening of the palace, and I couldn't miss it.

I was so deep in thought I didn't notice the sick feeling until the hairs on the back of my neck stood up. I sent my senses out, expecting to find

Quin. Nope. Not Quin. I turned in a slow circle, trying to figure out what I sensed. It wasn't like anything else I'd ever felt.

The buildings on my left were owned by the dwarfs and used to run their engineering businesses and access their various tunnels that stretched under the elven district. On the right was an open field. Beyond that was the fenced-off mage district.

The sensation wasn't coming from there. Nope. It was coming from the business district ahead of me, and I almost walked right into it. I shivered and pulled my phone out. But who would I call? There weren't many allies left who weren't acting strange.

I texted Quin and Tracy and waited.

The feeling grew and crept closer. Whoever it was knew I was there. I swung my head around, frantically searching for an escape route. But if I ran, I'd be prey. The tension drained from my shoulders when I remembered Cavil's words about how I could flash anywhere without a circle.

Just before I flashed away, I reconsidered. If I left and it attacked the elves, dwarfs, or mages, I'd never forgive myself. I used my senses to pinpoint the building where it originated, then shook out my hands. "Okay. I've got this."

I flashed to the roof of a building across the street from the feeling and examined it. The creepy feeling came from a square, one-story wooden structure resembling a shed or outbuilding. It had a couple of spelled windows so no one could see in. Great.

The feeling grew as I considered my options. I could box it in, destroy it, or go in and have a look. The last one was out of the question because who knew what I'd be walking into?

Destroying it was my best option. But how? I'd learned to create, not destroy.

"Do not go in that building."

"Gah!" I swung toward Bastien. "Where the hell did you come from?" And why hadn't I sensed him?

"Tracy sent me. I flew in from that direction." He pointed toward Dragon headquarters. "What is wrong with you?"

My eyes grew wide. "Am I acting strange?"

"No stranger than usual. But you should have sensed me."

He was right. I'd been so focused on the odd feeling I wasn't paying attention to anything else. "I wasn't going to go in. My best option is to destroy it, but I want to know what's causing the sick feeling."

He crossed his arms. "I see. And if you set something off?"

I hadn't thought of that. "What do you think I should do?"

"Call your mate."

"Nope. He has the bond locked down."

"What did you do?"

I threw my arms in the air. "I didn't do anything." When his eyes narrowed, I turned back toward the building. "Can we focus on the task at hand?"

"We need to know what they're doing."

"They can sense me. If I get closer, they'll know."

Bastien tapped his chin. "Let's use that to our advantage." Before I could answer, he morphed into his dragon form, and a long stream of dark fire smashed into the building.

"Are you out of your mind?" I screeched.

He dove off the roof and flew in tight circles around the destruction.

I held my breath, waiting for the flames to die down. My senses were on alert and focused on the building.

Bastien waved his tail, and the fire died.

The strange sensation I'd felt since I left the Conservatory disappeared, replaced with demon magic so thick I almost choked.

"Whoever it was left, Bas."

He hovered over the building and didn't respond. After a few seconds, his head lifted, and he met my eyes.

Run! Blasted through my head as hundreds of rat-sized demons poured out of the wreckage.

I reared back, my heart thudding so hard it hurt. The demons turned as one and skittered down the street toward Elven territory.

I flung out my hand and formed a tall wall.

They thudded against it seconds before Bastien doused them with fire.

The ones who remained turned and came back in my direction. A few curled into balls and rolled into the nearby field toward mage territory. Vines appeared, wrapped around them, and raised them in the air. An elven trap.

Others climbed the nearby buildings. Three came over the edge of the roof, saw me, and charged.

I flashed to the other side.

They followed.

Hundreds of the things converged on me from every direction.

I tried to form a shield, but wasn't fast enough.

Two latched onto my legs. I spun in circles and batted at them as they bit down, drawing blood.

One stood on two hind legs and chittered what sounded like a laugh.

Memories of Quin and me against all those shifters flooded my mind as more flowed onto the roof. "The Bellicose use the same tactics over and over again," I muttered.

A second later, I wasn't thinking about anything as the little assholes piled on top of me.

My arms came up to protect my face as a thousand needle-like bites pierced my clothes.

Concentrating was hard, but I closed my eyes and willed them banned. Silvery magic leaked out of me, and the ones who came in contact with me melted to dust. It wasn't enough.

I willed the silver circle to expand. More of the little critters melted away.

An ear-splitting roar sounded somewhere close.

I panicked and slapped the little shits. I punted a few off the building and spun in circles, slapping and kicking. Just before I exploded my magic, a massive green and black head lowered in front of me and the demons ran away.

My scream pierced the air.

Green fire lit in Drake's eyes. *You fear me now?*

"You startled me." Heart in my throat, I raced to the edge of the building, peered over, and concentrated on banishing. I'd barely cleared the roof before elves and dwarves poured onto the streets, dressed for battle. A large group of dragons flew overhead in formation. A couple peeled off and attacked something on the street. Several mages popped into existence.

"What did you do, Jenella?"

I swung toward Drake's voice and almost fell off the roof when I saw his icy glare. "Piss off, Drake."

He crossed his arms.

I didn't have time to deal with his issues. "They're bringing demons in right under our noses."

He moved to the edge. "Under your nose."

"I seem to recall stupid naïve me putting you in charge before I realized what a cold bastard you are. So it's *our* noses." My head might not have been right at the time, but I couldn't bring myself to care.

He didn't respond.

A pang of guilt reverberated through me. "Look. I'm pretty sure you and everyone at the palace are cursed against me. It's not your fault." I still resented it.

He gave me a long, considering look, then shifted into his dragon form and flew off.

"What in the world did you stir up now?" Razazia's voice came from behind me.

I closed my eyes, took a deep breath, and swallowed the pain before turning my attention to her. "They're bringing demons through right under our noses." I motioned toward the blackened hole that used to be a building. "They're using a magic I've never felt before."

Her eyes narrowed. "Right on my doorstep, too."

"Yes."

Bastien landed and switched to his human form. "Drake caught a few thoughts. They're practicing for when they invade and enslave the hybrids."

I almost snapped at him, then closed my eyes to tamp down the anger. It wasn't his fault Drake didn't talk to me. "Razazia, will you monitor this area, please?"

"What do you think I've been doing?"

I turned my attention to where elves and dwarfs searched through every building in the area, hunting the little demons. "Just keep your eyes, ears, and senses open, please." I flashed to the edge of the nearest flashing circle and tried not to think about what a mess everything had become.

I stood on the palace's outer wall and looked out toward the city. If I squinted, I could make out Deva perched on top of Dragon Headquarters. I shivered and wrapped my arms around myself. With the weather turning cooler, I needed to carry a jacket. "Is there a reason you won't talk to me? Because we need your help."

The gargoyle king stayed silent and in his stone form.

"They're summoning demons or have some kind of agreement with them. That's kind of your thing. Or do the gargoyles no longer care about evil overtaking the world?" Stone on stone grinding assaulted my ears, and I felt his eyes on me. It took every ounce of control I had not to turn and look. "If we're going to save the coalition, and perhaps the world, everyone needs to work together. You included."

Nothing.

Drake's power proceeded his descent to the back lawn. He scanned the wall, spotted me with the gargoyles, and disappeared into the palace.

"The grand opening is today. Then we're going to the human world to break up the Bellicose before they enslave the hybrids. But we can't focus on them if rat-sized demons take over Allure. I'd really appreciate it if you'd consider helping." I turned and made my way to the stairs.

"Why do you not order me?"

I stopped in my tracks at the deep, commanding voice. "Like I said, we're all in this together. I don't want to order anyone to do what they should already be doing."

"And you think it is our responsibility to help you with your demons?"

"They're not my demons. And we all have many responsibilities, including you. What's not your responsibility is sitting here weighing down this wall."

The sound that came out of him sounded like a series of short grunts. It took me a few seconds to realize he was laughing. "Very well, we will round up the demons inside the pockets and move on to the city over the mountain."

I swung my head toward him. "Why are you on this wall?"

He hesitated before answering. "Great evil resides in many places around the world."

The blood drained from my face. "Are you talking about the curse?"

"We only feel the darkness."

"And the main square? You were there for quite a while."

He turned back toward the street. "Evil comes and goes."

Which meant he knew the Bellicose were coming and going from there. I rushed back up the stairs. "I'm going to need a contract, so we're clear on your involvement."

After we made an airtight magical contract, he turned back to stone. "Thank you." I flashed to the ground and headed toward the family entrance.

Mat and Emine sat on one side of the breakfast table, Drake on the other. "Good morning," I said with as much enthusiasm as I could muster. It sounded somewhere between a funeral eulogy and a zombie. Though I'd never actually met a zombie.

Drake twisted in his chair and inclined his head. "Jenella."

Mat stared at me with dull eyes. "Where have you been?"

"Busy. Why?"

"Because we have work to do, and you've been absent, as usual."

Helen came in, slammed a platter on the table, and left without a word. I watched her go, then turned my attention to Emine.

Calm blue eyes stared back at me. "You're useless in most situations."

They were getting worse. If our mother placed the curse, then she'd plant something in it to make me feel like I did as a kid. Helpless, useless, and scared. And she'd make Mat feel inadequate. He didn't seem to be there yet, but I didn't like how much more hostile the room was than the day before.

Though I was more frustrated and angry than anything, their behavior scared the shit out of me. I reached for my water glass with a shaky hand and took a sip. "Has anyone seen Quin?"

Mat set his fork down. "No."

I sent my senses out, but he wasn't on the property. I got so used to him being around that his absence was loud. Plus, I needed him to confirm the strange behavior. He said he was following Lily, so I hoped he'd come around soon.

We sat in silence except for the silverware clinking on our plates as we ate breakfast. I kept a death grip on my fork so I didn't scarf it down and run. When Lily and Alex popped up on my senses, I perked up. I waited for Quin to appear, but didn't feel him. I took another sip of water. "Lily and Alex are coming through the front gates." My voice sounded too loud in the silence.

Mat picked up his phone and tapped the screen. "I'll send Pablo to fetch them. Perhaps Lily can do your job since you're not interested."

The burning anger inside me flared, and I had to repeat the word 'curse' inside my head to calm it down.

Drake's head snapped toward me. "That is not the first time you've alluded to a curse."

"Because I think the palace is cursed, and it's got hold of everyone here, even you."

Emine and Mat's laughter filled the breakfast nook.

Drake didn't laugh. His green eyes examined mine, and he gave me a slight incline of his head. "I feel better when you're around."

Another lie. I sighed and returned my attention to my plate.

George led Lily and Alex into the room and shot me a dirty look as Helen swept in. "Lily and Alex." She took Lily's hands, her previous crappy attitude absent. "Oh my. You're lovely." She patted Alex's arm. "And you are such a handsome young man. Sit. I'll get you some coffee and breakfast." She swept out of the room.

I watched her go, then scanned my dining companions. They looked normal. I jerked a thumb toward the door Helen used. "That's Helen. She's the griffin matriarch."

Lily slid into the chair beside Drake. "This place is beautiful."

Alex chose a seat next to Emine. "Lily was going to take a tour without telling you."

"Alex is a tattletale." Lily rubbed her hands together. "So, Mat, what's up with the ID that everyone says is fake? You messing with me?"

Humor danced in his eyes for the first time in days. "Everyone thinks it's fake, then?"

"Ahhh. I get it. The joke's on them *and* me." She leaned forward. "Gramps had to bail me out yesterday. I doubt he thinks it's funny."

As Mat shrugged, his eyes dulled. "Emine is the head of enforcers."

My gaze lingered on Mat for a couple of seconds before I turned my attention to Lily. "Wait. What? I get constant lectures on my safety and Lily gets funny games?" My decision to play along got me a speculative look from Helen when she swung through the door.

"Thank you, Helen," Lily said as she placed a coffee in front of her. No slamming things on the table for her, I noticed. "You don't know how to defend yourself?"

"I'm not a warrior by any means, but I can hold my own. Especially now that I have functioning magic."

"Huh."

I blinked in confusion when Mat smiled at her. My brother hadn't smiled at anyone since the battle. But he busted out the pearly whites for our new sister. "Lily is bored. She needs a challenge. I'm providing that. You are reckless and need to be reminded to think before you act. I also provide that. It's my duty as the eldest."

"I'm not bored."

"I'm not reckless."

"Lily is soooo bored. She needs to get out of here and back to her life," Alex said.

The crazy was back in Emine's eyes as she leaned forward. "So you took out some tainted wolves yesterday? What was that about?"

Lily eyed her for a few seconds before she answered. "We were just walking down the street, and they jumped us. The elf enforcer didn't believe us because of my fake ID. Then Gramps, who followed us there, showed himself and confirmed my origins." She scowled at Mat, but I was pretty sure her heart wasn't behind it.

Drake leaned forward, the disdain gone from his eyes. "Alex has a type of mental magic even my aunt hasn't seen before. There is no immunity to it, and he is a master at finding the thoughts he's interested in. Even my barriers wouldn't hold if he concentrated hard enough. Once he becomes better at his craft, no one will be safe. Especially since he can use his mental magic as a weapon. Even dragons can't do that, though we can usually confuse people and alter memories. The Bellicose want him for those abilities and because he can shift into a deadly predator. It makes him a valuable weapon."

"He's not interested in being a weapon. He wants to learn to shut it off so he can live his life." Lily focused on her breakfast.

"He wants you to stop answering for him." Alex was a smart kid. By the furrow of his brow, he knew something was off, but he either decided it wasn't his problem or was sneaking into our heads, trying to figure it out. Probably both.

I tore my eyes away from him and tried to ignore the mood shift. "Does it work on vampires?"

"I've never met anyone who can block me, though you came close. With vampires, I have to work harder to read their thoughts. Lily and I are pretty sure our parents adopted us because we were too powerful for anyone else to handle."

"We don't doubt they love us. But yeah. That's probably why they took us in. I have to go to that stupid dinner at Ara's on Friday, and then we'll head out on Saturday. That attack proved we're not any safer here than we were at home. I suggest you compare notes with our parents," Lily added.

Drake's elbow dug into my side as he turned toward Lily. "Jonas and Ann Marie are working with me. I'm rooting out and eliminating the Bellicose."

"Then you're doing a shit job because they're setting up base camps all over the Treasure Valley. They were outside Dragon Headquarters when you were there, for fuck's sake." Her face flashed with concern when we all stared at her. "What? It's true."

I elbowed Drake harder than I needed to and cleared my throat. "Drake's doing a great job, but it's a little like playing whack-a-mole."

Alex pushed his plate away. "That's a good way to describe it. Lily's assessment is a little too harsh, but she's not wrong. From what I've seen, these guys only recruit lower-level paranormals. You guys treat low-powered people like humans treat poor people. After a while of being treated like crap, they build up resentment and anger. It only takes someone power-hungry enough to come along and harvest their anger, and you have a revolt."

"In this case, it's demons. I spotted one of their leaders recently."

Everyone's eyes turned to Lily again. Mat leaned forward as if what she said was the most consequential thing he'd ever heard. "What did he look like?"

Lily blinked. "Dark hair and eyes, about six feet tall, lean muscle. He knew we were hiding in the shadows and smiled at us."

"The fake Jaques." My voice had a slight tremor. Not because of the mention of Jaques, but because everyone was acting so normal.

Mat disappeared, then reappeared. Apparently, the no flashing in the castle rule no longer applied to him. He shoved an old family portrait in front of Lily. "Is that the demon you saw?"

Lily examined it, then set it aside. "Demons lie. They cheat, lie, and prey on any fear they can find." She tapped the picture. "They found yours. That is the man I saw, but it wasn't Jaques. A demon is using that form to prey on your fear."

"I know. We already fought him once. His demeanor was all wrong."

"How do you know it's not him?" Emine asked.

"Because I can feel blood relations. That demon didn't register." Lily tapped the picture again. "Our mother used to go by a different name and wear glamor. She was pissed about Jaques' death. Something about him having the most potential. I think she was already pregnant with me when all that shit in Mahri went down. She never referred to you two as her kids unless something triggered her. She was a cold, cruel bitch."

Emine rested a hand on Mat's arm. "Just to be clear, what do you mean you feel family relations?"

She jerked a thumb toward her chest. "I get tingling or stabbing in my chest when I come across blood relations. The closer the relation, the stronger the sensation. It's off the charts around Jed and these two. It's a little different with Ara and Quin, lighter somehow, and even lighter still around Roman."

"Interesting." Triumph laced Mat's voice.

It didn't go unnoticed by Lily. She stiffened.

I bit my lip to keep from blurting out how they were all cursed.

Alex cleared his throat. "Lily didn't want to meet you because her biological mother tried to make her a darker version of you, Jen. She thought she could use my sister to steal the ruling magic back. The woman convinced her you would either kill her on the spot or lock her up. Lily believed her after the way Jed treated her, so she avoided coming to Allure to let her magic out until it built up to dangerous levels. She's still convinced you're tricking her but is putting on a good front because she'd do anything to protect me. Our parents promised her they'd protect her from you until she made up her own mind. I don't sense she's there yet."

Her fists clenched. "I would have preferred to go through my entire existence not meeting you. No offense. My point is the demon didn't register as family, so it's not Jaques."

Mat's dull eyes bore into Alex. "Is that so?"

"I'm only telling you because the threat level in your voice makes me want to smash your brain." He held up a hand. "Which I will do if you come for Lily."

I'd had enough of the weirdness. "Nobody's smashing anyone's brains." I held up both hands. "And no one is going to hurt Lily. Geez, Mat. You think *I'm* the one that causes trouble?"

Drake dragged his eyes away from Alex. "You should heed that warning, Mathias. Alex and Lily are very protective of each other. He's only helping us because he thinks it's the right thing to do for his sister. In contrast, Lily sees helping us as sacrificing herself for her brother. Neither of them will hesitate to act to defend the other. They are Jonas's children, after all."

"Whoo whee. This has taken an interesting turn. But then, it always does when Jen's involved. So, Lily, what happened with the wolves yesterday?" Emine's smile didn't reach her eyes, though a tinge of crazy reflected in them.

"I gave my statement to the enforcers."

Emine held up her drink. "That you did. But I want to know what really happened. Get me?"

Lily unclenched her fists. "Those wolves were outside your checkpoint yesterday. I even reported it to the castle guards, who gave me the fake ID. We walked when we left Meemaw's place because I had family overload. Something was off with that neighborhood, so I reported it to Glac. When they didn't find anything, we went to check it out. Stupid of me, I know. We killed a few of them. Also stupid, considering I'm a hybrid with a questionable ID. They transferred that nasty magic to us, even though we both took the immunity potion and we had to decontaminate. The enforcers released Elsie, but not us. Gramps vouched for us and swore the elf commander, or whatever he is, to secrecy."

"You're cool." Emine took a bite of toast like it was any other day. "I cleared you this morning."

I focused on Emine's normal behavior for a few seconds too long, then refocused on Lily. "To get this conversation back on track, where was this demon you saw?"

"Roman says they're not there anymore, so it doesn't matter. I raided one of their offices and gave the info to my parents, so I'm sure you have it."

Drake stretched an arm across the back of my chair as if we were still a normal couple on a regular day. "Our latest information is that they want to kill Jen and Mat and take over the Coalition."

His tone was too casual, as if he looked forward to it. My heart pounded in my chest, and I had to cross my legs to keep from running away.

"That doesn't match what I know about demons." Lily tapped the table. "Demons feed on chaos and negative emotions. Specifically, human emotions. They don't care about paranormals or taking over anything. Their goal is only ever chaos."

My eyebrows drew together. "We've already thought about that, but don't have answers. How do you know so much about demons?"

"I don't sleep much so I read a lot. That, mixed with the huge number of ancient books in Mom's library, means I've learned a lot of useless shit. My point is, look at how causing problems here helps them reach those goals."

"Lily's right," Alex said. "They already made sure a big chunk of people moved out of the pockets and into the human world. Including kids dumped by their parents with new powers they can't control. If it weren't for our parents, they would have already revealed themselves."

I held up a finger. "We're aware. And grateful. I'm going to learn how to create you a pocket to retreat to."

Emine rolled her eyes as she stood. "I hate to break up this merry little reunion, but I have to get to work."

Mat stood with her. "I will walk you out. I hope you know you are welcome here. You can use the family entrance in the back. I will reset the wards."

Lily watched them go, her intelligent eyes assessing. "What's up with the Jekyll-Hyde routine?"

I let out a nervous laugh. "Besides the fact that you don't fit in one of his neat little boxes?" I didn't want to bring up the curse. The two hybrids had enough problems of their own, so no need to dump mine on them.

"I don't fit in anywhere, so he might as well not try. Here's my theory. The demons learned most of the royal family died and had a window of opportunity to stir up trouble before you were old enough to rule. Then they figured out the second queen was desperate. So they team up with her to create chaos using the hybrids. It would have worked, but they didn't account for a First leading the outsiders. So, they had to step up their game."

"They're trying to mind control supernaturals and inject them into the human world to create chaos?" I shook my head. "It's too easy. There's got to be more to it."

Drake's spine snapped straight. "Perhaps. Perhaps not. They seem to think Alex is the key to whatever they are after."

"I can't get much from them because they're so singularly focused on their tasks." Alex rubbed his eyes. "I just want to live my life. Not fight demons."

"Same." Lily stood. "Well, I still have to get a dress for that stupid dinner. It's been real. It's been fun..."

"I'm going on a field trip today to absorb more mimic abilities. I can't wait to show you what I can do."

"Sure. Alex?"

CHAPTER SEVEN

By the time I escaped the palace, I was ready to tear my hair out. Everyone was hostile toward me. Even the urban sprite, Charlotte, who was as timid as they came, made a snotty comment. I needed to figure out the curse before it got such a hold on them they'd never recover.

The Ogre district was located downtown, about six blocks from Dragon Headquarters and nine blocks from the main square.

Ogres were once brutal creatures who crushed anyone who dared look at them the wrong way. Over the years, they had somewhat mellowed. They still had short tempers and were ferocious in a fight, but over the last five hundred years, they had developed an unnatural obsession with making money. Their district had rows and rows of shops and other businesses, each one trying to outdo the other.

Crowds of paranormals clogged the main street and lined up for the various sales. I took small sips from at least twenty different factions. The street was so crowded I had to limit the intake. I went back to taking a sip from those who bowed to me.

When I reached the end of the street, I stopped and craned my neck at the gigantic department store. I'd seen similar stores at a mall in the human world, but didn't have a chance to browse through them because Quin went crazy and tried to kill me.

Inside, I forced myself not to plug my nose against the scent of ozone and body odor. Crowds of paranormals shoved each other out of the way as they fought to see a display table featuring dwarven-made weapons. A massive hologram with blinking red letters floated above it that read 'Discounted.'

Someone blasted magic on the other side of a display. Glass shattered, and shouting erupted as the crowd pushed in to see what was going on or to take advantage of an opening.

I had to jump out of the way when two ogres latched onto the collars of a witch and a mage and tossed them past me and out the door like they were bowling balls.

The crowd in front of me parted before I regained my senses. Two massive ogres appeared and made their way toward me.

I locked my knees and took a sip of their magic.

Ogres were unique because they didn't believe in the fates. Instead of relying on magic to provide their match like the rest of us, their matches were determined in gladiator-style fights. They held the massive spectacles once every three months, based on moon cycles. Each ogre who wished to mate was entered into a bracket-style tournament to determine who matched with who. The first, second, and third-place finishers from each side matched accordingly. The rest had to wait until the next quarter. They weren't particular about which sex they matched with, either. Only that their fighting skills were balanced.

Their rulers were a couple who shared equal power and could beat all the other ogres in the tournament. The two queens who stood before me displayed their battle scars with honor. The putty-colored one on the left wore a loincloth and band around her breasts. Her one eye swept over me. "Your Grace. Please tell me you've come to recruit us for your war."

The dusky blue-colored one wore a short sheath and had an equal number of battle scars. She rolled her two eyes. "Of course not. She only recruits the weaker factions."

I swallowed back a snarky reply about how we asked for volunteers, and they didn't show up. "I have some questions for you. Do you have a place where we can talk?"

"Of course. Follow me." The one-eyed Ogre Queen latched onto her match's arm and yanked her toward the back of the store.

They led me to an office with a torn-up couch and holes in the walls. A desk in the corner only had three legs and was propped up by books. A pile of broken glass twinkled under the harsh lights.

I found a spot on the wall with the fewest holes and leaned against it.

The two of them took a seat on what looked like cement blocks. "Welcome to our throne room," Two-eye said. "My name is Queen Burma, and this is my match, Queen Romilda. I don't believe we've formally met."

I inclined my head. "Thanks for seeing me, Queen Burma and Queen Romilda. You can call me Jenella."

Romilda's eye narrowed. "Yes. I've heard that you are not fond of formalities."

I perked up. "You did? Where?" When she continued to stare, I waved a hand. "Never mind. I wondered if either of you had curse-breaker skills. And if so, I need your help."

The two-eyed Queen Burma smirked. "So you did not read our note?"

I tried to remember if Verity gave me something from them but came up blank. "Note?"

"The one our courier delivered on the street."

I remembered Tracy taking an envelope from an ogre. "I'm sorry, but I didn't see it."

The aggression rolling off them made my legs weak, and I was grateful for the wall holding me up. I needed to be crafty with my response to calm them down. "I apologize. My workload has been overwhelming, with the castle reopening and the Bellicose planning an attack on the hybrids. What did it say?"

One eye leaned forward. "We will tell you if you include us in your war."

Their fighting skills would be valuable. That is, if I locked them into a contract, ensuring they wouldn't get too carried away. I glanced at the broken furniture. If it was even possible to restrain their love of violence. "Sure. If you agree to my terms, I'll bring you to the next battle."

"Even if it's in the human world?"

I wasn't sure about that one. No way some ogres would pass as even slightly human. Most were eight to nine feet tall and twice as thick as the biggest human. And half of them only had one eye in the center of their forehead. "I'd be glad to call you if our troops need backup in a human world fight. But I'll definitely call you first if we have a fight in Allure."

The two stood and stomped out of the room without answering.

I leaned against the wall and considered my options. They knew something, and I needed to find out what. I pulled my phone out and texted Tracy.

If the ogres didn't help, we'd figure it out another way. But only so many curse breakers existed. I knew about a few mages, but had to contact them through Mat. And in his current state, approaching him wasn't an option. If the ogres wouldn't help, I'd go to Ann Marie next. She knew more about magic than anyone. And Lily said she had an ancient library. I hoped she'd let me use it.

The two queens barreled back into the room. Two-eye crossed her arms, her muscles bulging. "We accept your offer but have some conditions."

I tucked my phone in my pocket and tried to look confident, even as my shoulders tightened. "Okay. Let's hear them."

"We refuse to go near the dragon tower. When called to battle, we will gather our bravest warriors and fight until the blood of your enemies is smeared across the land."

"What's wrong with Dragon Headquarters?"

She waved a meaty hand. "Nothing. We will not disturb the dragons in their time of mourning."

"Do you think it's cursed?

"No, the Vinculum Tenebrism does not extend there."

"The what?"

Her one eye rolled so hard it looked like it spun. "Vinculum Tenebrism. The curse we explained in the missive. It was placed in the palace during the last battle. An ogre who works as a palace guard informed us of the strange feeling before the repairs began."

The ball of anger inside me fought to escape. "You knew all this time and didn't say a word?" My words came out in a growl.

The two-eyed queen held up a hand in the stop gesture. "No, no. We only discovered it three days ago. We sent you everything we could dig up."

I swallowed back the bitter taste in my mouth. "Can you break it?"

They shared a look. Or I thought they did. It was hard to tell with the one-eye-two-eye thing going on. The two-eyed one stepped forward. "It has advanced too far. The only one who can break it now is the First Gorman, and he went to sleep without passing on his power."

Tracy and I agreed to meet in a park near the main square. I was a few minutes early, so I found a bench to sit on. Other than one time when I first met Jedediah, I'd never sat in a park and relaxed. And that was a human park, so it was much different from the park in Allure.

A mage couple taught two kids how to control their magic. A group of fairy children played chase around a tree, trailing colorful magic behind them. Nearby, three elves sat in the grass, and the surrounding area became lush. A family of duck shifters led their six chicks toward a pond on the other side. An orange dragon swooped over the park on patrol while a brown wyrm dragon twisted around the trees to my right. A group of wyverns followed him, then veered toward the mountains beyond the palace.

My relaxing moment didn't last long. Sparkles caught the corner of my eye as the Pixie Queen descended on me. She landed on the back of the bench and threw her hands on her hips. "What are you doing, Jenella?"

"Hey, Sylphira. I'm waiting for Tracy. Do you want to join me?"

She crossed her arms. "I do not believe the previous two queens ever took time to daydream."

"My grandmother called them small moments in her diaries. She'd sneak away and sit on the beach in Mahri. Though I doubt my mother ever stopped to appreciate anything."

She didn't answer for a few seconds. "It is lovely."

"Yes. What are you doing here?"

"A group of pixies settled in the park until we finished the new sanctuary. They called me when they spotted you."

"I sensed them." And chose the bench furthest from the group. "I apologize if I scared them."

We sat in companionable silence for a while. "What is wrong with you?"

I tore my attention from two dueling kids at the center of the park and focused on her. "What do you mean?"

"You seem lost."

No way I'd tell the Pixie Queen what was bothering me. "I'm fine. I just have a lot on my mind."

She chuckled. "Don't we all."

My phone buzzed, and I yanked it out of my pocket. My eyes narrowed when I saw the name. "Sorry, I have to take this." I flashed to the edge of the park before I answered. "What do you want, Colonel Ballard?"

"Jen. Thank the fates. My family is under threat. We're being pursued and request sanctuary under the displacement law."

My heart jumped to my throat. Colonel Ballard was in trouble with his faction if he was requesting sanctuary. The law allowed anyone shunned by their faction with nowhere else to go to request help from the crown of Ahl. It was the law I used to bring the hybrids into the coalition. Which meant the former shifter alphas were after him. Or were using him. I started pacing. "See, that's a problem. You followed me on my first case, then set me up with those cat shifters because your alpha ordered it. I can't trust you. So, I'm going to need an explanation."

"I didn't know who you were when we met. I got an order from the Cauldron in Allure to look for black magic near the park. They used me. I discovered it a few weeks ago and approached the Shifter Alphas for help, not realizing they'd turned traitor. And Alpha Roberts was one of my closest friends. I thought I was sending you a legitimate job."

"Sure. And you didn't bother contacting me when you figured out what was going on."

"I was unaware half the shifters were on the wrong side. Not until the Alphas showed up in Hospa a couple of weeks ago. A short time later, I got the bulletin from your office. I gathered my family and ran. We're headed your way now and request you shelter us."

I swallowed. Travis said they used shifters to test me, and I just assumed Colonel Ballard was a traitor. If he was a victim of the war, then I needed to help him. The only problem was I didn't buy his story. "The former alphas are in Hospa?"

"Not anymore. They're traveling south with a large group of shifters. Some split off to follow us."

I needed Drake or Titus, the Crown Juror, to read him and his family. Which meant I needed to take care of the curse. Or find a place to stash the bears while I worked on it. I rubbed my eyes. "I'll allow temporary sanctuary if you agree to have your mind read by a dragon and/or a juror. If your intentions are honorable, I'll help you."

"Agreed. We have nothing to hide."

I strolled back toward the pixie queen, who perched on the back of the bench, and watched me with intense eyes. "Will you be arriving on a transport or through the gates?"

"The gates in about ten minutes."

"I'll meet you there." After I hung up, I focused on Sylphira. "I'm sorry, but something's come up, and I've got to go."

She shot into the air, buzzed around my head twice, and landed on my shoulder. "Oh no, you don't. I'm coming with."

I texted Tracy the update and turned toward the main flashing circle. And stopped in my tracks. Cavil said I didn't need to use flashing circles. I could flash from the park to the gate. I dismissed the idea as soon as I had it and picked up my pace. If I was going to lead, I needed to follow my own rules and set an example. Which meant using the flashing circles.

We landed at the gate, and I moved toward the guard station. Several vampires lurked in the shadows and cloaked dragons flew overhead. The city was still on high alert. Four gate guards turned toward me as I approached. Two of them were shifters. I waited for a warning tingle but got nothing.

They bowed as I approached, so I took a sip of their magic. "Your Grace, Your Highness. What can we do for you?"

"I'm meeting a family of bear shifters here. They've requested sanctuary."

A vampire stepped out of the shadows. "Where are your guards?"

I jerked a thumb toward Sylphira, who swung from one of my curls. "I brought a friend as backup." Though they were small in stature and numbers, pixies were vicious and deadly. During the battle, they killed several enemies by using their dust. Not a single pixie got so much as a scratch.

He didn't have time to respond because a group of around fifteen massive brown bears stepped through the gate. The lead bear, an enormous boar, stepped forward and shifted into Colonel Ballard. "Hey, Jen. Sorry to bust in on you like this. I couldn't think of anywhere else to go."

I waved a hand. "It's fine." I turned to the mage and the witch. "Test them for demon magic and mind control before you let them through. Then have one of the dragon patrol read them." The shifter guard flinched. I patted his arm. "Your former alphas used him to set me up. I want to make sure it doesn't happen again."

He nodded. "I understand. It still stings."

I bet. Their entire faction was torn apart. Worse than even the witches. At least the witches had a new president. The shifters were still in transition. Which left us with two of the major paranormal groups fractured. That, along with the curse, meant the Bellicose was winning. Again.

After the dragon guard cleared Colonel Ballard's family, I led them toward the palace. Some of them shook, while others clung to each other. Fear was unusual behavior for bear shifters, so their trek across the country had to be bad. Some bears had cubs, so I didn't ask many questions. I needed to stash them somewhere safe for a while. After I solved my own problems, I could help them if they still needed it.

I led the group past the castle and down a street and stopped in front of the gates of a Victorian-era house. It was a nice place with its wrap-around porches and gleaming white trim. I tapped on the wards.

A witch sauntered onto the porch. When she spotted me, her eyes grew wide, and she scurried inside.

My own eyes narrowed. I recognized her from the protests at the palace.

A shrill whistle came from my shoulder. "That's not good."

"Cavil is a god trying to establish himself in this realm. He might be unaware of the problems with the witches."

"So he's a dumb god. Got it."

I wouldn't say he was dumb. My impression of him was the opposite. He was so smart he'd gained the respect of two of the three Firsts, the last sorceress, and me. Not to mention the massive financial empire he built in a few short weeks. But he needed to catch up on the political climate.

I glanced at the bear family. If they were traitors, I was confident Cavil could take care of them. If they weren't, he could hide them. It was a win-win.

The god appeared on the other side of the gate. He wore an electric pink T-shirt and acid-washed jeans. His face, along with the surrounding area, lit up when he spotted me. "Jenella! It's nice to see you." The light dimmed when he spotted my companions. "Who are your friends?"

"This is Sylphira, the Pixie Queen. The bears are seeking sanctuary from their traitorous former alphas, and I wondered if you could take them in. Colonel Ballard is an enforcer who can help you set up security both here and in the human world."

Cavil scanned the bears, then stepped out the gate. "Can they be trusted?"

"Undetermined. I hoped you could help with that." I pointed toward his house. "In return, I'll point out your witch is loyal to the former president of covens and recently helped with the human protests in front of the palace."

The god didn't seem too surprised by that news. "Thank you. She will be taken care of."

Colonel Ballard flinched. "Not all shifters are traitors. Or even most of us. Especially not my family. I'm just a small-town enforcer who got set up and met Jen in the process. I wouldn't have asked her for help if we had anywhere else to go."

My head ached, and I was eager to work on the curse, so I waved a hand. "I'll send someone to help you monitor them."

Cavil's spine straightened. "I am a god. I can determine their sincerity without help. As can you." White magic shot from him and swirled around everyone, including me.

"Neat," I said as I caught what he did. The ruling magic did something similar during a council meeting before I fixed it. "Before you say no, bear shifters have excellent noses. They can smell lies from a distance and might catch something you don't as you hire your staff."

His lip twitched. "I will take them in on a trial basis. They can use the guest house out back."

My shoulders relaxed. "Thank you."

Colonel Ballard opened his mouth to thank me, closed it, then inclined his head. The emotion in his eyes almost made my knees buckle.

"Well, this has been fun. See you later, Jen. Nice to meet you, handsome god. Bye, bears." Sylphira zipped into the air, her wings buzzing as she flew away.

I held up a hand to stop Cavil from swinging the gate closed. "Wait!"

He stopped and raised an eyebrow.

"I sort of made a prototype of a pocket. When you have time, will you stop by the Conservatory and take a look? It's the weird house on the edge of dwarven-elven territory."

"Only if you take my advice on how to improve."

"Sure."

Chapter Eight

Tracy and Bastien stood outside my favorite deli. I stared at Bastien for a beat too long, so he leaned forward until his black eyes were even with mine. "I am not cursed."

"Are you sure? Because everyone at the palace has an excuse for their behavior, too."

"I am not acting strange."

I shrugged. "If you say so."

His face grew as hard as stone. "I have not been to the palace in quite some time."

"Then where have you been?"

"With Tracy at your place, in the alchemy village, and Dragon Headquarters."

I opened the door to the deli and waved them through. "Is anyone acting strange at Dragon Headquarters? I haven't been around the palace as much as everyone else, and Razazia says I have some immunity. But it makes me want to run away whenever I come close to it. What about Deva?"

"It is not a curse. I've seen her cope with many losses throughout my life, including the loss of my father and siblings. She mourns for as long as she needs to, picks herself up, and carries on. She is not one to ignore her feelings."

I sensed an underlying lesson, but ignored it. "So, she's not acting out of character?"

"No."

I rubbed my arms. "The whole thing has me worried and on edge."

"Me, as well."

Thaddeous, the Deli's owner, wasn't behind the counter, so we didn't waste time with small talk. As soon as we settled at a table, I held out my hand. "Do you have that letter the ogre on the street handed you?"

Tracy pulled the thick envelope out of her jacket and set it on the table. "Sorry about that. I got distracted and forgot I had it."

I stared at the envelope for longer than necessary, my heart pounding out of my chest. "What if it's too late?"

Bastien pushed it closer to me. "What if it's not?"

I picked up the envelope and dumped the contents on the table. A folded letter and pocket-sized book fell out, along with a small pink stone commonly used to hold hologram spells.

Tracy picked up the stone to examine it while I unfolded the letter.

Your Grace,

A palace guard approached us and requested we visit to investigate an anomaly. Though we could not enter the grounds because of your overkill of security, we could determine the existence of an ancient curse that was not present before the glorious and bloody battle we were not invited to. It is called Vinculum Tenebrism. A nasty curse was planted somewhere inside the building and is growing roots. Though slow-acting, it soaks into its victims' bones after a certain level of exposure. It is our recommendation you clear the palace of all living beings.

Enclosed is the information required to break the curse, along with our proposal to join your army so we may pound your enemies into dust and bathe in their blood.

Your loyal subjects,

Queen Burma and Queen Romilda of the Ogres

"Ha! I knew it!" I handed the letter to Tracy and opened the book. Or rather, a manual that explained the Vinculum Tenebrism curse in detail. I read the first two pages and closed it. "I need to evacuate the palace now!"

Tracy slapped a hand on my arm. "Wait. Let's see what this hologram is first."

A hologram of the First Gorman popped into existence. "My lovely creations. If you are seeing this, I have succumbed to the second queen's demands. Please don't despair. I will do what I can to fight these atrocities, as will the First Cynthia. Do what you can to carry on until my return. Should I not return, you can visit my resting place." He melted away, and a map of a jungle took his place with a small red 'X,' marked on it.

I leaned forward. "He knew where my mother planned to put him?"

Bastien shook his head. "The First Cynthia could curse. Gorman was the curse breaker. Anitta may have figured out a way to subjugate them."

My stomach soured when I realized my theory might be right. We theorized that a First might have woken up when we investigated the bug magic.

Cynthia created several magical species, including the kelpies, who were always a pain in the ass. She also created the chimeras who kidnapped me when I was a new detective. If two Firsts worked with the Bellicose, we were in trouble. And if it was only Cynthia, then we needed to wake Gorman. Something I planned to do what seemed like a million years ago. He could help us not only break the curse but defeat the Bellicose. If he wasn't working for them.

I threw all my ifs out of my head because they didn't matter unless I saved my family. Shoving the information about the curse back into the envelope, I stood and strode toward the door.

Tracy caught up with me outside. "What are you doing, Jen?"

"I'm going to kick everyone out, seal it, and comb through my mother's diaries. Then I'm going to find Gorman."

"We will accompany you," Bastien said.

My eyes settled on him. "No. You need to stay away from the palace. I can't have you cursed, too."

He blinked. "Did you just tell me no?"

"Yep."

"Interesting. Ara is still sane, as is Calvin. You have more people than us."

I shook my head. "Calvin needs to stay focused on countering the Bellicose magics. And Ara's preoccupied with Lily and Alex. I need you two to stay sane and alive. Please."

"Drake will kill me should I not protect you when he cannot."

Because of his loyalty, he'd go anyway if I said no. And if anything happened to me, I'd never hear the end of it. "Fine. But stay outside."

"Stay with her, Tracinia," He growled as she shifted into his dragon form and launched into the air.

I flashed to the flashing circle at the palace, raced through the family entrance, and down the main hall.

"What is the meaning of this?" George, the griffin patriarch, asked from the sweeping staircase.

"George! Clear the palace! It's cursed, and it's affecting everyone!"

"Nonsense." He descended the stairs. "We do not have time for your games, Jenella."

"It's not a game!"

Tracy's hand landed on my arm. "This isn't the way to make your case."

Mat descended the stairs, his eyes hard. "What game and what case?"

"Someone cursed the palace, and it's rubbing off on everyone who spends enough time here. We need to evacuate and seal it until I find the First Gorman to break the curse."

Mat shook his head. "Have the ogres been spreading their rumors again?"

My eyes narrowed. "What do you mean, again?"

"They tried to peddle those lies the other day. I dismissed them."

I threw my hands in the air. "It's not a lie. You're acting strange, and so is everyone else. Can't you see it?"

"What I see is a queen who refuses to take her duties seriously. Perhaps you should pass your crown to Lily."

I knew he wasn't himself, but the knife that stabbed through my heart sure felt real. So real that I almost doubled over.

Drake strode through the door. His eyes flared. "You stink of deli, ogre, and Bastien. Have you two turned him against his own family?"

Tracy's grip on my arm tightened. "Oh, hell to the no."

The red-hot anger inside me, mixed with the pain, stirred as I grasped her hand. I focused on projection and persuasion, opened my mouth, and yelled, "*Leave the palace now!*"

My words reverberated throughout the building and soaked into the walls. Paranormals streamed down the stairs and clustered around the doors, their eyes glassy while they followed my order.

Mat and George turned on their heels and strode toward the family entrance. Tracy tried to follow, so I tugged her hand and used a little persuasion. "Not you, Tracy."

She released my hand, shook her head, and coughed. "How in the hell did you do that?"

"My magic is all about intent. I added a little of Drake's, too, I think." It was the same mental magic I'd used when the dragons were mind-controlled and attacked our transport. I'd have been thrilled to use it again if the situation didn't suck so bad. I moved toward a wall and leaned against it.

My order didn't affect Drake for long enough. He stopped by the doorway and stood there watching people leave. His eyes met mine, lit up and narrowed as he made his way through the scrambling crowd. "You dare use my magic against me?"

"Yes. You found it amusing not so long ago."

His fists clenched as he leaned down and got right in my face. "It's no longer amusing." A plume of smoke streamed out of his nose.

I swallowed and tried to calm my pounding heart as I waved it away. "Because you're cursed."

Without another word, he turned and stomped out the door.

Tracy bumped my shoulder. "I mean, you may have a point about Drake. He's really pissed."

"Yeah." I rubbed my aching chest.

"These people are all glaring at you."

"Yeah."

"I wasn't sure I believed you until I saw it."

"I know."

She drummed her fingers on her leg. "You should have used your persuasion thingy as soon as you suspected a curse."

"I don't like making people do things. My panic and anger got away from me."

"And rightly so. When you said Mat and Drake were acting strange, you failed to mention they'd turned into asshats."

I brushed a curl out of my face and tried to hide the pain of their words. "They didn't mean it. The more time they spend here, the worse it gets."

"You still need to make them pay."

A ragged laugh burst out of me and echoed off the walls.

The clusters of paranormals moved faster.

It took longer than I expected for everyone to clear out. When I was sure they were gone, I put a solid seal over all the windows and outer doors, saving the family exit for last.

After I sealed it, we headed toward the flashing circle.

Tracy pulled me to a stop and pointed. "What do you suppose that's about?"

Bastien and Drake stood nose to nose in the practice field to the right in their dragon forms. A mass of palace guards and staff, including many of the griffins, gathered around them.

I shifted my weight from one foot to the other. "Are they having an argument?"

"Looks like it, though having it in their heads takes away the drama."

It really did. Neither of them made a sound except for the occasional wing rustle, tail wag, or head bob. "Their stances are aggressive. Sort of."

"Yeah."

Bastien smacked Drake across the face with his wing and launched into the air.

As one, the entire crowd turned toward us.

I took a small step back.

Tracy latched onto my arm. "Say something. They need an explanation."

I concentrated on projection without persuasion. "The palace is closed until further notice. Set up temporary offices at the Leadership Council building."

"What about those of us that live here?" Helen asked in an icy tone.

I swallowed when several paranormals crossed their arms and nodded, the tension in the air so thick I couldn't breathe. I hadn't thought about that.

"Nest inside the new Palace Guard barracks, Helen. We'll find temporary housing for the rest of you," Verity said from my left.

"No, we will not." Helen pointed at the palace. "You might hate it here, but it is our nest. Many of us have nowhere else to go."

"Why kick us out of our home?"

"What are you hiding?"

"The queen's trying to kill us!"

"Get her!"

The crowd surged toward me, including Drake and Mat.

"Stop!" I used a little persuasion. When they stopped, I continued. "I understand this isn't ideal, but the palace isn't safe. Until it is, it's closed."

"She's crazy! The queen has lost her mind!" someone shouted from the back of the crowd.

I looked to Mat for support, but he leaned against a tree, his arms crossed, his eyes glowing. My gaze turned toward Drake.

He huffed, smoke billowing into the air. He melted into his snuffy form and charged. *Detain the queen!* Boomed through my head, along with a mental nudge.

I grabbed Tracy and bolted toward the flashing circle. Not sure where to go, I flashed to our house.

"We can't stay here," Tracy said as we made our way toward our rooms.

"Where else can we go?"

"Somewhere the angry mob won't find us."

I shook my head. "They'll calm down once they're away from the palace for a while. I think. Drake acted normal the other day when he'd been gone for a few hours."

"Do you really want to take that chance? I mean, Drake already learned how to worm his way through our wards."

Not only that, but I gave him permission to come and go as he pleased. I perched on the edge of my bed and rubbed my sour stomach. "They're not after you, so you can leave. It won't matter where I go. Drake can still find me." For the first time since I met him, my stomach didn't flutter at the thought of him finding me. Instead, a bone-deep sadness washed over me. "What if it's already too late?"

"Don't think like that. Verity stood up for you, and she's there more than Drake." She tapped her chin. "I'm not leaving you. Let's reset the wards and strengthen them. We'll stay here and flash away if he attacks."

It wasn't the greatest hideout, but it was the best we could do. Besides, I wanted to learn more about the curse and see what my mother said about Cynthia and Gorman in her diaries.

Two days later, I rubbed my eyes and stretched. We'd been pouring through my mother's diaries. Tracy hadn't read them before, so she had to take frequent breaks. Looking up at the movement, she shook her head and closed her diary. "This is awful. How did anyone ever let that woman have power?"

My head throbbed, so I rubbed my temples. "I've often wondered how she turned out like she did when my grandmother was such a good ruler." Another throb of pain caused me to rub my eyes. Drake kept trying to enter my mind. He hadn't attacked the house, but flew over frequently and tested the wards once or twice. "I thought a First was near Mahri, but now I'm not so sure." I tossed the diary I'd been reading onto the coffee table.

"We can't stay here." I'd texted Verity, and she seemed fine, but I could still feel Drake's anger. "Did you read that book about the curse?"

"Yes."

The book the ogres gave me was small and written in a mixture of Latin and Ancient Mahri. The Vinculum Tenebrism curse darkened bonds and turned people against their friends and family. It required something solid to hold it and was generally directed at one person.

We theorized it was meant to rip away my support network and weaken the respect for my rule. It was slow to take hold, though, and took several months to fully engulf people. Like the ogres said, the amount of exposure determined the strength. Which meant that some of the palace's occupants would be further along in absorbing it than others. Like Mat and Drake. I hoped we cleared the area in time to save them. The book said if left to fester, it would become permanent.

"What if the curse doesn't wear off?"

"It will. Have faith." Tracy held up a finger. "You said a First was near Mahri?"

I was grateful for the change of subject. "Celia. The First to the centaurs, among others. But Drake said two opted for permanent death. After I woke Razazia, only two who my mother put to sleep were left to find. I'm unsure which ones. If the ogres are right and Cynthia is our culprit, then let's hope the other one is Gorman."

Tracy picked up the diary where my mother discussed him. "Then let's go over this with a fine-tooth comb and see if we can find out where she put him."

"Sure." We wouldn't find anything. I'd been over the diary a hundred times since I agreed to wake the other Firsts.

When my headache increased, I went to the kitchen to order food from the magichef. I peered out the back window as Drake landed in the alley behind the house and melted into his human form.

"Drake's out back. I'm going to talk to him."

"Be careful and don't leave the wards."

I stepped out onto the porch. "Hey, Drake."

His eyes flared with anger. "You shut me out of your wards."

Tears filled my eyes when I realized the curse still had him. "No. I added magic that denies access to anyone cursed."

"I am not cursed," he growled.

My heart ached at the waves of anger rolling off him. "You are."

He didn't react other than to lean forward. A tug in my chest warned me when he drew on my magic. I backed up a step. A green sheen covered the wards, then disappeared. He crossed his arms. "You really think I'm cursed."

"I think everyone at the palace is cursed. But it's supposed to wear off after you're no longer exposed."

His face hardened. "A place you insisted I work."

I hadn't insisted as much as given him an office. No one told him he *had* to work out of it. I leaned against the porch railing. "I'm going to break it."

His eyes met mine, and a sinister smile lit his face. "You think you can?"

"Yes. I won't let it take you."

He let out a clipped laugh. "That's rich coming from a spoiled, useless child."

I flinched at how much he sounded like my mother. "You're not your-self, so I'm going to let that slide." I leaned forward. "You once told me that your age means you have knowledge I don't."

"Correct."

"Then use all that ancient knowledge and fight it." My eyes burned from the tears that wanted to fall. "Use everything you are and everything good you've got inside you and fight it."

"I am not cursed." He didn't sound convinced.

I wrapped my arms around my stomach to hold back the pain. He was fine at the PISD, so I hoped he'd recover on his own. If not, I'd have to find Gorman soon. "Please."

He glanced down the alley toward the flashing circle. "Unlike you, I will not abandon my responsibilities."

I was done with the conversation, so I turned toward the house but paused. "If you care about your responsibilities, or your promises for that matter, then fight it." I slipped inside and closed the door.

A minute later, the bond slammed shut, and he flew off.

"He's in a jungle somewhere," Tracy said as I carried our food into the office. She glanced up. "What's wrong?"

"Drake couldn't pass through the wards."

She dropped the diary, shot out of her chair, and hugged me. "I'm sorry, Jen. We'll figure this out. I promise."

The pain of his words struck me harder than when my mother said them, so I hugged her back and let the tears fall.

Chapter Nine

My trauma dreams had been replaced with a real-world nightmare, I thought as I got ready for the day. Based on a few scattered comments in the diaries and the hologram map the ogres gave us, we'd narrowed down Gorman's location to somewhere in the Amazon Rainforest in the human world. Which wasn't much help, considering how vast that area was. Brazil only had one pocket, which wasn't even close to where we suspected my mother had left Gorman.

The pocket of Santuário was near Manaus, Brazil, a modern human city. Only one transport went from Allure to Santuário and didn't leave for three weeks. That wouldn't work for us, especially with the Bellicose activity.

Ann Marie sent me a report about twenty hybrids who disappeared over the last couple of weeks. I hadn't heard from Drake since the ward incident. Though Mat made several decrees that threatened to erase all the progress I'd made in making allies. Since I'd officially taken the throne, he couldn't enact them without my signature. But knowing my brother, he'd figure out a way around me.

The whole situation hurt, and I hated it. Worse, I was clueless about what to do. I stomped down the stairs and eyed Bastien, who was stretched out on the sofa, sound asleep. A deep rumble came from his chest. I braced myself as the whole place shook.

Tracy sat at the kitchen island and shot him a look. "Sorry, Jen. He's been out chasing those rat demons and hasn't slept for days."

"It's fine." At least he wasn't cursed. "Cavil said I can flash anywhere in the world with a thought. I think that's our best bet for getting to Gorman."

Her perfect brow furrowed. "I mean, that's *one* way. But you haven't even tested it."

True. "Do you have any ideas?"

She shook her head. "Nope."

My phone let out a shrill ring, and we jumped.

Bastien shot to his feet. A long plume of smoke streamed from his nose.

I coughed to cover a laugh. "Sorry. I thought it was on silent." I saw it was Quin and put it on speaker. "Hey, Quin. Where have you been?"

"Lily is going to expire. I cannot revive her."

"Wait. Slow down. Where are you?"

"At the edge of a river beside a paved road."

Sirens sounded in the background. "Can you move her before the humans show up?"

"No."

"Stay with her. We're on our way," Bastien said.

My heart leaped into my throat when Bastien swooped over the scene below. A human medical vehicle sat on the side of the road along with others that I assumed belonged to law enforcement and a big red truck used to extinguish fires. A large black truck was lodged in the side of a van down a ravine at the river's edge.

Several humans gathered around the two vehicles. I spotted Quin sitting on the ground to the side, a bandage on his head and some kind of device around his neck. A human woman leaned down and shined a flashlight in his eyes. I bet he loved that.

I focused on the van where several more humans wearing clothes too heavy for early fall worked. Lily was inside, her essence weak.

"What do we do?" I asked Tracy, who rode in front of me on Bastien's back.

"We'll have to follow them to wherever they take her and intercept."

"They're going to take her somewhere?" I screeched.

Bastien's laughter boomed through my head. *They will transport her to a healing facility.*

"Oh." It wasn't much better than the dungeons and other nasty places running through my head. If they witnessed how fast she healed, we'd be in trouble. "And Quin?"

Tracy leaned forward. "No doubt he plans to go with her and help her escape."

"Can you talk to him, Bas?"

I already am. It is equally enjoyable as carrying my cousin's mate on my back.

When I was a teenager, I teased him about giving me a ride on his back. I never expected him to allow it, though. It didn't occur to me I'd won our little pissing contest until that moment. With Lily down below bleeding out, Alex missing, and everyone at the palace cursed, the victory seemed hollow. "Yeah. I'd rather be with an uncursed Drake, but here we are."

He huffed.

Quin's head tilted up a few seconds later, and he gave us a slight nod. He had a plan.

A few minutes later, they pulled Lily out and hooked her up to a thin board, then several men lifted her and carried her toward one of their vehicles. Quin followed behind, limping. I had to give it to him; he was a great actor.

Bastien flew low over the screaming vehicle until it turned a corner on an abandoned street. *I'll convince them to pull over. We will only have a couple of minutes to extract Quin and Lily.*

I removed my hands from my ears and braced myself. Bastien didn't have spikes to hold, and wrapping my magic around him seemed wrong, so it was awkward. "I'll flash them away. Meet me at Lily's house."

"Wait. Where is her house?" Tracy asked.

I frowned. "Um. It's beside Cavil's farmhouse with a maze in the field."

I can sense your magic. We'll find you.

I patted his back. "Be careful when you land. Ann Marie set the wards, and they're strong."

The vehicle's screaming cut off as it rolled to a stop, and the back doors opened. Quin spilled out with Lily in his arms. I flashed to him, slapped my hands on them, and reappeared in front of Lily's house. "Ann Marie needs to know what happened." I flashed away before Quin could answer.

Ann Marie stepped out of the house when I touched down outside her wards. "What happened?"

"They crashed the vehicle Lily and Alex were in. She's with Quin but hurt."

"Where?"

"I dropped them off at her house."

Ann Marie burst through the ward, slapped a hand on me, and flashed us to the front porch of Lily's house. "Can you heal her?"

"I think so, yes." Healing was one thing I'd figured out on my own.

Lily was on the kitchen table on her back. The right side of her face looked like it had been through a meat grinder. Her arm hung at a weird angle, and I won't describe what her legs looked like, but it was bad.

I raced to her and put a hand on her cheek. Silver magic shot from my hand and surrounded her. A couple of sickening snaps and pops later, her wounds sealed, and her coloring returned. I sat back and waited for her to wake up. She didn't. "What's wrong with her?"

"Move." Quin nudged me out of the way and pulled a plastic bag full of blood out of his suit jacket. He grew fangs and poked a hole in it.

Ann Marie lowered herself to Lily's other side. "She doesn't need blood."

"Oh, yes. Because vampires are at their peak performance without it."

"Don't be smart with me, young man."

"Do not call me young."

I rested a hand on Quin's arm. "Stop it. She's not waking up, so it can't hurt to try."

Ann Marie and Lily vanished.

Quin disappeared a second later.

I sensed them upstairs and headed in their direction. Ann Marie was inside what I assumed was a bathroom with Lily. Probably cleaning the blood off her. I leaned against the wall and waited.

"Jenella, can you bring me clothes?" Ann Marie's voice was thick with concern.

I dug around her bedroom until I found comfortable clothes and helped Ann Marie dress my new sister. When we settled her on the bed, I stepped back and used my senses. She was alive. Healthy even. "Are you sure she doesn't need blood?"

Ann Marie shook her head. "She never has."

I glanced around. "Where's Elsie?"

"In Allure, gathering her things," Quin answered.

So she was still alive. Another thought popped into my head. "How in the hell did the Bellicose surprise them?"

"They rammed into the van."

I rubbed my eyes. "How did they not sense it? Alex gets in everyone's head, even if he knows it's dangerous. Lily can hear as well as Ara and sense magic."

"Interesting how she uses those senses, yet you do not."

"Not the time for a lesson, Quin."

"They convinced humans to do their bidding."

"So, humans drove the truck that rammed them?"

"Does your hearing present a challenge?"

I bit back a smile. I'd missed Quin.

Bastien and Tracy landed outside the wards, and Ann Marie waved a hand. A few seconds later, they sauntered in.

Bastien scanned the room, his eyes landing on Lily. "How is she?"

Ann Marie tilted her head. "You've all become attached to my kids."

I hadn't. I didn't even think of Lily as a sister, not really. Once the curse was gone, I needed to work on that.

"The dragons are fond of Lily and Alex," Bastien answered.

"She is my granddaughter and the heir," Quin said.

Her unfocused gaze turned to the window. "You can give her blood if you think it would help."

Quin inclined his head, tilted the bag, and dripped the blood into Lily's mouth.

She coughed and sputtered, then reached out and ripped the blood bag from his hand. Her fangs descended, and she attacked it.

As one, we scooted back. When it was gone, Quin took the empty bag and pulled out another.

Her eyes fluttered open. A gold sheen rolled across them and melted to red. "What the fuck are you doing here?"

I liked Lily's house. It was spacious and homey and smelled like eucalyptus and sage. Sort of. The overall feel was clean and comforting.

I perched on a chair in her office and watched her fingers fly across a keyboard at vampire speed. I bet she burned through human technology at an alarming rate. The stuff wasn't built to last, and they didn't have tech mages to help them preserve electronics.

"You're sure you didn't see anything, Gramps?"

"I did not," Quin said from the shadows of the corner behind her.

Tracy sat beside me and rubbed her eyes. "Hey Lily, can we crash here for a couple of days?"

Her fingers froze. "Why?"

Heavy footsteps pounded down the hall, and Jonas appeared at the door. He scanned the overcrowded room. "What in the hell did you do to my son and Drake?"

I frowned. "I didn't do anything. Drake got cursed, along with everyone else at the palace. Alex was outside my jurisdiction when they crashed."

His eyes narrowed. "Why does it feel like a lie even when you tell the truth?"

"Because you made up your mind about me before we ever even met?" The words slipped out before my brain engaged. But I didn't take them back because they were true.

He leaned against the wall next to Bastien. "Perhaps."

Lily's eyes scanned the occupants of the room. "Everyone out. Alex is missing, and I don't have time for drama."

I didn't want to push her, so I led my group out. Jonas stayed and closed the door behind us.

The back of Lily's property was gorgeous. A huge deck with three seating areas spanned from one end of the house to the other. Flower gardens lined several paths that cut through the pristine lawn and led to the surrounding fields. A grove of tall trees that looked like something out of a dream took up the left side. I stepped onto a path and leaned over to look at the golden flowers.

"What the fuck do you think you're doing, you bitch?"

I took a sip of gnome magic, then focused on the tiny man. "Excuse me?"

The grizzly-looking gnome took two steps back and removed his hat. "My apologies. No one told me the fuc...the queen was coming to visit."

"Don't mind him," Ann Marie said as she exited the back door. "He lost his manners when he lost his family. We haven't been able to stop the cussing since Lily rescued him."

I raised an eyebrow. "Oh?"

The gnome cleared his throat. "They're just words."

I wagged a finger. "Nope." I sniffed a flower and stood. "Tell you what. You stop with the disgusting language, and I'll help find your family."

He wrang his hat. "You can't. If Lily can't find them, no one can."

"You think so?"

He stared at his toes. "The damn words hide the fucking pain."

"If there's one thing I've learned about pain and anger, it's that taking it out on others doesn't solve your problems."

His eyes darted to Ann Marie. Then they met mine. "You can find them?"

"I can't make any promises, but I can sense other paranormals from a distance." I bent over to meet his eyes. "Do we have a fucking deal?"

His mouth turned up. "We have a deal, though I might slip from time to time."

I stood. "As we all do."

Ann Marie lowered herself into a chair. "Sometimes is much better than every other word."

He shot her the stink-eye and disappeared into the grass.

I took the chair across from her. "So, Lily really rescues strays?"

"Yep. Though, where the rest of the family finds hybrids and mixed magic couples, Lily finds cussing gnomes and powerful gods."

I grinned. Lily was a kind of unique strange I admired. I wondered if all hybrids had that kind of energy. The smile melted off my face at what they were up against. "How's the Bellicose situation?"

"It's not going well. The other leaders don't want to do anything, and we don't have the time or energy to force them."

They had too many responsibilities, especially since I insisted Jonas reclaim control of the shifters. "Any idea who the new alpha will be?"

"Nope. Jonas is wary of the candidates."

"That's my fault. It was a shock how Gabe and Linda betrayed us, and I might have been a little harsh. What can I do to help?"

Her blue eyes scanned me. "Are you kidding me right now? You've got enough problems of your own to deal with. You let us handle this."

Bastien landed in the backyard, lowered his head, and blew smoke, probably at the gnome. He stomped over to the path and shifted into his human form. "Glacintial is with young Alex."

Ann Marie stood. "Are you in contact with them?"

"Somewhat. One of my dragons sensed Glacintial nearby. He followed them to an abandoned garage down by the river and tried to reach out. Neither Glacintial nor Alex answered, and they disappeared from his senses. He suspects Glacintial cloaked them. The garage was empty when we raided it."

She nodded. "Tell me when you find their location."

"You don't seem as worried as I thought you'd be," I said.

"Because you don't understand what Alex is capable of. I'm confident he can save himself. If not, he'll wreak so much havoc we'll find him."

CHAPTER TEN

IT TOOK FOREVER TO move from one place to another using human transportation. Lily begrudgingly agreed to let us stay for a couple of nights. Something about not getting a moment's rest because of the constant stabbing in her chest. In exchange for a place to stay, she made us agree to go with her to look for Alex.

I stepped out of the vehicle, stretched my aching back, and craned my neck. The warehouse sat on the far side of the city from where Lily lived. Images of the lab near Ferine floated through my mind, and I swept them away. "What is this place?"

Lily slammed the door, then flinched. "Alex will have a fit if I ruin his car. It's the intake warehouse. Maria supplies our rescues out of it. If anyone knows where to start, it's her."

I tried not to gape at how human she looked as she walked. That had to be hard, considering her vampire skills. "I'm not following your logic."

Bastien shoved me forward. "It doesn't matter."

I shuffled inside behind Lily, then held the door open for Tracy and Bastien.

A woman greeted Lily, then turned her skeptical brown eyes to us. "You're a boggart," I blurted.

Maria's eyes sharpened. "Correct. Which is handy when outfitting your rejects."

The only other boggart I'd ever met was Mat's assistant, Pablo. "Yeah. Sorry, I didn't expect to find another boggart here because your kind are rare."

"Ah," She tapped her chin. "I forgot Pablo worked for your brother. Lily, your guests need some water."

Tracy drifted toward the shelves and bent over to examine some potions. "Where do you buy these?"

"From a hybrid supplier here in the city."

Bastien stood by the door, his spine straight as he tilted his head. "Who's hiding in the back?"

Maria's eyes flashed with anger. "None of your business."

Lily shoved a bottle of water into my hands. "Whoa. Let's tone it down a notch. Maria, this is my supposed sister, Jen, and her friends Bastien and Tracy."

"You know better than to bring purebloods into my establishment."

I raised an eyebrow. "Aren't *you* a pureblood?"

"I'd like to meet your contact," Tracy continued, as if she couldn't hear the conversation. "I like their style."

Maria jammed her hands on her hips. "I'm matched with a dwarf. So, no, I'm not a pureblood."

I smirked. "By that logic, none of us are purebloods. Bas and Tracy are a couple, and I'm matched with a First." I ignored the stab of pain at the thought of Drake.

She tapped her chin. "You got me there. Come. Let's talk somewhere else."

As she led us through the maze of supplies, a shelf containing tiny drinking glasses caught my eye. I stopped and leaned down to see them better. Then chuckled when I realized they were in the shape of a tiny potato. The human city's name was printed just above the plastic yellow feet glued to the bottom. Drake would love it. "Can I have one of these?"

Tracy took the tiny glass from my hand. "A shot glass shaped like a potato?"

I shrugged. "It's funny."

"Help yourself," Maria took it from Tracy and wrapped it in thin, white paper from the shelf above. "But you'll pay for anything you take."

I slipped the funny little glass into my bag and pulled out a twenty-dollar bill. I didn't know how much things cost in the human world. "Is that enough?"

She snatched it out of my hand. "Perfect. Now stop browsing my shelves and follow me."

Maria led us through a set of swinging doors. The kids inside the classroom sat in front of laptops and stopped talking when we entered. A hybrid woman stood at the front, her arms crossed.

Lily disappeared and reappeared beside her. The two exchanged words, and the woman dropped her arms. "We have visitors tonight. This is Lily First. She was rejected by her pureblood parents and adopted, just like many of you. The three at the back are here to learn about our lives so they can help us." Her last sentence sounded bitter.

"This is Queen Jenella of Ahl." Maria motioned toward me. "Her companions are Prince Bastien and Princess Tracinia of the dragons. Like your biological parents, they are a matched pair."

I didn't like the tone she used. Before I could say anything, Bastien marched toward the front. "We are nothing like them. For one, we don't have children. And if we had hatchlings, we would not leave them to fend for themselves."

"Hatchlings?" Tracy's voice was barely a whisper as we shuffled toward the front after him.

"These are the children who we've found abandoned over the last six months," the woman at the front of the room continued. "We're learning how to human."

I wished I could take her class. Her magic had a unique feeling. I sensed she came from four different magic factions, but couldn't pinpoint two of them. When my eyes swept the room, twenty kids stared back at us. Every single one was part witch, shifter, or chimera. The second side of their magic varied. A million questions spun through my head.

A witch-shifter hybrid in the front raised her hand. "Are you here to kill us?" She directed it toward me.

"Of course not," the teacher's voice carried a warning.

"We're here to learn," I said.

"Learn what?" someone asked.

"That's a good question. Why don't you tell me what you think we need to understand about you."

The kids were hesitant at first, but some were eager to talk to us. As a result, I learned a lot about how the hybrids operated. When the other kids saw we didn't plan to hurt them, they opened up a little. Their stories of abuse and abandonment were heart-wrenching. It took every ounce of control I could muster not to march back to Allure and bust some heads by the time we left the warehouse.

"How is this still happening?" I asked.

"Hell if I know," Lily said as we pulled out of the parking lot.

My eyes burned with tears, and I blinked them away. "Have my efforts helped at least slow it down?"

"Yes. Two years ago, we had three times as many kids. But it makes me wonder what's happening to the ones who aren't being abandoned."

I flinched at her words and wondered if I created a bigger problem by trying to help. I needed to put programs in place to help hybrid kids. Or something. I added it to my to-do list. "Where are we going?"

"It's Fall. We're going to get pumpkin spice lattes and take a walk. Then, I want to show you something."

"A pumpkin what?"

Her face lit up. "You'll see."

"This is not a good idea." Bastien's eyes scanned the street near a bar that Lily insisted we visit. She parked a few streets over and demanded we finish our delicious lattes and walk through a hybrid subdivision. "Drake often scans this area."

"I'm not scared of Drake. Besides, Lily wants to find Alex, and I want information about the Bellicose. Preferably not filtered through a curse. Also, I'd like to find the gnome family. You can't find things if you don't look." I sent my senses out. The neighborhood was full of hybrids and mixed magic couples, with a large concentration of darkness on the far edge. I pulled back before the influx made me dizzy.

Tracy took Bastien's hand. "It'll be fun. Jen's never been to a bar before."

"No shit?" Lily motioned me to take a right toward a parking lot. "Then good luck with this one."

I tried to tamp down my excitement. Tracy was right. I'd never even considered going to a bar, especially in the human world. "It'll be another new experience."

She shook her head. "They don't like purebloods here."

"It'll be fine. I'll mind my manners."

"I don't think your manners will matter."

Tracy dropped Bastien's hand and readjusted her purse so she could access her potions faster. "I mean, Bas and I are a mixed magic couple, so we could fit in. But Jen will stand out like a sore thumb."

Lily snorted. "If you say so."

She had a point. Dragons didn't buy into the anti-hybrid movement, and Bastien was intimidating on a good day. No way they'd blend in better than me. I sent my senses out again. "No one in this neighborhood feels tainted, but a huge concentration of Bellicose magic is on the other side."

"Yeah. It's one of their apartment complexes. Mom set a barrier to shield the hybrids. Do you sense Alex?"

"No. But Quin's following us."

Lily glanced back. "He's been following me since I met him."

He told me as much. It didn't seem to bother Lily, though. "Are you familiar with curses?"

"Somewhat." Lily opened the door and waved us in.

The bar was quaint and smelled of fried food and booze. A big block of a man stood behind the bar with a towel over his thick shoulder. A few customers occupied the rustic seats. All hybrids.

I latched onto Tracy's arm. "This place is great."

Lily pulled me toward the end of the bar and shoved me toward a stool.

The massive man behind the bar stomped toward us, his eyes scanning the place as he moved. "What are you doing, Lily?"

"Hey, Dale." She pointed at me. "I'm taking my sister out for a drink."

His eyes flared. "Sister?"

I nodded. "We just found out."

"Your titles are useless here, so keep your heads down and don't cause any trouble. If you do, I'll throw you out on your asses."

Bastien grunted.

I fought not to squirm from excitement. We got warned not to start a brawl in an actual bar! Something I'd only seen in human movies. "Sure."

The guy took our drink orders, and I watched in anticipation as he poured them.

He slid them in front of us and gave me a puzzled look before turning his attention to Lily. "Where's Alex?"

"They wrecked my van on the way home from Allure and took him."

"And you recruited the Queen and the Dragon Prince to help find him?"

"Not exactly, no. But they might be handy in a pinch." She downed her drink in one swig.

My eyebrows drew together. "Do you come here a lot?"

"It's where Alex and I unwind. Dale's great, but he usually decides what we drink."

I took a sip of mine and savored the fruity taste. A hybrid at the end of the bar stood, threw some money on the bar, and left. I swung toward Tracy. "Can I do that?"

Her brow furrowed. "What?"

"Stand and dramatically throw money on the bar."

"Sure. When we're ready to go."

Lily cleared her throat. "Sorry, Dale. Jen's never been to a bar before."

"I noticed. So, *Jen*. How long do you plan to stay in the area?"

He said my name like it was a cuss word. "I have no idea. It depends on a lot of things."

"Oh? Like what?"

I leaned forward. "Like how long it takes to save the hybrids from being enslaved or wiped out, including you and your bar. Tell me, *Dale*, what properties go into the spell that eliminates and protects from the black bug magic spreading through this city? How many apartment complexes do the Bellicose have? Where do they plan to take hybrids? How many labs where they torture and kill people exist nearby?"

"I'm a bartender. How the hell should I know?"

"Exactly." I jerked a thumb toward Tracy. "She knows how to eliminate the magic. As can I." Though I wasn't sure that was true, I sold it by sweeping my hand in a circle. Silvery magic swirled around the room and settled into the building. "Now your bar's protected from just about anything they throw at it. Important with a huge Bellicose presence on the edge of your neighborhood." I leaned forward. "If you'd like, we'll retreat to the pockets and leave you to your fate, but I doubt it would go well for you."

Tracy snatched the drink out of my hand and slid it toward Bastien. "Sorry. She doesn't drink often."

The guy ignored her. "Protected how?"

"Holy shit. You're as fast of a learner as Cavil." Lily sipped her drink.

"Thank you. He said my magic stems from his realm, so that makes sense." I pointed at Dale. "And what I mean is, it can't be destroyed, and demon magic can't harm your property."

The guy's eyes narrowed. "Why would you help me?"

I shrugged. "Why not?"

"Because purebloods hate us, and the royal family has done nothing for hybrids."

"Untrue. We have people all over this city watching over you, including two Firsts." Technically, there were two Firsts, but I wasn't sure how much protecting Drake was doing.

He scoffed. "Bullshit. As a bar owner, I hear things. And, other than a few vampires, I haven't heard of an extra pureblood presence."

"Yeah. Because of rule number one inside the pockets. Just because you can't see people doesn't mean they don't exist."

Lily downed the rest of her drink. "The damn vampires who hide in every shadow, right?"

"Among others."

Dale's eyes slid to Bastien. "I see."

Tracy rubbed her temples. "No offense, but you really don't. Have you, by chance, had any reports of shifters acting strange?"

"No. Though, some have come for a couple of drinks almost every night."

I leaned forward. "Want me to block their entry?"

"No." He glanced at Lily, who had her eyes closed in a vampire trance. "I want to go back to the life I had before your shit oozed into my world."

Lily's eyes snapped open. "Ha! Me, too. Finish up, people. We have some hunting to do."

I stood, slammed a couple of hundreds on the bar, and headed toward the door. "Thanks for the drink, Dale."

The human world was boring. Everyone avoided each other, and the roads were deserted at night. No one made eye contact. And when they did, they'd give us this strange lips-only smile. Lily took us to downtown Boise, where most of the bars were still open. As we strolled down the sidewalk, I counted seven dragons patrolling the skies. "Has the Bellicose been spotted here?"

Bastien tilted his head toward the sky. "I'm unaware of any."

"So, why are so many dragons in the area?"

"Without a Bellicose presence, they shouldn't be here." After a few seconds, the dragons turned and flew away. "I've redirected them."

"Thanks." I sent my senses out several blocks and only sensed hybrids, vampires, and dragons. No Alex and no gnomes. Until the hair on the back of my neck stood up and I had a sudden urge to run. "I've got a bad feeling about this. We need to leave."

"Do not flash." Quin's dry voice came from behind me.

I eyed the humans who trailed down the sidewalks on both sides of the street. "I'm not that stupid, Quin."

"Past behavior predicts future behavior."

Lily threw her head back and laughed. "Can you send your senses out as we drive?"

"Yes." I'd never sensed from a moving vehicle and wondered if it would skew the results.

"She can," Bastien said at the same time.

Lily cut down several side streets as we made our way through the city. I found two offices that didn't feel right, but nothing more. Quin disappeared right after he swooped in and insulted me, but he stayed close. I paused when I noticed a concentration of vampires a few blocks away. "Why is there a vampire house in the city?"

"It's the house of Roman," Lily said.

Roman was Ara's brother, and one of our best spies. "I heard he went crazy and his second took over several years ago."

Lily tapped the steering device. "He's a little long-winded, but sane. They don't bother humans."

"How does he avoid being noticed?"

"He registered his house as a sober-living home."

I had no idea what that meant, but let it go. "Okay." I cast my senses in the other direction.

When she stopped at a fuel shop across from an apartment building teeming with Bellicose, I had to plug my nose to keep from getting sick off the fumes and dark magic stench.

Lily leaned through the window as we waited for the fuel to fill. "Anything?"

"Yes." I pointed toward the apartment complex with my free hand. "But no Alex." I let go of my nose when I realized how nasally my voice sounded. "When they kidnapped me and Deva, they didn't stay in this area. He could be anywhere."

She rubbed her eyes. "That's what I'm afraid of. Bastien, is Glac still on his trail?"

"They were together when I lost contact, so I assume so."

"Why do humans insist on using such stinky fuel?" I asked.

"Because they don't have magic, genius." Lily wrenched a hose thing out of a hole in the car and placed it on a hanger. "Though some cars run off batteries."

"You should drive one of those," I mumbled. "We could have our tech mages retrofit it to recharge itself."

"I'm sure you could." Lily hopped in and shut the door. "Then let's search for the gnomes and head back to my house. I've scoured the area where Flemming said he lost his family and couldn't find them."

I gasped for air as we left the stinky area behind. "Is that your gnome's name?"

"Yes."

"How did he lose his family?"

"They were new to the human world and chose an abandoned property. When the people who owned it decided to tear down the house, the gnomes didn't recognize construction equipment. They scrambled to safety when they started tearing up the land. He lost them in the shuffle."

I wouldn't recognize what humans used for construction, either. "How did you find him?"

"He moved into a plant in a nearby office building. I happened to work there at the time."

We drove in silence until the human houses became more spread out. She turned onto a street lined with what looked like brand new houses, and we moved at a snail's pace as she navigated through the maze of roads. "Is this where you got the idea for your maze?"

Her shoulders shook with laughter. "No, but I see where you'd think so."

When she pulled back onto the main road, I pointed toward an enormous store across the street. "Four gnomes inside the building." I motioned toward where I sensed them. "That area."

Lily pulled in and parked. "Are you sure? Because I've checked here."

"Yes. They're in the back."

She opened her door. "Stay here. I'm going to sneak in and see if I can talk to them."

"Or, I could just flash us inside," I said.

"They have security cameras. Stay here." She slammed the door and disappeared.

I tapped my knee while we waited. "This is boring."

"I agree," Bastien growled. "Hybrids make things so hard for themselves."

Tracy twisted in her seat. "It's not like they have a choice. I mean, they need to pretend they're humans to survive."

"Right. We need to break the curse so I can learn how to make them their own pocket. Driving around like this is a waste of time. Especially since Drake already knows where the Bellicose are."

"Agreed." Bastien leaned between the seats. "What about Alex?"

"We'll find him. But it'll take years doing this." If Drake were sane, I'd ask him to fly me over the city so I could sense him.

My head snapped toward the building. "Why is Quin following Lily?"

Bastien leaned back and folded his arms. "Who knows why that crotchety old vampire does anything."

Tracy opened her door and stepped out. "Hey, Jen. Is something off about this place?"

My senses only registered the gnomes, Lily, and Quin. "No."

Lily appeared. Four gnomes of different sizes squirmed in her arms. "Got em."

One kicked her in the boob. The woman, whom I assumed was Flemming's match, screamed as Lily shoved her into the back of the car.

I took a sip of their magic as she closed the hatch.

Lily rubbed her boob and shook out her hands. "They didn't believe I had Flemming."

They most likely sensed her darkness, too.

"Silence!" Bastien roared from inside the vehicle. He put a little dragon mental magic behind it.

"Neat trick." Lily eyed Tracy, who stood a few feet away, rubbing her arms. "What's up with your friend?"

I sent my senses out again. A dragon who wasn't there before flew near the area. I also felt a mass of black about two blocks away in the opposite direction. I opened my mouth to say something, then snapped it closed when I recognized the dragon. A feeling of doom came from Drake, and my mouth went dry as I tilted my head toward the sky.

Bastien fled the vehicle, shifted, and launched into the air.

The deafening roar came a split second before the bond flew open. Drake's rage, along with a menacing feeling, flooded me.

Bastien smashed into him, and the bond slammed shut.

The darkness grew, and I spun toward the store as several tainted shifters swarmed around the building.

Quin's sword appeared. "Flash them away, Jen."

Beside me, Lily's claws and fangs extended. "Oh, hell no."

Drake tossed Bastien aside and twisted his enormous body toward us.

A human car buzzed by without slowing, so he was still partially cloaked. My shoulders relaxed a bit, but I didn't take my eyes off Drake.

His green eyes glowed as he reared his head back and drew in a breath.

Adrenaline shot through my system. "Don't you do it!"

Drake growled.

"I mean it, Drake. If you try to fry us, I will never forgive you."

His massive head turned as his anger cranked up a couple of notches. He hovered and drew in a breath. A second before his green fire streamed toward us, I threw my arms around Lily and Tracy and flashed away.

CHAPTER ELEVEN

THE SOUND OF BIRDS and other creatures sang a cheerful song. Roots coated in thick moss stuck out of the ground. The foliage surrounding us was dense and wet, the air thick with the pungent smell of decaying plants and animals. The deafening roar of the nearby waterfall almost drowned out all other sounds.

My shirt stuck to my body from the humid air as I released my death grip and spun in a slow circle.

Lily retracted her fangs. "A jungle?"

"Um, yes, though I'm not sure which one." When she gave me a flat look, I continued. "I panicked, okay?" I sent my senses out and pointed down a narrow path. "We need to go that way."

Tracy shook her head. "I mean, we could have gone back to Lily's house."

I swallowed back tears. "Drake blew fire at us. Even though he said it was impossible for dragons to hurt their mate. Even when he swore he'd never harm me. I wasn't thinking."

"That's brutal. But what the hell made you think of a random jungle?" Lily asked.

"Right. Well, it all started when Cavil told me I should be able to flash anywhere in the world. Everyone at the palace is cursed, and the ogre queens say their First was the only one who could break it. It all spun through my head when Drake showed up."

"So, you panicked and flung us into a jungle?"

I shrugged. "The only thing I thought was we needed to be as far away from him as possible. And then how I needed to wake Gorman to break the curse. I suspect he's around here somewhere."

Tracy shook her head. "Why would Anitta, someone who hated getting her hands dirty, store him here?"

"Good question." I pointed down the trail. "We could wake him and find out."

Lily crossed her arms. "Your own match turned on you, eh? That sucks for you, but Alex isn't here. Take me back."

"I will. But you won't find your brother if you're spending your time hiding from a cursed First. We might as well look for the guy."

"What do you mean, cursed?" Her voice was a couple of octaves too high. "You got us here, so you can take us back."

"I could, yes." I turned my attention to Tracy. "What do you think?"

"We can look, but based on the way Razazia attacked you when she woke, it might not be a good idea."

"Yeah." I examined the trail and made sure the bond was closed tight. "We don't have much time before Drake finds us." I closed my eyes to think, since pacing wasn't an option in the thick jungle. It wasn't fair to drag them with me to find Gorman. Especially Lily. "You're right. You didn't sign up for this. I'll take you home." My eyes drifted toward the game trail, where my senses pushed me. And come back alone.

Lily sighed. "Finding this guy is important to you?"

"Yeah. I think our wonderful mother was working with another First and cursed the castle when she wrecked it. Everyone who spent a lot of time in it was acting strange. The Ogre Queens said the building has an ancient curse on it." I waved a hand between Tracy and me. "We have our own house and weren't there as much. But Mat, the griffins, Verity, and Drake are all cursed. I threw them out of the palace and sealed it. The Ogre Queens' booklet said it should wear off without exposure." I hoped they were right. Judging by Drake's attack, I doubted it.

Lily's shoulders sagged. "Is this a pocket?"

Hope rose inside me, and I tamped it down. I'd search alone, but help would make the search easier. "No, though one's not far away. We could find a hotel while we search if you want. Or I could take you home. It's up to you."

Tracy shook her head. "Bastien's headed this way, and I bet anything Drake isn't far behind." She eyed a nearby tree. "I mean, it would be best if we avoid the pocket. Have either of you studied jungle survival?"

I could have hugged her. She was the best friend in the world.

Lily eyed our surroundings. "I've seen some shows on TV. You?"

"I can use spells to repel bugs and purify water. Jen can create shelter. We'll make the rest up as we go."

"Hopefully, it won't take long," I said as I stared down the trail.

"Doesn't matter how long we're here. From what I've seen on TV, living in the jungle without supplies is a death sentence." Lily pulled her phone out and checked it. "No signal. We're probably going to starve and end up with some rare disease."

"We have a lot of advantages that humans don't. People on TV don't have magic, and we don't get diseases." I started down the trail. "The faster we find the First, the sooner we can go home."

Tracy waved her hand, and my body tingled. "A bug-repellant spell."

"Except it won't work on me," Lily said.

"Mine does. I mean, I've been working with Quin for ages to create spells that work on vampires, so they should work on you, too."

Lily hopped over a root. "For the record, I don't like this idea. All I want to do is find my brother and protect the hybrids. I don't care about your First or your curse."

"Nice rhyme." When she huffed, I continued. "Sorry. If I hadn't panicked, you wouldn't be here. But a lot of people are looking for Alex, and Glacintial is with him. We'll find him."

Her fangs popped out, then retracted. "Fine. Head toward the water and keep a lookout for bamboo. We can use it for drinking cups."

I created what passed for three metal cups. "I've got that covered."

It wasn't long before I realized trekking through the jungle sucked. It was too thick, and even the small trail had all sorts of critters scurrying across it and roots sticking out, causing us to trip. I didn't want to flash because I wasn't familiar with the area and wanted to keep my senses open.

Tracy and I used magic to clear the path, which made it easier, but we were still moving too slow.

I was about to give up when a rustling sounded to the right.

I froze.

Tracy bumped into my back. "Oh, sorry."

Lily swung toward the sound. Golden-red flashed across her eyes as her fangs and claws extended. My skin crawled when her vampire aura ramped up.

A large cat shimmied out of a tree and crouched low.

"Not a shifter," I said.

Lily charged.

The cat pounced backward and bounded into the thick jungle.

She retracted her claws and fangs and grinned. "I'll take care of the predators."

I turned back toward the trail. "That's handy."

"Not always. I can't go to a zoo or rescue stray kittens. But it's great when dealing with toxic bosses and office gossips. And jungles, I suppose." She kept her creepy magic out as we walked, and all kinds of critters fled from the path.

"A zoo is one of those fenced off areas where humans hold animals, right?" I'd read a report about an elephant shifter hiding inside one when enforcers were after him.

"Yeah."

"Vampires aren't meant to view captive animals. But I like that you try."

"Whatever. This jungle blows." She used the end of her shirt to wipe sweat from her face.

"No shit." I eyed the mist from the thundering waterfall. "It's going to be dark soon. We need water and to find a place to stay the night."

We had to leave the stream and the path behind. The jungle smell changed based on the amount of decay and the type of plants or animals nearby as we trekked through the thick overgrowth. I found it fascinating. I concentrated on that instead of the choking heat and humidity pressing down on us. Lily could regulate her body temperature, but Tracy and I had to mop sweat off our faces every few minutes. Tracy dried our clothes every time we stopped to drink water.

I created a handkerchief and mopped my brow as we sat on a rock by the stream. "We're probably only going to go a couple of miles per day at this pace."

"Agreed." Tracy stood. "I mean, we could try to climb to higher ground to see the area so we could flash or go fluid. Because Bastien is getting close, and we don't have much time."

Sadness settled over me at the thought of Drake, and I rubbed my aching chest. "This is all my fault. My stupidity might kill us."

"Or it may have saved us. You panicked and made a snap decision, but it doesn't mean you were wrong." Lily said.

My eyebrows drew together. "You don't blame me? What about how I delayed your search for Alex?"

"Of course I blame you. But it gives us all a chance to take a step back and reassess. As my mom says, most things are both a blessing and a curse. This is one of those things."

I sighed. "Thanks. And Tracy's right. We need a faster way to move through this place."

"It would be nice to move more than a few yards before dark."

We alternated between flashing when we could see and walking when we couldn't. By the time the sun sunk over the horizon and the jungle's night sounds exploded, we were close.

"I'm going fluid to see if I can spot anything. You two wait here." Lily disappeared.

It was almost fully dark by the time she returned. "There's a cliff ahead, with a small clearing at its base."

I stood. "Is he there?"

"This is your gig. How am I supposed to know?"

"How far?"

"About a mile."

I flashed us a mile ahead and hoped I didn't land in the middle of a poisonous plant. When we reappeared, we were in the clearing. I sighed in relief, then turned my attention toward the cliff. Goosebumps rose on my arms as power rolled from it in waves. I rubbed them as I thought about what to do next. The cliff reminded me of the blocked caves in Mage Mountain, except for the climate. The boulder blocking the cave was so similar it had to be the place. "Should we camp or try to wake him?"

"It gives me the creeps." When our heads whipped toward Lily, she shrugged. "Yeah, yeah. I'm the creepiest thing out here. But there's something different about this place."

"Yeah. It's like there's a spell blocking it," Tracy agreed.

I sipped the magic. "It doesn't feel like Razazia's resting place."

"No, it doesn't." She closed her eyes. "Bastien will be here around midday tomorrow. We can camp here tonight and figure it out in the morning."

Tracy perched on the bank of the crystal-clear stream, not even trying to hide her amusement. "You've got this!"

Lily stood naked in the center, claws and fangs out as she stabbed into the water. "If parasites crawl up my hoo-hah, I might never forgive you."

"Is that even a thing?" I asked, a huge grin on my face.

"I saw something like that on TV once." She stabbed again, slipped, and caught herself so fast it was a blur. Water splashed down a few seconds later, drenching her.

I doubled over laughing, then stood and wiped my eyes. "I can heal you from that, but I'm going to tell everyone about it for eternity."

We were starving and wanted to eat before we slept. I created a shelter at the edge of a stream that included comfortable beds. Drake's magic was always available to me because we also shared a mage bond. Though I wasn't a mage, I wasn't about to call it a god bond. The term sounded downright arrogant.

I tried to conjure food, but it came out as a brown blob that Lily called shit. So, we came up with other ideas. While Tracy and I discussed it, Lily stripped naked and extended her claws, stating naked vampire fishing was our safest option.

We could have used magic, but watching her was too fun. So much so my stomach ached from laughing.

Tracy and I stifled our laughs when Lily grew still, her claws poised to strike. Something moved under the water. I put a hand on Tracy's arm and waited.

And waited.

After a few minutes, I let go and crossed my arms. "This is dumb."

The words barely left my mouth when Lily struck.

"*Grrrraaaahhhh!*" She spasmed and dropped to her knees.

"Lily!" I raced into the water.

Then backpedaled when she straightened and held up a long, slimy-looking thing, a triumphant smile on her face. She shook her head as if to clear it, then started smashing the thing on a rock. "Got it!" She flung it on the bank.

I scrambled away, splashing water everywhere. "What is that thing?"

"An electric eel." She climbed out of the stream and retracted her claws. "I think I peed my nonexistent pants."

Tracy bent over the thing and shuddered. "What did it do to you?" She flung a drying spell toward us. "She needs fresh clothes, Jen."

I created something resembling clothes and handed them to Lily.

She held them up. "Why are they mismatched and lopsided?"

"Um." I stepped closer.

She balled them up and disappeared into our shelter. She came out in her old clothes with a bright smile on her face. "We have food!"

"Yay, us." My stomach turned at the thought of eating the slimy critter. "How do we eat it?"

"It's an eel. We need to use the fire to cook it."

"If you say so."

Clouds rolled in as Lily used her claws to tear the eel apart under a lighting spell. "My dad took us fishing when we were kids. He taught me how to clean fish, but I've never cleaned an eel before." She sliced into it again. The process was bloody and gross. After removing a good portion, she ran her eyes over her work. "I think I got it."

"Great." I couldn't keep the disgust out of my voice. "Is this how humans eat?"

"Some of them, yeah. Why don't you tend the fire so you don't panic and accidentally transport us to Antarctica or something?"

I ignored the insult. "Sure. How?"

Tracy threw her head back and laughed. "I've got it."

Lily sliced the eel into chunks. "Can you conjure us a big metal pot? Stainless steel would be best."

I conjured a huge shiny pot. Every time I created, the magic came easier. "Good enough?"

"Works for me." She washed the bloody chunks and put them inside.

We built a makeshift stick rack over our fire. She put the rest of the meat on sticks and handed me one. "Hold it over the fire and make sure it's cooked all the way through."

My stomach fluttered with excitement as I followed her instructions. After a few minutes, I couldn't help myself. "I'm doing it. I'm cooking," I blurted.

"Yes, you are." Lily tried to share my enthusiasm, but it fell flat.

"Jen grew up sheltered and gets too excited when she learns something new." Tracy rotated her chunk of meat. "She's made huge strides but still thinks these things are cause for celebration."

Lily shrugged. "This little side-trip might be really good for her."

My excitement died as my eyebrows drew together. "How so?"

"It'll be a good confidence builder. It's also a chance for us to build a relationship."

Tracy nodded. "Agreed."

I shook my head. "If you gain any more confidence, you might out-confidence Mat, and then you couldn't tease him."

She threw her head back and laughed. "No one could out confidence Mat."

My own laugh escaped. "It wasn't something I noticed until you pointed it out, but yeah. His confidence is off the charts. I envy that."

She pulled a chunk of meat off the stick and broke it open. "Don't. You need more confidence, but that level would hit different coming from you."

We stayed up and talked. When the conversations drifted to our childhoods, Tracy won the most spoiled award. Her parents were great. After her mom died, her dad overcompensated by showering her with attention.

Lily had it even worse than me. No one cared about her at all until she found Jonas and Ann Marie. She described her time with our mother as 'cold.' She was taught to shut up and do as she was told. If not, Anitta beat her into submission. Until she got too strong to handle. Then she got dumped on Jed. At least she found people who loved her, helped her work through her issues, and gave her a good life.

It gave me insight into why she thought I didn't care enough to fight for the coalition. My new sister was loyal and had very strong principles. Her story also made me grateful for the griffins and Mat. And even more determined to break the curse.

CHAPTER TWELVE

"UGH. MOVE OVER," I grunted.

"I'm as far over as I can go."

"Me, too." Tracy sat up. "It's tight in here."

"I should have made a bigger shelter." I flipped over and eyed Lily. "Can you do something besides the vampire staring thing?"

"I'm listening for predators while you sleep. You should find something to do other than bitch at me."

"You don't need to listen for predators because they all run from you." She raised her middle finger.

I couldn't help but laugh. "Sorry. That was rude." I sat up and looked around. Tracy was on her back, her fingers drummed on her stomach. Lily was still in her vampire stupor. "Why are we on edge?"

"Because we've been trekking through the jungle for no apparent reason and we're hangry," Lily said.

Tracy sat up. "I mean, it's also the atmosphere. It feels like I'm waiting for the other shoe to drop."

Lily pointed at her. "Exactly. Which is why I'm listening for predators."

I settled on my back and turned my head. "Aside from being abusive, what was our mother like?"

The glow in Lily's eyes made me want to take the question back. "You sure you want me to answer?"

"Mat sugarcoated a lot of stuff about our parents. I'm pretty sure Jaques was part demon, the same way you're part vampire. I don't remember much about her."

Lily shifted to face me. "Angry and bitter was her go-to. She was also demanding. Whiny at times. She always complained about how her money and magic were stolen. She thought someone ripped her off the throne and handed you everything, and it pissed her off. The woman drilled coalition laws into my head as part of a scheme to win it back. Then she'd beat the hell out of me when I'd ask a question. She didn't care about anything else, including me. I hated her."

"Why would she think you could steal the ruling magic?"

"Because she was delusional. Her schemes were stupid, and even she didn't believe they'd work. But she craved power and would do anything to regain it." She shuddered.

"That's awful."

"Yeah." She cleared her throat. "My mom, Ann Marie, worked overtime to help me deal with the shit she dumped on me. It's why I don't hold the anger like you."

"Yeah. I need a better coping strategy. How long did it take to work through it?" I asked.

"Years. I still work on it when something comes up. We're both lucky to have escaped and found people to teach us how to be better."

"That's an understatement." I couldn't imagine how I would have turned out had I stayed with my parents and Jaques. "Is that why you help save people?"

"Pretty much. Most of the hybrid kids we pick up haven't been harmed physically, but the emotional and mental scars are there. I understand them."

"Me, too, in a way. I've been working to stop that nonsense for the last couple of years. Mat doesn't think my methods are appropriate."

"What methods?"

"The Bellicose created a whole campaign to convince the factions the hybrids didn't belong. I used their own tactics against them, and Mat called it propaganda. So I backed off and didn't use it like I wanted to."

"No shit?"

"Nope. I wanted to create our own full-on campaign, complete with shaming and moral restructuring."

She chuckled. "I can imagine Mat's face when you pitched that idea."

"He looked pained."

She let out another soft laugh, then her face grew hard. "You should have done it, anyway."

"You think so?"

"Absolutely. I understand where Mat was coming from, but I don't believe for a second that you'd use that tactic in every situation. Those assholes deserve that and more for all the trouble they've caused."

I was silent for a long time while I pondered her words. "Thank you."

"You're welcome, even though I'm not sure what you're thanking me for. You've got great instincts. But you need to build the confidence to use them, even if overconfident Mat disagrees."

"That's easier said than done. He's been my father figure most of my life. It's difficult for me to go against him."

"I bet. Especially since he made sure he was the most important person in your life through isolation."

"You make it sound abusive."

"That wasn't my intention. He's a good guy. I'm sure he did his best, but he's not infallible."

"Oh, I know."

"As hard as it is, you need to remember his ridiculous amount of confidence is as much of a front as your agreeable demeanor. Alex could help you with that if we find him. He's always telling me I'm not the boss of him."

A laugh bubbled out of me. "I'll keep that in mind."

Someone shook me, and I knocked the hand away. "Stop it."

"Wake up, you idiot. We need to hurry." Lily's voice sounded strained.

I shot up and looked around. "What?"

"Bastien's almost here. If you want to wake the First before they get here, you need to hurry," Tracy said from outside the shelter.

I checked the bond with Drake. It was still closed tight, so I sent my senses out. He was close. "Shit." I scrambled out and dissipated the shelter. "Let's go. I'll flash us to the cave."

We landed where we stood the day before, and Tracy spun in a slow circle. She pointed. "Lily and I will wait over there. When the First attacks, we'll swoop in and help fight him."

"What should I expect?" Lily asked.

I shook my head. "It depends. Drake and Razazia both attacked me because they thought I was my mother, so Gorman will probably do the same."

Her face twisted in disgust. "How in the hell did they mistake you for her? You look nothing like her aside from your eyes."

I shrugged. "It doesn't matter why. Just be ready."

They slunk into the dense jungle. The last two times I woke Firsts, I didn't do it on purpose. With Drake, my magic reached him through the wall as I patched it. Then, it connected to Razazia without my help. Both before it got fixed. Which meant I didn't have a clue how to wake Gorman. I concentrated on the cave and tried to send the magic I used to sip from paranormals into it.

Nothing happened.

"Hurry, Jen!" Tracy screeched.

I swung around to see her head tilted toward the sky.

I craned my neck to see what she was looking at. Two dark dots appeared on the horizon. One bigger than the other. They were moving fast.

"Holy shit!" I flung the full force of my magic into the cave.

Rock exploded.

One smashed into my shoulder before I remembered to make a shield to protect myself. A cloud of dust blocked my vision and made a beacon for Drake and Bastien.

Rumbling from inside the cave made me take a step back. Lily appeared beside me. "Is that normal?"

"Um."

The sound of dragon wings drew closer.

Jenella! Drake's voice boomed through my head.

Heart racing, I bolted toward the cave.

A hand latched onto my arm and stopped me with an abnormal amount of strength. "What the hell are you doing?"

I shook off Lily's hand. "Drake yelled in my head, and I panicked."

"Well, stop doing that. It's not normal."

The ground shook, and we flung out our arms at the same time to keep our balance.

My heart pounded out of my chest as the two dragons descended toward us.

Movement caught the corner of my eye inside the cave. I swung that way and braced myself to fight.

A filthy man in what used to be a white robe stumbled out. He rested one hand on the side of the rock and rubbed his long white beard with the other. His teeth were too white when he smiled. "Are you the heir? Please tell me you're the heir, and you've come to free me from this hell."

That was not the reaction I expected. I cleared my throat. "Yeah. I'm Jenella. The third queen. Are you Gorman?"

Thwap, thwap, thwap.

The sound of dragon wings drowned out his answer.

Lily latched onto my arm, and a swirl of green filled my vision as she whisked me away. When we stopped, Drake and Bastien perched in front of the new First.

Drake's green eyes scanned the jungle. They landed on me, and the bond opened.

Anger and darkness gushed through and slammed into my chest. "Curse," I croaked as I sunk to my knees.

Lily disappeared, then reappeared with the tattered man and pointed at me. "Fix that."

Tears fell as I tried to hold on. The darkness threatened to consume me. Drake took a step forward, and I threw a box around him. Except I couldn't concentrate long enough to anchor it, and it dissipated.

"Do you see?" Drake's deep, smooth voice came from somewhere around me. "I tried to save her from it, but can't fight any longer."

"I see," came an unfamiliar voice.

Foreign magic shot into me, and I hit the ground face-first. "I don't see!"

People were shouting, and someone roared.

I lay on the ground and fought to move. My body wouldn't obey, and my brain spun too fast to concentrate. A silvery glow formed in front of my eyes, and my brain shut off.

My bed was moving, I thought as my senses came back online. I jerked to a sitting position. I was in the air, propped against my favorite spike on Drake's back.

A man with white hair and a long white beard sat in front of me. "Very good. It worked. I am Gorman the First. Pleased to meet you."

I blinked.

A hand landed on my shoulder. "You and your boy-toy are good now. Gandalf there saved the day."

I swung around and focused on Lily. "Gorman."

"Whatever."

"The First Drake protected you from the curse as long as he could. It is a good thing you found me when you did, or I am afraid all would be lost." He didn't sound upset by the idea.

I rubbed my face. "Did you recognize the curse? Was it Cynthia's? The Vinculum Tenebrism?"

His too-thin face fell. "I'm afraid so."

I'm sorry, Drake said inside my head.

If you land, I can flash us back to Lily's.

Only if you accept my apology.

Pretty sure I made it clear if you blew that fire at us, I'd never forgive you.

It wasn't aimed at you.

Sure, it wasn't. And this whole mess is on me. I've known something was off for a couple of weeks.

I checked the bond and found it wide-open. Thick guilt and self-hatred waited for me on the other end. "Stop that right now," I said out loud.

He descended toward a clearing on the edge of the jungle. *I promised I'd stand behind you.*

You did. But I'm not listening to this. You'll pay for that fire, but no more apologizing for a curse you couldn't control.

I listened to your concerns and closed the bond to protect you.

Is that why you closed it? Because I think you did it to hide the curse from me.

I thought we were talking about forgiveness.

I flashed us to the street outside Lily's wards. We barely touched down when Jonas and Ann Marie stormed out the front door.

Lily pulled us through and turned to face them. "Hey."

Amber flashed across Jonas's eyes. "Where have you been?"

I raised my hand. "My fault. I wanted to wake Gorman, and I took Lily with me in a panic."

Gorman flashed his perfect teeth. "It's so good to see you again, Jonas. How did you avoid Cynthia's curse?"

Jonas's eyes narrowed. "What do you mean, Cynthia's curse?"

"I have a theory on that," I interrupted. "I think destroying the palace was a distraction. Everyone who spent a lot of time there is cursed." I pointed at Bastien. "Bas, Tracy, And I are safe because we've been working at the alchemy coven or out of our house. The ogres told me Gorman could break it. They even gave us a map."

Ann Marie examined Lily from head to toe. "And you don't find that a little too helpful?"

"Yes. That's why Tracy and I did our own research. I didn't intend to take Lily with me. I panicked when Drake came at us right after we found the gnomes."

Jonas's eyes settled on Drake. "You're cursed?"

"Not anymore. Gorman freed me, but not before I infected Jenella."

"I'm good," I said.

"There you are!" came a tiny voice.

I swung toward the street. "Hey, Sylphira."

The pixie queen eyed the wards. Sparkling pink dust dropped from her wings, and she zipped through. "Queen Jenella. Thank the fates you're here. You need to come back to Allure right away."

Ann Marie crossed her arms.

Sylphira paused long enough to mutter a 'sorry,' and turned her attention to me. "Ward breaker dust. Works every time. Anyway, Prince Mathias has locked down the pocket. No one gets in or out until you're found. Enforcers are raiding private homes and businesses. You must stop him."

I swung toward Gorman. "Mathias is my brother, and he's cursed. Will you help?"

Gorman rubbed his beard. "How did everyone around you become cursed?"

"Did you not just hear that entire conversation? The Bellicose destroyed parts of the palace and somehow slipped it in. I noticed everyone acting strange, but it took me too long to figure it out and evacuate. The Ogre Queens said it would wear off."

"If it is the same curse as Drake's, it is rather simple and takes some time to take root. Cynthia isn't normally so lazy. When did you wake her?"

"I didn't. What do you mean, the curse is simple? The Ogre Queens insisted they couldn't break it."

"Did they? Huh." He shrugged.

Tracy linked her arm with Bastien's. "It doesn't matter. What matters is we break it now."

I turned my attention to Jonas. "How close are the shifters to finding a leader?"

He rested a hand on Lily's shoulder. "We're on round two of ten in the testing phase. These things take time."

"Any changes to the situation in the valley?"

Amber ran across his eyes, and he blinked it away. "I relied on Drake to monitor the Bellicose."

An extra helping of guilt flooded the bond.

I ignored it and paced so I could think. "Your attention needs to be on finding Alex." I pointed at Bastien. "Have you heard from Glacintial?"

"No, but he's an experienced dragon. He won't let the mental mage out of his sight."

"Let's hope not. Will you work with Jonas and Ann Marie on that?"

"Yes."

"Drake can work with that vampire guy in the city...."

"Roman," Lily said.

"Right. Drake can work with Roman." I turned back to Jonas. "What else can I do to free up your time so you can find Alex?"

He blinked. "The shifters take a lot of time. I hoped the testing would reveal someone. None of the candidates are powerful enough to make it through the tests."

He was trying to run two factions and find his son. As powerful as he was, he was only one man. "That's a problem."

Jonas blinked. "A time-consuming one, yes."

Ann Marie crossed her arms. "I'll take over the hybrids so he can focus on his shifters."

I shook my head. "That's an option, but you also need to focus on finding Alex. Is there a hybrid powerful enough to lead them other than you?"

Everyone's heads turned to Lily.

She held up a hand. "No. I'm not leading shit."

I grinned. "Any ideas?"

"Dale," she said with conviction.

It took me a minute to place the name. "The bartender?"

"Yes. Nothing happens in the hybrid community without him knowing. He'd be a great leader."

"I'll keep that in mind," Ann Marie said. "But we don't have time to train him right now. I'll take over the hybrids while Jonas handles the shifters. We can make time to find our son."

I decided it wasn't really my business and let it go. "Great. Now, who's going with me to break the curse?"

Chapter Thirteen

Drake, Sylphira, Gorman, and I flashed to the gates of Allure. Tracy and Bastien stayed behind to help Jonas and Ann Marie. Bastien didn't believe Dragon Headquarters was cursed because the dragons weren't acting strange. I still planned to stop by and have Gorman check on Deva.

A wall of guards met us when we landed at the city gates. I took a sip of magic from each of them as I approached. A high-level mage stepped forward and bowed. "Your Grace."

I eyed the line of gate guards. Some wore shiny new uniforms. New hires, I realized. "What's going on here?"

"Regent Mathias has ordered a lockdown."

Drake rested a hand on my back. "Why?"

She swallowed. "Because the queen is missing, and demons are active in the pocket."

"Thank you." I pulled Drake through, and our small group headed toward the empty flashing circle.

"See what I mean?" Sylphira launched off my shoulder, her sparkling dust coating my hair. "I'm going home. I don't have dust to protect myself from curses."

"Thanks for coming to find me. You're a great friend."

A smile lit her face. "I really am." She took off toward downtown.

I concentrated on the dust she shed and accessed the magic I stole from her. While trekking through the jungle, I'd thought a lot about how I'd used Mat's magic. In my mind, it was a separate pool that I purposely drew from. Now that it was a color running through mine, the execution was different. But if I concentrated hard enough, I could still use it.

By that theory, accessing the other magics I'd absorbed should be similar. So, I did that with hers, concentrating on dissipating the dust. I still wasn't sure whether Sylphira was a friend or using me to gain status, but I knew pixie dust could do many things, and I didn't need another spy.

I imagined hers as a pink pool inside me and let it flow through my skin. Then, I had to tamp down my excitement when the dust disappeared. Gorman didn't need to see how inept I was.

Drake stepped into the flashing circle with us, and I cut my internal celebration short. "You're not going to fly?"

"No. I'm staying with you."

A few weeks earlier, I would have been thrilled at the idea of him tagging along. But that was before the curse. It was difficult to switch gears from being weary of him to complete and total trust. No, not difficult. Impossible, I decided. On top of that, I didn't trust the new First, Gorman. He was too cooperative.

I flashed to the main square. "Gorman, will you check Deva first? Then we can concentrate on the palace?"

Gorman spun in a slow circle, taking in the main square. "This has not changed much since I left."

"On the surface," Drake said as we made our way toward my favorite street. "There have been many advances in technology, clothing styles, and language. You'll need to learn them."

The look of disdain Gorman shot him unnerved me, and I had to grit my teeth to keep from lashing out. He warned me the other Firsts hated him, but until then, I'd never seen it. I also would not tolerate it.

Drake's lips twitched, and he sent me a warm, calming feeling. It wasn't until that moment that I realized how much I missed him. We still needed to hash things out, but I couldn't help but soak up the squishy, warm feeling as we started up the steps of Dragon Headquarters. "We'll fix it if necessary, then leave. Try not to piss Deva off, Gorman."

"I have no plans to unsettle the Dragon Queen. She is simply not someone I like."

I didn't care what he liked or didn't like, but I didn't comment as we blew past the guards and made our way to Deva's temporary office.

She stood in front of the window, looking out over the city. "Hello, Gorman. I wish I could say it's nice to see you again."

He cleared his throat. "Deva. I hear you may be cursed. Fitting, really, considering your lovely disposition."

She spun and examined Drake. "What is different about you?"

"I am no longer cursed. The others who work at the palace are, though. Jenella found Gorman when she realized something was wrong."

I held up a hand. "I've known something was wrong for a while, but not what. And, for the record, I always planned to wake Gorman."

"Pity," she drawled. "Some things are best left undisturbed."

Some kind of magic shot out of Gorman and smashed into Deva.

A small stream of fire shot from her. Drake shoved me behind him.

Gorman ducked, but not fast enough, and his hair caught fire. He reached up and patted it out. "Deva is not cursed."

My mouth dropped open at the exchange. "Holy shit. I did not realize you two hated each other that much." I moved back to Drake's side. "Sorry for interrupting you, Deva. I wanted to make sure Anitta didn't do something to you, too."

Her eyes softened. "Of course, love. I understand your misguided concern. I lost many magnificent dragons, and my heart hurts for each one. Grieving will take time. Tell me, how did you allow yourself to be cursed, Drake?"

He shook his head. "It was a slow process. A negative thought here and there, followed by a slight nudge to turn against Jenella. She noticed and kept insisting I was cursed. I disagreed until the thought of courting her was no longer appealing. Then, I had to admit she may have a point and closed our bond."

My fists clenched to fight the sudden urge to smack him for brushing off my warnings. "It's not just him, but the entire palace. I've been working from my house and haven't been there, so it didn't affect me. The Ogre Queens said I had some immunity."

"Perhaps." The look she gave Gorman was pure venom. "You cannot trust some Firsts."

"Nor can you trust all dragons," he retorted. "Queen Jenella is not cursed. And I owe her my life for the brave way she rescued me."

I scooted closer to Drake. I might have resented him and his recent actions, but the new First's personality grated on my nerves. "Right. So, Deva. I'll leave you alone and let you mourn. Please reach out if you need anything." I held up a hand. "Bastien and Tracy are helping Jonas find Alex."

She tapped her temple. "He told me. It's wise to focus on finding him. I will help when I can. Perhaps I'll send the dragons Lily befriended. Flintous and June were quite mischievous while she was here, and I fear they need more duties to occupy their time."

My eyebrows drew together. "Did Lily cause trouble?"

"No, love. She is a delight, and there was only one incident. Her and two of my dragons spent too many hours in the hotel bar."

I opened my mouth to ask her to tell me more, but Drake nudged me toward the door. "Come, Gorman. We need to visit the palace."

Deva was acting so strange. Maybe it was how she mourned, but I suspected there was more to it than that. I glanced at Gorman and realized it wasn't the time to bring it up.

We landed inside the family flashing circle. Tents covered the back lawn, along with some new buildings. Griffins and palace guards rushed toward us, fire in their eyes. I threw up a wall, and they bounced off. "Gorman."

His eyes scanned the griffins, who threw magic and used claws as they tried to break through. "Oh, my. This curse is much worse than I imagined."

"Can you break it?" I asked through gritted teeth.

"Perhaps. I can free people outside of its influence, but I will need to find the roots and eliminate them for it to truly be gone." He turned toward the palace and nodded. "I shall use my precious energy to free your people first."

"Great idea." It didn't escape me how he called them 'my' people.

I let go of the wall I'd created as his magic fanned out among the crowd. One by one, the griffins and palace guards dropped to the ground. Gorman's magic covered the tents and new buildings, coating them in what felt like a thick syrup before moving on. Everyone it touched fell unconscious.

Anger lit inside me, and I spun toward the new First.

He held up a hand when he noticed my glowing eyes. "It is a side effect, nothing more."

Drake nudged me out of the way and wrapped his hand around Gorman's throat. "Fix it."

"Fine," he croaked. "You are no fun." He waved his hand.

When the griffins stirred, I latched onto his arm and dragged him toward the Leadership Council building. Drake stayed so close I could feel his heat on my back.

"Nice of you to join us," came Mat's rough voice when we stepped into the main meeting area.

The stadium seating was gone, replaced by desks. The palace staff who filled them stopped what they were doing and twisted their heads toward me. Every single person's face reflected contempt.

The hair on the back of my neck stood on end. "What the hell?"

My brother's golden eyes were unfocused and glowed a sickly brownish-yellow color. He wore his greasy hair tied back, and his stench told me he hadn't showered in days. Anger radiated off him in waves.

Drake pushed Gorman toward him. "Fix this."

Gorman shook his head. "I need to restore my energy before I can take care of this many cursed paranormals."

"How long will that take?" I asked.

"Around fifteen minutes if I have proper nourishment."

Drake handed him a plate of food. "Eat."

I turned my attention to Mat. "What's up?"

"Did you once again forget that you're the queen?" He eyed Drake, then the griffins who filed in behind us. "Where is Lily?"

"Home. You knew that." I took two steps toward him and stopped. "You're cursed, Mat. And it's clouding your judgment."

His katanas appeared in his hands, and he charged.

Adrenaline shot through me as I backpedaled.

He followed.

I flashed away.

When he appeared in front of me, I sprinted through the tangle of desks, shoving furniture in his way. "Stop, Mat! This isn't you!"

One of his blades swiped at me, coming so close to my face a lock of hair fell to the ground.

Hands reached out and grabbed me from all directions as the rest of the cursed staff came at me. One caught a chunk of hair and pulled me back, while another kicked my knee.

There were too many to fight off without hurting them.

A fist landed in my stomach, and I doubled over.

An ear-splitting roar shook the building, and paranormals dove out of the way as Drake barreled through them in what I called his snuffy form. His koala bear head swung toward me, and his mouth opened, revealing long, sharp teeth.

Griffins rushed to restrain people.

Someone screamed, tearing my attention away from them as a katana swung toward my throat.

I threw my hands out in front of me and put myself in a containment box.

Mat's blade bounced off with a 'clink.' He smashed into the side, roared, and flung his magic toward it.

When he stepped back, I opened my mouth to reason with him.

He attacked again. His short swords sparked as he tried to carve his way to me.

Emine appeared beside him. "Release the shield." She aimed an enormous gun at Drake.

He smashed a paw into the side of her face. A bullet pinged off him, then my shield, and lodged in Mat's arm.

Mat grunted and charged.

I formed a box around him, and he smashed into the side of it.

Fire in her eyes, Emine raised her weapon again, so I restrained her, too.

I stood on my tippy-toes as I searched for Gorman.

The crowd of angry staff surged toward me, but the griffins formed a line to hold them back.

I slammed my hands on my hips and focused on intent and projection. *"Everyone who is not Gorman or Drake, sit!"* As one, they all sat down, including the griffins. I hated treating them like that, but I was struggling to contain the ever-present ball of anger inside me. *"Gorman, break the curse!"*

Drake shifted into his human form but kept his scales on the surface. He leaned against my barrier. "Gorman is not reliable. He often boasts about being able to do things beyond his capabilities."

"That would have been great to know before we got here, but it's unsurprising. He's too nice."

Drake's lips twitched. "Never trust the ones who are too nice."

"Exactly."

Gorman finished his meal and meandered through the palace guard. He stopped, bent over, picked something up, then continued toward us. One of the magic-laced tablets used by the staff, I realized. He raised his head, a carefree smile on his face. "This is the most useful thing I have ever seen. Tell me, are there similar gadgets now?"

I clenched my fists. "The curse?"

Drake reached over and plucked the tablet from his hands.

Behind him, Mat pounded on the side of his box, his face bright red. Emine summoned a new tool and pried at a corner, trying to free herself.

Gorman tapped his chin. "Oh, yes. I should take care of that right away. It can cause widespread damage if left unchecked." His eyes slid back to the tablet. "Fascinating."

"Do you plan to free these people today, or should I find a hole to put you in until you regain your strength?" Drake asked.

"A hole? When I've been asleep for over two hundred years? No, that won't do."

I took a deep breath. "Free. These. People. Now." The words came out between gritted teeth.

"Temper, temper. To free them is easy. But they must avoid the root so the curse does not regrow." He smirked. "But you've already accomplished that, haven't you?"

"Gorman," Drake growled.

I took another sip of Gorman's magic so I could eventually learn how to break my own curses.

"Fine. It's planted inside the newly built walls at the front and back of that monstrosity you call a palace. It will take some time to dissolve, as it's grown quite strong." Gorman shook his head. "Cynthia used to be much better at curses. I can't tell if its weakness is a trap. Perhaps she created it to be easily broken." He pointed at Emine. "I'll need you to release your prisoners."

I released Mat and Emine.

The box I created for myself was small, so when Drake stepped in front of them, I couldn't see around him. Mat's war cry echoed through the building as he attacked.

Booming gunshots sounded, and I lost my hearing as Drake and Mat tumbled away, fists flying.

Gorman folded his arms, a huge grin spread across his face.

I wondered if waking him was a mistake. "Now, Gorman!"

He sighed. "I normally charge thousands of dollars for this service."

"Good point. My price for waking you is breaking the curse, so once that's done, we're even." When his eyes narrowed, I leaned forward. "Or would you like to go back?"

With a huff, he waved an arm. "Very well. I shall pay your price." The building vibrated with the force of his magic.

Emine melted to the ground, her weapon dissipating. Mat went limp, his throat still in Drake's grip.

I dissipated my cage and shuffled toward Emine as she came to. When her eyes fluttered open, I held my hand out to help her up or blast her. I wasn't sure which, since Gorman turned out to be such a pain in the ass. "Hey, Emine. Want to hear the ridiculous situation I dragged Lily into?"

She blinked. "No way! I missed it? Life is not fair sometimes." She ignored my hand and hopped to her feet in a fluid motion. "Why don't I want to kill you?"

Our griffin matriarch, Helen, burst through the doors and raced toward me. Tears streamed down her face as she swept me into her arms. "I have failed to protect the nest."

"No, you haven't. It's not your fault the Bellicose cursed the palace, so don't take that on."

"Explain," Mat's gravelly voice came from behind me.

I explained how I figured it out and how I found Gorman. "Gorman said he needs to kill the root of the curse before we can go inside. It might take some time."

"How was it placed there?"

"The First Cynthia set it, but she didn't do it right or something."

"When?"

"Either during the battle or when it was being rebuilt."

"Holy shitballs," Emine said. "That explains a lot."

My muscles relaxed at the crazy reflecting in her eyes. "Why aren't you at work?"

"Long story that involves planning your demise." She shook her head. "Mat and I were a little nuts."

"Weird, considering your regular, sane demeanor."

She cackled. "Right?"

I started toward the door. "Where's Verity?"

Verity and Charlotte had locked themselves in my pre-meeting waiting area and set up a makeshift office. Charlotte looked up when I entered, and her face flushed.

Verity lifted her head and shook it, then blinked. "What was I doing?"

I waved a hand. "Doesn't matter. You were cursed, and it's wearing off, so you might want to take a break." I shut the door behind me and headed toward the window overlooking the main floor. Everyone was stirring, and it didn't look like Gorman missed anyone, but I still didn't trust him.

"I'm not taking a break. There's too much to do."

I angled toward her and examined her face. "Okay, then what decrees did Mat make while I was gone?"

He hadn't made many, but the ones he made were doozies. Having locked down Allure, he sent out hunting parties to find the little rat demons and ordered the gargoyles to leave. Not that they'd listen. They never did unless their king wanted them to.

We'd just finished reversing everything and issuing new orders, including my new no-bowing policy, when the door opened and Drake strode in. When our eyes met, I had the sudden urge to cry. As fast as it came, it was gone. "Is everyone back to normal?"

"Gorman believes so. He will start on the palace tomorrow. He will need access."

"We'll just take that break now." Verity dragged Charlotte from the room.

"Sure." I turned my attention back to Drake. I didn't blame him for his actions while cursed, but I couldn't shake the resentment and mistrust. "How are you feeling?" His eyes were dull as he examined me. "That bad, huh?"

"I failed in my purpose. Worse, I've once again violated your trust. Lily made a good point that I'm doing a shit job of rooting out the Bellicose Leadership. I'm still unsure who they are or where to find them. My sole focus should have been on them and courting you, but I couldn't accomplish either."

"That's a big load of crap." I pointed at him. "Lily hasn't been here in the trenches fighting like we have. She didn't see how hard we fought or even how many resources we'd sent to the valley to help the hybrids. As far as our relationship is concerned, I'm glad we took a step back." I leaned forward. "In case you haven't noticed, I can be a little impulsive. Sleeping with you the first chance I got was a mistake. Especially when you made it clear you wanted to court me first."

"It takes two to tango."

I drew a blank on that one. "What?"

"It's a dance. My point is, you weren't the only one who made an impulsive decision."

"Right. And you're not the only one who got cursed. If there's one thing I've learned about my mother, it's that she's great at screwing up other people's plans. That's not your fault, so don't take it on. We have enough problems."

"Yet your anger toward me is still present." A tsunami of guilt sprinkled with hope flooded the bond. "And you said you'd never forgive me for the fire."

"Yep. You were an ass and it will take me a while to adjust to having you back. And I won't forgive you for trying to kill me. I just haven't decided how you'll pay for it yet."

"I can't wait to see what you come up with." He ran a hand through his hair. "You're too forgiving."

"I agree. But a wise multidrakelandarnarian recently told me the bond allows us to understand what our mate feels and helps us adapt to them. When you treated me like crap, it confirmed my suspicions that something was wrong. It also gave me the push I needed to fix the problem. Now it's solved. The question is, where do we go from here?"

Our eyes stayed locked for a long time as a tangle of emotions flowed back and forth. After a few minutes, he shifted his weight. "I will start our courtship over and attempt to regain your trust. I believe I owe you a picnic. As far as my purpose, Jonas thinks the Bellicose will bring their leaders in soon. I'll follow that lead."

A small smile ghosted across my face. "Sounds good to me." I held up a hand. "Wait. I got you something." I fished around in my bag and pulled out the present I'd bought at the warehouse. As soon as the paper fell to the floor, I held it out. "I bought this tiny potato glass with feet for you. Maybe you could use it to store what's left of your pride."

His shoulders shook with laughter as he reached out and took it. He examined it and laughed harder. "I shall treasure it always."

CHAPTER FOURTEEN

A SHIVER SHOOK MY body as I once again stood on the outer wall. The god Cavil's power proceeded his appearance at the gates. He eyed the overattentive griffins lining the wall, then reached out to touch the wards. Daylight formed in a small circle around him.

I made my way to the stairs and waved when he noticed me.

Cavil was a big guy. Almost as big as Drake. But where Drake was dark and stormy, Cavil was bright and sunny. Lily liked him more than she'd admit, too. It was the only reason I trusted him. The guy was way too nice to like without a reference. I met him inside the gates. "Thanks for coming."

"Hello, Jenella. Ann Marie created your wards?"

"Yes. And hundreds, if not thousands, of people have added their magic to them."

"I've never seen anything like them. Doesn't the magic of others create loopholes?"

I couldn't help the laugh that escaped me. "The only one powerful enough to create a loophole is my consort. He even locked me out at one point."

"Impossible."

"It was back when my magic was fractured. Or suppressed. I'm not sure which."

"So it would not happen now?"

I'd never paid much attention to the wards or people accessing the palace. It never crossed my mind to try. "I have so much to learn."

We headed down a trail in the woods to a gym the palace guard used to spar during inclement weather. I opened the door and waved him in. The windowless building looked like a storage facility on the outside, and I was pleased to see the bright colors and plenty of lighting as we stepped through the door.

Cavil eyed the orange and yellow pads and white walls. "These colors are pleasing."

"Yeah. They make up for the lack of windows."

"They do." He walked to the center of a yellow pad. "I'm unfamiliar with your full capabilities, only that you have creation magic and can mimic those under your rule. What did you want to learn today?"

I conjured a ball of silvery magic. "I've absorbed the powers of hundreds, if not thousands, of paranormals and might be able to use some of it. Sort of. Will you help me figure it out?"

He shook his head. "It isn't something I can do, but I can help with the principles."

"You said I've been mimicking my brother's magic my whole life. I used pixie magic the other day and got the basic idea. It would be handy to use the witch and mage magic." Or the ogre's ability to break curses.

"Very well."

An hour later, sweat dripped down my temples, and my nerves were fried. I could do small things with the power I'd taken from others, but it was difficult and took a lot of concentration. "Do I need to absorb more?"

"Most likely. You said the mountain colors were vibrant. Perhaps that's the key. Instead of absorbing from multiple people, I suggest you master one faction at a time. Once you have a vibrant color and can access it, move on to the next."

I rubbed my eyes. "That will take forever."

He shrugged. "Most leaders have years to master this ability."

And I didn't. I needed to learn fast. Which meant visiting each faction and sipping from everyone I saw. It would be exhausting. "Okay." I picked up a towel. "Did you have a chance to visit the Conservatory?"

"I did. Your creation is interesting, though lacks detail. The dwarven prince liked it, though I do not understand why."

"Yeah. It was my first try. I've been practicing in my backyard and have done better. I think it would help if I could channel power, rather than trying to create from memory. And I still can't figure out climate."

"I agree."

I tapped my foot to keep from pacing. "Can I ask you an unrelated question?"

Cavil's blue eyes scanned me with a fierce skepticism I hadn't seen from him before. It made me trust him a little more. "Of course. You are the queen, are you not?"

"Last time I checked. Why are you here instead of helping Lily find Alex?"

The color drained from his face, and his massive power pulsed, almost blinding me. "What do you mean?"

His relationship with Lily wasn't my business, but she needed the support. Besides, I liked the idea of playing matchmaker. "Um. Someone ambushed them, leaving Lily for dead. They took Alex. Quin saved her and called me. She's fine, and a dragon followed Alex. She considers you a friend, so I thought she could use your help."

He ran a hand through his hair. "My farmhouse is under what the hybrids called construction. However, I have new ideas for decorating. If you don't need my services, I'll go oversee it. Perhaps I can convince Lily she needs my help."

I choked back a laugh. "Go ahead. I'll text if I have questions."

Cavil started to bow, thought better of it, nodded, then marched toward the door a little too fast.

I grinned and turned toward the darkened doorway. "They're a good match, don't you think?"

Mat stepped out. "I don't trust him."

"There's no way he'd hurt Lily. I'm almost sure she's the only reason he's still in this realm."

"Perhaps."

My eyes swept over him. "How are you feeling?"

"Ashamed. Embarrassed. And a little off kilter."

I rubbed my stomach. "Drake feels the same way. He doesn't trust Gorman."

"Drake is right not to trust him. Gorman can twist a curse and hates the dragons. I believe he has his own reasons for helping you."

"Yeah. Sylphira, the Pixie Queen, is doing the same thing. She's gains status amongst the other leaders by claiming to be my friend and being seen with me."

Mat's face pinched in disgust. "Why don't you do something about it?"

"Because I don't care about their posturing for status. They're all equals who have invented a political game. It's a waste of time and energy." I raised a hand. "I'll still use their perception of status if it benefits the coalition."

His lip twitched. "You are becoming a true queen."

The words were like a punch to the gut. It wasn't the first time someone in my inner circle said something similar. "See, that's the thing, Mat. I'm not becoming anything. I've been the true queen since I was six. Though no one knew it, and I didn't want to admit it." I rubbed my chest. "But I've always known in here. The only difference is that now I'm making the effort."

My brother wasn't one to show much emotion. But the feelings that swept across his face in that moment almost brought me to my knees. He pulled me to him and hugged me with his whole heart. "I am sorry for holding you so close that I suffocated you. For letting my own fears drive my decisions. I never meant to make you think you were less than you are or to clip your wings. You're growing into the woman I always knew you could be."

I stepped back and swiped a tear from my eye. "That's never going to happen."

"I disagree. All those years spent protecting you were meant to shield you from the evils of the world. I thought I was doing the right thing. The evidence of my mistake slaps me across the face every time you allow me a glimpse of how capable you are."

I blinked back more tears. I loved him every bit as much as I always did. Curse, power struggles, and all. And there was a time I would have sold my soul to hear Mat say those words. But I'd become a different person. So, although I appreciated his approval and knew he'd never let me fall, I no longer needed it to feel whole.

It was a revelation that both stung and seemed right. "Thank you. And I love you, too. I understand how hard decisions are when fighting your own demons." I held up a hand. "For the record, I appreciate everything you've done for me, from raising me to keeping me safe from mother. I often wonder how you do everything you do while making it look effortless."

We stood there in a companionable and awkward silence. When I shifted my weight, he moved toward the door. "What do you have planned for today?"

"I'm going to see how the witches are faring and introduce myself to their new vice president. Calvin says he has them under control, but I want to see for myself."

"You want to absorb their magic." It wasn't a question.

"That, too. But I'm worried about the power vacuum created by not having an established leader for two major factions. And I can't effectively lead until I figure some things out."

"You worry too much about it."

"Yes. Do you want to go with me?"

"Do you think that's wise after I disciplined their former president?"

"I do. We could use your reputation to our advantage."

"I don't see where my presence will further your agenda of bringing everyone together."

I shrugged. "Some factions appreciate power plays."

His lips twitched. "Very well, I'll go with you."

The witches weren't adjusting well to Calvin's rule. Or some of them weren't. As Mat and I landed in the flashing circle in the witch district, a tingle between my shoulder blades started before we even took a step. I scanned the colorful row houses that comprised most of the district and noticed some witches pointedly ignoring us, while others glared. I took a sip of magic from them as we passed.

We made our way down the main street and took a right toward headquarters. Only six witches bowed. While others hustled down the sidewalk toward their houses before we reached them. I sipped their magic, too. "It's not exactly a warm welcome, but it could be worse."

Mat scanned the rooftops. "They're running like rabbits."

"But they're not trying to attack us."

"They would be foolish to attack you after feeling your power."

Because they didn't realize I sucked at using it. When we took a left heading deeper into the district, the row houses gave way to smaller one-story homes with vibrant gardens. They paled in comparison to the gardens in Calvin's village, but were still charming. Some houses had herb gardens in the front, while others had flowers. One house lined each type of herb with a smattering of purple, yellow, red, and pink flowers of different types.

Witch headquarters sat at the heart of the neighborhood in a sprawling antebellum-style mansion. Four large round columns with ornate trim supported the front of the two-story white house. One-story wings with dark blue shutters jutted out from each side. Several witches gathered on the second-floor balcony and glared as I touched the wards.

Mat stared them down. "If they don't let us in, what will you do?"

"They might have been loyal to their former president, but they're not stupid. If there's one thing our mother taught coalition members, it's respect for the crown."

"We shall see."

I sensed Drake heading our way and tilted my head in his direction.

Mat did the same. "Is he following you around again?"

"No." I rubbed my fluttering stomach and once again marveled at how the emerald green of his scales glittered in the sun. I dropped my hand when the thought of him rearing back to fry me raced across my mind. He landed on the street, not bothering to shift. "Hey, Drake." My voice didn't sound as enthusiastic as it once did.

He lowered his nose to my level, and I reached out and rubbed the side of his enormous face.

What made you decide to come into hostile territory? Amusement trickled through the bond.

"Just seeing how things are going."

A stream of smoke rose into the air above our heads with his laugh.

The front door opened, and three witches rushed down the stairs. The front one, a dark-haired woman with intelligent brown eyes, greeted us. "Your Grace. Your Majesty. Consort. What brings you here today?"

I pasted on a professional smile. "I just wanted to meet you and see how your transition is going. Mind if we come in?"

She stepped forward and held out a hand. "Not at all. Does the consort plan to shift?"

I will wait here and look intimidating. Many witches secretly support the Bellicose. Guard yourselves.

I took her hand, and she pulled me through the wards. They were good wards but not great, which baffled me because I knew they were capable of better ones. "He's fine staying out here. Thanks."

Mat touched the back of her other hand and stepped through, but stayed silent.

She led us toward the front door. "Please, come in. I'm Mel. The new Vice President. Calvin's not here right now, but I'll gladly answer your questions."

We followed her to a sitting room on the second floor with antique chairs and heavy curtains that hung across the large windows. A semi-circle of several ornate maroon and gold chairs stood in front of a gaping fireplace. The two witches who accompanied Mel didn't say a word as we took our seats. I bit back a laugh when a massive green eye appeared at the window, and one of them jumped.

Mel cleared her throat. "The consort can come in."

I shook my head. "He prefers to stay outside."

An awkward silence followed. The witches stared at us, and we stared back. The witch who didn't jump swept his hair out of his face. "I thought you were friends with the President's daughter."

"I am."

"Does she not update you?"

"She doesn't really associate with witches outside the alchemy coven because you bullied her for the last few years."

Mat's jaw ticked. "We would like an update on the transition of power."

Mel's smile didn't reach her eyes. "We deeply regret how the former administration treated Tracinia. Please understand it was only a few witches involved in, or even knew about, her treatment."

My left eye twitched at the lie. I thought about being diplomatic and letting it go, but Deva's voice telling me I needed to be myself in all situations rang through my head. I squared my shoulders. "We both know that's not true. She couldn't go anywhere without her own people attacking her." I leaned forward. "I understand it wasn't your proudest moment, but it's best to acknowledge failures, or you'll never move past them and do better."

"Fine. We knew the former president ordered her death. But many of us avoided that woman."

"I don't blame you." I motioned to Mat. "Like my brother said, we're here to find out how the transition of power is going. Not stir up trouble."

"Of course, Your Grace."

I opened my mouth to tell her to call me Jen or Jenella, but the words caught in my throat. They hadn't earned my first name. Calvin had, but not the other witches.

Mat shifted in his chair. "How many witches have defected to the Bellicose since the election?"

I glanced toward the window where Drake loomed. "We recently received information about several covens supporting them."

"As are many mages." The male witch's voice sounded bitter.

My attention turned to him.

He dipped his head. "I thought you wanted honesty."

"I do. And you're right. Our intelligence says most defects are shifters, witches, and mages." I held up a hand when he opened his mouth to speak. "I'd like to work together to address the issues causing them to turn toward that organization. So, let's share information. We'll tell you what measures we're taking, and you tell us how you're handling the problem."

"Very well," Mel leaned back in her chair.

Mat's intimidating magic amped up.

She stiffened, but didn't speak.

He didn't acknowledge their fear. "Many of the mages defecting are low to mid-level in power. They're seduced to take the side of the Bellicose with the promise of more power or forced into service by mind-control magic. To date, we have shut down fifteen labs in multiple countries in the human world. Our compound raids have recovered over five hundred unwilling and willing paranormals who worked for them. The witches we've recovered are mostly volunteers. Three local covens created and manned a lab near Seattle. They joined the Bellicose after the battle at the palace. Explain." His eyes flipped to me, and he added, "Please."

Mel leaned back and crossed her arms. "It's been a rough transition. Some older witches were fiercely loyal to the former president. They consider President Cordalia a weak substitute and are the ones most likely to defect."

The blonde male witch who jumped at Drake's eye shifted in his seat. "Can I be candid, Your Grace?"

"Sure."

"A certain segment of the population knew your mother was still alive and believed she should have remained queen. In addition, you started your rule in such a chaotic manner they don't trust you."

My heart jumped to my throat. I thought back to everything I had done since my coronation and couldn't argue the point. Most of the stuff wasn't my fault. But part of being queen meant I had to take responsibility for the good *and* the bad. I wiped my clammy hands on my pants. "Is that so?"

"It is part of the problem," Mel said.

"And the other part?"

The witches shared a look, and she met my eyes. "Your plans for the hybrids are a bigger issue than the chaos you've caused. Many witches don't believe the Bellicose started the alienation."

I leaned forward. "Oh?"

She shook her head. "Not me. We have many witch hybrids in our faction. We hide and protect them. But many believe you care more about hybrids than the rest of us."

I fought to keep my mouth from dropping open. When I brought the hybrids into the coalition, I expected my efforts would turn some factions against me, but didn't realize it would be perceived as favoritism.

"How big is this problem?" Mat's gravelly voice was barely a purr.

Mel squirmed under his intense stare. "It wasn't so bad until you acknowledged the mage vampire hybrid as royalty. It caused quite a stir and allowed the Bellicose an opportunity to recruit. Many of the most ardent anti-hybrid members are considering ditching the coalition over it."

My eyebrows drew together. "That doesn't even make sense."

All four heads turned to me.

I shrugged. "It's only been a couple of weeks since we found out we had a sister. Even less time than that since Mat added her to our family records. There's no way that kind of sentiment has built in such a short time."

"Correct," Mat growled. "And there's nothing wrong with setting an example by acknowledging our sister's position."

Mel held up a hand. "I'm unfamiliar with the details. Only that the sentiment exists."

I needed the coalition members to be on board with helping the hybrids, and I needed it yesterday. The fact some factions resented Lily's status wasn't good news. But I knew with a bone-chilling certainty that the coalition would crumble without them. And I wasn't willing to give up my progress over a few disgruntled people. "We'll work on that." I tapped my fingers on my leg. "Now, about the transition of power."

They were cautiously hopeful the witches would rally behind Calvin and that the chaos in their faction would end soon. I wasn't sure what to think about it, but I doubted the rosy picture they painted was accurate. Especially when we stepped out of the building and saw the glares Drake ignored.

I fought not to race toward him when his head turned and our eyes met. "Thanks for your time. Please contact my office if you need anything from the crown."

They bowed. Damn it. I needed to figure out how to stop that.

My mind spun as I headed toward Drake. I needed to appease the people who hated me for the hybrid situation. If they existed. I couldn't trust anything the witches told me. They were scared and grasping at ways to direct my attention away from them.

Drake must have sensed my unease because he launched into the air and made large circles over the witch district. Probably gathering information by scanning their minds. I loved that dragon when he wasn't cursed.

I came to a sudden stop and swallowed when I realized where my thoughts took me. My heart raced at the idea of being in love. My traitorous body shook. Needing to hide the panic before Mat picked up on it and started asking questions, I took a deep breath and closed my eyes.

"Jen?"

Too late. "Sorry. Freaking myself out with my own thoughts." I clinched my fists and glanced in the direction Drake flew. "You go ahead. I want to find out what information Drake's getting."

"Are you sure you're okay?"

I nodded a little too hard. "Um. Yeah. Fine. I won't be long."

He gave me a skeptical look as he stepped inside the flashing circle. "At least talk to Drake about whatever is going on inside your head."

"Sure." Wasn't going to happen. I needed to untangle my feelings before I said a word to anyone. Especially Drake. The curse had ruined my trust in everyone, and I didn't believe for a second Gorman would clear it without a fight. Because I'd had to fight for every inch I gained as a ruler and didn't see that changing anytime soon. My thoughts screeched to a halt when I realized Mat was still there. "I'll be fine."

"I don't believe you." He disappeared.

Drake made one more swoop over the area, then headed my way. When he hovered over me, I flashed to his back and hugged my favorite spike.

What happened just now? Your feelings are all over the place.

Panic attack. I'm over it.

He sent calming feelings through the bond.

"Where are we going?" I asked a couple of minutes later.

I promised you a picnic.

"Now?"

Yes. I understand there's a lot to do, but it won't hurt to take a moment and breathe.

I had to admit, taking a break sounded great.

CHAPTER FIFTEEN

WE LANDED IN A lush valley surrounded by tall trees. I flashed to the ground and spun in a slow circle as I breathed in the refreshing scent of spruce and pine. A bubbling creek danced through the golden meadow. "We're having a picnic here?"

"Not here, no." He pointed toward the creek. "We need to hike to it."

I eyed the trail. I'd had enough hiking in the jungle. "How far?"

"Not far." He held out a hand. When I didn't take it, he leaned toward me. "I am no longer cursed and will not hurt you."

I took his hand and let him lead me down the trail. The entire scene was surreal after how awful he'd been to me. And even though I understood it wasn't his fault, it still stung. "You tried to fry us."

"I was aiming for the Bellicose."

"Didn't look that way from where I was standing."

He squeezed my hand. "It should have. You're my mate. No curse, hex, or spell in the world could make me harm you."

"You came at me when I evacuated the palace."

"I still wouldn't have hurt you."

"You would have let the others tear me apart."

"I thought you were a threat to the coalition with your poor decisions."

"Still not a reason to attack me."

Drake paused. "What was the curse designed to do?"

"Tarnish and destroy bonds. It worked because now I'm hesitant around you."

"It played on my anger issues. I cannot change what happened, but I apologize. I should have listened when you raised concerns."

"You should have, yes. Look. I understand it wasn't your fault. It's just...." I shrugged.

"It's just what?"

"I don't want to fear you and wonder about the long-term effects."

"I see." He squeezed my hand. "I'm not a threat to you."

My shoulders relaxed a little. "I read up on dragon bonds, but a lot of information was missing."

"By design. Deva doesn't like giving away our secrets."

I understood her reasoning, especially if the other Firsts hated the dragons as much as Gorman.

We followed a well-maintained trail along the creek and around a bend. The trees parted and revealed a picnic table covered in a checkered tablecloth. Food containers lined the table in a stick-straight line down the center. Potted purple and pink flowers adorned each end of the table, their blooms cascading over the sides.

A sloppy smile formed on my face. "Wow."

He tugged me toward it. "Do you like it?"

"It's beautiful."

The picnic was amazing. We sat on opposite sides of the table, eating, talking, and laughing. We spent hours just enjoying each other's company. I learned a lot about him. Like me, he loved learning new things and going on adventures. They kept life exciting as he aged and helped him stay engaged.

I learned we shared the love of human movies and how he hated the formalities of being a First every bit as much as I hated the ones sur-rounding being a queen. And we both shared a love of the outdoors. I vowed to take him running on the trails around the palace. They were hard to navigate but fun. We kept our conversation light and laughed a lot.

I'd never been so comfortable with someone before, and I savored every second.

As the meal wound down, I rested my elbows on the table as the thousands of coalition problems and responsibilities pressed down on me.

"Stop that." He popped a grape into his mouth.

"Stop what?"

"Thinking about whatever made that crease in your forehead."

I sighed. "Thank you for this. It was fun."

"It was long overdue."

I took a sip of water. "Can I ask you a question?"

"Always."

"What was it like to be cursed?"

"I didn't notice it at first. Not until I snapped at you in my office. Despite this, I refused to admit the problem existed. Even after your numerous warnings, I couldn't stop the intrusive thoughts. But I understood you would not have kept insisting without cause, so I closed the bond on the off chance you were right."

"The Ogre Queens said I'm immune to most curses. The only thing I experienced was the need to run away."

"I wondered why you stayed away."

"It was part of the reason. Everyone being hostile toward me was a bigger factor."

"I resented you. The curse made everything your fault."

"So it was accurate."

He didn't laugh like I hoped. Instead, his eyes flared. "No, it was not accurate. None of the terrible decisions made over the last thirty years came from you. And Mathias is partially to blame for the recent poor decisions. The curse compelled him to take over, circumvent you, and give me questionable information. It urged me to follow his orders and blame you for them. I should have seen or sensed it, but I let it drive a wedge between us and failed at the purpose you handed me."

There was nothing I could say about that because he was right. I rubbed my eyes. "I should have done something as soon as I saw everyone acting strange. Instead, I didn't trust myself and thought I was losing my mind. And I'm so used to Mat taking over that I let that happen, too. Because of my lack of confidence, he almost ruined all my progress in building trust. We can't afford to engage in this nonsense if we want the coalition to survive. I'm trying to bring people together to fight for a common cause. I have some ideas."

His eyes searched mine. "And?"

"I want to recruit a coalition army." When he opened his mouth, I held up a hand. "My goal is to convince all factions to work together. If the witch debacle proved anything, it's that they don't even work well within their own factions, let alone as part of the coalition. That means there are a lot of paranormals who feel left out and might go to the side of the Bellicose. I want to give them an alternative place to belong."

"And Mat will block you."

"He might." I rubbed my thumb in circles on the back of his hand. "Which is why I'd like you to make sure I stand my ground."

I expected to feel something through the bond, but a tsunami of respect and joy was not on my list. "I would be honored. How do you plan to recruit this army?"

The leadership council building was quiet as I approached the door. Mat made himself scarce as I untangled his smaller orders. Some of them weren't bad, but others were doozies. Like how he ordered four blocks of homes and businesses surrounding a recent demon attack searched. And then he decreed Lily his heir, just in case he couldn't find me. I left that one because having a line of succession was a good idea. Though she'd think he did it to mess with her.

My assistant walked beside me. Or stomped. To say she was mad was an understatement. I turned my attention to her. "You should take the rest of the day off."

Her tight grip made the tablet she carried creak. "No."

"Okay, then consider taking a break tomorrow."

"It pisses me off how I didn't realize something was wrong with me."

"That was probably baked into the curse. I once read about one giving an entire village of humans dual identities. One minute, they were model citizens, and the next, they slaughtered a neighboring town. Not a single person remembered what happened. They woke up on the road between villages, bloody and weighed down with makeshift weapons."

"I thought it was against the law to mess with humans."

"It is now. This was a long time ago. Back then, we mingled with humans a lot more. The town that got slaughtered was anti-magic and was conducting witch hunts and killing a lot of women. The real witches, especially the male ones, took offense and bought a curse from a kelpie, which is always a bad idea. Kelpies don't like to curse, but when they do, they're doozies.

"When the witches released it, instead of stopping the witch hunt, it got everyone killed. My grandmother had to step in and break the curse and negotiate with the humans. She advised against going down that path in the future."

"Huh." Verity opened the door and waved me through. "And this curse?"

I shook my head. "Gorman and the Ogre Queens agree it is one of Cynthia's, which means she's awake and working with the Bellicose. Though, according to Gorman, it's one of her mild ones. He's not sure if she's volunteering her services or making curses under duress."

"That's ridiculous. How do you even regulate something like that? Anyone could run around with a curse attached to them, and no one would suspect it."

"We need to convince ogres and trolls to help sense them. And put the kelpies and chimeras on high-alert. Their ability to create them might make them targets, too." I took a left and headed toward where the council members gathered. "I don't have a good relationship with the chimeras after the former director's actions, and the kelpies are a pain to work with on a good day. On top of that, the trolls and kelpies have a long-standing dispute. It won't be easy."

"What can I do to help?"

"Just keep your senses sharp and be you. Most leaders respect your no-nonsense attitude, so they might be more willing to work with you."

The group of leaders I'd tried to befriend were meeting in the same room I'd found them before. When we entered, the Centaur King stood. "Your Grace. What brings you here?"

I headed toward an empty chair. "I thought I'd touch bases with my newest friends."

His eyes narrowed. "No."

"No?"

"Whatever you're scheming, our answer is no. We fought in your battle and don't want further conflict."

"Understandable."

"On top of that, my contact within the hybrid community says you are messing with their politics now."

"Ha! Let me guess. His name is Dale, right? The bartender?"

He inclined his head.

"I'm not interfering with their leadership. Much. Jonas needs to focus on the shifters until they find a new alpha. Lily, the new Vampire Heir, suggested Dale for a leadership position, but Ann Marie took that role."

He leaned forward, his eyes glowing. "The Vampire Heir, who is also your long-lost sister."

I shrugged. "And a valuable member of the hybrid community. Why does the suggestion bother you?"

"Because he has no desire to lead, and I want what's best for him."

"I didn't get the impression he's easy to push around."

"He is not. And will make a fine leader one day, but it is not your place to insist."

"Sure. It doesn't change the fact that the hybrid discrimination is ridiculous." I tapped the table. "But right now, they're in trouble, and we need to step in and help before the Bellicose exposes us to humans. I have some ideas but need your help. Can I count on your support?"

The Pixie Queen launched into the air. "You have mine. I can't wait to kick some demon ass."

I grinned. "Thanks, Sylphira."

The Minotaur King cleared his throat. "We dislike war. I don't have a problem with you taking the fight to them, but we will not take part if humans are involved."

Verity stood. "That's just dumb. If this council doesn't stop their nonsense and support Jen, then we're all screwed. The Bellicose won't stop with taking one throne. They want to rule the world. And if human history taught me anything, it's that world domination never ends well for the royalty of small kingdoms."

A bee buzzing in my ear made me turn my attention to Sylphira, who was bent over laughing. She held up a hand, laughed some more, and straightened. "You would make a fine Pixie, Jenella's assistant."

"Her name's Verity," I said, unsure what she found so funny.

She squared her shoulders. "The pixies stand with my friend Queen Jenella and her brave assistant, Verity."

All but three leaders agreed to support me in my efforts. The encounter reminded me of why I hated politics. It made me think about Lily's question. What did I care enough about to die for? I'd focused on only myself for most of my life. Worrying about the people of the coalition took a back seat to my own issues. I didn't care until recently and wondered if it was because they were a massive puzzle I needed to solve. I still doubted myself and never believed I was doing enough.

The words Jaques often used rang through my head. *'You're a nobody! A nothing!'* He repeated that so many times. When he wasn't repeating it, he called me useless. I was a little kid, so I believed him. Because, in my undeveloped mind, if I wasn't worthless, I would have stopped the beatings.

As an adult, I understood none of it was true, but his words were like a deep scar slashed across my soul. Ones that flared up, cut me off at the knees, and skewed my perception sometimes. I needed to figure out how to work around that scar. Because no one would follow a leader who didn't believe in herself.

My shoulders slumped as we made our way toward our makeshift office. "I have more ideas I want to implement for the meeting."

Verity set her note tablet on the tiny desk in the corner. "Okay. But can they wait until tomorrow? I planned to take the rest of the day off, like you suggested."

"Sure. Take a couple of days if you need to." It would give me time to think before I acted.

As I moved through the tents and new buildings scattered across the palace grounds, checking on everyone, I sensed Drake inside a blue tent. The urban sprite and his assistant, Charlotte, jumped to her feet when I entered. Drake's chair groaned when he turned to look at me.

A smile spread across my face. "Is that thing going to buckle? Because I'd like to be here to see it."

Charlotte snickered and flapped her wings. "I said the same thing, but he won't use a better chair."

Drake shrugged. "It was empty and had a privacy spell, so I took it."

He knew damn well whoever owned it wouldn't kick him out. "That sounds tyrannical."

His lips twitched. "One must do what they can to prove a point."

Which meant he forcibly stole the tent from someone, and the person knew why. "Sure. If anyone complains about my decisions, I'll send them your way. Any news about Alex?"

"As you should. Glacintial knows where Alex is, but won't reveal the location. Deva refuses to break his confidence, though she agreed to monitor the situation."

I lowered myself to a chair. "Why is he keeping it a secret?" The white dragon had been around for a long time and took guarding Lily and Alex seriously.

"Because Alex doesn't want him to. The kid is smart and more cunning than he looks. He is attempting to gather information. Glac says Alex convinced the Bellicose he's under their control but is not."

"It's a dangerous strategy. If they could chain Deva and steal her magic, they can do the same to Alex."

"They never controlled her. Besides, my aunt fought them, so they restrained her. Alex is pretending to cooperate."

"Have you told Jonas and Ann Marie?" I wasn't sure about them, but Lily was going to have a fit when she learned about it. Her protection of Alex echoed the way Mat protected me in his uncursed state.

"Glac is keeping them informed. Jonas wants to keep Lily out of it."

"That won't last long."

"Agreed." Drake's eyes scanned me. "Are you okay, Jenella?"

"Yeah. You?"

He shook his head. "I don't trust Gorman."

"You don't think he'll break the curse?"

"He'll break it, but he'll make sure the situation swings to his advantage when he does. I'm still not sure why he's been so cooperative. It's not in his nature."

"I wouldn't call him cooperative, exactly." I tapped my chin. The curse was placed during or after the battle, and I didn't feel it until everyone's behavior changed. Even then, I convinced myself I was imagining things, especially when they all had explanations for their behavior. "I need to ask Cavil what he knows about curses. When Lily and Alex got into that fight with the wolves, she said they had to be decontaminated, even though Ann Marie gave her a potion to make her immune to bug magic. I feel like an idiot for not noticing, but some of their nasty magics spread like a curse."

"Calvin recognized it. The curse in their magic was weak and easily circumvented."

"He didn't mention it." I turned my attention to the urban sprite. "Are you okay, Charlotte?"

Her cheeks flushed. "I am now. But, um, I kind of, sort of knew something was off, but I lacked the confidence to say anything."

"No kidding? Is that a trait of sprites? To sense curses?"

"No. But we're in tune with our environment. It wasn't my place to mention the feeling. I didn't want to lose my job."

"Have you not seen how Verity speaks to me?"

She coughed to hide a laugh. "It's just..." She shrugged.

Drake stood. "Charlotte's still settling in."

I nodded. "Yeah. Don't worry about stuff like that. I'd rather you overstep than have the whole palace turn against me."

"Okay. Should I hold this tent?"

"Yes. Have the palace guard replace the chimera symbol with the Queen's and place security around it." Drake took my hand and escorted me toward the council building. His eyes swept over the brown glow coming from the back windows of the palace. "You know that ever-present anger we both carry?"

"How can I forget?"

"I'm carrying a similar amount of guilt from everything that has happened since I met you and fear it will make you hate me."

I took a deep breath and turned my head until our eyes met. Heat flared between us, and it was all I could do to keep my knees from buckling. "I like you just the way you are, guilt and all."

A smile ghosted across his face. "Perhaps we can combine our disfunction and turn it into fuel to save the world."

I reeled in my emotions and dropped his hand. "Or something."

The gleam in his eye almost made me explode right there on the lawn. "Or something."

I swung around to run from the awkwardness. "Gah!"

"Eternally reminding you to use your senses is exhausting." Quin inclined his head toward Drake.

"Where have you been?"

"Working." He skirted around us and headed down the path.

I followed him. "Working? Or spying on Lily?"

"Assessing her. Roman is attempting to sharpen her skills but lacks the ability to hold her attention."

Ara's brother was a good choice to teach her. "Huh." I climbed the stairs toward my temporary office. "And you think you can do better?"

"Perhaps."

"Will it involve telling her to piss off the first time she calls you for help?"

"I did not tell you to piss off. I simply pointed out the obvious."

"Uh-huh."

"Lily's mage side is part of her as much as her vampire heritage. The only way she's ever going to live up to her potential is if she can use both skills together," Drake said, as if our little side conversation hadn't happened.

Quin breezed into the office and to the window overlooking the main meeting space. "Agreed. I have assessed the warehouse Ann Marie set up for her to practice and find it inadequate."

"The one by Calvin's place?" I'd noticed the warehouse when Drake and I flew over on the way to the village where Tracy's dad lived with his coven of alchemy witches.

"Yes. It is too small and lacks the obstacles necessary to use her physical skills while deploying magic."

"Huh." I took out my phone and texted Cavil to schedule a meeting with him. "Want me to ask Cavil for help?"

"No." Quin's eyes became unfocused. "Why are your griffins fluttering about like chickens?"

"They're not *my* griffins. They belong to themselves. And it's because of the curse. They feel guilty about neglecting their nest."

"Curse?"

"Yeah. I woke Gorman. He freed everyone who got exposed and is working toward breaking it. Or didn't you notice we disappeared in that parking lot? Or that we were gone for a couple of days? Or how we're all working in out-buildings and tents?"

"One would think you'd simply flash to safety when confronted with a horde of Bellicose. And I had some family matters to tend to."

"Right." Lily didn't say much about the dinner she attended at his house the night she and Mat fought demons. But I knew Ara and Quin were beyond pissed at how their son, Jedediah, kept her a secret. I had no desire to learn how they handled the situation. "I woke him and brought him back to break the curse on the palace. He thinks it's Cynthia's work."

"And what do you think?"

"I always suspected a First was behind the Bellicose, so it doesn't surprise me. What bothers me is that she's not the only one. That pyramid we got sucked into in Pyron had a complicated magic signature to it that not even Drake recognized. It wasn't a curse."

Quin turned his attention to Drake. "They call their leader a king, not a queen."

"Correct," Drake drawled. "And it wasn't demon magic. We're dealing with someone we haven't met."

"Interesting." Quin stood. "I am going to pay my granddaughter a visit. Perhaps you can create a pocket for her to practice in?"

"I plan to, but figuring it out might take a while. I'm still absorbing magic, so I can rule."

He vanished.

Chapter Sixteen

The orange glow of the sunset took my breath away as we circled the pocket and checked in with Drake's dragon, vampire, and elf patrols. I couldn't remember when he'd recruited the elves. Though it didn't surprise me, considering Razazia reclaimed her position as their leader.

I tried to untangle my thoughts, but it was impossible, considering all our problems, the decisions I had to make, and everything I was feeling inside. I needed time to think without interruption, but I didn't want to go back to the house Tracy and I shared. People displaced from the palace already thought I didn't care about them because I'd spent so much time away.

Then, there was the rumor my mother started about me stealing her throne. I didn't. But some witches believed it. She even had the curse suggest Lily rule and never told her. The last thing she wanted was a crown, let alone the responsibility of a coalition that rejected her and everyone she loved.

The thought of losing my entire support system to something that dumb made my stomach sour. I needed to put pressure on Gorman to speed up the process and move everyone back inside. Except I didn't trust him to do it right, which meant I also needed to figure out how to use the power I absorbed. I wished I could go back and warn my child self not to mess with the ruling magic, no matter the consequences. It would have solved a lot of problems to have all the tangles worked out before the Bellicose gained so much traction.

The turmoil among the witches and shifters was also a problem. We needed them if we were going to defeat the Bellicose, but Jonas's heart was with the hybrids. I wondered if he cared as much about the shifters as he once did. I hoped so.

And I still didn't have the full cooperation of the Leadership Council. It would be so much easier to rule without their input, but they were necessary if I wanted to rally the people. Maybe I needed to shake things up.

Drake descended toward the palace and flashed to the ground. He shifted into his human form, wearing a green dress shirt with rolled sleeves and black slacks. My mouth watered at how good he looked.

The twinkle in his eye told me he knew exactly what it did to me. "What's got you so wound up?"

"Everything."

An older man with silver hair and piercing blue eyes stepped around a tent. "Jenella. Drake. Welcome home."

I grinned. It was good to be home. Especially since the griffin patriarch was acting like himself. "Hey, George. How are you feeling?"

His face flushed. "Much better. Thank you. Helen and I would like a word with you, if you will." He motioned us inside a brown tent.

My heart thumped so loud I could hear it. It felt as if I were a kid again and in trouble. I squared my shoulders. "Sure."

Helen jumped out of her chair when I stepped through the door, or flap, and rushed toward me. "Jenella. I'm so sorry." She wrapped me in a warm hug.

"Not your fault." I patted her back.

She released me. "I've never had a hateful thought toward you or my family and should have noticed something was off."

I raised an eyebrow.

Helen waved a hand. "Frustration, confusion, and the occasional angry thought, sure, but not hate. I should have known."

Drake rested his hand on the small of my back. "The curse was designed to go unnoticed."

"True. Everyone had explanations for their behavior." I shook my head. "The ogres said I have some immunity, but I'm not so sure. It was almost like it saw me as an outsider. Speaking of which, has anyone seen the First Gorman?"

"The Ogre Queens came and got him," George said.

"Do me a favor and watch out for them."

"He has never been honorable," Drake added.

George inclined his head, patted my shoulder, and left.

I turned my attention to Helen. "Will you watch the staff? If you see the slightest sign that something's wrong, text me."

A bright smile lit her face. "Great minds think alike. I am already working on it."

"Thank you. And I'm glad you've recovered."

She squeezed my hand as tears brimmed her eyes. "I am so proud of the woman you've become. It's everything we'd hoped for and more." With a slight bow toward Drake, Helen swept out of the tent.

I watched her go as I blinked my own tears away. "Do you think they'll be okay?"

Drake rubbed small circles on my back, causing small lightning bolts to shoot through my body. "They will. We'll make sure of it."

I didn't respond as I turned and headed toward the Leadership Council building and my temporary office.

Footsteps pounded up the stairs. I dove between the bed and the wall and curled into a ball in the corner as the door burst open.

"Jenella!" The man's voice sounded as rough as the scars on his hands looked.

Heavy boots thudded on the floor as he rounded the bed.

I curled tighter, and a single tear ran down my face, splattering on the hardwood floor.

Golden eyes peered at me from the end of the bed. The man's face fell. "Oh, Jenella." His eyes filled with so much pity I couldn't look at them. "I won't ever harm you or let anyone else hurt you. I vow it." He stretched a hand toward me as his contract made my head tingle. "But we need to go. They've caught up with us."

The sound of a door slamming against the wall came from the first floor. We'd only arrived two days earlier after taking a ship across the sea. I reached my tiny hand toward his larger one. He swept me into his arms, and I stiffened.

Soft voices sounded outside the room.

The man's head swiveled toward the door as he set me on my feet. "Stay behind me."

I followed his orders. He hadn't hurt me or thrown me in a cage, though I wasn't sure he wouldn't when we got to where we were going.

Two men and a woman with long brown hair burst through the door. The first man swung his sword toward the golden man.

He blocked with one dagger, then stabbed the man in the throat with another. A second man threw a spell at us, and he turned his attention toward him.

The spell thrower fell at my feet in a pool of blood. I watched as it soaked into my new shoes. I raised my head in time to see the woman conjure a gun. Her blue eyes focused on my protector.

She hesitated, then blinked.

He lowered his daggers. One fell to the floor with a 'thunk.'

The woman disappeared without saying a word.

I bent over to pick up the dagger.

A flash of steel from the door out of the corner of my eye was the only warning I got before the knife sank into my forearm.

The man threw me on his back without making a sound, and, with a flash, we reappeared behind a bus station.

He lowered me to the ground and examined my arm. "I need to remove this."

I reached over and pulled the knife out of my arm without making a sound. The pain was always worse if I made noise.

The man ran his golden magic through my already healing wound, then pulled out a cloth and cleaned me up. "Are you okay?"

I blinked at the question. No one had ever asked me that before. "Yes."

His eyes narrowed. "Can you mute your magic?"

I shook my head. I didn't have as much magic back in Mahri when the other man dragged me to the cage. It grew a few moments after we escaped, though I didn't dare tell him that. I didn't want to anger him.

The golden man shoved me behind him as three women dropped from the roof.

He attacked them with a ferocity I wanted to copy when I got bigger. Then, no one could hurt me or put me in a cage.

A fourth woman came from the other direction and morphed into a big cat.

I peered down at the dagger still in my hand. The man, my brother, didn't take it away, and I didn't understand why. The other man would have broken my arm and taken it, then backhanded me. This man just...let me keep it.

The cat pounced.

I used all the strength my six-year-old body could manage and jammed the dagger into her belly and sliced up.

She fell at my feet. I used both hands as I stuck the dagger in her eye. I released it and stepped back, my eyes wide and my skin feverish. She wasn't breathing. Dead. I'd killed a woman.

The man turned and saw what I'd done. His eyes drifted to me, and his face grew hard.

I shrunk back against the building and curled into myself.

He removed the dagger from the cat's head and kneeled in front of me. "Thank you for your help. But never do that again."

Silent tears ran down my face, and I swiped them away with my bloody sleeve.

His face formed into a grimace. "Come. Let's clean you up and have a talk."

I turned back as he led me away and saw a sea of corpses floating in the air, on the ground, and hanging on the walls of the building. All people I'd become responsible for killing.

I jerked awake and tried to figure out where I was. Home, I realized. I sensed Drake downstairs, his feelings neutral. Good. Hopefully, he didn't notice the turmoil inside me from the dream.

The cold water felt good when I splashed it on my feverish skin. At least it wasn't the same old dreams I had about the cage and my parents' supposed deaths. I'd call that a win. The water I kept beside the bed was empty, so I padded downstairs. And stopped short when I saw Drake stretched out on the sofa, still in his clothes. His head rested on a throw pillow, and his eyes were closed. But I knew he was awake.

I continued to the magichef, ordered water, and leaned against the kitchen island. "I know you're awake."

With a twitch of his lips, one green eye opened. "I didn't mean to pry into your dreams."

"But you did."

"Correct. I felt your turmoil and needed to investigate."

"Oh?"

"Yes. I worry about your nightmares."

I took a sip of water. "When?"

He sat up. "What?"

"When do you worry about me and my nightmares?"

"The nights when I feel your sheer terror." He tapped his chest.

I set the glass down. "Are my dreams the reason you never sleep?"

"No. I never sleep because I've gotten plenty over the last couple hundred years."

I supposed that was true enough, but I didn't want to traumatize someone else with my past. "Sorry. I don't have those dreams often."

He rubbed his eyes. "There's nothing to apologize for."

I motioned toward the stairs. "If you plan to sleep here, we can have Rayar build another bedroom or...."

A wicked smile spread across his face. "I would like nothing more than to sleep with you. But you consider us being together a mistake. And I want to court you properly."

"I'm right here. Have been for weeks." The words barely left my mouth before I regretted them.

Even more so when the smile melted off his face. "It scrambled my brain, and with everything happening..." He shrugged. "We had a picnic."

"And it was great." I pointed at him. "You and me, we don't have a lot of time. And when we do, we don't make the effort. How do we change that?"

"We can take small moments, I suppose."

Stealing a moment here and there sounded great. "I'll hold you to that." When I reached the stairs, I stopped. "This dream was different. It was about Mat trying to protect me from assassins. I think Emine was one of them, but she left." I closed my eyes, trying to remember the details. "The end wasn't right, though."

"I see." Drake's voice was extra gentle. When I didn't respond, he continued. "I'm going to be gone for a while. Jonas requested I help find Alex and I want to keep my eye on the Bellicose residences."

"Any word on his whereabouts?"

"Glac still won't disclose the location."

I turned and met his eyes. "Be careful. I have a bad feeling about the whole thing. There's a council meeting in a couple of days. Will you be there?"

"Yes."

As I sank into bed, I thought about the dream. Drake didn't see. At the very least, he didn't understand what Mat's vow meant. Though, he may have understood the symbolism of the sea of corpses. I'd caused so many deaths in my short time as queen. If I could go back and do things differently, I would.

I squeezed my eyes closed. If only I'd known how my actions would affect everyone else, I would have...what? Changed things? Been less selfish?

No. I wouldn't have been able to get over myself without living through the whole mess. And it wouldn't do me any good to rehash the past. I needed to figure out how to move forward and make fewer mistakes.

The details requiring my attention were never-ending. Mat and I used to have a grievance day once per month to settle minor problems, but I changed that to an 'as needed' basis and moved to an electronic grievance form. I eyed the latest one filed by the Kelpie Queen. She wanted us to reassign twelve troll-occupied bridges to her and re-home the trolls. The Troll King's response to her proposal was colorful, to say the least. Mat had already given them several solutions. So, I denied the requests and sent those solutions for reconsideration.

A knock on the door interrupted my thoughts. "Come in."

Verity strode in, her eyes bright and her hair clean. She held up a hand. "Don't say a word. I was going to take a few days off, but here I am." She scanned the small office. "Where's Quin?"

"I think he's hanging around Lily's place. He said something about training her." I missed him and his sarcasm.

"Huh." She shrugged. "I've got a bunch of work to catch up on. Are you going to be around today?"

"Yep. And tomorrow. I'll probably head to Ann Marie's after the Council meeting."

"Anything you need for the meeting?"

"As a matter of fact, there is."

CHAPTER SEVENTEEN

"I DON'T UNDERSTAND," TRACY said as she watched Verity straighten a section of the circular table I created. It stretched around the auditorium, with gaps every six chairs to allow access to the center. "I mean, I see what you're trying to do here, but why?"

"There's nothing wrong with giving everyone a seat at the table," I parroted Ara's words as I raised the two places where Drake and I would sit. They were only a couple feet higher than the others. "It's ridiculous how the council members maneuver for position. If we're going to work together, all leaders need to be equal."

"So, instead of fighting for the front spots, they'll fight to sit closer to you."

I hadn't thought of that. They were so ingrained in their power struggles that they would absolutely fight over something so stupid. I crossed my arms. "How do I keep that from happening?"

She spun in a slow circle. "You and Drake need to be in the center and at an equal distance from everyone. And add a couple of levels for the ones who bring staff with them."

Drake would hate having his back to half the leaders, I thought as I created two levels of smaller seats behind the circle.

"What if we do assigned seats and rotate them at each meeting?" Verity asked.

"It's just so...strange."

I examined my work. Verity's desk was now behind the two throne-looking chairs. I hoped the seats for staff were adequate. The only part I hadn't changed was the top levels where we allowed the public to sit during open meetings. "My goal is to end their game and make a point with actions instead of words."

"Well, this will certainly make a point." Tracy trailed me as I created name plates for each seat, intermingling rulers of smaller groups with large ones. "What will you do with all the extra space in the center?"

"Not sure. Do you have any ideas?"

"Not a one."

Verity took a stack of name plates from me. "We can figure it out later."

"Exactly. Right now, I need to convince them to help with the effort to save the hybrids and to allow their people to join my army."

Tracy crossed her arms. "They will not like this."

I rubbed my aching eyes. "I know."

Mat and I stood in my makeshift office, peering out at the council members as they assembled. He'd been quiet, but I assumed it was because he had so much to catch up on. My eyes flicked to his face. "Where's Emine?"

"She's on her way. Where's Drake?"

"He's here."

The conversation died as the Firsts came through the front door. Jonas led them, Drake by his side. Gorman and Razazia strolled in behind them. The four of them together were a commanding presence, and the other leaders stopped what they were doing to gawk. I leaned forward. Gorman had cleaned up and trimmed his white beard into a close-cut style, making him look like a kindly grandfather. Though, he didn't have a single wrinkle on his face. Razazia gave him a sharp look when he said something.

"What do you think of Gorman?" I asked.

"I think he needs to break the curse. You?"

"It's obvious he's playing us, but I can't figure out how."

Mat rubbed his chin. "Interesting. Yet you trekked through the jungle to wake him."

"And I'd do it again if it meant saving my family." Especially since almost everyone I cared about got swept up in my mother's agenda. Either by the curse or by dealing with the fallout caused by her actions. Everyone except for Tracy and Bastien. They saved themselves by being absent. A deep loneliness settled into my bones. I missed spending time with Tracy and Quin. And I missed not worrying about the coalition every minute of the day.

Mat shifted. "Of course you would. But he might become a problem."

"He might. All four of the Firsts could. And a fifth one might be awake and already a problem. Gorman thinks Cynthia was present at the last battle. Something about how no one else could contain and transport that type of curse."

"And you believe him?"

I shrugged. "I wouldn't put it past Anitta to wake a First and coerce her."

He ran a hand through his hair. "You never call her mother anymore."

"Nope. She doesn't deserve the title."

A hundred emotions reflected in his eyes. "When I came of age, I moved out of Ara's residence and tried to avoid her and father. She captured and tortured me until I agreed to move to Castle Mahri. I'm glad you never really knew her. Yet I still struggle with her death."

I felt nothing for my mother. Though my heart ached for Mat. He had been through so much in the name of a family that treated him like shit. Me included. "Thank you for all you do. I'm sorry for everything I put you through the last few years. What can I do to help you grieve?"

His lips twitched. "I am not grieving as much as I keep waking up, thinking she's still alive with a knife to my throat. And you have nothing to be sorry about."

Unsure what to say, I nodded.

The door swung open, and Drake strolled in, sniffed the air, and frowned. "Am I interrupting?"

"No," we said at the same time.

Amusement flowed through the bond. "Where's Emine?"

"She's on her way," Mat said as he turned his attention back to the Council. "What surprises do we have for the Council besides their new seating arrangement?"

"I want everyone working toward the common goal of saving the coalition. The walls that divide the factions need to be torn down. It's going to take some time." I hesitated before I continued. "Those orders you put out while cursed caused a panic. I need to address that. If we have time, I'd like to have a listening session and hammer out our differences."

"I wish I could take those orders back. What can I do to make amends?"

"We're going to have to be honest. I've given you and Emine seats at the mage leader's table. The Council will see that as an admonishment."

He inclined his head. "You're demoting me."

"You're still regent. I can't do this without you, so demoting you would be a disaster." Especially since he took care of so many details I wasn't ready to deal with. "Once we settle the Bellicose situation, we'll plan the transition to take place over a couple of years."

The door swung open, and Emine swept in. "Whoo, whee. Looks like a full house today. What did you do to the seating arrangement?" Her eyes bounced between me and Mat. "Awe, man! I interrupted something."

It took everything I had not to smile. She was crazy, but it was good to have her back. "Hey, Emine. No, you're not interrupting."

My mind still swirled as we made our way to our seats. At the last minute, Mat and Emine split off and took the assigned seats between Jonas and the Pixie Queen. Pablo, his assistant, scrambled to sit behind them.

Many leaders who usually attended remotely were there in person. A few were still wandering around the center of the circle. I folded my hands on the desk and waited.

"What is this?"

"Where are our seats?"

"This is an insult! I will not sit by that man!"

"This is no way to treat the more important rulers."

The complaints continued, some louder than others, as they meandered around the circle. A few refused to sit in their assigned seats and stayed in the second row with their staff.

Drake leaned back in his chair and folded his arms. "This is going well."

"If my effort to create unity baffles them, wait until they hear my plans."

"They like their power plays," Verity said from behind me. "Then you come along and go all King Arthur. Except they're too whiny to be considered knights."

I spun around. "Who's that?"

She waved a hand. "No time to explain. Your projection spell is the red one. The blue one is the hologram spell. Tracy set it to cast in the center of the room so everyone can see."

Despite my best efforts, a wide grin spread across my face. I knew Tracy would figure out a way to use the blank space. "Thanks. And I want to hear the story of the king you mentioned."

"You can look it up on the internet. It's common human lore."

After all the members were present and the doors closed, Drake leaned forward and smashed his finger into the red magic. "Take your assigned seats or I will seat you."

The protesting leaders scrambled toward their places.

Eyes glowing, he gave those who didn't comply fast enough a pointed look.

"What's that about?"

"I'm a patient dragon, but I will not allow them to disrespect you."

My heart turned all mushy. Once everyone settled, I activated my projection spell. "As you can see, I've made some adjustments to the seating."

"Why?" someone shouted.

"Because every leader here contributes to the coalition. Every group of citizens is important to its success. I wanted to remind you of that."

"It's preposterous," the Kelpie Queen said from her place on the other side of Drake.

He swiveled his head toward her. "How so?"

She visibly shook as she squared her shoulders and activated her projection spell. "Because many of us have spent years fighting for status. It's disrespectful to strip it away."

He leaned forward and rested his elbow on the table, his muscles flexing. "What status?"

"I started in the fifth row and worked my way to the third. It took ages. And the baby queen thinks she can come in and ruin it within a handful of meetings? I won't stand for it."

"Oh?" I leaned around Drake to meet her eyes. "What advantages did all that hard work give you?"

She crossed her arms. "Respect."

The Troll King laughed from his seat halfway down the circle. "You did not earn that seat, you stole it. Just like you steal bridges."

"This is not the place to litigate your petty dispute, love." Deva said from her seat on the far side of the circle. "This formation is much better for open communication between leaders."

She always had my back. "Thank you, Deva. That is exactly the point."

"Queen Deva," the Chimera King corrected.

Deva, Drake, and I focused on him at the same time.

He held up a hand. "We are at a formal meeting where proper protocol is the standard."

"Your Grace," Drake growled.

The Chimera King's beady eyes narrowed. "The girl killed one of my people in cold blood. Respect is earned, and she has done nothing but create division with her love of the filthy hybrids and nasty dragons. Dragons who unseated the Regent and installed their First in his place." He leaned forward and snarled. "Then there's her inappropriate relationship with the Vampire Consort. It is disgusting how they don't even try to hide it."

My nose wrinkled in disgust. "Ewwww."

"Do not sit there and say it's not true when we all know it is!" He shifted to his chimera form.

I'm not sure what came over me, but the ball of rage I kept controlled exploded. A wave of magic blasted through the chamber and blew everyone's hair back. Drake flooded the bond with his soothing feeling as I fought to control it. It helped. I directed the flow and snatched the Chimera King out of his chair, slammed him in the center of the circle, and forced his shift. "Titus?"

"Got it, Your Grace." He made his way through an opening in the circle, stretched out a finger, and placed it on the Chimera King's arm. "He's not working for the Bellicose. He just hates you and thinks Deva and Drake are running the coalition."

"Thank you," I said, as Titus made his way back to his seat beside Verity. I scanned each leader's face before I spoke. We didn't have time for their pettiness, but if his thoughts were the general sentiment, I'd never earn their support. Some leaders didn't like me, but not as many as I thought. "Anyone else here share that sentiment?"

Murmurs broke out as everyone looked around.

I rested my elbows on the desk. "As *Deva* pointed out," I gave the naked, pinned Chimera King a sharp look. "I've rearranged the seating for better communication. The whole point is to stop the power struggles. Every group contributes something unique to the coalition and has a seat at my table. Including the..." I turned to Drake. "What did he call your family and my sister?"

Amusement trickled through the bond, though his face remained hard. "Nasty dragons and filthy hybrids, I believe."

"Right. Including the wonderful, loyal, patient dragons who have saved your asses more than once in the last year, and the well-rounded, honest, hardworking hybrids you threw out like the trash."

"What about your relationship with the Vampire Consort?" Razazia asked, just to stir the pot.

Ara's tinkling laughter rang through the chamber, but she didn't answer the question for me. Quin sat beside her, examining his nails.

"Not that it's any of your business, Lady First, but Quin is a treasured friend, a valued mentor, and a key advisor." I leaned forward. "As you know, power corrupts. Quin helps ground me with his brutal honesty.

Without him and my other advisors to check my power, who knows what I would turn into? Perhaps I'd become my mother."

Several people flinched.

Razazia's eyes sparkled as she stood. "I have been observing Queen Jenella since she traveled to the Southwest deserts and woke me. She is not above asking for help, listening to advice, or criticism. I have tested her patience on more than one occasion and she has not lashed out." She paused. "Though I've never called her consort and family vile names."

I wondered if she paused because she was envious of the Chimera King for testing me before she could, or if she liked my response. It was hard to tell with her.

With the wave of a hand, she continued. "But that is not the point. Queen Jenella has earned the loyalty of the dragons, the vampires, and the elves. The fact the Vampire Consort, who does not like anyone except his match, is loyal to her should tell you the type of leader she is becoming."

"That is debatable," the Kelpie Queen scoffed.

Razazia's focus shifted to her. "Is it? Because she has earned the respect of many leaders by listening to them and buying them delicious sandwiches from the leprechaun deli, instead of using force. She woke and reunited the Firsts her predecessor worked so hard to eliminate. Jenella had no idea where our loyalties fell before she acted. No, she woke us because it was the right thing to do. A stupid yet honorable action. Then, she earned the heart of Drake the First, a feat no other woman has accomplished in thousands of years. And she has earned my loyalty, another difficult task. If you stand against the queen, you stand against me.

Drake inclined his head. "And me."

My heart jumped into my throat when Jonas stood. "Queen Jenella has earned my respect through her fair dealings and perseverance. She has risked her life to save my adopted children, both hybrids. She does not take herself too seriously. That trait alone is worth following." He motioned toward the Chimera King. "But I wouldn't advise pissing her off." He waited for the laughter to die down. "I stand with Queen Jenella."

I could have passed out. Not in a million years did I expect to have the support of the Firsts, other than Drake. I blinked to clear my spinning head. "Thank you for your kind words, Razazia, Jonas. I cannot tell you how much I appreciate your support."

I took Drake's hand and kissed it. "As for the rest of you, you'll need to decide for yourselves if I am worthy. I won't ask for personal loyalty, but I believe all our people are worth fighting for, no matter the faction. I've reseated you to stop your power plays. Because as long as we're fighting each other, the Bellicose wins. If we care about our people, we cannot let that happen."

The next part would be tricky. My heart pounded so hard I could hear it. I swallowed the lump in my throat and let my gaze drift to Mat, who sat two seats away from Jonas. His face was unreadable, his eyes filled with pride. It gave me the courage to continue. "We're going to fight. Their reign of terror and campaign to divide us stops now. We're going to end the demon summoning, the mistreatment and killing of our people, their lies, and their hold over us."

"How do you propose we accomplish this rather ambitious goal?" The Centaur King asked.

"By taking the fight to the human world."

The council chamber exploded with chatter. Some leaders shouted while others sat in their chairs with their mouths open.

"That will expose us to humans!"

"We won't be safe!"

"It's too risky!"

"The queen is right."

"Have we forgotten our past?"

I let them debate the issue as I scanned their emotions. Most registered as shocked. An acrid fear feeling came from others. But there was a small number who seemed either relieved or determined. I could build on that.

As the chatter quieted, I squared my shoulders. "This won't be easy. And, although we'll take measures to hide our activity, there's no way to defeat them without exposing magic to humans. It's an enormous risk that might not work out in our favor. Especially if we don't pull together. I'd like your thoughts on the matter, but let's go through our agenda first.

"Today's meeting will be a little different," I continued. "We have a long list of problems and not much time to solve them. I'll make decrees as we go so we can move on to our discussion about taking the fight to the human world. Nothing will be tabled, so try to stay on topic." I met the eyes of as many leaders as possible, then released the Chimera King. "Please take your seat. Verity, if you will, please."

A list of agenda items appeared in the center of the circle.

We were halfway through the agenda when the doors in the back opened, and Ann Marie and Lily strode through. Ann Marie branched off and moved toward the chairs I'd reserved for the hybrid leadership, while Lily settled in one between Jonas and Mat. The seat reserved for the Shifter Queen.

I fought not to laugh when several leaders gasped. "Any more updates?" I asked.

The groaning of rocks echoed throughout the room as the Gargoyle King stood. "We banished the horde of small demons and moved on to others. Twelve larger ones found themselves banished from Allure overnight. There are currently none within the pocket. It is possible the practitioners will bring them back. It is, at best, a temporary solution."

"And the ones in the human world?"

"Thick magic protects them."

The Chimera King shot out of his chair. "It is not appropriate for a filthy hybrid to sit in the front row."

I wanted to face-palm. "Do I need to pin you down again?"

Jonas's eyes flashed as he lifted his head from something Lily showed him on her phone. A chill ran down my spine when he turned it as slow as molasses and settled his gaze on the Chimera King.

He flinched and lowered his eyes.

I squared my shoulders. "Anyone who has a problem with my sister, Princess Lily, Daughter of Jonas the First and the Sorceress Ann Marie, Heir to the Throne of Umbra sitting between her dad and her brother, please stand."

If Lily's glare were daggers, I'd be dead.

About ten people stood. The Kelpie Queen cleared her throat. "She may be all those things, Your Grace, but she is not the Shifter Queen."

"Correct. And everyone here knows it. Jonas, as the acting Shifter Alpha, can choose who sits there." I scanned the nine other people who stood. As far as hybrid hatred went, I'd call the small number progress. I met Quin's unblinking eyes, and he gave me a slight shake of the head. I sighed. "And I don't believe for a second any of you would care if she weren't a hybrid. What will it take to extinguish this hatred?"

"Time," Ann Marie said from her position near the Kelpie Queen. "Which is the one thing we don't have." She stood. "I recently sent my adopted kids to Allure for their safety. They were harassed, followed, and detained by Enforcers. If it weren't for the dragons and vampires, it would have been much worse for them. But I wouldn't have considered sending them here a year or two ago. It's progress, but it is not fast enough."

"I agree. It's not only a waste of our time, but not your business where Princess Lily sits. So sit down." I added a little persuasion behind the order and turned to Drake. "Consort."

Drake launched into all his team's efforts to root out the Bellicose inside the pockets and the areas in the human world surrounding them. Even cursed, he'd made progress.

When he was done, the Fairy Queen stood. "I don't mean to sound crass, but what about Allure? Shouldn't the pockets be our priority?"

"The pockets *are* a priority." My eyes scanned the room, even though I didn't need to. The ruling magic told me how people felt about the subject. "How long do you think the pockets would last if the Bellicose alert humans about them?"

When no one answered, I leaned forward. "In 1947, one of our experimental transports wrecked several miles outside the pocket of Pyron. A rancher recovered it before we could, though the occupants flashed to safety. It set off human mass hysteria. They've been watching the skies ever since. There has not been a single transport malfunction that humans haven't seen or reported. If a war between the hybrids and Bellicose breaks out, how long will it take before mobs hunt us? What do you suppose they'll do when they notice cars and people disappearing as they enter our gates?"

"They'll wait outside and shoot us as we come and go," Mat spoke for the first time. "I gave the order to mind-wipe an entire group of militia in Texas a few years ago when they discovered one of our gates and did just that. My choice not to kill them cost us time, and they posted videos on their internet. What should have taken a couple of days to clean up cost us two years. Imagine that scenario times a thousand."

The room erupted as everyone talked at once.

I leaned back, rubbed the chills on my arms, and let them argue. Mat didn't tell me about that mess, though he acted fast when Verity and I got kidnapped by dragons in the human world, so it didn't surprise me. When the shouting wound down, I rested my elbows on the table. "The open discussion begins now."

The room exploded again.

Drake folded his arms. "I thought you said you didn't have any surprises for this meeting."

"I didn't. Lily gave me an opening by sitting beside Jonas, and I took it."

Pride filtered through the bond, but he didn't comment.

CHAPTER EIGHTEEN

THE MEETING TOOK TWELVE hours. I was ready to rip my hair out by the second hour of discussion. By the fourth, I had to create barriers so the coalition's royalty would stop launching themselves or their magic at each other. Things settled down after the sixth hour, but not in a good way. The group found a common enemy. Me.

"It is unbecoming of a queen to hold the coalition's leaders against their will!" someone shouted.

"Unlike you, we have things to do besides worry about the hybrids," The Chimera King said.

"You cannot do this!" the Kelpie Queen screeched.

"Stop using diplomacy."

"Gah!" I butt-hopped toward Drake at the dry voice in my ear. "Damnit, Quin!"

Quin's eyes narrowed from the previously empty seat beside me. "Make your case as if you are speaking to Mathias and stop allowing them to insult you." He leaned forward to address Drake. "I assume she did not plan this, but took advantage when the opportunity presented itself?"

Drake raised an eyebrow.

"Of course she did. A good idea should one ignore its impulsive nature. But useless if you do not take charge and *lead*." He disappeared.

The rulers continued shouting as I thought about his words. How would I handle this idea if I were to present it to Mat? The immediate answer was I wouldn't present it on impulse. I'd think it through and come up with a solution that got me where I needed to go. If he was resistant, I'd make an argument that played on his love and worry for me.

My thoughts drifted back to the look of sheer terror on his face when I made my first kill. The dream was fresh in my mind, and although I'd repressed a lot of that mad dash to safety, I'd never forget that look. Not because of my horrific act of killing. But because it was the first time anyone had ever cared about me.

I turned my attention to the angry and tired faces in the crowd. I couldn't treat them like Mat because he cared about my well-being. The council only saw me as a tool. Someone to be used and manipulated for their own purposes. Like Sylphira, the Pixie Queen used me for status. And, if I were to be honest, I thought of them the same way. Tools to be used to win the war. I didn't understand the first thing about many of them on a personal level. And I sure as hell didn't know what they wanted enough to cut a deal.

Drake's hand landed on my bouncing leg, bringing me out of my thoughts.

"What do you want?" My voice sounded much more confident than I felt.

Silence.

"What is it you want from the coalition?"

"Peace!" someone shouted.

"Respect!" a stern voice said as the crowd quieted down.

The Manticore King stood. "I want my people to thrive."

Several leaders agreed.

Sylphira flittered into the air. "Mine want to spread their dust freely without worrying about other factions."

Ann Marie burst out laughing, and everyone turned their attention to her. She held up a hand. "Sorry. I just find it funny how you want these things within your grasp when the hybrids don't have those options."

An awkward silence followed.

"Perhaps you should explain, honey," Jonas said in a calm, unassuming voice.

When I turned my attention to him, I noticed the excitement in Lily's eyes as she soaked up the drama. I couldn't help but smile. She winked and turned her attention to Mat, who said something in her ear.

Ann Marie stood. "Hybrids work jobs where they have to pretend they're human. They can't use magic outside their houses. So, we created a sub-society in the city. We've opened businesses and developed hybrid-only subdivisions to give them a safe space. Humans still drive through and exist around them, so they must be constantly on guard. Shifters must search for remote locations to shift and use the buddy system to avoid being spotted. Lily always monitors how fast she moves and fights her nature to blend in. And then there are the children."

She closed her eyes. "So many children, we don't have enough homes for them. Every mixed-magic couple and adult hybrid has taken in at least two kids. The lone shifters who search for them sometimes keep kids for months before we find a suitable placement. Your children. The ones you spent thousands of years claiming to cherish, who are now thrown away without a second thought. Many have been abused, neglected, or are filthy and starved when we find them." She pointed at Lily. "It took us years of love, therapy, and patience to give our kids a chance to become stable adults. And they're the lucky ones. Some never recover from what you've done to them. Many hybrids and mixed magic couples dedicate our entire existence to their recovery. And now another problem you created crash-landed on our doorstep.

She clenched her fists. The room was so silent you could hear a pin drop. When she opened her eyes, the sadness was gone, replaced by blazing anger. "Fuck you. Fuck you and your peace and tranquility. Fuck your respect. And fuck any of you who will abandon us to clean up another pile of your shit!" She slammed her fists on the desk as she lowered herself into the chair.

I cleared my throat. "Thank you. I'll do anything I can to help, and I hope the other leaders will see the error of their ways and work to make amends." I rested a hand on Drake's to calm my nerves and scanned the crowd. When my gaze landed on Lily, the words just came out. "I'm a young queen and am told I'm a little impulsive."

A smattering of laughs broke out when I gave Quin a pointed look. "Until a couple of years ago, I lived a sheltered life. My brother believed it was the best way to keep me safe and help me heal after we spent nearly a year escaping assassins our own mother sent after us. Make no mistake, it's because of his efforts and the efforts of Jonas and Ann Marie we still have a coalition." I lowered my eyes. "You should thank them when you have a chance."

I scanned the room with my senses, then squared my shoulders. "My vision for the coalition is simple yet complicated. I'd like to see the factions set aside their differences rather than isolating and competing for status and power. There's no doubt we're stronger when we work together. A few days ago, someone asked me what I'm passionate about. What I will kill and die for. And after pondering the question, I've concluded that besides my friends and family, I would kill or die for you. Now I ask you the same question. What will you kill or die for? Your people? The coalition? Or your status? Because I believe the first two are worth it. And the last means nothing to the Bellicose, who will enslave, mind-control, and kill us all, regardless of status. Take your time, but not too much. Because our time is limited unless we work together to stop them."

After a few seconds of silence, Drake leaned forward. "Who stands with the queen?"

Deva stood. "The dragons will continue to support the queen."

"As will the vampires," Ara drawled.

Mat stood. "The Bellicose has kidnapped and recruited many mages. Those who remain are angry and want revenge. Therefore, the mages stand with the queen."

Sylphira shot into the air. "The pixies support the hybrids and stand with the queen." She was good at making herself relevant.

Razazia stood. "The elves support the queen, and I will help my old friend, Jonas the First, save the hybrids."

The Ogre Queens stood. "Ogres will break limbs and pound skulls to protect the hybrids."

Ann Marie's eyes teared up as leader after leader stood and declared their support. Lily's mouth hung open. Pride reflected in Quin's eyes. The same pride I felt.

In the end, around three-quarters of the leaders agreed to help. Some still sneered at me, but their respect for me grew.

It was hard not to replay the meeting in my head. I wondered if I'd gone too far or if my words were too cheesy. If the other leaders would choose my side, or if they'd pretend to further their own agendas. I took a deep breath of crisp air and peered over Drake's side. People looked like ants from high over Allure.

Stop thinking about it. The leaders will come around. Drake's words rang in my head as he made a large circle around the front gates.

I doubted some would ever come around, but I had more support after the meeting than I did going in, so I considered it a win. The wind whipped my hair sideways. I shivered and leaned over and admired the changing trees. It wasn't cold yet, but the weather was changing. Soon, I'd have to bring a coat. Or learn to create one. I closed my eyes and imagined a professional navy blue coat that matched my suit. When the material formed in my hands, I opened my eyes and held it up. Laughter bubbled out of me.

The 'coat' was so thin it was almost transparent. One sleeve was too short, while the other one was too long. The holes were too small to fit the big clunky buttons. One side hung low, while the other would barely cover my stomach. I rolled it into a ball to work on it later when my concentration improved.

Drake flew over the witch district, where a large group of witches met on the lawn of their headquarters. They'd organized themselves into covens. Tracy's dad, Calvin, stood in the center, addressing the crowd. *Do you think Calvin will convince them to help?*

Yes. He's more charismatic than the former president and has a moral compass. Aside from a few, the covens never fully supported the former president's plans. He is earning their loyalty, but it will take time.

It wasn't long ago I believed I could step into my role, make a few changes, and everyone would fall in line. Ruling people was a nuanced skill. And as much as I believed in my vision for the coalition, I'd have to become better at identifying subtleties to achieve it. I wasn't above being a little manipulative, either. But I sure as hell didn't want to become my mother.

My other option was to be flexible and patient. Except I didn't have the time or personality for it. The Bellicose activity decreased since the battle at the palace, but not because they were done. No, their leaders were licking their wounds and patting themselves on the back for placing the curse and kidnapping Alex. They'd make their move soon, though. And if they stole Alex's magic, like they did with Deva, we'd be in trouble.

How am I going to do this?

Drake slowed, descended, and landed a couple of blocks outside the neighborhood on the road leading toward the castle. I flashed to the ground as he shifted. "Do what?"

I waved my arms. "All of this. I need the leaders and their people to follow me, mobilize an army, move them to the human world undetected, and eliminate the Bellicose. All while two major factions are in chaos, one of my closest allies is in a funk, and the other is fawning over her new granddaughter. On top of that, I need to light a fire under Gorman to break that curse. It's a mess."

Drake's eyes searched my face. "You're already doing it."

"I'll admit I'm doing a great job pretending." I wrapped my arms around myself. "But I'm still a hot mess with a giant ball of anger just under the surface and a bone-deep fear of my crown. All that shit I spewed at the meeting?" My mouth went dry, so I shook my head. For all my posturing, I wasn't sure I believed my own words.

He pulled me to his chest and ran a hand down my back. Goosebumps broke out over my body when his hand came to rest on my hip. "Few leaders have one hundred percent confidence in their decisions. Those who do are tyrants." He leaned back, his eyes sizzling with heat and hunger.

"And you are not a tyrant. Don't forget the reasons you took the throne. I saw the complete devastation on your face when you witnessed the carnage in that lab. And I helped you kill your own mother to save your people. You stepped into your role for the right reasons. And you're making steady progress."

"It's not enough."

He shook his head. "I doubt it ever is. All you can do is take one step at a time."

A tear streamed down my face. "I don't even fully understand my magic."

"You will." He swiped the tear away with hands way too gentle for such a big guy. "Can I give you some wisdom that has come with age?"

"With or without emotion?"

His lips twitched. I'd once accused the ancients of removing emotion from every situation. "Without, of course."

"Sure."

"There will always be a threat to the crown. Not everyone will like you or agree with your decisions no matter what you do, and they will sometimes push back. Some will take it to the extreme, like the Bellicose. The best rulers mitigate the threat by negotiation and empowering their people to make their own decisions. I believe you will be an outstanding leader because it comes naturally to you."

I leaned into him and soaked up his warmth. Then I snuck my hand under his shirt. Lightning bolts shot through my body when his thumb ran across the small of my back, just under the hem. I made feather-light circles on his bare stomach in response. "What would my grandmother do?"

"Lissa didn't need to win over anyone except the other Firsts." His soft lips touched my neck right below my ear, and I shivered. "The Firsts ensured the magical factions added her leadership as a central part of their structure."

My hands stopped. "I have her magic, right?"

He kissed a trail from my neck to my collarbone, and I lost my train of thought.

Drake leaned back and met my eyes. "Yes. And it shows."

My body shuddered at the heat in his eyes and his ragged voice. I stood on my toes and touched my lips to his.

His grip tightened, and he deepened the kiss.

My arms slid around him as I sank into his heat. I slid my hands to his back and pulled him close. My entire body lit on fire. I'd missed his touch.

"Hmm hmm." A throat cleared behind me.

Our bodies broke apart. Chilly air replaced his warmth, and I wrapped my arms around myself. "Yes?"

The Troll King bowed. "My apologies for interrupting. I wanted to inform you I've dispatched trolls to occupy the bridges in the hybrid areas."

My face stayed blank as I tried to shift gears.

Drake's hand landed on my back. "Thank you. Ensure they don't bother the humans or hybrids."

The Troll King spread his hands. "How are they to make a living?"

"They can make a living inside the pockets," I said. "We'll recall and punish trolls who bother a human or a hybrid."

He sighed. "Very well. I will spread the word. But our numbers in the human world may dwindle."

"That's fine." We had plenty of vampires and dragons monitoring the situation. I wondered why Drake deployed the trolls. I'd support the questionable decision, but I didn't like it. Trolls were greedy and unreliable on a good day. And there weren't many of those since the Bellicose moved in.

He bowed again. "Very well. I will frame it as a kelpie-free vacation, and perhaps they will see reason."

Neither of us said a word.

"I will report back to you on what they find."

I inclined my head. "Thank you."

He stumbled toward the bridge, extended a long, meaty arm, and climbed under it.

Drake put his arm around me and kissed my temple. "We need to speed up our courtship. I'm unsure how much longer I can restrain myself."

Butterflies erupted in my stomach, and I tamped them down. "Why did you deploy the trolls?"

He dropped his arm and chuckled. "I thought you did."

"He did that on his own?"

"I assume so."

"And we let him."

"Yes."

"We're a couple of idiots. No way they're not going to out us."

"It's not a bad idea. The Bellicose knows you're close with the dragons and vampires. They won't expect trolls under bridges in the human world."

"Until they out us."

He patted my butt. "There is that."

"Yeah. There is that." I meandered toward the checkpoint leading into the neighborhood. "If we have rulers sending their people into the valley, we'll need a base there, too. And a staff."

"I'll check with Jonas and see if there's a house we can rent."

I held up a hand. "Let me check with the god Cavil and Prince Leebol of the dwarves first. Maybe I can make them a pocket to hide our activities better."

He raised an eyebrow.

I forgot to tell him about the terrarium I created at the Conservatory, so I filled him in. "It was so close. I think I need people with the specific magic types present, though. Or figure out how to be a conduit rather than trying to create the pocket from memory. If I take power from the source and weave it, it will be more accurate."

"I was unaware you learned how to weave spells."

"I haven't. But I can ask Tracy to teach me when she has time."

"Mmm. Hmm."

"You don't think I can?"

"You can do anything you put your mind to. However, taking on such a large project without practice is risky."

I sighed. "Yeah. But I can't think of another way to shield them all, so it needs to be a priority."

CHAPTER NINETEEN

LILY STOOD ON THE other side of the wards. Her brownish-gold eyes glowed, and the tip of a fang touched her lips. "No."

I fought not to fidget. "Oh, come on. There's no way we can help the hybrids from Allure. We just need a place to stay while we work."

"Not a chance. I already have Gramps and Elsie screwing up my life. I don't need you and your entourage helping them. Especially since I can't trust you not to whisk me off to some jungle for your own purposes."

"That was the only jungle where a First rested, so you don't have to worry."

"No."

I gave her my best puppy-dog look. "Please?"

Her eyes scanned the group I'd brought with me. Olwen, the Snow Elf King, stood a few paces away from Verity and Titus, Emine's brother Rayar, beside him. Drake loomed over us in his dragon form. Mat and Emine stood between his green toe and Bastien's black one. Tracy peeked over Bastien's shoulder.

Lily shook her head. "I don't have room for this many people."

"Liar." I eyed the expansive field behind her house. "What if we build a couple of guest houses in the back and stay there?"

"Still no."

I crossed my arms. "Fine. But when they're attacked, you'll have to explain to the hybrids why we didn't make it here fast enough."

Her shoulders slumped. "Damnit. I hate you royals."

"I'm sorry you hate yourself."

"Burn," Emine whispered.

"We need a staging area with solid wards, and your house is in the perfect location," I continued.

Lily rolled her eyes. "You'll build the guest houses. And make human kitchens and bathrooms, not that fancy schmancy magic crap you have in the pockets."

I turned toward Rayar. He was one of the most powerful architectural mages in the world. He was also a genius.

"I can ensure it fits in with a farm aesthetic and gives human vibes."

I frowned. "Vibes?"

He shrugged. "Reflect archaic human styles."

I jerked a thumb in his direction. "See? If you let us build in your back field, Tracy and I can create a ward to hide our activities. You won't even notice us."

"Except for the dragons launching into the sky and the stench of magic in the air from whatever you cook up."

"Okay, so maybe you'll notice. But no one else will."

She shook her head. "No."

My shoulders slumped. "Fine. We'll find a place in the middle of the city."

Her eyes narrowed. "Damn it, Jen! Fine. But I better not find a single pile of dragon scat on my property. And no roaring or whatnot."

A trail of smoke escaped from Bastien's nose.

"They're shifters. They can scat in the human-style bathrooms."

Emine threw her head back and laughed. "Scat in the toilets?"

Lily yanked me through the wards and shook a finger at Drake's massive nose. "You'll need to shift or no admittance."

Drake and Bastien morphed into their human forms. Bastien stayed naked to irritate her. Tracy slapped him on the ass, and he huffed as he glamoured clothes.

Lily glared at him while she yanked the others through. "If you stay, you help me find Alex and stay quiet. I don't need the police showing up because of a noise complaint."

I spun in a circle. There wasn't a house for miles other than a half-finished farmhouse-ish mansion where The God Cavil's small house used to be. "I don't think you have to worry about it. What happened to the cute little farmhouse?"

"Cavil happened." Lily's voice held a hint of bitterness. "Apparently, the house wasn't fit for a god or something, so he's expanding while trying to keep the style."

"He's failing," Mat mumbled.

Lily clinched her fists, then relaxed them. "He's trying. It's the best we can hope for at this point."

She led us toward the back of her property, pointed to three locations where we could build houses, and then insisted on supervising. I didn't blame her for being cautious. She barely knew us, and we could overpower her if we wanted to. Considering her history, putting that much trust in us had to be difficult.

I shoulder-bumped her as the rest of the group helped Ray mark out the utilities and floor plans. "Thanks for this."

Her hard eyes scanned me. "This is nothing compared to losing my brother and not being able to find him."

"We'll find him. Even if we need to pry the location out of Glacintial."

"I hope so." She bit her lip. "He should have escaped by now."

My heart ached for her. If Deva couldn't escape them, I doubted Alex could, but I didn't want to say it. I had faith in the dragons and knew Glacintial would step in if he thought Alex needed it. "We'll find him."

She didn't respond.

"What are you doing here?"

I almost didn't jump at Quin's question. Almost. "We need a base of operation if we're going to help the hybrids."

His eyes narrowed. "And it must be here?"

"Do you own any land in the human world big enough to house us? Because we don't. We tried Jonas and Ann Marie's place, but they're holding tests for the new Shifter Alpha there. I can't be near it without it looking like I'm picking the winner."

"I am not your housing broker, nor do I care where you lay your head."

"Real estate agent," Lily corrected.

I bit back a smile. I missed Quin hanging around. "Lily was kind enough to let us use this field."

"Manipulated is more accurate," Lily said. "Hey. Do either of these dragons have culinary magic?"

"Drake does. Why?"

"Because we're going to need some snacks." She pointed toward the maze. Cavil stepped out of it, followed by Colonel Ballard.

"You can ask him. His food is delicious." My mouth watered at the thought of it. Cavil stopped at the edge of the field and bent down. Probably talking to Lily's foul-mouthed gnome. "Has Flemming's language improved?"

"I can't answer that on the grounds it may incriminate him." She stepped around me so fast I didn't see her move. "He's happier, though. More content. Thanks for helping find his family."

I waved a hand. "It's the least I could do with all the help you've given me."

Quin disappeared and reappeared in front of Cavil, and the two exchanged words.

Colonel Ballard trotted across the field. "Jen! Verity! It's good to see you."

Verity's face lit up, and she joined us at the edge of the field. "Colonel! I haven't seen you in forever. How are you?"

Right after I got my first case, mind-controlled dragons kidnapped the three of us, along with the Vampire Prince, Jedediah. We escaped, only to have Jedediah take off and leave us to deal with the fallout. The jerk.

Colonel Ballard took her hand and bowed. "Good to see you, Rookie. How's life?"

"Great. This is my match, Titus. Titus, Colonel Ballard. The Enforcer who helped us the day I met Jen."

Lily disappeared while they exchanged pleasantries and reappeared near Drake. He smiled at whatever she said and winked at me as they strode toward the back door of her house.

I tamped down the flutter in my heart and turned my attention back to Colonel Ballard. "How's the security detail working out for you and your family?"

"Surprisingly well. Cavil is easy to guard and cares about his staff. My family owes you one."

"Nope. You don't owe me anything, and I don't trade in favors."

He inclined his head. "Very well. Then thank you."

I watched the blur I knew as Quin as he made a sweep of the perimeter and disappeared into the house.

Rayar waved me over, so I left Verity with Colonel Ballard and headed his way. "What's up?"

"We'll need a privacy ward before we can start building."

"Let's eat first," Tracy said. "I mean, I'm hungry, and we need to make sure we don't do something Lily won't like."

"Sure." I eyed the back door of her house, not wanting to invade her kitchen. "Let's wait on the back porch."

We were a few steps away when Lily burst out the back and slammed her hands on her hips. "Are you kidding me?"

I glanced around. "What?"

"You've got a dragon who can make a feast with the wave of a hand, and you're hoarding him."

I nodded. "It's my right to horde him. I told you he's amazing when not cursed."

"No shit." She pointed at Cavil. "You're going to help serve."

A blinding smile lit his face, though he tamped down the daylight he shed when he was happy. "I swear I will serve food to you any time you ask, Lily."

She shook her head. "Nope. No contracts. Just help serve the food."

I'd never had a meal like that one. Drake's food was always excellent. But the atmosphere was unlike anything I'd experienced. Lily had shoved two picnic tables together, and we lined both sides. It made conversation easy. Instead of sitting by myself at the head of the table, I sat across from Lily and Cavil, smashed between Tracy and Drake. For the first time in my life, I felt like I fit in. If only for a moment, I was just a friend and a sister having a meal with the people I cared about. I tucked the moment away so I could pull it out and savor it later. It was perfect.

Until the topic turned to the Bellicose.

"Roman and his vampires are adequate spies, but demons come through in many locations," Quin answered a question I hadn't heard Drake ask.

The smile melted off my face. "The gargoyles are working on it. They banished the ones in Allure and are here now. But whoever is summoning them can still bring more through."

Lily shrugged. "Then we need to take out the people summoning them. Problem solved."

"You make that sound easy." Drake pushed his plate away. "We wasted a lot of time trying to track down their king. It led Tarquin and me to evidence of Anitta's existence. Still, I didn't find a single clue implicating her involvement with the Bellicose. She covered her tracks well."

"No shit? Did you find anything, Gramps?"

"Unlike the First, I am a detective." Quin sat at the end of the table on the other side of Lily. "Of course I found information. But only after Jen and I discovered a unique magic. I suspect it stems from the one they call the king."

I sucked in a breath. "You're talking about the pyramid?"

"Yes."

"It was strange and complicated. Even Drake couldn't identify it."

Lily leaned forward. "And how many hybrids have you two been around?"

"Correct." Quin rested his elbows on the table.

"You think their leader is a powerful hybrid?" The answer dawned on me, and my heart started pounding out of control. "No."

"Perhaps."

Lily's head swung between us. "Want to let the rest of the class in on the revelation?"

"No." Quin folded his arms.

"Not a good idea until we have proof." My wide eyes found Mat's.

His face was blank. "Careful, Jenella. You do not want to go there."

Lily threw her hands up. "How come I'm the only one who's lost?"

Tracy shook her head. "I mean, I'm lost, too. Who do you two suspect?"

"Me, too," Verity said.

"As am I," Titus agreed. "I think it's best if they keep it to themselves."

"Agreed," Colonel Ballard said from beside Verity.

Emine took a bite of food, her crazy eyes calculating. She knew.

The sound of an engine interrupted us. Lily and Quin disappeared. Cavil followed.

"Tread carefully, Jen," Mat growled. "Accusations like those could end relationships if you're wrong."

"Yeah." I leaned into Drake's arm and closed my eyes, trying to remember the weave of the strange magic. I only remembered how perfect it felt, and I couldn't unweave the spell. But then, that was before my magic got fixed. I hadn't learned the ruling aspect of my new power, though I was getting pretty good at spell weaving with Tracy's help.

Ann Marie and Jonas interrupted my thoughts when they came around the corner. Ann Marie's eyes scanned us, and she inclined her head. "Looks like we missed the party."

"Not much of a party. And it's not like I invited them," Lily said.

"I told them to set up here. It will give you something to do other than stew over Alex. You need that, firefly."

Lily said nothing, but she didn't need to. Her scowl said it all.

Drake waved a hand, and several sweets replaced the leftover food. "You can join us for dessert."

Jonas stepped onto the porch. "What do you plan to build here?"

Rayar, who'd been quiet the entire time, cleared his throat. "Lily said we can build three houses no larger than three bedrooms in the field."

"Hmm." He moved a lawn chair to the end of the picnic table and motioned for Ann Marie to sit before getting his own. "I am at an impasse with the shifters."

CHAPTER TWENTY

I broke out in a cold sweat. "What do you mean by impasse?"

He rubbed his eyes, his dark circles more prominent. "Gabriel and Linda spent years finding the most powerful and competent shifters. When they left, they took the ones who lived with them."

Mat's eyes flashed gold. "And they did it right under my nose."

I shook my head. "So, there's no one left to lead the shifters? Not a single person out of the millions throughout the world?"

"None that have come forward to test, no."

I pinched the bridge of my nose. "Holy hell. Can this coup be any dumber?"

"It cannot." Quin stood.

Lily rolled her eyes. "You *have* made some terrible miscalculations, but it wasn't like you knew it was coming."

"No, but you did. As did Jonas and Ann Marie. Yet none of you said a word." Mat's rough voice was barely a purr. "Nor did you bother checking on the shifters. We're all to blame."

Jonas shook his head. "I disagree. The shifters are no longer my responsibility."

I swung toward Drake. "What did you say about the other Firsts blaming you for the dragons coming through the gate and wrecking it?"

Delight filtered through our bond. "For thousands of years, they rejected me and blamed me for the actions of others. Actions I had no control over. The other Firsts are only friendly now because they've finally discovered they are not infallible."

"Right. They held you responsible. Made sure you didn't fit in. Wouldn't allow you to create a magical species." I held up a hand when Jonas opened his mouth to talk. "Refused to let the dragons have a seat on the Council. Yet it's okay for them to create an entire magical species and abandon them. And unlike you, they *chose* the responsibility. And now you're out there working your ass off to save them, even though you don't have a magical faction." I pointed at Jonas. "While you shrug and wash your hands of the situation because you found a new cause. Am I getting this right?"

"No, you're not." The entire deck shook with Jonas's growl.

"She has a valid point," Drake growled back.

"I never once shunned you or treated you like the others."

"You did. Often."

"Name one time."

"It's not my fault your memory is slipping. Figure it out yourself."

"Enough!" I gave the command a little push. "You created them, so the shifters are your responsibility. You trusted Gabe and Linda, and they burned you. No matter how you look at it, you carry as much blame as the rest of us."

He stood so fast his chair fell over, his eyes glowing amber. "I have a missing son and a shitload of hybrids to rescue. I cannot take care of them and lead the shifters!" Tremors rolled through his body, and he grew a few inches.

I stood in a slow, deliberate move. It wasn't as badass as I had hoped because we were packed shoulder-to-shoulder on a picnic bench, and I had to climb out. I took three steps toward him. "If you shift here, I will knock you out so hard you won't wake up for three days."

"You're not helping, Jen." Tracy's voice was barely a murmur.

Drake's hand landed on my shoulder. "No one is telling you to abandon the hybrids."

"Good. Because I wouldn't want to become you."

I held up a finger to stop Drake's response. "I'll tell you what. You clean up your mess, and I'll clean up mine."

Mat stood. "The hybrids are not your mess. They're mine."

"Yeah. Me too, I guess." Emine made a lazy attempt to stand, then sank back onto the bench.

Lily threw her head back and laughed. "This will be fun to watch."

Ann Marie crossed her arms. "I'll lead the hybrids until the shifter mess gets straightened out." She pointed at me. "You can pile all the blame in the world into the back pasture, and all you'll have is a gigantic pile of nothing. Now sit down. All of you."

She made a good point, so I changed the subject, though I didn't sit back down. "Let's move on to privacy wards so Rayar can start building houses."

Verity stood. "Sounds better than fighting over decisions you can't change."

I stood on the edge of the field, watching the others mill around, making plans, and wondered how long it would take to build the houses if I added my creation magic to the efforts.

Ann Marie shifted her weight. "I can almost see the wheels turning in your head."

My eyes landed on Cavil, who stood beside Lily like a too-good-looking sentry, watching Bastien, Jonas, Olwen, and Drake argue. Titus and Verity stood on his other side, their heads together, talking. Rayar walked in a straight line nearby.

"No shit. I can't wait to see what she comes up with. It's like human Christmas every day when Jen gets ideas," Emine said from my other side.

Tracy dragged a lawn chair over and lowered herself into it. "Yeah, but she's usually right."

I looked around for Quin but didn't see him, though I sensed him on the far side. "I wonder if I could add my creation magic to Rayar's."

"Absolutely. If you can use it." Ann Marie raised an eyebrow.

She knew I hadn't ever done anything like it before. I wondered if Lily had told her about my issues or if she had figured it out herself. I dismissed the thought because it didn't matter. An idea formed, and I grinned.

Emine rubbed her hands together. "Oh, boy. Here we go."

Lily's wards buzzed, and I flashed to the front. Razazia, the team who took care of the wards in Allure, Ara, and Sylphira, the Pixie Queen, three more architectural mages, some extra climate and tech mages, and a few ogres, stood on the other side.

"What the actual fuck?" Lily's voice came from behind me. She stopped in her tracks when she saw Ara. "Oh. Hey, Meemaw."

"Lily! Thank you for inviting us." Ara blew through the wards like they weren't there and wrapped her in a hug.

My sister patted her awkwardly on the back. "Um. I didn't." She stepped back and pointed at me. "Does she always move into other people's houses and take over?"

Ara's shrewd eyes landed on me. "No. Never. It makes me curious what she's up to."

Razazia cleared her throat. "Mind if we come in, little hybrid?"

Lily spun toward her. "As a matter of fact, I do. Who the hell are you, and why are you here?"

I waved a hand. "Razazia the First, meet my sister and Ara's heir, Lily."

"Charmed, I'm sure."

I leaned toward her and mock whispered, "She inherited the power of Lilith."

Razazia's eyes swept over Lily. "Shame it was wasted on such an uncivilized creature."

Ara's magic amped up.

When my skin crawled, I rubbed my arms. "Razazia, mind your manners, please."

She sighed. "This is a waste of time. It took your mother more than a decade to create a pocket."

I nodded. "I'm aware. But she didn't have Prince Leebol and his team. Nor did she have three Firsts, a god, Ann Marie, and Lily.

Lily slammed her fists on her hips. "*You* don't have Ann Marie and Lily."

"I'm with Jen," Ann Marie said. "And I suggest you help, too." She pulled Razazia and the others through the wards.

"With what?" Lily pushed my shoulder a little too hard. "What are you scheming?"

"I'm going to create a pocket for the hybrids." I motioned for the group to follow and headed down the path that led around the house. "Stay on the path, or the gnome will cuss you out."

"This is such bullshit," Lily said as the group made their way to her back field. "I don't want people traipsing through my field at all hours of the day and night to access a pocket. That's *if* you can pull this off. Which I doubt."

"I can."

"You don't know that!" She swung toward the Dwarven Prince. "Unlike Jen, you understand a thing or two about engineering. Do you believe she can do this?"

His eyes bounced between us. "Perhaps. The Queen is very powerful."

She threw her hands out. "See! Even your expert has doubts."

"What's the worst that could happen?"

"You could blow up my entire property. Expose us to humans. A million things could go wrong."

"They won't."

"You don't know that!" she repeated, her voice two octaves higher than normal.

"Once the pocket is formed, we can move the gate to a more convenient location," Prince Leebol interrupted her rant. "And don't worry. We have measures in place if things go wrong. I am an expert engineer and can somewhat direct the flow."

"Ann Marie and Tracy can help, too. And my bond with Drake will keep me stable. He helped regulate my emotions when I..." I trailed off. No need to tell the group about the interrogation of my mother. "Well, he can monitor me and step in if needed. Your back field is the perfect place for a pocket."

"Do you mind if I walk through your house to memorize the layout, Lily?" Rayar asked as we approached.

"Yes, I mind. This is nuts."

"Help yourself," Ann Marie said at the same time.

His eyebrows drew together. "I won't touch anything or snoop. I just need measurements and such."

Lily crossed her arms. "Fine. At least that way, you can rebuild when Jen blows it up."

Quin appeared in front of Ara and kissed her cheek. "I did not expect you."

Her tinkering laugh echoed across the field. "It's good to see you, my love. Are you enjoying your visit with our granddaughter?"

"Boot camp is more like it," Lily grumbled.

They ignored her as they zipped across the field toward Mat.

"How do you want to do this?" Ann Marie asked.

"I'll defer to our expert."

We all turned toward Prince Leebol.

Two hours later, I stood at the field's entrance, the others in a cluster around me. The gnome family rested on my feet. "Okay. Here goes."

"Regulate yourself, take your time, and don't create it all at once," Cavil instructed from behind me. "Take a small sip of each type of magic, weave it, anchor it, then repeat the process."

"If the weave isn't tight enough, release it and try again," Ann Marie said.

Tracy moved to my side. "And don't be too optimistic. I mean, don't create too much with your first try."

"Concentration is key to creation," Cavil continued. "You must visualize the exact thing you want to create."

"She can't extract magic from the Firsts," Razazia moved to my other side. "Except Drake's, of course. We created our magical species using a combination of our own magic and Lissa's. Because Jenella inherited her abilities, she can mimic any supernatural species created from Lissa's magic, but not ours."

I conjured a ball of silvery magic, held it toward her, and pointed at a greenish-yellow strand. "Yours is this one." I pointed to a deep orange color. "That's Jonas's."

Cavil stepped around her and grinned. "That white streak is mine. Jenella descends from my realm. Our rulers can store all magics, no matter the origin, as long as they have access to the source."

Razazia's face paled. "Lissa lied to us?"

"I doubt it. From everything I read in her diaries, she considered you friends. If she said she wouldn't absorb your magic, she probably didn't. On the other hand, my mother most likely used your own power to put you to sleep. But I swear I won't use it against you unless it's necessary." The magic contract snapped into place.

She blinked. "Very well. What do you want us to do?"

"Stand behind me with the others." I waited until she moved, then met Cavil's eyes. "Monitor me and have Drake pull me out if I lose control."

He inclined his head and moved to stand beside Lily.

I took a deep breath and imagined a bucket like what I'd seen the maintenance crew do when they recharged the wards. I went down the line and added more from each person in the group behind me, then concentrated on the look and feel of the various pocket wards. A mixture of Allure's and Mahri's was best considering the location. And I began to stitch.

I used Ann Marie, Rayar, and Cavil's magic for the shell, then weaved in Mat, Emine, Lily, and the entire team who maintained the wards in Allure for security and climate. After each layer, Leebol would check it and approve the construction.

When he approved the shell, I tied the layers together and moved to the inside. Unsure what to do, I paused. Building the pocket was an impulsive decision, but I had to at least make it inhabitable. Which meant I needed to know what people wanted. When a thought struck me, I mixed Tracy's magic with Rayar's and my own to create the main space and a few shells of buildings, then used Drake and Bastien's magic to form the skies. Razazia and her elves helped form the flora and fauna, and I used Jonas to create spaces for shifters to live and roam. Then, I moved back to the climate mages and anchored the climate to the human world, using a boost of Cavil's magic to create daylight. Lily, Quin, and Ara's magic allowed me to make the night.

Strong arms wrapped around me at one point, but I didn't stop. I sifted through every detail I'd ever learned about the various pockets, the hybrids, and the surrounding area. As soon as one idea left my mind, another one formed. The last thing I created was the gate, using Mat's magic for the base and Jonas, Ann Marie, Lily, and Cavil's magic for access permissions. Verity and Titus's power shored up the security.

As soon as I tied the last anchor, I pulled myself out of the trance. Black dots danced in front of my eyes, and my head swam. I swayed and shook my head. Bad idea. My knees buckled.

"Jenella!" I heard the voice, but it sounded like it came through a tunnel. Was that Drake? No. It was Mat, I thought. Was Mat cursed again? Why would he yell at me?

I blinked away the dark spots and rubbed my face. "I'm trying to sleep." It came out in a mixture of a mumble and a growl.

"Perhaps killing yourself over a pocket is not the wisest choice."

I focused on the voice. "Hey, Quin." I jerked to a sitting position when I remembered what I'd been doing. My head bounced off something, and I rubbed it. "Ow."

"Jenella, are you okay?"

"Yeah." Arms came around me from behind, and I was pulled onto a lap. Drake's scent washed over me, and I snuggled into his chest. "My head's still spinning, but I'll be fine. The pocket?"

He stood in a fluid motion, blinked, and swayed.

"Did I drain you?"

"Perhaps." When I landed on my feet, he wrapped an arm around my waist to hold me up. His deep laugh rang in my ear. "You have rendered Ann Marie speechless."

"What? Why?"

He pressed his lips to my ear. "Perhaps using my mental magic to understand what people want you to create is not the best idea."

"I didn't. At least, I don't think I did."

"See for yourself."

CHAPTER TWENTY-ONE

THE ENTRANCE TO THE pocket was between two large trees that weren't there before. The magic emanating from the wards felt different from the ones my mother made. I bit my lip. "Did I screw it up?"

"No, but it's different."

"What do you mean, different?" If it wasn't secure or inhabitable, then we could fix it. But if I created an unfixable monstrosity, it was a waste of everyone's time. And Lily would be more perturbed than she already was. "Is it at least viable?"

Sheer delight swirled through the bond as Drake kissed my temple. "You are the most amazing creature I've ever met. Go see for yourself."

I tiptoed to the gate, leaned over, and peeked through. "Holy hell." I stepped the rest of the way inside.

The pocket was massive. Allure was a metropolis and one of the biggest pockets in the world. But this one stretched as far as the eye could see. To the right, a replica of Lily's house sat. Along with her weird maze field and Cavil's house, only it looked more finished. Unlike the originals, both were a bright blue color. A purple-paved human road stretched behind them where their back fields used to be. The houses were flipped around, facing the road.

To the left was a copy of Jonas and Ann Marie's farm, the barn hot pink rather than red. Another road branched off and led to a distant town. They were all crooked and winding. Round and triangular buildings dotted them.

I flashed to the center, where a fountain bubbled with turquoise water. A quaint town hall sat on the far end, with empty, lopsided buildings ready for businesses lining the circle. Five roads branched off, leading to neighborhoods smattered with fully formed colorful houses of different sizes and shapes. There wasn't enough for all the hybrids, but it was a good start if they were inhabitable.

But the town wasn't the focus. Purple-blue foothills rolling into peach-colored mountains surrounded it on three sides. The breeze carried a sage-pine scent mixed with spring flowers. Groves of trees spread out behind the town hall, reaching for the sky and casting long shadows. They were a mixture of trees I'd seen in the jungle, native trees, and others I'd admired during my travels. They all had red, yellow, and orange leaves. The needles on the pine and spruce trees were purple. Farm fields sat on the right, the soil a grayish color. The left side had a massive meadow that stretched for miles where the hybrids could build onto their town, the grass more blue than green. The sky, on the other hand, was more green than blue.

I sighed. "Well, I tried. Maybe I can do it again in a few days."

Lily appeared. "What the actual fuck, Jen? How many hybrids do you think there are? And how are we supposed to maintain this?" She waved a hand through the air.

"Maintenance wouldn't be a factor if I had done it right. Magic maintains the wild areas, and your gnome would help with your personal space." I spun in a slow circle, taking in the beauty of the strangeness. "I didn't mean to make it so colorful and big. Everything's off, so I doubt it will sustain life."

"She used my mental magic to pluck wants and needs out of everyone's heads." Drake pointed past the closest foothills. "I smell swamp coming from that direction."

She planted her hands on her hips. "I have a magichef in my kitchen instead of a stove. How am I supposed to stock it without dragons?"

Drake raised an eyebrow. "Do you want dragons here? Because my aunt will send some to live here if you do."

She shook her head. "I'll think about it. This is just...."

"Ugly. But can it sustain life?" I eyed the turquoise water in the fountain. "It was my first try. I'll do better next time."

"It'll sustain life." Ann Marie stepped out of a building, Jonas trailing behind. "It's the most stable and detailed new pocket I've ever seen."

My chest puffed out. "Really? So, it'll work?"

She nodded. "It's too bright, and the colors are off, but it'll work. Anitta didn't add all this to her pockets. She created a shell and ordered paranormals to create everything else."

I bit my lip. "Oh." That would have been much easier and more accurate. And I wouldn't feel so drained. "So, if I create another pocket, I need to dial it back?"

"You can, yes. But it won't be quite the masterpiece." Her eyes scanned me. "Just how much magic did you have stored?"

"Too much," Lily answered for me. "She felt like she was going to explode. Using it to create this monstrosity probably saved our lives."

I rolled my eyes. "I've been using my magic daily, so I was fine. It's possible I tapped into Drake's power and drained us both. Will it work for the hybrids as a temporary shelter?"

Jonas dipped his hand in the center fountain. "We can't move them all at once without the humans noticing, so it'll be a slow process. And some won't move to a pocket no matter what we offer."

"We need more gates, too. We can't have a bunch of traffic going in and out of one place," Ann Marie added.

"There's one across the street from your house. I'll need to add one to that bar Lily took me to so that Dale guy can send people through, or maybe the warehouse where the boggart hands out supplies."

Silence.

"What?"

No one answered as the others started filtering into the town's circle. Rayar and the Dwarven Prince walked together in deep conversation. Cheesy smiles on their faces.

Emine moved from building to building, opening doors and peering in, then stomped toward us. "The buildings are cool shapes, but empty."

"I wanted the hybrids to make them their own."

"Uh-huh. And the multiple climates? What's that about?"

"Some hybrids need the different climates to thrive. I wanted them to have a place."

She shook her head. "I never took you for an overachiever. Weird."

"Jen cares," Mat said. "And she is trying to prove it."

My face puckered at the statement. "Are you still cursed?"

"No."

"You sound like you are," I mumbled.

Quin and Ara appeared beside Lily, and Ara hugged her before she could dodge.

I snickered at the grimace on her face. Like Deva, Ara always got her way. Lily would learn soon enough if she hadn't already.

I pointed toward the round houses closest to Lily's place. "Those three are the guest houses. We'll stay there while we root out the Bellicose."

Everyone left except for the group I brought and Ara, though she and Quin planned to stay at Lily's house in the human world. Rayar made an agreement with Jonas and Ann Marie to bring his team back and help build regular buildings and finish the strange ones I'd created. Cavil loved the bright colors of the pocket and asked Lily a bunch of questions about them.

My eyes drooped as I dragged myself toward the stairs of one of the three houses. The place was sparsely furnished. A sectional and six-person table took up the main room. The kitchen sat to the left behind stairs that led up to three bedrooms.

Tracy and Bastien were staying with us but took Ann Marie flying so she could understand the strange new pocket. Mat and Emine were in the kitchen with Drake as he stocked the ugly hot-pink magichef. I yawned and dragged myself up the steps, then fell face-first on the bed, half asleep before I landed.

Heat wrapped around me, along with the scent of home. I cracked an eye open, grinned, and slung my arm across Drake's chest.

"Hmm." He slipped an arm around me and pulled me tighter. "Too early."

He wasn't much of a morning person.

I feathered soft kisses from his jaw down his neck in response, soaked up the hunger filtering through the bond, then rested my head on his shoulder. It was nice to wake up beside him. But I had things to do, so I couldn't stay. "Go back to sleep. I've got to do some work before Verity breaks down the door."

His arm tightened. "Hmm."

I couldn't help it. I laughed. "At least there's no trail of smoke this morning."

A soft kiss landed on my temple. "I don't want Lily to kick my ass for burning down her new pocket."

My laughter echoed off the privacy wards in the bedroom. "She would, too."

He released me and sat up. "She would try."

I slid out of bed and headed toward the odd-shaped bathroom.

Tracy and Verity were at the small table, their heads together, when I made it downstairs. "Where's everyone else?"

Verity shrugged. "Emine's bringing in enforcers and mental mages. Titus and Bastien left with Mat to help Jonas with something. No one's seen Drake."

"He's right here," came his deep voice from behind me. His green eyes swept over the empty table. "Did you eat?"

"Yep," Tracy said as she looked over some papers in front of her. "Did Deva mention she was going to send this to me?"

I went to the magichef and ordered coffee. "Send what?"

"She sent a decree naming me Princess of Dragons."

I handed Drake his coffee. "You've been with Bastien for years. Why does it surprise you?"

She shrugged. "I'm not a dragon."

"My aunt is grieving. When she grieves, she plans."

Tracy shook her head. "I don't want to be a princess of anything. I like my life the way it is."

"Welcome to the club." I took a swig of coffee.

Verity cleared her throat. "As someone who recently upended her entire life, not to mention her value system, I have to say that sometimes you just have to deal with what life throws at you."

"I agree," Drake said. "Deva recognizes you for what you are. It's a compliment. I doubt your life will change much with the declaration, but if it does, it's best to roll with it, or she'll steamroll you."

Tracy sighed. "Fine. But I'm not going to tell dragons what to do."

"Wise." Drake did a slow stretch that accented his muscles.

I tore my eyes away from him and gave Tracy a half-hug. "I'll tell them what to do for you. If I'm not around, make Bastien do it."

"I'm sure that will go well. What are we going to do today? Do you have enough energy to do anything?"

"Great change of subject." I set my cup down. "Drake has people stationed all over the human world, so he's in charge."

"We will visit the areas where the Bellicose are living. The vampire, Roman, and his house found two more locations this week. We have eyes on them but haven't discovered what they're doing at those locations." He conjured a plate of fruit and some toast and slid them in front of me.

"Thanks. My energy is okay. I'll come back and rest if I need to." I'd need to be at full power if the Bellicose attacked the hybrids. Especially since I planned to create a dome to hide the fight from humans.

"I need an office to keep in touch with the palace better," Verity said. "Maybe an entire command center."

"Bring in tech mages to hook it up. Allure's pocket team should be back today, so ask them to find someone they can work with. Mat can help you contact more mages if you need them."

"Will do." Verity held up her phone. "I'm letting Charlotte handle things in the palace."

"How's she doing?"

"Great, actually. She enjoys working for Drake."

Drake's lips formed into a small smile. "I have vowed to protect her and her family should they need it."

Sprites were resourceful and, more importantly, survivors. But also a small segment of the paranormal population who sometimes needed help. I bet the Urban Sprite Queen, Charlotte's grandmother, was happy about his oath. She was part of the group of leaders I tried to befriend when they were banding together to help protect each other.

"I'm glad you like her." I stood and took my dishes to the magiwash. "Let's get busy."

CHAPTER TWENTY-TWO

MAT ONCE SPENT TWO months teaching me field coordination. After reviewing Drake's efforts, I realized how basic the lesson was. He had twenty dragons sweeping over the city in varied shifts. Vampires were hidden in every shadow. Hybrids drove around in their cars and reported to him as we passed. It opened my eyes to how much work he'd done. Not only in gathering information, but in building relationships with the hybrids.

We landed on top of an office building in the city, and I flashed to the roof. I shuffled to the edge of the three-story structure and scanned the surrounding area as he shifted. Two dragons, three vampires, and a smattering of hybrids were inside the building. A few blocks over, I sensed a mixture of bug magic and the magic used to control Deva. "Do you sense that?"

"Yes. It is common around the apartment buildings."

"Is it new?"

"The location has been there for a while. The magic has changed since we occupied this building."

"Did you tell Lily about it?"

"No. I reported it to Jonas and give him regular updates."

"Right. Any sign of Glacintial?"

"He checks in every day and claims Alex is fine."

"What are the chances they have Glacintial and control the message? Because if Alex were free, he'd contact his family."

His hand landed on the small of my back. "It's a possibility. Which is why I have many people searching for him. I want to show you our operation."

I tore my senses away from the strange feeling. "Sure."

Drake's field headquarters took up the third floor of the office building. A hybrid-owned business occupied the first two floors. He picked the location because the established business made it easier for the team to come and go without raising suspicion.

We stepped through the door, and everyone in the office lifted their heads to stare. A red-headed dragon hopped to his feet and bowed. "Your Grace. Consort. Welcome."

My eyes narrowed. "Are you the dragon who hung out in the bar with Lily?"

His face turned as red as his hair. "Er. Um. My name is Flintous, Your Grace."

A purple head popped up. I recognized her as the one who often checked me in at Dragon Headquarters. She waved. "Hey, Jenella. Um. Your Grace. Yes, Flintous is Lily's drinking buddy. As am I. We volunteered to help find Alex."

I liked how the dragons took in and befriended Lily and Alex. "Does Lily know you're here?"

"Well, no. Drake thought it best we didn't tell her."

I swung toward him and raised an eyebrow.

His lips twitched. "Lily's protective instincts are in overdrive. Jonas advised against it."

I scanned the office. Six hybrids clustered around a table, their faces blank. A middle-aged woman sat near the back office, her eyes wide and mouth open. A human. No, not wholly human. She had death magic. I made my way to her desk.

Drake followed behind me. "That is Susan. A human-mage hybrid who Roman and Lily befriended. Roman asked me to give her a job and protect her."

I stopped in front of her desk, intrigued by her magic. "Hi, Susan. It's nice to meet you."

Her eyes scanned me, then Drake. "And who are you?"

"I'm Jen. I'd love to learn your story."

"Not much to tell. Until a couple of weeks ago, I thought I was human. I worked with Lily and knew she was different, but not how different. Roman's been my landlord for years under a rent-to-own agreement. He told me I'm touched by magic, which I always suspected. Didn't realize he was a vampire until he told me. He insisted we move to a safer area."

"We?"

"Me and my daughter."

"So, you were raised human?"

"Yes."

"And Lily knew you were part mage?"

"Possibly. She worked in my former office. Money occasionally appeared on my doorstep, and an anonymous donor paid off my mortgage. I assume it was her."

For all of Lily's fear of her dark side, she had a heart of gold. "And have Drake and Roman treated you well?"

She swallowed. "Yes. Is that a problem?"

A laugh escaped me. "No. I've never met a human-mage hybrid and was curious. If you need help with anything, call my office. My assistant is around your age and raised in the human world. She's a full-blooded mage and can help you adjust, or at least give you someone to talk to who understands the struggle."

She waved a hand. "Oh, I'm not struggling. As a matter of fact, my daughter and I have never been happier."

"That's great. But keep the number."

She nodded. "Sure."

"Let me introduce you to the other hybrid leaders." Drake motioned to the group gathered around the table. "The hybrid leaders each oversee a specific district within the city. Unlike us, those they lead have varied magical abilities."

I inclined my head. They peered back with sour expressions. "Where's Dale?"

A witch-mage hybrid stood and crossed her arms. "I'm the leader of this group, Sheila. What can we do for you?"

"Sheila thinks she's in charge," a full-blooded wolf shifter said. "The rest of us follow Jonas and Ann Marie. My name is Charles. I'm responsible for Southeast Boise and a lone wolf who got lucky and found an elf to match with. People call me Chuck."

I inclined my head. "Nice to meet you, Chuck. I'm Jenella, the Queen of Ahl, who got lucky and matched with a multidrakelandarnarian First. I motioned toward Drake. People call me Jen."

Chuck's baritone laughter filled the room. "Good to meet you, Jen."

"You, as well."

There were three other leaders. A witch-elf hybrid whose ears with slightly pointed ears, a giant-dwarf who looked like a burly human, and an ogre-mage who didn't look human at all but hid it well with facial hair. They introduced themselves.

I turned my attention to the woman, Sheila. "You're in charge of West Boise?"

Her eyes flicked to her colleagues. "I am. There are three subdivisions in my area with over six thousand hybrids and mixed magic couples."

"And two Bellicose apartment complexes."

"Correct."

"They're on the edge of hybrid subdivisions," Drake said.

"So you have one neighborhood without a Bellicose presence?"

"Yes, though it's near the one with the big apartment complex."

"Is it the most active one?"

The leaders shared a look.

Chuck cleared his throat. "They were all active until Alex First went missing. Now, they're silent. They make supply runs, never keeping the same schedule, but that's about it."

Sheila pointed toward a counter with a couple of appliances, some paper cups, and condiments. "Help yourself to coffee."

My stomach clinched. I couldn't work human appliances and refused to make a fool out of myself in front of the hybrid leaders.

Drake felt my fear and moved toward the counter. "I'll get it."

My muscles relaxed. "Thanks." I tapped my chin. Something about Sheila rubbed me the wrong way. It was the same feeling I'd always had around Gabe and Linda. Everyone told me I could trust them, even after they let the kids in their pack bully me. Even Mat brushed it aside, saying the behavior was normal amongst shifter packs. But they always unsettled me. Since the Shifter Alphas betrayed us, I wasn't willing to dismiss the feeling. "So, Sheila. What are your plans for all those people when the Bellicose attacks?"

"If," she corrected.

"When."

She shook her head. "They've left us alone so far, and there's no evidence they want to enslave us other than one document Lily First found. There's no way of telling if it's part of their plans or a brainstorming idea."

I slid into a chair next to Chuck. "Oh?"

"Look. I understand they're dangerous, but I don't want to scare my people."

"And if you're wrong?"

She shook her head. "You don't understand hybrids. They're powerful, resilient, and take care of each other. I doubt they'll allow themselves to be enslaved."

I fought not to grind my teeth. "Do all of you share her opinion?"

"No." Chuck rested his elbows on the table as Drake set a paper cup in front of me. "The hybrids in my district are spread out. There's been minimal activity, but I've alerted them and made an evacuation plan so they can at least evacuate their children."

"As have I," the ogre-mage added. "I'm in charge of North and Northwest Boise. There's one apartment complex in my district, and we've already started moving people out."

"Where are they going?"

"Staying with friends or family in other areas of the city where there's less activity."

The ogre-mage hybrid rubbed his beard. "I lead those who live Nampa and Caldwell. We've found some offices in our area, but no apartment complexes. I have my people monitoring the situation."

"As do I," the witch-elf hybrid said. "I oversee Meridian. We have a large subdivision of hybrids who are aware of the situation. We're coming up with defense strategies, so we can move fast should they strike."

The giant-dwarf grunted in agreement. "I disagree with Sheila's nonchalant attitude. There are not as many hybrids in my district, but our inability to work together will be our downfall."

"I agree. I have the same vision for the entire coalition." The urge to pace was strong. "There were several demon attacks in Allure. They brought them in right under our noses. The gargoyles are patrolling now and the attacks have decreased. Several are now in the city looking for them."

Sheila's face flushed, and she clenched her fists. "You're not our leader. We don't need your pitiful help. Especially since you can't even protect the pockets."

I turned to Drake. "Did she just infer I'm pitiful and weak?"

His lips twitched. "I believe so. Though she assumes the same about me."

I shook my head. "I'm surprised you haven't eaten her yet with that attitude."

"You said you wanted to build rapport with the hybrids, so I haven't even shown her my pointy teeth."

"You're so much better than me."

"Better? No. But patient, yes. It comes with age."

"I suppose."

Chuck coughed to hide a laugh. "My district will take any help you want to provide."

"Great." I turned my attention to Sheila. "You lack situational awareness."

"You're wrong. I am well aware of the threat and have more information than you."

"Is that so?"

"Yes."

Drake rested his hand on mine. I wasn't sure if he planned to restrain or caution me, so I ignored it. "Yet, I've had one conversation with you and can tell you lack leadership skills." I held up my free hand when she opened her mouth to protest. "You ignore the intel because you think you're smarter than everyone else. Despite overwhelming evidence of danger, you deny it. Good leaders put aside their egos for the sake of their people. I bet you haven't given a single thought to what would happen to them should the humans become involved.

"I understand there's a lot of resentment within the hybrid community, and rightly so. The coalition should never have treated you so terribly. I'm sorry about that. It disgusts me and goes against everything we stand for. I've worked to reverse it since the day I took the throne and will continue to do so. But, if you think for one second that I'm not in charge of every single paranormal on this planet, including you, you're mistaken. If I wanted to, I could swoop in here, order you all to move to Allure. And you'd have no choice but to follow."

Her pen snapped in two when she clenched her fists. "That's tyranny."

I inclined my head. "Correct. And it's not in the best interest of the hybrid community." I didn't mention that Jonas scared the hell out of me. It wasn't relevant to my point. "So, I gave you someone who understands what rejection feels like." I motioned toward Drake. "And he's given you regular dragon and vampire patrols, a safe place for you to meet, and a bunch of other resources he didn't tell you about. I've given you my consort. My heart." I twisted my head toward the corner. "Lily, Quin, come out of the shadows, please."

They appeared behind me.

"My two biggest allies, and women I consider family, have also given you their hearts. Meet Tarquin, the Vampire Consort and one of my most trusted advisors. He and Bastien, the Dragon Prince, are working to keep your people safe, as are several others. They've been here for weeks watching over you. As a result, I guarantee I'm more familiar with the situation than you believe.

Sheila's face screwed up in disgust. I followed her gaze and realized it was directed toward Lily.

Lily's eyes met mine. Yeah, she was not happy I outed her. I turned my attention back to Sheila. "Let's drop the pissing contest and get to work."

CHAPTER TWENTY-THREE

AFTER HOURS OF GOING over details, my head spun. The only one who didn't have a plan to evacuate was Sheila. And she oversaw the largest district. The only reassurance I had was knowing Dale's bar was there, and he might have a plan.

As we exited the building, Quin and I stood out like sore thumbs in our expensive business clothes. Though, humans in the area didn't give us a second look.

"How did you figure out we were eavesdropping?" Lily asked as she led us toward a human vehicle.

"I sensed you. Quin can hide his essence. I can find him if I concentrate, but he's great at sneaking up on me. How did you find us?"

"None of your business."

Drake's anger filtered through the bond.

I spun toward her. It would have looked badass if the icy fall breeze hadn't picked that time to gust, flinging my hair across my face. I brushed it away. "What did you do?"

Lily held her hands up. "Don't look at me. I didn't do anything."

Quin's eyes scanned me. "In an attempt to save your life, I may have created a blood bond."

In an out of character move, Drake wrapped a possessive arm around my shoulders. "He can find you anywhere."

I racked my brain, trying to remember when he could have done that. I came up blank. "How?"

"I fed you my blood to heal you faster after you were injured inside the pyramid in Pyron. It did not occur to me at the time that I had consumed your blood at the mall."

I balled my fists. "Are you kidding me?"

"I rarely joke."

"So, what? You can order me around like I'm one of your vampires now?"

Lily watched the exchange with wide eyes. When Quin didn't answer, she answered for him. "No, but he can find you."

"What do you mean, no?" My mind whirled as I tried to think back to anything that pointed to Quin using a blood bond to influence me.

Drake shook with laughter. "It's not *him* who can order *you* around. You're the one in control, and he hates it."

"Correct," Quin said in a dry tone. "I am uncertain how it happened. Blood bonds must be intentional, and this was not."

I shook Drake's arm off my shoulder. "So, when I ordered you to show yourself," I pointed to the office building. "You had to comply."

"Yes."

"And we can find each other anywhere because of it."

He inclined his head.

I stopped in my tracks when a thought punched me in the gut. "Does Ara know?"

"Open communication is essential for maintaining a centuries-long relationship."

"So yes. What does she think about it?"

"She thinks it's hilarious," Lily answered for him. "Aside from the fact that no one besides her has ever snared Gramps, she likes being able to keep tabs on you."

"I bet. And if I don't want this blood bond?"

Quin shifted his weight from one foot to the other. "You may break it at any time or transfer it to Ara or Lily."

"I see." I continued walking, so I didn't burst out laughing. "Where did you park, Lily?"

She caught up with me. "You're not going to cut him a break?"

"Nope." I liked the idea of knowing where Quin was. If I used it right, he couldn't jump-scare me. As a bonus, it might give me practice using the magic I'd absorbed.

"That's something I'd do."

"Well, we *are* sisters."

My phone buzzed against my hip as I climbed into a brand-new minivan. I pulled it out and checked my texts.

Tracy

> Strange activity near the bar.

> Where are you?

> I think it's Alex.

On our way.

"Head to Dale's bar."

Lily turned onto the main road. "Why?"

"There's strange activity. Tracy thinks they found Alex, so you might want to hurry."

She scanned the area. "I can't go any faster. There's too much traffic."

I raised my head and eyed the other cars, wondering if I could flash the entire vehicle to the bar.

"Humans won't forget an entire car disappearing," Drake said.

"I wasn't going to do anything," I lied.

"Sure, you weren't. I didn't even need to read your mind to guess what you were thinking. You're too much of an adrenaline junkie to not have the thought."

"That's rich coming from you."

"Yes."

Quin cleared his throat.

"Fine." I slid my phone back into my pocket. "How do you deal with traveling everywhere like this, Lily?"

"You get used to it. Don't worry. It's only a few minutes away."

The bar was quiet when we arrived several minutes later. I sensed Tracy and Bastien deep inside the neighborhood.

Lily must have sensed them, too, because she veered away and headed in their direction.

When she slowed to turn a corner, Quin disappeared from the front seat.

"You gonna call him back?" Lily asked with a snicker.

"I would, but I need him on my side. Have you seen him fight?"

"No."

"His fighting skills are pure artistry. Aside from that, I consider him a friend. If I screw with him for my amusement, he won't fight for us, and our friendship won't last long. I'd like to keep both."

"You're no fun."

"Sure I am. Just not at the expense of others."

She slammed on the brakes. "Holy hell."

Very few things surprised Drake. He did a great job of pretending he wasn't ancient, but he couldn't hide his lack of surprise from me. As a result, I could count on one hand the number of times something caught him off guard. The scene before us was one of them.

A massive lion stood on the back of a white dragon in the middle of the road, a chain around his neck. It branched off and connected him to an identical one on the dragon. Dark tendrils of magic swirled from the chain and wrapped around Glacintial's mid-section, then flowed back into Alex. It was unlike anything I'd ever seen.

Based on the wrecked front lawns and houses, it looked like the two of them had gone on a rampage.

A cloaked Bastien hovered above them. Liquid dripped from what looked like nowhere as Tracy dropped a potion.

The lion let out an earsplitting roar.

Hybrids darted in every direction, dragging kids and pets as they attempted to flee the area. The dragon turned his white eyes toward Lily's van and sucked in a breath.

I flashed the entire car to the next street over and fumbled with the sliding door. "How do I escape this thing?"

Lily reached up and pressed a button. "Did you not just flash an entire van? You don't need to use the door!"

I flew out of the van and scanned the scene. A woman with red hair flashed people out, then blinked back in for more. A tall, skinny man herded a group of kids around a house.

Lily nudged my shoulder. "I've got the hybrids. Go help Alex!"

Right. I slapped a hand on Drake's arm and flashed us back to the street where Glacintial and Alex were chained together.

Drake morphed into his dragon form as soon as our feet touched the sidewalk. My stomach twisted as I flew head over heels through the air. By the time I realized he'd tossed me toward his back, my face was heading straight toward my favorite spike. At the last second, I flashed and landed on my ass. "A warning would be nice."

I am not feeling nice. Do something! He cloaked us and launched into the air.

I stood and leaned over his side. I closed my eyes to concentrate. The magic was foreign, yet familiar, and woven in a complicated pattern. It wasn't the same as what we'd found inside the pyramid. "No," I whispered when the answer smacked me in the face.

Drake flew away and landed on top of a nearby house. Bastien swooped in again, and Tracy threw a spell like the one she used on bug magic but with a twist.

It wouldn't work. "Tell them to leave."

Jenella! No! Drake's voice boomed through my head as I flashed to the sidewalk near where Glacintial spun in circles, as if he were looking for an escape.

I scanned the street but didn't see anything to escape from, so I sent my senses out. The apartment complex was still there, but didn't feel any different. When I refocused on Glacintial, he stopped and swung his head toward me. My body filled with adrenaline and I crouched, ready to fight. If I had to, I'd pull an Emine and attack him with crazy.

But he didn't do anything other than stare.

Lily appeared beside me. "The hybrids are heading to the bar or out of the area. That's not the same stuff as what's around the apartment buildings."

"No, it's not. Is this entire neighborhood full of hybrids?"

"Yes. Why?"

I tilted my head to where Drake and Bastien hovered. *These chains have magic I've never seen. Can you two make sure everyone evacuates?*

Hybrids tore out of their houses and raced down the street toward the bar. *Done. Be careful.*

Thanks. I turned my attention back to Lily.

Glacintial sidestepped away from us as he continued to try and free himself. Dust rained down on the other side of the street when he rammed into the front of a house.

Tracy jogged toward us from the other direction. "It's not bug magic."

"No, it's not." I leaned toward the chain at the same time Lily did, and we bumped heads. "Ow. Can you sense magic like me?"

"Not like you, no. But I'm pretty good at guessing."

Alex peered over the side of Glacintial's back.

Lily glared at him. "What the hell were you thinking? You can't single-handedly fight a bunch of sycophants. We're helping, and you'll have to deal with it."

His massive block of a head dipped.

"Is he talking in your head? Is Alex okay?" Tracy asked.

"He's hanging on. They escaped and flashed here to try and get help, but those chains will lead the Bellicose right to them. We need to hurry."

I tried to relax and sift through the different magics. "I feel a different type of demon magic and a similar, but stronger, spell they used to restrain Deva. The weave is more complicated." I tilted my head.

"A mixture of mage, witch, and shifter magic," Lily said.

"Yes. It's also got dragon and whatever Alex is mixed in. But something else." I hissed when I realized what it was. "Something much more complicated. Then there's the seal. It's too simple." I had to take the chance. "I'm going to dissipate it. You two head to the bar."

"No."

"Not a chance."

"I mean it. I don't know what I'm doing, and if the shell isn't as simple as it seems, we're screwed."

"You cannot curse the cursed," Quin's dry voice came from behind us.

My muscles relaxed. I didn't have to be as vigilant in protecting Tracy and Lily if he was there.

"I took a potion to protect me after the whole castle incident," Tracy said. "You're the one in danger."

"You have a potion?"

"It's an experiment."

"Right." Tracy was always testing new potions. I turned my attention back to the problem. If I concentrated hard enough on intention, I could do just about anything. Even dissipate a complicated spell. "Keep an eye on them, Quin. If this goes sideways, run."

"Oh, yes. I'm sure leaving you to suffer alone is the correct choice."

Tracy's hand landed on my shoulder. "We do better together."

Lily flipped her claws and fangs out. "I'm not leaving my brother *or* you."

I glanced at Glacintial, who stared back at us, white fire in his eyes. Right. I needed to hurry. I focused on the magic I stole from Gorman to try and feel for a curse. A dull brownish-gray stream formed, and I sent it toward the chain.

It flickered and held. I took a deep breath and wiped my hands on my pants. The demon magic was simple and not nearly as powerful as we'd seen before. And the complicated weave holding it all together lacked finesse. Almost like it was an afterthought. "Lily, can you dissipate the weave?"

"Not without something awful happening."

"Okay. Here goes nothing. If this doesn't work, go fluid and run as fast as you can. Take Tracy with you." I put my hand on the chain and sent the intention to unweave the spell. My intention moved up the chain as slow as molasses. I held my breath as it wove around Glacintial and continued toward Alex.

Clink. The chains fell to the ground.

"Oh, shit." They wiggled like snakes as they drew into themselves and curled into a pile. I flung an arm around Tracy and backed up.

Glacintial shot into the air, a naked human-shaped Alex clinging to his back.

The chains went still, and I let out a relieved sigh as I swung my head toward the fleeing hybrids. "Let's head to the...."

Boom!

The air left my lungs, and the world spun as I tumbled through the air.

I threw up a shield, but it was too late. Pain exploded in my left arm and head. My back and legs burned as I skidded down the road, the rough surface ripping and melting my clothes. When the motion stopped, my head pounded, and I fought to stay conscious.

The explosion should have killed me. It was the first coherent thought. Then I realized I still held Tracy in a death grip. Pun intended. I healed her and sat up. My head bounced off something hard. "Ow."

When I started to dissolve the shield I'd formed around us, I hesitated. Outside, waves of cursed magic floated and rolled through the subdivision, soaking into the homes, vehicles, and roads. It hovered for a few seconds and floated down like feathers, coating everything it contacted.

I let out a breath when I realized it had avoided the little bubble locking us to the street.

"What the hell is that?" Tracy's shaky voice came from beside me. "Is that from the chain?"

"Yes. It's a curse or something. The chains were boobytrapped." I tried to dial down my magic sight to see through the stuff. It didn't work. "Can you sense Bastien?"

"Yeah. He's near the bar."

I touched the bond with Drake and found a ball of fear and anger on the other end. *We're okay. I made a shield before the explosion.* The pounding in my head eased, and I wondered if Quin and Lily had made it out. Then I shook off the thought. I needed to escape before I could worry about them.

Can you flash through the curse? His mind-voice was clipped. I needed to learn how to do that. Mine sounded more like an instruction manual than a person talking.

I'm going to try. I refocused on Tracy. "Drake's okay."

"Bas says they'll clear an area for us to land. He's pissed."

"Yeah." I linked arms with her, closed my eyes, and flashed to Drake.

The bright fall sun shone above, and the cool wind whipped my hair back. "We did it." A thought struck me, and I spun back toward the neighborhood.

A pair of angry green eyes blocked my view.

I blinked. "It was a trap."

"Which is why I tried to stop you. No way the Bellicose are going to take a dragon and a mage of Alex's caliper and let them escape without planting something nasty." He wrapped an arm around me and pulled me close. "That was not your smartest moment."

I took a few seconds to soak up his heat and stepped away. "It was terrifying."

"Never do that again," Bastien said from behind us.

I ignored him and examined the glassy-eyed hybrids who crowded the parking lot. "How many escaped?"

"Not enough. There were several still inside their houses. There is a dark, cursed bubble across four blocks of the neighborhood."

"Alex and Glacintial?"

"Inside the bar." He tapped his temple. "The curse didn't harm them. When Alex discovered how to manipulate their mind control magic, he released several shifters. They were not pleased and chained them. Glacintial believes the Bellicose leaders allowed them to escape to set the war in motion."

"Are you sure they're okay?" I didn't notice the curse on the palace at first, either.

Lily and Quin appeared on the other side of the parking lot, and I breathed a sigh of relief.

Until the screaming in the distance registered. "Are those sirens getting closer?"

Bastien stomped toward me. "You blew up an entire neighborhood in the human world."

"Not my fault. I was trying to save it." I trotted to the back of the bar and eyed a small grassy area with two young trees growing out of it.

Bastien's heavy footsteps followed me. "It was a trap, and you walked right into it."

I spun toward him. "It wasn't a trap."

He raised an eyebrow.

"Okay, it was a trap. But not for me."

"It was a message to my parents," Lily said as she joined us. "What are you doing back here?"

"We need to help these people."

Drake turned his head toward the squalling noise and handed me a bracelet. "Put that on. It should glamour you well enough to hide your torn clothes. Bastien and I will monitor the authorities."

"I'm going with," Tracy said. "Don't do anything drastic while we're gone, Jen."

Lily waited until they left, then pointed toward a man in a blue-gray uniform. "He works for the gas company and plans to tell them it was a leak."

I eyed the putrid bubble hanging over the neighborhood. "And when the humans walk right into a curse without knowing?"

She shrugged. "It might not affect them. If it does, it's not our problem."

I rubbed my eyes. "Not your problem, you mean. Because humans harmed by magic are my responsibility."

"No shit? That sucks." She crossed her arms. "You could always push the mess off on Mat. It might put a dent in his enormous ego."

"That's not...We don't...Never mind. I'm going to build a gate here for the hybrids to use." I'd never built a gate other than the ones I made to access the new weird pocket. They were attached where this one would be remote. I'd read about them in documents the Dwarven Prince gave me. "It's closer to the hybrid neighborhoods."

"Uh, huh. And if a human finds it?"

"The gates don't let humans through."

Dale, the scary bartender, stomped up, his eyes glowing an eerie amber. "What the hell are you doing to my bar?"

"Um."

Lily slapped a hand on my arm. "Hey, Dale. Jen built us a pocket and would like to put a gate here."

His hard eyes scanned me. "Is that so?"

My mouth went dry. I swallowed. "Yes. It was my first try, and it's strange, but it will work as a safe place for hybrids to go. This is the perfect location. It's blocked on three sides, and there are two trees to anchor it. Plus, humans don't think twice about people coming and going from a bar."

He scanned the trees. "I want control."

"That's not how gates work."

"I don't care. If I allow you to use my property and herd my people, then I control it or no deal."

I turned to Lily and jerked a thumb at him. "Why isn't he the leader of this territory instead of that worthless Sheila?"

They both burst out laughing.

If I were going to build a gate, it needed to be one like Allure's. Our gate was several miles away from the anchor where the pocket was located. I'd studied the magic every time I went through, but never enough to duplicate it. But with my new flashing abilities, I could go anywhere and study anything. "I'll be right back." I flashed to the gate of Allure.

CHAPTER TWENTY-FOUR

THE SOUND OF CAR tires crunched on the road when I landed. I scurried up a hill and behind a tree. After the vehicle passed, I wrapped my jacket tighter, approached the gate, and tapped my chin. I knew better than to touch the wards. The last time, they drained me and left me with only Mat's magic. At the time, I thought his magic was my inherent power.

A motor rumbling from somewhere down the mountain jolted me out of my thoughts. I needed to hurry. I sent out a small tentacle of my new silvery magic and tasted the gate wards. The spell was complicated but not much different from the one I'd built into Lily's pocket. Except for the alarms.

I jerked my magic back at the realization I'd probably set them off and turned to leave.

"Your Grace, what are you doing out here?" a stern voice asked.

I turned toward the voice and tried to look innocent. "Sorry about that. I was trying to understand gate magic."

The woman's eyes narrowed. "Why?"

No way I'd tell a random gate guard I'd built a new pocket before the leadership council learned the news. I raised an eyebrow.

Her lips twitched. "Come on inside, and I'll show you the alarm system and the monitoring spell."

The alarm console was a sphere made from witch magic, with a shell similar to the one Tracy put on the balls she made for Quin to use. Blinking lights blazed as a truck drove through the outer gates.

The guard pointed. "The outer shell is a shield. It protects us from the wards."

I'd never taken the time to think about how the gate was monitored. "May I?" I motioned toward the sphere.

"Don't touch the lights."

"Sure." I found a spot on the top and set two fingers on it. The shell was more basic than Tracy's, but the magic inside felt like the outer wards. I focused on the lights. Razazia's magic mixed with pixie dust. I pulled my hand away. "Thank you."

"Can we do anything else for you?"

"No, I'm good. Thanks." I strode out the gate and flashed back to the bar.

Blue and red lights assaulted my eyes. I blinked and leaned against the tree I'd planned to anchor the gate to. Too late now. Human police flooded the area and herded hybrids. I watched as they pulled a woman from a group and questioned her out of hearing distance from the others. Healers examined the injured. Several authorities ran around with no discernable pattern.

"Do not move."

I flinched, but didn't jump at Quin's voice. "What are they doing?"

"They are questioning people."

A man in a black uniform glanced our way, turned, and headed in the other direction. "Can they see us?"

"We look like bystanders. Should they ask, we heard an explosion and came to see what happened."

I scanned the crowd but didn't see anyone I knew. I sensed Drake, Bastien, and Tracy on the roof. Lily was inside the bar with the scary bartender, Glacintial, and Alex. "I guess the gate can wait."

"Perhaps dismantling the chain without a thought was not the best idea."

"Yeah. I suspected a trap and tried to neutralize it, but I'm still learning. They might have figured out I was the one to free Deva."

He gave me a flat look.

I held up a hand. "I did the right thing."

"You saved two people at the cost of hundreds."

I winced. He was right. Worse, the dryness was gone from his voice, which made it seem more ancient and powerful. It wasn't often he showed that side. "You're saying I need to slow down and think before I act?"

"Yes."

He'd been telling me the same thing since we met. But his lack of calling me stupid added gravity to the situation. My eyes drifted back to where a black cloud still hung over several houses. "The way they set it off is odd. Almost like an emotional response, rather than a well thought out plan." And if I'd sensed that magic right, then I needed to warn Ann Marie. "How long do human police take to question people?"

"I am not the foremost expert on human authorities." The sarcastic Quin had returned.

I sensed Drake and Bastien launch into the air as I watched the police meander around. A sandy-haired authority lifted his head, met my eyes, blinked, and then returned to his duties. I sucked in a breath and concentrated on the others. More than half were hybrids. I knew Jonas and Ann Marie were smart, but it never occurred to me they controlled the police. Which meant they probably had as many plants in the local and state government as we did. Or more, since they could fit in better. A glimmer of hope lit inside me. We might get through this without drawing too much human attention.

Movement out of the corner of my eye caused me to turn my attention to Drake, Tracy, and Bastien as they shuffled in from the main street. They stopped a few feet from us and scanned the scene, their eyes wide.

Tracy sidestepped toward me. "What's going on?"

She was acting so human it caught me off guard. It took me a few seconds to answer. "Um. We heard an explosion."

Quin's elbow jabbed into my ribs.

Right. Act human. "It might have been a fight."

A human police officer patted a crying witch-shifter hybrid on the shoulder and strode toward us. "Any of you see what happened?"

Drake's rough demeanor morphed into a country-boy manner. He wore a cowboy hat, boots, worn jeans, and a T-shirt that had seen better days. "No, sir. We came for a drink and saw the commotion."

The guy turned his attention to Quin, who shook his head.

I cleared my throat. "We heard the explosion, but didn't see anything."

His eyes scanned Quin's expensive business suit, then my dress clothes.

My heart pounded in my chest. I hoped Drake's glamour held until the authorities left. When I used to wear glamour earrings, he said my magic burned it away. And my power had grown since then. If the humans saw my ripped-up clothes, I was in trouble.

I let out the breath I'd been holding when he dismissed me and refocused on Quin. "You folks often drink at this bar?"

"No," I answered for him. When the guy's skeptical look landed on me, I fought not to squirm. I needed to come up with an answer fast. "*My sister!*" I realized my voice was too loud and toned it down. "My sister comes here. We were going to meet her for a drink."

His eyes narrowed. "I see. And what's this sister's name?"

"Lily First," I answered without hesitation.

He wrote something down. "Stay here until you're released."

"Sure."

He eyed me for a few seconds before he turned and picked his way through the crowd, heading toward the front of the building.

"Your aptitude for lying to the police is beyond reproach." Quin's dry tone told me he thought the opposite.

"Do you think she'll vouch for us?"

Quin folded his arms. "Perhaps. If not, time in a human jail may teach you how to lie better."

I ignored Drake's growl. "He caught me off guard. How was I supposed to know he'd ask a bunch of questions?"

"It is not difficult information to find."

He was right, as usual. I stupidly thought my limited experience in the human world had prepared me. I didn't understand it as well as I originally thought. It was something else I needed to work on.

We didn't have to wait long before the guy returned and released us. I sighed in relief and turned to Drake. "I wanted to build a gate to the new pocket here. Is there a better place? Something central to hybrids?"

"This is the most central location, but there are others. Have you discussed it with the proprietor?"

"Sort of." And we'd draw attention if we sauntered up to the front door. "Is there a way inside without being seen?"

We walked until we were about a block away. The silence was eerie. Cars sat abandoned on the street, their doors left open. One had a seat built for a small child in the back. Houses were empty, with wide-open doors, and several children's toys littered the lawns. I wondered where they all went.

"Stay alert and do not cause a scene." Quin disappeared.

Drake's arm snaked around me. "The curse didn't affect these hybrids. They have evacuation plans in place and activated them."

I nodded. They were safe, but the ones a few streets over got caught up in it. Families with children. And it was once again my fault. The last thing I wanted to do was hurt or kill more people. "How do I become less impulsive?" The question slipped out before I thought. The irony of my impulsive question about being less impulsive hit me, and I suppressed a groan.

"Experience," Bastien answered. "And a better listening ear."

"Thanks, Bas. Very helpful."

"I mean, he's not wrong. But you're better than you were when I first started guarding you," Tracy said.

True. I'd come a long way, but still dove in without thinking when someone was in danger. And Bastien was right about my listening ear. Several people told me to think more before I acted. "Okay. How do I gain experience without making mistakes?"

Drake pulled me to his side. "You can start by paying attention when I yell your name in a mad panic." He kissed my temple.

Tracy chuckled. "Or when anyone does. I mean, I'll always have your back, but maybe slow down when in dangerous situations."

Was slowing down snap decisions in tough situations even possible? I doubted I could do it without a lot more experience. Not wanting to talk about it, I changed the subject. "How do we get inside the bar?"

"Let's wait until the police clear out," Drake said. "If they do. Humans are touchy about these situations. The authorities might not clear out today or even tomorrow."

We waited several hours before the hybrid police cleared the humans out and took over. When the last one pulled out of the parking lot, we strode toward the front door.

Hybrids glared at us. Some made rude comments. Others clustered together in fighting stances. I knew they hated us, but never expected the open hostility. Dumb of me, considering even Lily had animosity toward us.

She sat at the end of the bar, her arms crossed, while Alex talked with his hands. Glacintial loomed behind them, sipping a beer.

I headed her way. Drake rested a hand on my hip to stay close.

Tracy shimmied past a hybrid and plastered herself to my other side. I scanned the bar again and realized several pairs of eyes tracked me. "Are you guys guarding me?"

"No, just walking with my friend."

"I like being close to you."

Bastien crowded close to Tracy. "The patrons here are not your biggest fans. You need guards."

"Okay." It was good to have people that cared. Even though I didn't sense danger from anybody in the room. I slid onto the barstool next to Lily and eyed the glass in front of her. "Is that orange juice?"

"Mimosa. Dale decided I wanted to celebrate finding Alex."

Drake's hand rested on my shoulder. "That is rather clever."

She held up the glass. "More like a smartass comment through a forced drink."

The barkeep sauntered in our direction. His eyes scanned Bastien, who stood next to Glacintial, then Tracy, who took the seat on my other side. "Drinks? No? Then show me this pocket you created."

I squirmed under the scrutiny of several pairs of eyes. Some glared, but others had hope. "I wanted to talk to you about that. With the police outside, I can't use the area we discussed."

"We didn't discuss an area. You told me where you wanted the gate."

"Yes. Which means we discussed it. I wondered if there was a more concealed place."

His eyes darted between me and Lily. "Is she always this difficult?"

"Yep. But count yourself lucky it's her and not our mother. She'd have just waltzed in, taken over your bar, and either killed you or bulldozed right over you like you weren't there. Jen's much nicer when she bulldozes people."

"I'm not bulldozing anyone. The hybrids need an escape hatch, and I'm trying to solve the problem."

"Everyone's right," Tracy said. "Jen's pushy, but she's also trying to help. And her mother would have killed you if you questioned her. So, is there a better place for the gate?"

Dale leaned on the bar in front of her. "If you use that spell you have in your hands, I'll forcibly remove you from the premises, little witch hybrid."

Her eyebrows drew together. "How did you know I wove a spell?"

He grinned. "I'm a satyr-centaur hybrid. I have a keen nose."

"Leave her alone, Dale," Alex mumbled, his voice a smidge darker than before his kidnapping. "The Dragon Prince is about ready to launch himself at you."

I held up my hand in the 'stop' gesture. "A place for the gate?"

He clomped to the other side of Alex and opened a small door. "Follow me. And bring all your purebloods with you, including the looming white dragon."

We filed behind the bar into a small but clean industrial-sized kitchen. Dale opened a door on the left that led to an empty room. "This is my match, Darla's office, but she won't use it. We can sneak people in and out if you put the gate here."

I rubbed my chin. "What about their vehicles? The magic I sampled in Allure allows for an outer gate where cars park and an inner gate for access. They can't leave them in your parking lot."

"We have people who can transport them here," Lily said. "If they want to bring their cars later, the one on my property is wide enough to drive through."

I didn't realize she'd followed us. She was getting good at hiding herself. "Okay. I'm going to pull magic from everyone. You might want to warn them. I'll also make it so Dale can restrict and monitor access."

"Oh, Sheila will love that," Alex drawled. "She doesn't like it when Dale takes over."

"I don't care." Nor would I trust that woman with gate access. She rubbed me the wrong way.

I held my hand out to Lily. "Give me your hand and feel how I do this. Keep your morbid thoughts to yourself and don't help."

Her face scrunched in disgust. "I won't. Dale doesn't need a bunch of human crazies descending on his business."

"It wouldn't be the first time," Dale said.

"That was an accident!"

"Pay attention to how I do this, especially to my intentions. It might give you insight into why you give your magic cruel little surprises."

Chapter Twenty-Five

THE ACCESS POINT WORKED well. The monitoring station? Not so much. Instead of a perfect sphere that tied the gate to the controls, my creation was more of a fried egg shape. Or something. The shell reflected a map lit up in different colors I couldn't interpret.

"Well, it sort of looks okay," Tracy said as she leaned over the oval. "Are those dots moving?"

"Yeah." I rubbed my temples, trying to figure out what I did wrong. "Don't use the monitoring until we figure out what it's showing."

"You don't know?" Dale asked.

"It's my first pocket," I explained. "Ann Marie said it's stable. And it's not like you need to monitor it from here." I didn't mention it was an experiment.

The look he gave me cut to the bone.

"It's fine," Lily said.

He shook his head. "You're going through this gate first. I'm not risking a hybrid on what's clearly a hair-brained idea."

I crossed my arms. "Why aren't you in charge of this district again? Because I can guarantee you, Sheila wouldn't try to order me around." She'd been quiet after my comments at the office building.

His eyes sparkled, giving away how amused he was, despite his serious face. "My bar, my rules."

I huffed but didn't argue with the scary barkeep. I liked the guy.

Drake nudged me out of the way. "Jenella is a fast learner and very good at magic. I'll go first."

"No," Glacintial said. "I am the lowest-ranking paranormal, aside from the bossy bar owner. I will go first."

"And me." Alex tried to push past us. "I don't even have a rank."

I pointed at him. "You're Lily's brother and, therefore, mine. Sort of. Besides, your parents would kill us if we let anything happen right after finding you."

"Nothing's going to happen." Alex had a certain darkness to him he didn't have before. It wasn't a spell, but more like his shine wore off a little, leaving him tarnished.

I opened my mouth to say something, then closed it. It wasn't my business.

Drake nudged me aside and stepped through the gate.

I held my breath as I monitored him. A sense of wonder and amusement came back at me. "He's fine. Let's evacuate people."

Jonas came through, Drake on his heels. His eyes locked on Alex. We scrambled out of the way as he stomped toward him and wrapped him in a hug.

My heart melted. It was heartwarming to see how much he cared about his adopted kids.

He released Alex and focused on me. "What in Sam Hill are you doing, Jenella?"

"The Bellicose booby-trapped and chained Glacintial and Alex and then let them escape. When I broke them, it set off a curse in this neighborhood. I'm helping evacuate hybrids. This gate gives them easier access than Lily's place."

Drake stepped between us. "We'll talk about it later. The gate is safe."

I stayed and watched as Dale and his match, a moose shifter, led hybrids through a few at a time. I told Tracy and Bastien to go, but they wouldn't leave my side. Drake loomed behind me and growled at anyone who dared glare as they passed. It was a disheartening and hopeful experience. The hybrids hated me. I hoped to build trust and rapport by building them a pocket, but based on the murmurings, it didn't help.

I kept my face neutral, even as I came to the realization it would take more than building a pocket for them to even remotely warm up to me.

When the crowd thinned, I took Drake's hand and followed Bastien and Tracy through.

The gate spit us out on the side of a twisted road. Hybrids wandered around, exploring. Some wore smiles, while others were wide-eyed with shock, probably from the strange colors and shapes. We passed the center square, or trapezoid, where the squeal of children's laughter rang through the air.

"You're quiet," Drake said.

"We need to hire a hybrid-only enforcer unit. They won't trust anyone we send from Allure."

"Give them time. They'll come around." Bastien opened the door to the house and waved us through. "Many are relieved to have a safe place to retreat."

"I suppose." I kicked off my shoes and padded toward the kitchen. "The whole coalition is a mess and I keep making it worse."

Tracy plopped into a chair. "You can only do so much. I mean, it's not like you aren't trying to bring people together and heal the wounds Anitta caused."

"But it's still not enough." I slumped onto the love seat. Thanks to my friends and family, I somewhat succeeded in keeping my freedom as I took the throne. As a result, I wasn't cooped up in an office all day. At least it wasn't the cage I'd imagined back when I thought I could dodge the responsibilities that came with my position. Instead, it felt more like I dove into the center of an ocean without a life jacket and was one poor decision from drowning.

I leaned back and closed my eyes against a wave of mental fatigue. I needed to do better. More. If I didn't, I'd drown and take a lot of paranormals with me. Maybe I needed to rely on my training and stop trying to pretend to be a regular paranormal. Because I wasn't, nor would I ever be, normal. The ball of fear and anger inside me was a testament to that. It was also something I hadn't dealt with. Like so many other things.

Drake nudged me over and sent reassurance and other calming emotions through our bond as he took the seat next to me.

A rough laugh escaped me. "You got my feelings wrong again."

"I never misunderstand your feelings. What I send is always what you need."

Bastien cleared his throat. "You're not as bad as you think, Jen. And much more effective than I once believed you'd be."

I soaked up Drake's reassurance, cracked an eye open, and focused on him. "But?"

"But you keep trying to single-handedly solve problems. You're more powerful, so you believe you're more effective."

"And you don't want to put anyone else in danger," Tracy added. "So you charge in to fix everything yourself."

"Correct." Bastien leaned forward and rested his elbows on his knees. "The coalition is like a pyramid. You are the top piece. The leaders are the two or three layers below you. The rest of us branch out from there. You keep trying to reform it into a circle. You can't. The quicker you realize it, the faster others will rally behind you."

Drake stretched an arm across the back of the loveseat. "And you feel responsible for your mother's reign of terror. Which is not your fault."

"No, but the problems she caused *are* my responsibility."

Bastien shook his head. "Not all of them. The leaders vying for position during the power vacuum caused some. It is their responsibility to adjust. Yours ended with ordering them to check themselves, which you did."

He had a point. Rather than throwing my weight around, I tried to cooperate with everyone to gain allies. All because my mother was such a tyrant. On top of that, when I thought of her, I only saw her hateful, glassy eyes as she died on Drake's back. "What do you mean I keep trying to make the coalition into a circle? Are you talking about the new council formation?"

"He means treating subordinates as equals is not the best strategy. Nor is projecting a false front." Quin said from the doorway. "As I have pointed out many times."

I didn't have time to respond because Lily, Alex, Glacintial, Jonas, and Ann Marie strode through the door.

Jonas pointed at me. "You really screwed the pooch this time."

I raised my head off Drake's arm. "Gross."

Lily chuckled. "It's a saying. It means you screwed up."

"I don't care what it means. It's disgusting. Don't use that saying again when scolding me."

Jonas dropped his arm. "You've screwed up the entire hybrid community in a matter of two days, and you're worried about my phrasing?"

"Yes. And why are you here? Don't you have shifters to sort out?"

He frowned, his anger melting away. "What happened to you?"

"I messed up and didn't notice a trap on the chains. You don't need to point it out. But you and Drake also screwed up. You, by dragging your feet and allowing the hybrids to become complacent, even though Lily and Alex have been up to their eyeballs in the mess. And Drake knew the territory leaders would sell out their people in a heartbeat but said nothing. I'll forgive him because he's been busy chasing after my naïve, impulsive ass. But you knew there was a problem, had the power to fix it, and did nothing."

"We didn't have any problems until you showed up," Ann Marie snapped.

"Bullshit. Sheila has always been a problem. All you need to do is go to her territory and mention her name, and you'll find out what the hybrids think about her. Dale pretty much runs the neighborhood he lives in. He would have been the better choice, but you left an incompetent sellout in charge." I pointed at Jonas. "You screwed the pooch. I just piled on."

"Gross," Lily snickered.

I raised my middle finger.

Drake snatched it out of the air. "Jenella's a little grumpy."

"Jen's right," Alex said. "Shiela sold out her territory to eliminate Dale and Darla. Glac and I thought we could outsmart the ones who kidnapped me, but they have some powerful people working for them."

Drake and Bastien leaned forward at the same time.

"Who?"

"What powerful people?"

"One or more of their leaders uses sorcery. The second magic on the chains was complicated but not as bad as the pyramid in Pyron, which was nothing I'd ever felt before. The First Cynthia created the curse. She's handing them out like candy. Aside from the one I set off in the neighborhood, the palace has a Vinculum Tenebrism curse. The First Gorman is sure she created and placed it. I'm fairly certain the one activated today snags and enslaves people, but I haven't learned how to read curses yet, so it's a guess."

Everyone except Tracy gawked at me.

"You knew all that and said nothing?" Drake asked.

"I was too busy feeling sorry for myself."

Glacintial lowered himself to the arm of the couch beside Alex. "It would have activated even without your intervention. They weren't after you, but Ann Marie. I do not believe they knew you were in the area."

My eye twitched. "Are you sure?"

"He is," Alex said. "The question is, what are we going to do about it?"

I patted Drake's thigh. "My consort will work with you to come up with something. I need to return to Allure and check on some things." I stood and sauntered toward the door.

Lily, Quin, Bastien, and Tracy followed me.

I stopped on the front porch. "What?"

Quin leaned against the railing. "The Dragon Prince makes a valid point, but remember what I said."

My eyebrows drew together. "Which time?"

His eyes didn't roll like a normal person. Instead, he appeared in front of me and ramped up his creepy essence. "You do not need to conform, nor do you need to take on a persona. You simply need to be yourself."

"And work on your confidence," Lily said. "If you can become half as confident as Mat, you'll be good."

So, the opposite of what Bastien said. "Sure. Thanks." I slapped a hand on Bastien and Tracy and flashed to the gates of Allure.

"That's handy when we don't end up in a jungle," Tracy said. "Why did you need to leave so fast?"

"I want my palace back. It's not fair to make the griffins handle it alone. And I don't trust Gorman. He's..."

"Slimy. I think so, too."

Bastien watched the gate guard scan Tracy's magic. "My aunt will help you should she see past her grief."

I shook my head as I waved my magic over the scanner. "She's been there for me every step of the way, so I don't doubt it." Even though she manipulated me into summoning my mother, I believed her intentions were good. And I couldn't imagine having a mental connection to one person as they die, let alone several. "She needs time. Let her decide how long she grieves."

"Who are you, and what did you do with the selfish girl I once knew?"

"Oh, don't worry. She's still in here somewhere."

CHAPTER TWENTY-SIX

THE FALL WIND WHISTLED through the trees behind the palace as I stepped out of the flashing circle. Griffins circled, and people darted in and out of the tents the palace staff used as makeshift offices. But none of it caught my attention. A line of paranormals on the other side of the field snaked around the edge of the palace wall and out onto the street.

Instead of going inside to confront Gorman, I pivoted toward the massive tent outside the Council Building. Several paranormals greeted me while others started to bow, caught themselves, and dipped their heads. I took sips of magic as I went, careful not to overdo it.

Inside, so many people talked at once I couldn't separate the conversations. The line snaked around several ropes made of vines and ended at a table on the far side. Razazia sat at the center, three leaders on each side of her. She waved me over. "Hello, Jenella."

"What are you doing?"

Her face lit up. "Your very pushy assistant asked me to lead the recruitment efforts for your army."

I scanned the line. Every faction was represented by the potential recruits. "And you already have this many people?"

"More, actually. Tell me, was it her idea or yours to give me this assignment?"

"Mine. I thought it would give you something to do."

She threw her head back and laughed. "This is a dream. I pick up all sorts of gossip. For example, how the Manticore King adores you. And the Pixie Queen thinks she's your friend. Adorable."

"Sylphira *is* my friend. And I like the Manticore King. He's honest and cares about his people."

"Oh? Interesting." She typed something on the tablet in front of her. "How big do you wish this army to be?"

I hadn't thought about it. I didn't think many paranormals would be interested. Now that I saw the lines, I wondered why so many were. "Are you asking them why they want to join?"

"Answering a question with a question. Lovely. And yes, we ensure they are volunteers. We will not accept anyone coerced or ordered to join by their ruler."

"Good. How many do you have so far?"

"Two thousand. Though it will be closer to five by the end of the day."

We didn't even have a structure or leadership in place yet. My eyes trailed down the line. Some looked eager, others looked bored. A few had unreadable expressions. Most were mid to low powered. "Try to identify people with leadership abilities. Judge it based on potential, not power level."

"Are you sure that's wise? After all, power level is everything."

"I'm sure. We'll screen them better later."

She leaned her elbows on the table. "Well, this just got a lot more interesting."

I shivered when an eerie feeling washed over me as I climbed the steps to the family entrance of the palace. I half expected the back door to creak as I reached a shaky hand out to open it. Though, I knew Helen and George would have a fit if a single one fell into disrepair enough to squeak.

I tried to ignore the deafening silence as I padded through the mudroom and down the wide hall to the center of the foyer and stopped at the base of the sweeping staircase. "Gorman?" My voice echoed through the cavernous space.

He didn't answer, even though I sensed him and the Ogre Queens inside the palace. I let my feet lead me up the stairs toward them. I found them on the third-floor landing. They sat in a circle, holding hands. Their combined magic looked like thick gray smoke as it floated to the ceiling and spread, entering the open doors and soaking into everything.

I leaned against the doorjamb and frowned as I sampled it. It didn't feel like curse breaking magic, though I'd only sampled that type of magic a couple of times. The stuff was more concentrated and felt more like ownership. When my eyes settled back on them, they jumped to their feet.

"Your Grace." Gorman bowed. "We didn't expect you today. The palace isn't safe."

I crossed my arms. "No? Because it didn't repel me like before."

They shared a look. "Well, the curse itself is gone, but there may be fragments. We are cleaning those up now. I thought you were staying in the human world."

"As did I," Mat's gravelly voice said from behind me. "But plans change."

I called him and explained my suspicions. He already knew what was going on because he was Mat. And Mat was always a step ahead of me. He'd been monitoring the ogres inside the palace through the new monitoring spells Tracy installed. Spells that were hard to detect.

I nodded. "They do. Like how I didn't plan to wake Gorman, but was told he was the only one who could break the curse. Or how I slogged through a jungle to find him instead of working on the massive problems the coalition faces."

Mat nodded. "Don't forget they disrupted the task force."

"Seems counterintuitive, doesn't it?"

"It does, yes."

Voices and wing beats echoed throughout the palace as the griffins poured through the doors below us.

Gorman held up his hands. "I can explain."

I raised an eyebrow.

"Cynthia and I are matched. We hid it from everyone except Lissa for years. We attempted to keep the secret when she chose to sleep, but Anitta found out."

"And though our grandmother kept the information to herself, our mother blackmailed you," Mat said. "Tell me, did she pit you against each other? Or spin your heads around to the point where you lost your way, so you followed her?"

Gorman's face pinched. "How did you figure it out?"

Mat took two steps toward the ogres. When they puffed up, ready to fight, he turned his attention back to Gorman as if they weren't a threat. "How do I know my own mother's tactics?" He shrugged. "She never missed an opportunity to manipulate the powerful."

Boots pounded on the stairs as the palace guard returned.

I glanced that way. "Did she even put you to sleep like the other Firsts?"

"Yes. Then woke us a couple of years ago to help with her creations." He shook his head. "I caught on, but Cynthia liked the idea of changing the coalition. She was loyal to Anitta for a time. When I told her how I had doubts about what we were doing, she went straight to the second queen. She locked me up and used demons to extract my magic, then set a trap for you by putting me back to sleep."

My mouth went dry. She knew I planned to wake the Firsts. I hadn't told anyone my plans, not even Drake, until just before I woke Razazia. "When?"

"About two years ago. She learned you woke Drake and theorized since you woke one First, you would wake us all."

"And if I didn't?"

"She didn't care, since she planned to extract your power and kill you. Anitta forced an oath from me to work against you for the rest of my days if you woke me. I am still under that oath."

I scanned the Ogre Queens. "And you?"

"We are loyal to our First," the one-eyed queen answered.

"And your oath to the Coalition?"

They shared a look. "The oath to our First came before our oath to the Coalition."

Before I could process her words, they charged.

Mat's blades lit up a second before I flashed away. When I reappeared, Gorman had a gash in his arm.

Powerful magic boiled out of him. Mat braced himself on the railing as it pushed him backward.

A meaty fist came for my head and I ducked. Plaster rained down when the hit landed on the wall instead of me.

I created a chain and wrapped it around her torso. I'd absorbed a lot of ogre magic, but couldn't figure out what to do with it, so I flashed away.

The two-eyed queen barreled into my stomach.

Sharp pain shot through me as a loud crack came from my ribs. I smashed onto the marble floor. There went my shoulders. Thankfully, I remembered to tuck my chin.

Jenella! Drake's panic flooded me.

You're not helping! I blasted solid magic into the queen's face.

She reared back and raised her fist. It came at my face so fast I didn't have time to form a shield.

Wingbeats sounded a second before a massive beak bit into her shoulder.

She screamed and fell to the side.

I stumbled to my feet and wheezed while I waited for my ribs to heal.

Across the room, Mat was cornered by Gorman. Magic pinned him to the wall, his short swords at his feet.

Another griffin barreled into Gorman's back and latched onto his neck.

Palace guards flooded the area and swarmed the ogres.

"Stop!" I used persuasion.

Everyone froze. I needed to work on ordering some people and not others.

I formed Lily's handy boxes around the two queens and Gorman, ensuring they were isolated like the human police did with the hybrids outside the bar. Only they did it without boxes.

After I released everyone else, Mat rubbed his chin. "Why did you not do that when you first came upon them?"

"I wanted to see what they'd do."

He shook his head. "Not smart."

"We know exactly where they stand now." And we had another major faction without a leader. Solve one problem by creating two more seemed to be how my rule was going to go. "Thanks for the assist, George."

The Griffin patriarch turned his massive body toward me. "You're very welcome. I will have someone check the nest to ensure no others are lurking."

I inclined my head, turned, and headed toward my office.

Mat's heavy footsteps followed.

When I got to the door, I motioned toward the empty desks outside of it. "I'll text Verity and work on getting the staff back. What's the word from the mages?"

Mat strode to the conference table and scanned the documents left out when we evacuated. "The two I found who can guard against curses said the ogres broke it two days ago. It wasn't as complicated as they led you to believe. These pages are blank."

I waved a hand. "Verity buys privacy potions from the alchemy witches to ensure no one except me can read them."

"She is a good assistant."

"The best."

"I came in after they left last night. My office was not touched, nor were our apartments. The monitoring spells showed the ogres stayed in the common areas."

I crossed my arms. "Strange, isn't it? How Cynthia's curses aren't very strong, and Gorman didn't do much while he had access to the place?"

"Yes."

"Were they forced to stick to Anitta's oaths, but did the minimum? Do you think we can save them?"

"Perhaps. Emine believes you can release them from their oaths to mother."

"I suppose I could if I knew how." One more thing to add to the 'things to learn' list. It grew longer by the day.

He rubbed his chin. "What are you going to do with them?"

"Move them to the council building to make a statement. How long will it take for the enforcers to question the Ogre Queens' inner circle?"

"A day or two."

"Perfect."

"It's barbaric," Verity said as she patted the box that held Gorman. "How do you feed them?"

We stood in the council chambers where I'd flashed the three prisoners. The First and the Ogre Queens stood in their tiny boxes and stared at us.

"It's humane compared to what I could have done. And they're immortal, so they won't starve."

"Immortal or not, they still need to pee, right?"

I frowned. Yes, they did. And the boxes I made weren't big enough for them to lie down and rest.

"Let them figure it out, dear. Perhaps it will do them some good to sit in their own filth for a while," Ara said from behind us.

I rubbed my arms when her magic crawled across my skin. "You think so?"

"Yes. I also suggest regular flaying. It is very effective in disciplining vampires, so I assume it would work with ogres."

Verity's mouth dropped open. "Oh, hell no." She strode toward the desk where she sat during meetings. "I will not take part in torturing people."

Ara's tinkling laugh rang in my ears. "I forget how human you are. You could always show mercy, but I have found the method ineffective."

I rubbed my face. "I haven't decided what to do with them yet."

Ara tapped her chin. "There are so many ways to inflict pain."

A shiver ran down my spine. "Yes." I led her away from the ogres. "But that's not why I asked you to come. I wanted your thoughts about something."

"Of course, dear. Take your time. But dealing with traitors and liars in swift and painful ways is always the best option."

I didn't comment as I headed down the hall to my half-dismantled makeshift office. "Bastien said I'm trying to make the coalition a circle instead of sitting on top of a pyramid. Quin says I need to ignore him and be myself. Lily thinks I lack confidence. I wanted your opinion."

She blinked. "I do not have thoughts on the matter."

I sighed. "From my perspective, the structure of the coalition is more of a scatter chart than a pyramid."

"I believe what the Dragon Prince is alluding to is that you cannot give them your power. Listening to our opinions and suggestions is fine. But decisions made on behalf of the coalition are yours and yours alone."

That made sense. And what I'd been doing. Sort of. "My second question is, how do I organize and mobilize a massive army to fight for a fractured coalition?"

Ara threw her head back and laughed. "Lissa used to do it by giving them a common enemy. Anitta manipulated and used intimidation. You, dear, already have a common enemy and have done an excellent job convincing the rest of us to fight against them. And you can be manipulative when necessary. Perhaps you should create an action plan and present it as a group effort."

"You mean make my goals theirs? Without discussion?"

She sauntered to the window overlooking the chamber. "Or lay out your plans and expect them to follow. Many paranormals regret rejecting their hybrid children and would jump at the chance to make amends."

"Do you think that's why there's so many volunteers for our army?"

"No. The turnout is due to Razazia's recruiting efforts. She is quite efficient when she wants to be."

And that worried me more than anything else about the First. I wondered what she was up to. Ara had vampire spies everywhere, so I trusted the information she gave me. If she thought the people were coming around, then I needed to believe it. But I didn't have some cosmic plan to present them. Or any plan at all aside from rough ideas. "Thanks."

Verity was right, I decided as I stood in front of the boxes and eyed Gorman. He and the two queens needed food, water, and bathrooms. The only thing keeping them in the small boxes accomplished was easing the ball of anger in my gut.

Emine slammed her hands on her hips. "I dunno. The dungeons at The Caudron are at capacity with all the turncoats we've rounded up. Adding these three would give them someone to rally behind. You could expand the boxes and create a commode and bed. Don't your dragon buddies have culinary magic? They can feed the traitors."

"They're grieving. I don't want to bother them."

She cackled. "Bothering people is your thing. Use it." She plopped into a chair. "Or don't. They'll live either way."

"Fine. I'll ask." A long box with three sections formed behind the prisoners. After anchoring them, I added the cots I'd seen enforcers use inside the jail and small compost toilets, though I couldn't make them work. "I need to practice using the magic I've absorbed. I'm still inept at even the most basic stuff."

"Sure. But you're not an angry little shit anymore. That's progress."

I merged the old boxes into the new ones. "Oh, the anger is still there." Drake helped regulate it sometimes, but he had his own anger issues. It had to be exhausting tampering down both. My hope was it would go away on its own, but as time passed, it just hung there and waited to lash out. Not that I'd tell Emine about it.

When the boxes merged, I moved toward Gorman's much larger cell. "Why didn't Cynthia use her full power on the curse?"

He pursed his lips. "Neither of us wanted to bring down the coalition we worked to build. The experiments we took part in would have been diabolical if we'd fully cooperated. Your mother lost her ruling magic and could not overpower us."

"Then how did they use you?"

"Demons can be quite persuasive. The spreading spell you recently encountered had a curse that allowed it to spread and infect paranormals but not humans. My magic countered it enough to give you a chance. I am under oath to work against you, but the oath did not state how."

"So you tweaked it to make it easier to break?" Emine asked.

"To dissipate. By attaching it to the spell itself and coding the curse breaker portion to dissolve when anti-demon magic touched it. It was quite brilliant, really."

I held up a hand. "How did it work against me?"

"By allowing it to exist at all, of course."

"And the Ogre Queens?"

"They were simply following my orders, like the ogres have done for centuries."

"Just to clarify, the oath to work against me was to my mother?"

"Yes."

"And you weren't released when she died?"

He tapped his chin. "I don't believe so if she is, in fact, gone. She's rather hard to kill."

Images of her bloody death flashed in my head. "Oh, she's dead. I saw it myself."

"Perhaps." Gorman winked.

It took a few seconds to realize he was working against me. "Right. She planned to take my power. How?"

"I'm unsure. They have a sector of demons who can transfer power from one individual to another, so I assume she planned to recruit them."

It explained how they stole Deva's magic. "Why would they help her?"

"She worked with the demons regularly. Anitta is behind the Bellicose movement but does not run it, so she uses them to maintain power."

Emine leaned forward, her eyes flashed with extra crazy. "Who *does* run it?"

"I don't know. I never met them."

Chapter Twenty-Seven

Council meetings were becoming my least favorite part of being a queen. I disliked them so much I'd rather run through dragon fire naked than sit through the nonsense the other leaders brought up. Especially as I sat in my office and read through the speech Verity and I worked on for the last four hours.

"It's good, but not great. It needs more pizzaz," she said.

I rubbed my eyes. "There's got to be a better way to convince people to follow me."

"Your magic makes them want to. All you need to do is give them a reason. And wipe the scowl off your face. It makes you look like you hate your job."

If only it were so easy. "I like the problem-solving involved and, believe it or not, the people part. It's sitting in the office or in meetings for hours I don't like. I can't concentrate when I feel trapped. And trying to convince a bunch of paranormals to do something they don't want to do doesn't feel right." I tapped my chest. "Part of my trauma, I suppose."

She held up a hand. "The Council members aren't helpless children. And you're not making them do anything. You're persuading them."

My phone buzzed with a text from Ann Marie saying she was on her way. "Persuading them still feels wrong." I held up my phone. "Advisors incoming."

Verity stood. "Good. Oh, I added the God Cavil to your advisor's list, since he knows more about your magic than you."

I trusted her judgment, so I shrugged. "Fine with me."

My first official advisor's meeting was in the second-floor conference room, where Mat had pinned the former President of Covens to the wall with his katanas. Verity probably scheduled it there on purpose. I sensed Drake drawing closer as I took my seat at the head of the table.

King Olwen of the Snow Elves entered with Razazia on his heels. The involuntary flutter of her wings made her look extra perky. I frowned. "I thought you declined an advisor position."

"Yes. But I also vowed to back you and have become your top recruiter. Besides, you've proven yourself erratic. You need my help."

I held up a hand. "I'm not erratic, but thanks for your recruitment efforts. And for coming."

Drake strode in, scanned the room, and moved toward the chair to my right. He leaned over and gave me a light kiss. Butterflies erupted in my stomach.

"Not appropriate," Quin mumbled as he appeared in his chair on the other side of Drake.

Tracy took the seat across from Quin. "Where's Mat?"

"On his way, I suppose," I answered as I squeezed Drake's knee under the table.

Deva sauntered in, her bronze hair in a complicated braid piled on top of her head. She wore a long black skirt and a crisp white shirt. Her feet were bare. The sadness in her eyes made me want to burst into tears. She chose the chair beside Tracy without uttering a word.

Ann Marie and Jonas came in together and chose seats at the other end of the table. I didn't bother questioning why Jonas was there. Like Razazia, he probably couldn't help himself. As much as the Firsts wanted to detach and do something new, they wanted to protect the coalition more.

The god, Cavil, appeared at the door, a bright smile on his face. "Jenella. Thank you for including me."

"Sure."

He headed toward a chair by Jonas as Mat strutted in. His eyes narrowed when he saw the Firsts, but he didn't say anything as he took his seat. Emine came in behind him, a bag of popcorn in her hand, and took a center chair.

I waited for Verity to close the door and take her seat to my left, then cleared my throat. "We've got some information about the Bellicose leadership, and I need your advice about a few things. I'll try to keep this short."

Deva leaned her elbows on the table. "You've learned who leads them."

"We suspect it's one of our children, most likely Morten, though I can't be sure until I feel the magic Jenella found." Ann Marie could have been talking about the weather rather than her son with her matter-of-fact tone.

Deva's eyes turned predatory. "I see."

I held up a hand. "Nope. We're not turning on each other. I understand you've lost people and want revenge, but it's going to have to wait."

Her fiery eyes turned to me. "Oh?"

I fought not to cower under her glare. "I'm not saying you can't go after them. But let's do it right."

The fire in her eyes grew.

I clasped my hands under the table to hide the shaking.

Drake's growl almost blew my ears out. "Do not attack Jenella, Auntie. It will not end well for you."

She took a breath and nodded. "My apologies, love. My hunting instincts are unsettled since I lost so many dragons."

"No problem."

Razazia pointed at her. "This is exactly why she never had a seat at the table. Dragons are dangerous and can't control themselves."

I almost face-palmed. "Deva is family and welcome at my table any time. And if you came here to shit-stir, you can leave."

"The Bellicose have cursed a hybrid neighborhood and we have reason to believe they'll attack the others soon. Can we drop the bullshit and move on?" Jonas grumbled.

"Exactly." I activated the hologram spell with the Bellicose information on it. "Anitta planned this whole coup, but Gorman said she didn't lead it. We've found evidence of sorcery within some spells, along with an unknown magic."

"The magic on the pyramid from Pyron," Mat said.

"Yes. The Firsts Gorman and Cynthia have been working with the Bellicose. Though, Gorman claims they were coerced and doing the bare minimum. The one they call the King is possibly one of Jonas and Ann Marie's children. The creator of the complicated magic is unknown."

"Do you have a sample?" Cavil asked.

I met his electric blue eyes. "We have it contained in a safe location."

"I'll take you there to examine it when we're done here," Mat said.

Deva leaned forward. "It is not magic born of gods, if that's what you're asking."

Cavil rubbed his chin. "Good. I would still like to examine it."

"Sure." I altered the hologram. "The gargoyles found multiple groups summoning demons in Allure and banished them. They're working in the valley to do the same. Alex, Jonas and Ann Marie's adopted son tried to find information while inside." I tapped my temple to indicate his mental abilities. "Gorman claims the bug magic contains a curse to help it spread and his to keep it from becoming too lethal. Something about how it's tied to demon magic."

Tracy tapped the table. "Makes sense. I mean, I figured because curses are the only type of magic that spreads the way bug magic does."

Ann Marie nodded. "Calvin and I added curse breaking herbs to the potion and tried it on the one Jenella unleashed on the hybrid neighborhood. It didn't work."

I cleared my throat. "It was a mistake. Besides, they were after you, not me. My theory is Cynthia used it to signal Gorman while appeasing the Bellicose leadership."

Olwen flipped his silver-white hair over his shoulder. "And where is the First Gorman?"

"At the council building in a magical box," I answered. "Along with the Ogre Queens. They lied about the curse on the palace and I caught them using some kind of smoky magic to take possession of it."

"Did you absorb it?" The god Cavil asked.

"No. I scanned it. It felt intrusive, so I didn't bother."

"Gorman has more magic than curse breaking," Razazia said. "I wonder if he will talk to me."

"I don't see why not." I held up a hand. "Which leads me to my next question. How do I release him from a magical contract forced on him by a dead woman?"

Cavil shook his head. "You don't. Magical contracts last for the term agreed."

"Gorman was forced to make a contract with Anitta to work against me for the rest of his days. He doesn't want to, and I don't want to put him to sleep or imprison him."

"Why?" Mat asked.

"Because we don't need another major group plunged into chaos."

Quin's head cocked to the left a smidge. "Oh, yes. I am sure an ancient First can be rehabilitated."

"He doesn't need to be rehabilitated," Jonas said. "Gorman was always one of the better Firsts."

Ann Marie nodded. "You can't rescind his oath, but he can redirect it."

My eyebrows drew together. "How?"

"If he's agreed to work against you for the rest of your days, but the oath doesn't say in what capacity, then you can define an unintrusive way to meet the terms."

Verity squirmed in her seat, but shook her head when I turned my attention to her.

I drew a blank and shrugged. "Ideas?"

"Not without the exact wording."

"I mean, it could be something simple, like telling you a lie once per day at a specific time, right? And if you knew it was a lie, he's fulfilling his oath, but you're not affected by it." Tracy tapped her chin. "I'll go with Ann Marie and Razazia to question him and maybe we'll come up with something."

I nodded. "Thank you. The Ogre Queens are loyal to him, but don't have an oath. I'd like to let them go as soon as possible, but still need to discipline them. Before Gorman, they were eager to join our fight. I need ideas about that, too."

"We'll start with Gorman, then decide what to do with them depending on how cooperative he is." Ann Marie said.

"Okay." I swallowed and my eyes swept over Drake, who sat with his elbows resting on the table, his chin on his hands. Not a single emotion filtered through the bond. "It's time we took out the compounds we've been monitoring in the human world."

Jonas shook his head. "We can't. There are too many humans in those areas. If we start a war in the middle of the streets, they'll be all over us."

"I know."

The room went silent.

Tracy shifted in her chair. "Do you mean you know and want to put measures in place to hide our activity? Or you know and don't care if the humans see us?"

"Yes. Both."

Mat's jaw ticked. "That is a risky strategy."

"Yes."

Olwen leaned forward, and a snowflake drifted to the table. "It could throw the entire world into chaos."

"Yes."

Emine opened her bag of popcorn. When she noticed everyone looking at her, she shrugged. "Be prepared for Jen to do crazy shit, is what I always say."

I ignored the dig and glanced in Quin's direction and wished I hadn't. His navy-blue eyes focused on me in a way they never had. It was as if they pierced my soul and dug out my inner secrets. "It is the only route to a swift victory. If you elect to take it, you must consider every nuance and make sound, measured decisions."

The only time Quin said that much without sarcasm was when the situation was dire. I took a deep breath. "Agreed."

"Humans see what they want to see," Verity said in her matter-of-fact way. "If you're smart about it, you might be able to pull it off. Some will ask questions, but most will either make up an explanation to help them feel safe or dismiss it as an anomaly."

Drake leaned back in his chair. "Many of the Bellicose facilities are in human business areas. If we attack at night, it will decrease our exposure. Alex First suggested we use guerilla warfare to take out the smaller apartment complexes before we converge on the larger ones. I like the strategy."

Mat rubbed his chin. "It's still risky. And could cause many deaths."

"There's already been too much death," I said. "Just because they're lower to mid-level in power doesn't mean they aren't ours."

Olwen nodded. "True. But there are many safety measures to take before we deploy this strategy. You have many volunteers for your army, but it lacks leadership and structure."

"Correct. What's the fastest way to assign rank and create a structure?"

"Start with generals you can trust and allow them to appoint the other leaders. Though the generals will need guidance and structure to make sound decisions."

"I want three divisions consisting of varied magic types. We'll add more when other regions begin recruitment efforts. Each division will have one general with twelve companies, squadrons, or platoons. I don't care what they're called. Merit, rather than power level, will determine leadership positions. Meaning lower and mid-level paranormals who show leadership abilities can advance. Those twelve sub-divisions can be divided at the General's discretion. Thoughts?"

Mat rubbed his chin. "You've thought this through and didn't say a word."

"Yes."

My advisors were silent for a few seconds.

I threw out my hands. "Why is that such a shock?"

"Because until now you've lacked strategic abilities," Quin answered.

A laugh escaped Tracy. "Those of us close to Jen should have seen this coming. I mean, she's a puzzle solver and creating an army is a puzzle."

I pointed at her. "Exactly. The coalition is wounded and bleeding. If we don't start healing soon, we might bleed out. Forming the army and saving the hybrids is a good start. If you have an alternate idea, I'm all ears. If not, let's figure out how to make this one work. I'm fine with either choice. But I will not approve ideas unless they align with my goals."

"Which are?" Ann Marie asked.

"To end this coup, gain support of the factions, and earn the trust of the hybrids. Then, I want everyone to work together better. To value their people more, no matter the power level. We need to take measures so this doesn't happen again."

"I like the formation you proposed," Deva said. "We need to end this nonsense swiftly and decisively."

Drake put his hand over mine. "If we are to do this, we need to organize fast. Which means drawing on every resource we have at our disposal."

"And to create a structured, trained army with zero time to do it," Mat agreed. "The first step is picking trustworthy generals who are motivated to help with the efforts and understand command."

Razazia waved a hand. "I have taken on the recruitment efforts, but I will not lead an army."

"The attacks will need to be coordinated," Jonas said. "And communication spells established."

Ann Marie shook her head. "Although I like the idea of getting rid of the Bellicose and moving on with our lives, I don't like the risk. And the hybrids won't work with you."

I folded my hands. "We're doing all we can to right those wrongs. Use that to convince them I'm on their side."

"Not we," Jonas growled. "You. No one else is so much as lifting a finger."

"Did you not see the number of magic users who showed up to build your pocket?" Drake asked. "Jenella didn't order a single person to be present. They volunteered."

Ann Marie shook her head. "Creating one pocket doesn't make up for over twenty years of abuse."

"Nor should it," Mat said. "But it is more than I was able to do and far more than our mother would have done."

I cleared my throat. "I'm not looking for praise and won't argue about the past. We need solutions and to act fast. To do that, I need every single one of you helping."

Cavil raised his hand. "I don't see where I fit into this conversation. I've only recently come to this realm."

A smile spread across my face. "So glad you asked. I'd like you to become my minister of magic. Which means if this goes south and we are exposed to humans, you'll be our ambassador and use your overwhelming charisma to smooth things out. You'll also be responsible for our army's magical roadmap. With it, my generals can assign people to teams where they will be most effective. It will give you a bigger following and grow your sunshine aura."

"You want me to use my light magic on demons, even though I made it clear I didn't want to take part in your war."

"It would be helpful, yes. But I won't make either banishing demons or fighting for me a condition of your position. You can work behind the scenes."

Cavil inclined his head. "Very well. I accept."

"Thank you." I tapped my chin. "I want Quin, King Olwen, and Glacintial as my generals. You will coordinate with them, should they accept the position."

Mat leaned forward and rested his elbows on the table. "And what roles do you have for the rest of us?"

"You, Deva, Ann Marie, and Jonas need to coordinate people." I turned to Razazia. "I want you to continue to recruit and become my chief strategist."

Her eyes narrowed. "Why?"

"Because you're a sneaky bitch and we're going to need those skills. Start with taking care of Gorman and the Ogre Queens."

Her lips twitched, but she said nothing.

I turned my attention to Tracy. "I need you to work in logistics. Find the things we're missing and fill the gaps. Hire and move people around as needed. That sort of stuff."

She nodded.

I met Drake's eyes. A bolt of lightning shot through me when I saw the respect in them. "As we've all learned from previous battles, I suck at war. I need you to lead my generals."

His eyes danced with amusement. "I shall try."

I focused on the table to imagine different scenarios. "Alex is sneakier than Razazia. He should be included in this."

"No," Jonas growled.

"Absolutely not," Ann Marie said.

I shrugged. "If he's not included, he'll strike out on his own and probably drag Lily with him. But he's a hybrid and your son, so it's your call."

I hesitated to make my next statement, but it needed to be said. "The scary bartender needs to be in a leadership position. And Lily needs to be part of the army. Maybe she can lead a team in Quin's division."

Ann Marie jumped out of her chair. "Are you insane?"

"Most likely, if my family history is any indicator. But that's not the point. She's got the power of Lilith, so people will follow her. On top of that, she's not afraid of Quin, so they'll work well together. And the bartender..."

"Dale."

"Right. Dale has natural leadership abilities. I want him on our team."

"I'll ask them, but I don't like it," Jonas said before Ann Marie could respond.

"Noted." I used one of Mat's favorite responses. "Emine, while we're working in the human world, I need you to coordinate the Enforcers worldwide to raid any suspected Bellicose locations. Develop an intelligence branch to feed us information so we don't miss obvious things like bug magic inside The Cauldron."

She shook her bag of popcorn. "Like an anti-stupid task force?"

"Exactly. I want intelligence. A daily or weekly report about what's going on in every pocket. Tap the PISD and hire detective for it if you need to."

"What about the battle?"

"You might need to sit this one out, but we'll use you and the enforcers as backup if needed."

CHAPTER TWENTY-EIGHT

I threw my hood over my head to block the wind as I dragged my tired butt to the council building the next morning. We'd spent all day and a chunk of the night planning. In the end, we agreed on a mixture of small and large attacks with heavy hybrid involvement since they knew the area.

Ann Marie was convinced we wouldn't be able to hide our efforts from the humans. She was right, but the longer they hunkered down, the more time they had to perfect their experimental magic.

"You're quiet this morning." Drake handed me a hot cup of coffee.

"I'm starting to understand why you're not a morning person." I took a sip, then gave the cup a death stare while the burns in my mouth healed.

He chuckled. "I'm better than I used to be."

"No kidding? Then you must have been a total curmudgeon before," I teased. He was grumpy in the mornings, but not so bad he became an ass. At least, not to me.

He opened the door and motioned me inside. "I still am. You're just blinded by my good looks and winning personality."

"You mean that as a joke, but no statement has ever been truer. I've never seen a more beautiful creature, inside and out, in all three of your forms."

The smile melted off his face. "You mean that."

My heart pounded, and I closed my eyes. "Sorry."

His arm wrapped around me, and he pulled me against him. "Don't apologize for surprising me." He kissed my temple. "No one has ever thought me beautiful before."

"I find that hard to believe." I snuggled closer and absorbed his warmth and his unique scent. "They were probably scared to tell you because you're also terrifying."

His laughter was music to my ears. When a door slammed somewhere in the building, he lifted my chin and brushed his lips against mine. "We'll need to discuss my beauty later."

I stepped back. "I can't wait." We headed toward where we kept Gorman and the Ogre Queens.

Razazia stood in front of the clear magical box and shifted as we entered the room. "Jenella, Drake. I think we've found a solution."

Gorman stood as I approached. "Yes. We have discussed the oaths Anitta made me take. There were only four. We've discovered three got released upon her death. The vow to work against you was not specific."

I crossed my arms. "What were the exact words?"

"Pardon?"

"The exact words of the oath. What were they?"

"Oh, yes. Of course. I will leave out the swearing part, but the words were 'to work to sabotage the success of the third queen of Ahl every day for the rest of my life.'"

Razazia laughed. "It's vague. Though, it doesn't surprise me, considering Anitta had the critical thinking skills of a gnat. But it means we can find one thing to sabotage daily to fulfill his oath."

The door swung open and Jonas appeared. He moved to the box holding the two-eyed Ogre Queen. "What in the hell is this?" He waved his arm toward the clear magical boxes.

"They're temporary."

He lifted a finger and tapped it. "Huh. Looks like Lily's magic without the..." he waved a hand in a circle.

I nodded. "She taught me how to make them. I like her version better."

His lips twitched. "So, how do we release our old friend?"

"Gorman is required to work to sabotage Jenella's success every day," Razazia said. "Anitta didn't even have the decency to specify the requirements."

"She wouldn't," I said as I tried to think of something for him to sabotage. "Because she'd want to dictate his actions."

Gorman cleared his throat. "To be fair, I rarely saw her. Her demons would visit with orders."

"What demons and where?" Drake asked.

"Various places throughout the world. She's worked with demons since before the conception of Jaques."

Jonas waved a dismissive hand. "It doesn't matter. What matters is we clean up this shit show before the Leadership Council assembles."

I took a small step forward. "The oath doesn't say how many times, or what you need to screw up, correct?"

"Correct," Gorman agreed.

Razazia leaned against a support pillar. "His oath does not mention scale, so it can be a small thing."

I nodded. "Titus?"

Verity's match and my crown juror stood from the chair where he'd observed our exchange. "Yes?"

"Can you read oaths by touching him?"

"I can." Titus rubbed his chin. "Would you like me to extract all existing magical contracts involving you?"

"Please do." I dissipated Gorman's box.

I felt Drake tense beside me as Titus stretched out a hand and touched Gorman's. "It's the only one, though he lied about the wording. He must do everything he can to sabotage your success for all his days."

"Right, so not just one thing." I scratched my head. "And Cynthia has a similar oath?"

"Unknown," Gorman answered.

"Lie." Jonas tapped his nose.

"Then I need to learn how to dissolve a magical contract before we let him go."

"I can do that," Verity said from her desk. "I think. Maybe."

We swung toward her as a group, and I held up a hand. "Wait. What? You knew that and didn't tell me?"

She shrugged. "I'm not a hundred percent sure I can. It's something I've been practicing with Charlotte. The urban sprites weren't happy with her career choice and made her take a ton of oaths to keep their secrets before she came to work with us. I'm not great at it."

It would be handy if I could absorb her magic as she did it. "Show me."

Gorman raised his hands in a defensive position. "You would experiment on me?"

"Yes."

Verity shook out her hands and squared her shoulders. "Give me your hand, please."

He took a step back. "No. I won't have this."

I opened my mouth to order him to stop, but she lunged toward him and slapped both hands on his arm. He dropped to the ground, unconscious.

I bit my lip to keep from laughing when she jumped back and did a little dance. "Oops. I forget how many sins the old people have committed."

"Perhaps this isn't the best solution." Jonas's voice was laced with humor.

Though Verity understood our value system better, she still held onto her human beliefs. And no matter how much practice and training she had, touching people was still automatic for her.

Titus moved to her side. "Close your eyes and concentrate before you touch him again."

"Right." She took a deep breath, let it out, and closed her eyes. "Okay. I got this."

I reached out and sipped her magic when she activated it. It felt the same as always, so I backed off. I'd need to think about it later.

"This is complicated," her voice was barely a murmur. "There's a contract to sabotage each of you that kind of circles around his oath to the crown of Ahl. Like a mastermind constructed them."

"Focus on those. Keep your concentration and reverse them all if you can. Keep his oath to the crown," Titus instructed in a soft voice.

"Oooh. That one's nasty." Verity shifted her weight closer to Titus. "Easy. Not amusing. There it is." She ramped up her power level, then injected it in a way I'd never felt before.

'Crack!'

I got lifted off my feet and wrapped in scales before I registered the sound.

"*What was that?*" Jonas's voice boomed through the council chamber.

"Sorry!" came Verity's panicked voice. "It's a side effect of breaking an oath."

Drake released me and retracted his scales. "The question is not how you used the magic, but how you got it. Being a full-blooded juror mage, you should not have well-developed oath breaker abilities."

I swung toward him. "What do you mean?"

"It is not a magic found in this realm."

"I thought you said I could break oaths."

"Because you're the queen. This is different."

Razazia's wings created a breeze as she lowered herself from the ceiling. "We had a First lined up to come with us to this realm who had those abilities, but she got killed two days before we gathered."

I shook my head. "Magic decides those things, not us. And Verity's a brutally honest person, so it doesn't surprise me she got the gift."

Verity stood and stepped back as Gorman stirred. "Well, that got away from me. I accidentally broke all his oaths except the one to the Crown."

My head pounded by the time we left the council chambers. We didn't gain additional support. The leaders didn't listen to my declaration about complaining and reverted to their old, petty arguments. Drake had to roar twice to stop fights, and I had to slam two leaders into their chairs to keep them from starting a magic duel.

I rubbed my eyes as we made our way back to the castle, then bit my tongue to keep from exclaiming, 'I hate my job.' When the thought registered as a lie, my forehead crinkled. "Huh." I ignored the confused faces of my entourage and continued walking. "We don't have time for this," I ground out after taking a few steps.

Drake didn't need to say anything because the look he gave me said it all. He was getting sick of my impatience.

"You're right." I took a deep breath.

"Break it down," Mat ordered from behind me.

"The leaders without a passable human form have valid concerns. They're easy targets for humans. The smaller groups who don't have people to spare are also right to resist allowing their people to sign up for the army. Part of it is my fault. I've intimidated the leaders who still believe the hybrids are expendable, so they won't discuss the issue. They'll just keep voting against them. And I can understand the larger groups not wanting to risk the lives of even more of their people. I don't want that, either."

"But?"

"But the shifters and witches are the biggest problem. I trust Calvin, but I don't trust the individual covens not to betray us. And I trust Jonas, but not the shifters. They've always been sneaky."

"Yes. Gabe and Linda's betrayal proved that point." Mat's voice sounded bitter. "But most shifters are also fiercely loyal to Jonas. It may work to our advantage."

"Not if Morten is the Bellicose King, which I'm almost certain he is. If so, their loyalty will be split."

Drake squeezed my hand. "Not necessarily. Jonas is their creator and will always have a hold over them that no other leader can duplicate."

"Perhaps we should present them with a choice of strategies," Olwen said.

I didn't even realize he'd followed us. I stopped in my tracks and turned toward him. "What do you mean?"

"After Razazia went to sleep, the elves were lost without her. So much so, we almost went to war."

"I read about that. You came to an agreement without intervention."

"Correct. We saved ourselves a war by holding a summit. Each elven leader brought a proposal to the table. We used them to make an agreement."

"You're saying we should have a summit with the Bellicose?" As soon as the words left my mouth, I wanted to take them back. "Never mind. So, I should ask each leader to propose a strategy that works for them?"

"Or present them with several options and mold it into something most leaders can agree to."

I tapped my chin. "You're right. We should have thought about it before the meeting."

"Correct," Mat said. "We are not the dumbest leadership to ever exist, but it's close."

"It's because we're moving so fast. We need to pay more attention to detail. Let's meet in my office in an hour. We'll work through the night if we need to."

"Should I notify your advisors?" Verity asked.

"Yes. And see if Ara, Lily, and Alex want to attend. Invite the Pixie Queen and the Manticore King to represent the small groups and the groups without a human form."

"Done."

I picked up a nameplate and scanned the circle for a place to put it. It was the third meeting in as many days and I shuffled everyone around each morning, then again during the lunch break.

"This isn't how to win friends and influence people."

I shrugged as I sealed the nameplate onto a table. "Who needs friends?"

Verity chuckled. "Not you, apparently."

Mat came through the door, scanned the name tags, and groaned. "Yesterday, you sat me beside the Chimera King and now you want me next to the Kelpie Queen?"

"I want to see if she squeals like she did when I put her between Quin and Deva."

He pinched the bridge of his nose. "So, this is for your entertainment."

"No. It's to stop their stupid power struggles. The entertainment is a bonus."

"Then I will look extra deadly."

A sloppy smile formed on my face. "And ramp up your magic when she's contrary for no reason. Maybe it'll shake her up and she'll forget her argument."

He shook his head as he took his seat. "This is not the conventional way to solve infighting, but it's effective."

"Verity gave me the idea. She said a teacher used it on school children to break up friend groups."

"And stop bullying. He used assigned seating to keep the students who got bullied safe, though he didn't form the desks into a circle."

I rested my hands on my hips. "We have plenty of bullies."

"It's in the job description," Mat agreed. "How long will this experiment continue?"

"After lunch, I'm removing the name plates. If they fight for status again, then I'll start over."

He inclined his head. "The plans need to be finalized today. We've had thousands across the world request a position in your new army."

My head shot up. "Really?"

"Yes. They keep calling my office."

"Send them to us," Verity said. "I've got an entire staff working on taking their information and assigning rank. As soon as we have the Council's approval, we'll bring them in for training."

When I came up with the idea to form an army, I thought about the basic logistics but didn't know nearly enough to take on such a large-scale task. I tapped my foot. "Contact the highest ranking person in each pocket and have them sort out the pecking order and send it to the three generals."

"And if they choose their lackeys?" Mat asked.

I rubbed my tired eyes. "We solidified the leadership requirements yesterday. I think. If they don't comply, then I or one of my advisors will need to pay them a visit to sort it out."

His face softened. "Although you didn't want any of this, you are becoming an excellent queen."

I swallowed back the tears that sprung to my eyes. "Thank you. I still feel like I'm caged sometimes, but it's not as bad as I thought."

"Because you're changing it to fit your will."

I ignored the sick feeling in my stomach that gnawed at me when I thought about being trapped under a crown for life. "I'm trying."

Mat inclined his head. "That you are." He motioned toward the tables. "And you're making a difference."

I hoped so, though I had my doubts. I still didn't care enough and wasn't doing enough. Though, according to Deva, a good leader never feels satisfied with her efforts. "Thank you." I barely settled on my makeshift throne when the door to the chambers swung open and the leaders poured in.

I fought to keep my eyes open as the Fairy Queen droned on about how her people wouldn't make it in the human world. We'd already solidified our war plans, so Drake left to handle the implementation. Which meant he wasn't there to wake me up or conjure coffee. He'd spoiled me rotten, and I hadn't even realized it. I stretched and took a sip of water.

"Am I boring you, Your Grace?"

"Yes." The word left my mouth before my brain engaged. "But it's not your fault. I haven't slept much in the last few days. Please continue."

Her eyes narrowed. "This is a legitimate concern. Many of us will be stuck inside the pockets and unable to escape when the humans come after us."

"I understand. Though I doubt they'll find the pockets, even if they find the gates."

The room went silent.

"What do you mean?" The Manticore King asked.

"The gates aren't always near the pockets, but a portal. If they find a gate, we can move it to another location." I'd learned that from Prince Leebol. The gate to Allure was in the central Idaho mountains, but the pocket was deep in the rugged forest where there weren't roads or humans. In theory, I could move the gate if needed. Though I still had a lot to learn about how. "If we needed to, we could connect the pockets to each other and be done with humans. Though I'd hate to take that route because we use a lot of their inventions to advance our own society."

"Then it's settled," Deva drawled. "Can we move on now?"

Deva was the most patient dragon I'd ever met. If she was trying to move the meeting along, we'd gotten off track.

I squared my shoulders. "We can. Tarquin, Olwen, and Glacintial are the appointed generals. They're forming teams to infiltrate and take out the Bellicose bases as we speak. When we move on them, attacks on Allure and the other pockets might increase. Emine has the enforcers on alert and working with the individual pocket leadership. Coalition members need to be prepared to fight and help noncombatants. Especially since they can summon demons and spread curses. Thoughts?"

Tracy and I landed in the flashing circle behind the little house we'd lived in for the last couple of years. My heart ached with a sense of nostalgia as we headed toward the back door. "I'm going to miss this place."

"Me, too." Tracy opened the back door and waved me through. "It still feels like home."

I plopped down on the sofa and closed my eyes. "Yeah. I can't sell it, but don't want it to sit empty, either."

"You can rent it to a hybrid who needs a house in Allure."

I cracked an eye open. "Like Alex and Lily."

She grinned. "Or someone who the dragons and vampires aren't obsessed with for a change."

"I'm sure the neighbors would appreciate that."

We sat in silence for a while. "Jen, will we really be able to hide our war from humans?"

"Not a chance. Though Ann Marie is working on spells to keep our exposure to a minimum."

"Yeah. My dad is helping her with some potions. I guess they're friends now."

"That's good. Maybe it'll give the witches who don't support his presidency a reason to change their minds."

She snorted. "Fat chance."

"Yeah, it's a long shot, but one can hope."

"I love your optimism. And naivety. The combination is badass."

A laugh escaped me.

Then she laughed.

And it made me laugh more.

Before we knew it, we were both bent over, holding our stomachs, laughing.

I sat up and swiped my sleeve across my eyes. "I don't even know what's so funny."

"Me either. It's possible we're both so tired that everything is hilarious."

Chapter Twenty-Nine

THE COLD, DRENCHING TURQUOISE rain made my ears ache, and my nose run as I stood on the hill inside the hybrid pocket and looked over the swarm of paranormals gathered below. Hybrids intermingled with groups of elves, while blurs of vampires zipped through the crowd.

Bright wings fluttered as fairies carried supplies through the camp. A straight line of shifters marched toward the command tent, where Jonas strategized with my team. Cavil stood in the center of a mesmerized group of soldiers, his light shining brighter than before. Tearing my eyes away, I tried to count the different factions. It was impossible because there were clusters of just about every paranormal group in the crowd, including hybrids. "Isn't this overkill?"

Drake wrapped an arm around my waist and pulled me close. "It is. The hybrids are determined to defend their way of life, and your allies want to support the efforts."

I soaked up his warmth as I swiped a sopping wet curl out of my face. "How is everyone getting along?"

"The environment is...uncomfortable. The hybrids don't trust us, but tolerate our presence because they don't stand a chance without our help."

My stomach turned. If we couldn't hold it together long enough to take out the Bellicose, then we were screwed. I took a deep breath and snuggled closer. "Am I doing the right thing?"

"I'm unsure. But it may save a lot of lives. It also has the potential to mend relationships. Or it could backfire, and many more paranormals will die. It is the chance we take with every war."

For a split second, I wished he'd lied to me and told me everything would be okay. But he'd pledged his honesty, even when I didn't want to hear it. I'd just have to suck it up. "I hope I don't get everyone killed."

"It is a risky strategy, and you should prepare yourself for an unfavorable outcome. But if it's successful, it will solve many of our most pressing problems."

Risk and reward. And it was too late to change my mind, so I stepped away, squared my shoulders and nodded. "Let's go meet with the advisors."

As we made our way toward the command tent, paranormals stepped out of our way. Some still bowed, but most didn't. I took sips of magic, and stopped and chatted as we went, especially when I came across a group of hybrids. I knew they'd never fully trust me, but it didn't hurt to build a little rapport.

The conversation between my advisors died when we stepped through the tent flap.

My eyes narrowed as I marched toward an empty chair. "What?"

"The Bellicose were alerted to our plans. They've taken over the human courthouse and are holding multiple hostages." Mat's tone was conversational, as if he were discussing the weather.

I lowered myself into a seat. "Oh?"

Razazia examined her nails. "Even a moron would realize we didn't eliminate all the traitors."

Drake rested a hand on my back. "Razazia's right. We expected something like this to happen and planned accordingly."

I swung my head toward him and raised an eyebrow.

His lips twitched. "We won't do anything about it."

"We couldn't if we wanted to," Olwen said in an even tone. Though I could tell it bothered him based on the sudden temperature drop. "The human police have surrounded the building, and more are arriving each minute. If we take the bait, the Bellicose will simply kill the human hostages and blame you."

"They might do that anyway," Jonas interjected. "But I doubt it. They have as much, if not more, to lose as we do should the humans come after us."

Mat nodded. "Correct. We had to change our plans."

I folded my hands on the makeshift table. "How so?"

Lily zipped into the tent, smashed into my side, and landed in the chair beside me. "Sorry. So, Roman and his vampires are in the area. The police think it's a court-related situation. He'll update us on any new developments."

"Thank you, Lily." Mat turned his attention to me. "And to answer your question, we're going to attack all known hideouts at once." He flicked a spell and a hologram of the city formed over the table. "They have offices throughout Nampa and Caldwell, and their residences are scattered throughout the valley. All apartment complexes. We will send our groups out, eliminate their protective magic, and herd them to this park." He pointed to a green void on the map. "Ann Marie already set up a privacy spell with repellent to keep humans away. The bulk of our army will wait for them there, while the attack squads eliminate their offices and residences."

Jonas whistled. "That's too much distance. There's no way we'll be able to herd them all into that park. And a chase through the valley will be messy."

Deva shifted in her seat. "We could burn them to the ground and eliminate the threat. The humans would think they are being attacked by terrorists and we will remain hidden."

"Absolutely not!" Alex's exclamation drew everyone's attention. "You could start a war and kill thousands of humans."

"It wouldn't be the first time," Ara drawled. "We often do what we must to protect our own."

"True," I said. "And it's a viable option. But let's discuss alternatives." I could have patted myself on the back for my diplomatic answer until I scanned the pinched faces of my advisors and saw I wasn't fooling anyone. "Fine. It's not an option. I don't want to be responsible for human deaths. If we're going to expose ourselves, then I want to be seen as the ones protecting humans, not starting wars to save our own asses."

"Expose ourselves, eh?" Lily chuckled. "Jen's right. We need to be seen as heroes and protectors."

"Even then, they might try to eliminate us," Ann Marie muttered. "We need better options."

Quin conjured his sword and examined the blade. "Let's argue in circles while the Bellicose slaughter hybrids."

Drake leaned his elbows on the table, then removed them when it groaned under his weight. "I agree with the vampire. We will use the same strategy, but adjust it. Instead of several minor attacks, we attack all known locations at once. Should they pursue us, we'll lead them to the park."

Mat ran a hand through his hair. "And the humans?"

Everyone turned to me for a decision.

I rubbed my sour stomach. "Some of our army will need to be in the areas surrounding the Bellicose apartments to protect humans. We can't use the park."

Ann Marie nodded. "I don't like the park idea either. What are your reasons?"

"I have a bad feeling about fighting downtown. I've been in Lily's van as she tried to navigate the maze of roads. Jonas is right. It's too much distance to cover, especially since the bulk of their apartment complexes are at the edges of the city. Aside from the distance, they have our plans. So, let's change them and not tell anyone."

"Burn them down," Deva said in a sing-song voice.

"Slaughter them," Ara agreed.

My head started pounding, and I rubbed my temples. "I understand you're all pissed and want revenge. I am, too. But I'd like to make smart decisions for once."

Tracy coughed to hide a laugh. "Sorry. But Jen's right. How about we try to find an alternate strategy using the good parts of our original plan?"

"Like?" Drake asked.

She threw her hands in the air. "Like use the guerrilla style attacks without burning down the city. Or maybe taking out the Bellicose leadership without leaving a trail of bodies for the humans to find."

"Oh, they'd never find the bodies," Ara said.

"My fires are hotter than lava and very controlled," Deva agreed.

I face-palmed. "Ooooor, we could change the location we lead them to and then you can do your recruitment murder thing."

Razazia conjured a large leaf and fanned herself. "So we're going with a simple solution."

"Too easy," Jonas said. "They're not going to chase us into a trap, no matter where we set it."

I leaned back and folded my arms. "Then we take them out where they live. Increase the size of the attack teams. Make sure we have enough people in the area to fight and to protect humans." I held up a hand. "Before we do that, we need to expose our leak. Send the teams to the hybrid neighborhoods as planned, but have them observe and report. Tell them we need to check out the courthouse before we act. Deva, you and your dragons go burn their businesses down. Don't alert anyone or harm any humans. And make sure the fire doesn't spread."

"Of course, love." Her predatory smile sent shivers down my spine.

"Ara, send your spies to the neighborhoods ahead of our teams to gather information. Mat, Ann Marie, and I will go to the park and pretend I want to check it out. We'll make fake plans while Ann Marie pulls her spells. Drake, Bastien, and Tracy will go with us and stay cloaked. See if you can find their spies and don't reveal yourselves. I'll flash us back here if we're attacked."

"And if we're not attacked, but they're spying?"

"Then we feed them false information. They think I'm weak and Drake's running things. We play it off like we're helping the hybrids because he wants Jonas to accept him." I winced at my own words. I knew being rejected by the other Firsts was a sore spot for Drake, and using it as a manipulation tactic felt dirty. "Or we can pretend to hate the hybrids or something. Maybe contemplate whether they're worth saving." Using

Lily's insecurities didn't feel better. I closed my eyes. "I don't like using either of those tactics. It feels icky."

When I opened my eyes, the entire table stared at me contemplatively.

Jonas stretched his arm across Ann Marie's back. "And here we thought Jenella was so much less manipulative than her mother."

I almost heaved. "I'm not thrilled to have come up with the idea and doubt I can pull it off."

"It's good," Ann Marie said. "But we need to give them something else to attack."

I didn't respond because I was too busy sucking air in through my nose and exhaling out my mouth to keep from throwing up.

Jonas rubbed his chin. "We've got a couple of fields warded to hide us from humans. We fought a group of them there not long ago. Say you're going to park the army there until you figure out a new strategy."

"And the apartment complexes?" Alex asked.

"Nothing happens until our spies identify and kill the traitor. Upon their death, sew your seeds of doubt and manipulation, let the dragon fire fall from the skies, and the glorious blood rain from the apartment buildings."

The way Quin talked about death and blood was so poetic, my mouth dropped open.

Ara clutched her heart and grinned from ear-to-ear. "Such a romantic."

I cleared my throat. "Right."

Drake stood. "Ara will stay at central command. Reassign the extra members of the army to human protection and battle intervention. Ensure their skills are used efficiently. Everyone goes to their assigned locations and waits for Ara's command to proceed. As soon as the businesses burn, send the dragons to the subdivisions as backup." He held out a hand to help me up. "We only have one chance, so stay vigilant and do not fuck it up."

CHAPTER THIRTY

THE CITY FELT UNUSUALLY quiet as we flew toward downtown. A few lights from human vehicles moved down the streets, but not as many as during the day. I wrapped my coat tighter and leaned against my favorite spike. Bastien, with Tracy on his back, circled above while Drake made a zigzag pattern across the park.

In front of me, Ann Marie clutched another spike so hard her knuckles were white. "I thought this would be more fun."

"It *is* fun." I scanned the ground but couldn't see the paranormals I sensed. "They have about twenty shifters spread throughout the park. Raccoons or badgers, I think. Maybe both." I closed my eyes. "I still don't like using Drake and Lily's insecurities."

Use mine. I no longer care about fitting in. Drake sent a wisp of soothing emotions through our bond. *Ara has confirmed the death of three traitors.*

"Three?"

"It doesn't matter how many, as long as they're out of the way." Ann Marie shook her head. "And don't think for a second you're becoming your mother. She would have never have even contemplated the pain this idea would cause."

I took a deep breath. "Right."

"When you're ready," Mat said from behind me.

I flashed us to the center of the park near where I sensed Bellicose spies and eyed the large open space. "This is it?"

"Yes," Mat said. "It is the only park large enough."

I pointed. "I sense something in that direction."

"The courthouse where they took human hostages."

I waved a dismissive hand. "What happens to humans is none of our concern. No, this park won't work."

Ann Marie crossed her arms. "You should be concerned about the humans."

"Correct," Mat said. "We cannot attack the courthouse, but we must investigate."

"No need. When this is over, I'm ordering everyone back into the pockets. I would have done it already if Drake wasn't trying to appease Jonas."

Mat stomped across the grass and spun toward me. "You let him have far too much power over you. It is not his place."

I turned away from him and took a few steps. "I'm not having this argument again. The hybrids got themselves into this mess, so they can get themselves out of it."

"You are their queen."

"Not according to them."

"If you don't help us, then I'll make sure Jonas never speaks to Drake again." Ann Marie flashed across the park to retrieve her spell, then reappeared. "And another thing. If you don't like this park, pick another place, but you're going to help."

"Fine. But I'm not moving my army here."

"It's too late to change plans," Mat growled.

"I don't care. Jonas's support isn't worth waging a war in this park. Especially since you can't even guarantee the Bellicose will follow us all the way down here."

Ann Marie threw her hands in the air. "We don't want a war! We want them out of our neighborhoods."

"Then push them out. But I'm disbanding the army."

"And the humans?" Mat asked.

"Not my problem. If they expose us, we'll bury the story like we always do."

Ann Marie shook her head. "I'll tell you what. If you agree to help the hybrids, I'll let your army camp on my property until it's time."

I sighed. "Drake would like it if I helped Jonas."

Mat shook his head. "You are the queen, not *Drake*."

My shoulders slumped. "I just want everyone to get along."

He latched onto my arm. "Impossible. We'll abandon the plan to use this park. We have a week to gather our forces and develop a new strategy."

"Agreed," Ann Marie said. "Let's go tell the others the change in plans."

I flashed us to Drake's back.

When we landed inside the pocket, the camp was buzzing with activity. Witches and mages circled the tents, handing out spells, while the elves formed people into teams. Pixies swarmed above them, shedding sparkly dust all over everyone. The boggart lady who ran the hybrid intake facility, Maria, handed out supplies. Half naked ogres danced in a circle around a fire on the far side, pounding large clubs on the ground every few seconds.

Our command tent was in the center of the camp, so I headed in that direction. "How did we do?"

"We did fine. Now, we wait to see if they take the bait." Mat scanned the area. "How many did we reassign to Jonas's field?"

"Several teams," Ann Marie answered. "They'll be our backup if this whole thing goes south."

We gathered in the command tent. Holograms of the neighborhoods showed attack teams preparing to take out the Bellicose. As expected, many hybrids refused to move to the new pocket. In fact, many of them were going about their business, pretending to be human.

"I don't understand why they won't evacuate."

"They think they can defend themselves." Jonas stood at the other side of the table sipping coffee.

"They don't look too alert."

"Looks can be deceiving."

"They're out there mowing their lawns and playing sports."

Tracy slid into the chair beside me. "I mean, my dad and his covens have gone through and given them bug magic potions and taught their magic users your anti-demon spell, so they have a chance."

I knew they were working on potions for the hybrids, but didn't realize they'd already distributed them. "Your dad moves fast. I need more regular status reports."

Jonas set his coffee cup down. "Hybrids are resilient. They'll do okay."

His calm demeanor was getting on my last nerve. "How did you get coffee?"

His forehead creased. "I made it."

"Will you show me how?"

"No need. There's a pot right there." He pointed to a silver contraption on the snack table at the end of the tent.

I wondered over to the device and leaned down to examine it.

Tracy hip-checked me out of the way. "You need to work on your cluelessness."

I threw my braid over my shoulder. "Among a million other things." I watched as she pulled a lever and coffee came out. "Is there always coffee in there, or do you have to refill it?"

"You not only have to refill it but use soap and water to wash everything in between batches," Jonas's voice was more instructional than judgmental.

"No kidding? Seems like a lot of work." I took the cup from Tracy and eyed the condiments. I knew how to use those.

"Not as much as you'd think, especially if you do it as you go."

"Huh." I took a sip and returned to the most stable-looking metal chair. Though none of them were too sturdy. The coffee wasn't as good as Drake's, but not bad. "Where is everyone?" The three of us were the only ones in the command tent. I knew Drake took Glacintial to patrol and a few advisors went to get some sleep, but I was getting restless. I hated sitting around waiting.

Jonas lowered himself to the chair across from me. "How much combat training do you two have?"

"We don't have any," Tracy answered. "I mean, if you discount the several skirmishes and two major battles Jen dragged me into."

His lips twitched. "Those were primarily magic battles, correct?"

I wondered where he was going with the conversation, so I gave him my full attention. "On our end, yes. Tracy's effective at slinging her spells and potions from Bastien's back."

"And you?"

My cheeks heated. "I have a habit of exploding my magic in intense situations. It's not ideal."

"I see. Yet you plan to take part in a battle where humans are close enough to notice."

"Yes."

He leaned forward. "If your magic explodes, it will take out Ann Marie's shields and expose us. I don't know what kind of head up the ass strategy Mat used while raising you, or why Drake hasn't had the balls to point it out, but without training, you are a liability."

A lump formed in my throat so thick I had to swallow to clear it. I didn't like his criticism of Mat and Drake, but he had a point. I wasn't trained, nor did I understand my magic well enough not to circumvent Ann Marie's. "Quin mentioned it, as has Drake. I think." I couldn't remember if he had or not, but assumed he did, and I ignored him.

Tracy put a hand on my arm. "Mat spent her childhood trying to keep her alive. He did the best he could."

"I call bullshit. Because the best way to keep someone alive is to teach them how to fight for their own life. Mathias understands this, yet he didn't bother."

"I learned self-defense, but I'm no warrior. Most of my training focused on how to rule."

"Same with me, except the ruling part," Tracy said. "We can hold our own in a fight. Besides, Bas doesn't let me out of his sight when danger is near."

"Stupid." He tapped his chin. "I'd train you like we did Alex and Lily, but there's no time. This battle is going to be very different from the ones in the pockets. Bloodier. More vicious. I suggest you stay with your mates. If you get separated, flash to another First." He pointed at Tracy. "You need to wear armor and hightail it out of the action if things get hairy."

I stared at my coffee. "I don't need to become Lily. Mat wants me to work over-watch so Ara can fight. But I need the people to see I'm willing to go to battle with them, so I'm going to."

"Yeah. And I'll take a healing potion and stay with Bas, who always stays close to Drake."

"Very well." Jonas took a sip of coffee. "Just watch your asses."

My eyebrows drew together. "Why are you so worried about us?"

"For many reasons. But mainly because leaders who deal in hope, who strive for peace and unity instead of more power, are rare. It's vital we preserve them for as long as we can."

My heart stopped. And I fought the urge to hop out of my chair and dance the jig while singing, 'I won Jonas over.' Instead, I sipped my coffee and tried to pretend my hand wasn't shaking. "Thank you."

He stood. "Stay alive." Jonas swept out of the tent.

Tracy and I had huge, goofy grins on our faces when our eyes met, but I kept my mouth shut. I didn't want to jinx it.

Boom!

I flew out of my chair. A huge plume of smoke and rubble shot into the air as a large apartment complex on a busy road exploded. Dust coated the observation spell, and the hologram went dark. "What the hell is that?"

Boom!

Another one detonated.

One by one, the hologram spells went down. It was mere moments before our people planned to attack their residences.

I wrapped my arms around myself and tore my eyes away. "What the hell just happened?"

"They called our bluff." Drake turned to Quin. "Is everyone in place?"

"Yes." He disappeared.

"Activate the privacy spells now. Dragons go," Ann Marie said into her communication spell.

Drake's hand landed on my knee. "We've made contingency plans for this. Stay alert and keep the communication lines open."

"The police will evacuate and block off the neighborhoods. Hybrids not behind our spell will act like humans," Jonas explained. "Your people won't. Get them behind those spells."

"Activate all teams. Emergency protocol two." Mat said into his communication spell. "Bastien, have the dragons set fires so the police can't get too close. Jenella?"

My head spun with their rapid-fire orders. I shook it and sat up straighter. "Send teams to help evacuate the neighborhoods. Keep your eyes open for demons. Eliminate the Bellicose." I hated giving the order. Especially since many weren't working for them by choice. But protecting the coalition had to take priority. "Dragons, protocol one. Teams N and F use protocol three."

My advisors scrambled, everyone talking over each other as the camp came alive with shouting.

The god Cavil burst into the tent. "Where's Lily?"

"She left with Tarquin," Ann Marie answered.

"She'll be fine." I threw on my coat and flipped the hood up. "I'm glad you're here. You and I need to hit each of these neighborhoods and add the magic that repels humans to the privacy spell."

His eyebrows drew together. "The one worked into Allure's gates?"

"Yes. If the human authorities enter those neighborhoods right now, we're done."

He nodded. "Which ones should I grace with my presence?"

I blinked. "There's seven. You take these three, and I'll take the other four." I pointed them out on the hologram. "When you're done, you can either go to the bar and help us fight or return here. Lily and Quin are headed to the neighborhood adjacent to the bar."

Ann Marie moved toward the door. "I'm going to the warehouse. Send any hybrid refugees who won't go to the pocket there. Just tell them to head to Maria's."

Chapter Thirty-One

Chaos. No, not chaos. That was an understatement for the carnage and sheer destruction at the edges of the first neighborhood we went to. Blue and red flashing lights were everywhere, with some yellow ones mixed in. A small apartment complex and several homes surrounding it were flattened. Thick black smoke plumed from them. Hybrids dragged their children toward the human authorities, who handed them blankets or directed them behind a long yellow string.

The Bellicose are after hybrids. You can fight, head to a pocket, or go to Maria's. Drake's voice boomed through my head.

Several of the people on the ground tilted their heads toward the sky. Others looked around as if trying to figure out who spoke. A few ran toward vehicles.

A street over from the yellow string, our privacy spell formed a large dome, showing a tranquil neighborhood. Drake flew through and headed toward the center. Several hybrids were on their porches or in their yards. Others strolled down the street toward the destruction to join their neighbors. The dark feeling I associated with the Bellicose emanated from the far side.

After Drake descended and perched on top of a large house. I flashed to the gray box in someone's front yard containing our spell. I closed my eyes and added repellent intentions. It would put any human who wondered into the neighborhood back out on the surrounding walkways and roads. It didn't take long, which meant I was getting better at my magic. I only hoped I did it right.

Fighting broke out in the direction I sensed the Bellicose, so I flashed to Drake's back. We swept over our army as they clashed with one demon and a handful of others. They were fine, so we moved on to the next area.

I still wasn't good enough, I thought, as we left the third neighborhood.

The Bellicose are after hybrids. You can fight, go to Maria's, or head to a pocket. You will be welcomed in all pockets. Drake had broadcasted those words using different phrasing so many times they became background noise.

The fourth subdivision was the largest and had the biggest apartment complex. It was the one near Dale's bar and across a busy street from where I triggered the curse to release Alex and Glacintial. Our privacy spell stretched over both. The busy street would have been a problem, except Jonas ripped some of it up and blocked it off with a bunch of orange barrels. He explained they were commonly used in human road construction.

I swung my head toward the curse as we entered the privacy spell, then focused on the bar. Relief flooded me to see the sizeable crowd of hybrids clustered around it. I assumed they were trying to get to the pocket.

The flashing blue and red lights were at the other end of the neighborhood, and even more prevalent there than the other ones. Like the other neighborhoods, thick black smoke rose into the sky from what used to be the Bellicose apartments. Vehicles were backed up in both directions for as far as the eye could see on the cross street.

Unlike the other locations, nearly half of the bystanders were Bellicose. They crowded around a group of hybrid families. I covered my nose to block out the rancid scent of burned wood and dark magic as I leaned over to get a better look.

A large cat slunk behind a hedge, while several blurs moved through the shadows. The members of the Bellicose collapsed. Alex tilted his head in our direction, then disappeared into the shadows as several vampire blurs swarmed the bodies and remaining Bellicose and dragged them through the privacy spell. I averted my eyes because I didn't want to know what happened next.

Drake stopped blasting his mental message and descended toward a clubhouse, where I added repellent magic to the dome. The heart of the neighborhood was eerily quiet. I stood and sent my senses out and felt a mass of Bellicose in the adjacent neighborhood near where the booby trap curse had gone off.

Whoosh!

My skin prickled as something thick and ominous coated a few houses at the edge of the street. A curse, I realized. And behind it, a clump of Bellicose and demons packed in too tight for me to read without getting dizzy. I activated the communication spell. "The bulk of enemy forces are in subdivision six. Send everyone who isn't engaged in battle."

Sweat trickled down my temple. Dumb of me to waste so much magic on the repellent spell, I thought as I finished. But we couldn't have humans wondering through our battle zone trying to see what was going on.

"Jen!" Tracy's voice sounded muffled and far away.

I didn't dare break my concentration as I anchored the magic. One anchor, two.

A roaring sound came from the west as I set the third. I needed six more.

A massive paw wrapped around me and I tumbled through the air and landed face-down on a bed of fur.

"No! It's not anchored!" I untangled myself from the fur of Drake's snuffy form and concentrated on finishing them as he raced through the streets. I got two more anchors in place.

Hold on. I'm going to climb.

"Wait." I scooted toward his neck and wrapped my hands in his long fur as his, or maybe my, magic tightened around me. Our power mixed so often it was hard to tell. I stayed low and concentrated on the final three anchors as the world tilted.

When he came to a stop, I pushed myself to a sitting position. "No."

A thick black blanket coated a third of the houses on the west end. I yanked out my phone and texted Gorman as Bastien landed on the roof next to us.

"It's bug magic, but darker somehow," Tracy said from his back.

"Yeah, I feel it. It's mixed with something else. Maybe a curse. Where are the dragons with the potion?"

Drake crouched low and skittered closer to Bastien. *Five minutes out.*

A mass of paranormals burst through my shield, the other Firsts leading the charge. Jonas stopped, sniffed the air, then pointed in our direction. Mat stepped out from behind Razazia, said something, and flashed away. Gorman and his ogres split off and jogged toward the affected area.

Mat reappeared between Drake and Bastien. "I have a status update."

Drake melted into his naked human form.

I landed on the roof, wobbled, then latched onto his arm. "What's up?"

He scanned the houses, his gaze settling on the curse creeping through the neighborhood. Behind it, the hundreds of Bellicose waited. For us, I supposed. "The bartender has spent the last two days moving the noncombatants to the pocket. The last of them are going through the gate now. Lily is assisting him, but Alex is out gathering the fighters."

"I saw him. He was with a bunch of vampires."

"It is the house of Roman."

"Gah!" I slammed into Drake's side.

Tracy burst out laughing as she slid off Bastien's back. "Hey, Quin. What's the status?"

Quin kept his eyes on the curse. "The Bellicose abandoned the other locations and congregated behind that curse."

Mat nodded. "Half of our army is here, the rest on the way. Many will flash here. We have people disbursed throughout the homes getting into position. What's the status of the protection spell?"

"Done, though a few human authorities are still on this side."

Quin tilted his head. "The house of Roman and Lily's brother ejected them."

"You need to sit this one out, Jenella," Mat said. "We don't have much room to work, and both armies are large."

I opened my mouth to argue, but closed it when Tracy's elbow landed in my ribs.

She pointed toward what used to be the bellicose apartments. "I've set up a few monitoring spells, but we need more witches."

Drake's eyes glowed. "We didn't have many witches volunteer to fight, so they're spread thin. If we can trust the ones Calvin sent, more monitoring spells should be functional in a few minutes."

I pointed to one of the taller houses. "We'll set up command there. How many teams have communication spells?"

"All of them."

Quin's fangs elongated, and claws formed on his hands and feet. "*Do not* explode your magic." He disappeared.

I rested my hands on my hips. "Maybe the Bellicose are right about how I let others push me around."

Tracy shook her head. "There's nothing wrong with listening. Especially when you've surrounded yourself with the oldest paranormals in the world."

True. And I liked the honesty. "Let's set up our headquarters."

Drake and Bastien perched on the roof of the three-story house in their dragon forms. I assumed they stayed cloaked, but didn't bother checking as Tracy and I set up the command station and monitoring spells inside the attic of someone's home.

The scent of death clogged my nose as Ara wandered in, filthy and covered in blood.

She studied the holograms of the other neighborhoods. "Those are abandoned, dear."

"Yeah, I ordered everyone not engaged in a fight to relocate here. It looks like this is where they chose to make a stand. The question is why?"

Tracy dug through her backpack, pulled out a potion, and handed it to me. "Take one drop of this. It'll protect you from demon magic. I think."

"You think?"

"It will at least protect you from some, though you might be immune to it now, too." She started scooting mismatched chairs to the rickety table we found in the corner. "Who else is joining us here?"

I remembered the magic my mother threw at me disintegrating, but wasn't sure if I was immune, so I put a drop of the potion on my tongue and handed it to Ara. "I don't know."

Ara's eyes narrowed as she examined the potion.

"It'll work on you." Tracy waited for her to take it, then tucked the bottle in her backpack.

I deactivated the other areas from the hologram and enlarged the one we were in. "Any word on their leaders?"

"They were in the area before the explosions. My vampires lost them in the chaos."

Which meant they were still out there. I lowered myself into a chair. Two more monitoring spells came online, showing a side view of an entire Bellicose army. They were packed so tight I couldn't tell how many were there or what magic they had. "Were our suspicions correct?"

Ara walked around the table and poked a blank space on the hologram. "I'm afraid so."

"What about the one who uses the complicated magic?"

"We have not detected him."

Another view popped into existence, showing the back of their group. We all leaned toward it to get a better look.

"Well, this conflict has become slightly more interesting," Ara drawled.

All three of Ann Marie and Jonas's biological children stood shoulder-to-shoulder. The former Shifter Alphas, Gabe and Linda, sat at their feet in wolf form, with strange metal collars around their necks. Behind them, the First Cynthia's wrists and neck were shackled, a long chain stretched toward a massive demon with the balloon-like head and the body of a stick. The thing yanked the chain and dragged her toward the three hybrids.

"Are they treating Gabe and Linda like dogs?" Tracy asked, her voice tight.

I scanned the group surrounding the former alphas, trying to see anyone who looked too confident or out of place. There were several glassy-eyed witches and other paranormals. I refocused on the leaders. "Even if they're not, Jonas will not like the collars."

Ara took the chair to my right and activated our primary communication spell. "They are waiting for something."

A tangle of voices blasted through the room. There were so many, and it was so loud that I couldn't hear what anyone said.

The Bellicose leaders are here. It's Jonas's kids. I said to Drake as I felt for his emotions.

Disappointment, rather than surprise, came back through the bond. *We already knew it was one of them.*

They put collars on Gabe and Linda and have Cynthia in chains.

He didn't answer for a few seconds. *I have informed Jonas. Brace yourselves.*

A pained roar shook the house. I latched onto a beam as something below us crashed. *Tell him not to engage until Gorman breaks that curse!*

He won't listen.

I couldn't imagine how he felt. It was bad enough when we speculated one of their biological kids was leading the coup. But we never even imagined all three were responsible for it. My eyes slid to Ara, who'd recently learned her kids hid her granddaughter and heir from her for years.

She sniffed. "Do not look at me like that, dear."

I turned my attention back to the monitoring spells as a couple more views popped up. We could see most of the area, though there was still a gaping hole where the curse lingered.

An entire flock of dragons burst through the dome from the South, massive buckets hanging from their talons, Deva leading the charge. They split up and flew around the curse.

Several flying demons rose into the air to meet them.

Deva dove into the darkness and dumped her bucket on the Bellicose army. A massive wave of mental magic nearly knocked me off the chair.

Do not move! Her voice echoed through my skull so loud it sounded like a chorus of dragons.

I shook my head to clear it and wiggled my fingers to make sure I could. "That woman packs a punch."

Tracy leaned forward as a bronze streak moved through the monitoring spell. "What is she doing?"

Ara's tinkling laugh filled the attic. "She is toying with them."

The bronze streak I recognized as Deva zipped left, drawing the demons away, while dragons swept in and dumped their buckets of potions and flew away. She circled around and drew them to the other side so more dragons could do the same.

A glow emanated from the ground. As it grew, it drifted into the darkness. The curse turned from inky black to a gray haze. Gorman and the ogres.

Two more monitoring spells came online.

Uncloaked dragons swept in and dumped their buckets of potion. I wondered about Deva's grief. It did strange things to people. Like causing such a hunger for revenge, she didn't care about leading a flock of dragons into a war without using the element of surprise.

Not that I had any room to talk. I made dumb mistakes all the time, and I wasn't even grieving.

The tension in my shoulders drained when I sensed three times as many dragons come in from the north. I realized that she kept a few uncloaked to create a diversion. After all the crap I'd given Drake about how ancients could detach their emotions, I should have guessed. On top of that, Deva could manipulate any situation to her advantage.

Movement a couple of blocks over made me shift my attention to where most of our army waited. Jonas, in the form of a massive dinosaur, separated from them as he stomped toward the curse, leaving large gouges in the street. Lily and Quin clung to his feet with their claws and fangs out. Quin's sword was slung across his back. "What are they doing?"

"Holy shit!" Tracy jumped out of her chair.

My eyes widened as the gray fog cleared to reveal a mass of demons surrounding the Bellicose army. Some were flyers, while others slithered around, leaving long trails of goo in their wake. I watched as one turned to his neighbor, raised a massive spiked club, and bashed it in the head. The putrid scent of sulfur floated through the attic's window.

My heart pounded in my chest. We had a lot of paranormals join our army. So many I thought it was overkill. But theirs was twice the size. And they'd bunched together to trick my senses. "How many people do we have who can banish those things?"

Ara stood. "Not nearly enough."

"Deva, Drake, Lily, me, the gargoyles, the witches if they gather as a coven, and maybe Gorman and Razazia?" As Tracy listed them off, my stomach churned. There was no way we'd win this with all those demons.

"And me," I murmured as I pondered how they brought the demons in without the gargoyles knowing. The answer smacked me in the face. They didn't. "Are the gargoyles working with them?"

"The gargoyles work for no one," Ara answered. "Their primary function is to protect humans, and their allegiance lies with them."

Yeah, I knew that. I closed my eyes and tried to remember our agreement. I did a pretty good job of ensuring there weren't any loopholes. "No. If they helped the Bellicose, they'd break the contract with me. The gargoyles don't want demons living in this realm feeding off humans, either."

"So, why weren't they aware of their numbers, and why aren't they here?" Tracy waved a hand toward the monitoring spell.

I pulled out my phone and texted the Gargoyle King. "I'll find out."

Jonas made an abrupt left. Lily and Quin were gone. A massive box formed around a group of demons and turned blood red. Enormous blades shot toward the center. They whirled so fast that the demons trapped inside didn't stand a chance. When the box dissipated, the only thing left was a mass of jelly. A few seconds later, the stuff wiggled and plumed into the air with a 'poof,' leaving everyone in the area coated in dust. My new sister's magic was as glorious as it was disgusting.

I pulled my eyes away and moved toward the window. "Lily can't banish them all alone. Let's go."

Tracy latched onto my arm. "You realize they're trying to draw you out, right?"

My stomach twisted when I met her wide eyes. I'd never seen her face so tight. I swallowed. "Yes. It might be best if you stay here. Stay here, and if anything happens to me...."

Ara yanked my arm so hard pain shot through my shoulder. "None of that, dear. We will go into this battle as warriors and come out the other side as victors."

"Right." I rubbed my shoulder. "Warriors and victors."

Ara disappeared, then reappeared. "Do not explode your magic." She vanished again.

"That's Quin's line."

Tracy shook her head. "They're right. We need you to be measured and confident. When you exploded your magic in the last battle, it looked like you panicked."

"I *did* panic. Sort of. At least I let the burning rage inside of me take over."

"Yeah. I mean, it was effective, but don't do it again."

"I'll try not to." There was no point in making a promise I couldn't keep. I pulled her into my arms and hugged her with my whole heart. "You're a great friend, Tracy, and I thank the fates every day for bringing us together."

"That sounds so final."

I stepped back. "Not final, but I wanted you to understand how much you mean to me."

She swiped a tear from her eyes. "I feel the same way."

"Good. Don't forget, we're two badass women who cheated death as kids. We're stronger for it. And we're more powerful than them." I flashed us to the roof. "Now let's kick some demon ass."

"If you say so." She climbed onto Bastien's foot. "Don't do anything stupid."

I forced myself to smile and nod, then flashed onto Drake's back. *We need to help Lily banish demons.*

You do realize it's a trap.

Yes.
And they will feel your magic, even though we're cloaked.
Can you fly in a zigzag pattern? And move fast or something?
Hold on and don't second-guess yourself.

CHAPTER THIRTY-TWO

DRAKE'S STATEMENT RAN THROUGH my head, along with Quin and Ara's insistence not to explode my magic as we flew in an erratic pattern so fast the ground went by in a blur. The icy wind cut to the bone. I fastened my coat and sent my senses out instead of using my worthless eyes. Bastien and Tracy bolted toward Deva at the far side of the line of demons. Lily was with Quin in the shadows of a house. I pulled up my hood and peered in their direction. I couldn't see them, so went back to using my senses.

The putrid scent of sulfur, death, disease, and blood made me heave. I conjured a purple scarf, added a scent filter spell, and wrapped it around my mouth and nose. After a few deep breaths to calm my stomach, I refocused on the battle.

I cannot get to the side Jonas is on. There's too many flying demons.

Go to the center. I gathered my magic and concentrated on banishing.

He made a wide circle, sideswiped a flying demon, then sunk like a rock. *Now.*

I pushed out the intention of banishing. Silver magic shot from my body, blanketing the center section of the horde.

I'd barely released it when Drake switched directions and dashed out the other side, swooped around, and flew to the rear of the formation. His lungs expanded under my butt and I felt a tug at my chest a split second before bright green fire lit the evening sky.

The former Shifter Alpha, Morten, tilted his head in our direction. And smiled.

A shiver ran down my spine as the dragon fire smashed into their protective bubble.

I craned my neck but didn't see what happened because Drake was already moving. "What was that?"

They're using your ruling magic.

My mind went into a spiral. "What? How?"

He didn't answer until we landed back on the roof of the three-story house where we'd left the monitoring spell. Drake melted into his human form before I was ready, and I tumbled toward the ground. He caught me bridal style and set me on the roof. "You need to go back to Allure now. This entire battle is a trap."

"How the hell did they get ruling magic?"

"It doesn't feel like yours but your mother's. Yours has always been stronger and more aligned with Lissa's than hers."

I rubbed my eyes. "So my mother wasn't weak because she broke her oath?"

"A question to consider later. They have a weaker form of your powers."

I twisted my head in that direction. Not wanting to fall off the roof, I avoided pacing and settled for wringing my hands. "You said I'm stronger than them?"

"Much stronger. But you've used too much power already."

"If they have Anitta's ruling magic, then they can take out Mat and Lily."

"Yes."

"I need to warn them."

"I already did."

I slumped against the chimney. "Thank you."

"Don't thank me yet. This changes things."

Three massive flying demons rose into the sky two streets over and swiveled toward us.

Drake latched onto my arm. "Leave, Jenella."

When our eyes met, I gasped. The sheer resolve in those beautiful green eyes almost brought me to my knees. "No."

"They are hunting you. You need to go now."

"Not a chance."

The demons separated and started sweeping the neighborhood, sniffing as they went.

Drake pulled me to him and put his lips to my ear. "We might not make it through this."

I ignored the shiver that went through my body. "Or we might."

His arms tightened around me. "Think this through. If you die, the coalition dies with you."

I jerked back. "Mat has drilled the same point into my head my whole life. But I'm not running like a coward while all these paranormals die. If they go down, I go down with them."

His eyes searched my face. "What about the coalition?"

"The Coalition is doing just fine at tearing itself apart, with or without my leadership. Between the massive divides and sheer numbers of paranormals who defected to the Bellicose...." I closed my eyes when a sharp pang of guilt stabbed through my chest. "It feels like my efforts are too little and too late. I'm not so sure we'll still have a coalition, even if we win."

The resolve in his eyes sparked into confusion, then anger. "The Firsts will not let the coalition fall."

A tear escaped, and I swiped it away. "Okay."

He froze. "You don't believe me."

"I believe *you* will do everything you can. Maybe Jonas. It's the others I don't trust."

"They'll step up. They always do." He rubbed his thumb across my cheek. "Hold on tight and stay low. Please. We'll avoid demons and help the army you are so willing to die for."

The sudden lump in my throat kept me from responding, so I nodded.

As soon as Drake morphed into his dragon form, I flashed onto his back and crouched as low as possible.

It never crossed my mind that my lack of understanding of my various powers was going to bring down the coalition and get us killed. I always thought I'd be able to improvise or have enough time to figure it out, even as I told everyone I needed to hurry. Stupid. I threw the unhelpful thoughts out of my head as Drake banked toward the main area where the battle took place, then leaned over to get a better look.

Bodies and ash coated the streets. Trees that had brilliant orange and yellow leaves a couple of days before were now greenish-gray. Entire houses were destroyed. One was on fire, the flames flickering well above the roofline.

I sneezed to expel the acrid scent of rot, blood, and thick smoke, then wrapped my scarf around my nose.

Below us, the armies clashed. A new inky-black curse swirled around a group in the back. Razazia and Gorman hung upside down from a tree above them. "Are they hanging from jungle vines?"

Yes. Razazia will eliminate them after they've served her purpose.

Gorman released his misty curse-breaking magic, and it floated toward the ink and disappeared. Razazia's vine swung them out of the way before it hit. It retracted into the trees as she clutched Gorman to her chest and flew away.

A roar rattled my bones as Jonas stomped through a group of Bellicose soldiers. Deva swooped in from the other side and let out a long bronze stream of fire. She cloaked herself and flew away.

Two flying demons attacked a red dragon. The dragon bit an arm off when the demon tried to grab him. He latched onto the second one, spun through the air, then kicked out his talons and dug into the second demon. A purple dragon flew in and pummeled the armless one.

A horde of ogres ran through the Bellicose formation, swinging clubs, shovels, rakes, and other makeshift weapons. The two Ogre Queens raised their weapons and a war-cry erupted. They took off, obliterating everything in their path.

A bright light flashed from below, and several demons turned to ash. I squinted as I focused on the source. The God Cavil trailed Lily and Alex as they tore through the center of the Bellicose army. Several hybrids took advantage of the gap and pushed their ranks. Relief flooded me. The god said he didn't want to fight in my war but was willing to if it meant protecting Lily. She probably hated having the extra help, but she needed it.

Mat's blue katanas flashed to their right as he carved his way toward them. His head snapped the other way, and he started moving in that direction.

I followed his gaze and gasped. An entire line of long demons with accordion bodies swarmed the line, cutting a path through both armies to keep Mat separated from Lily and her group.

"There!" I pointed toward them.

I tightened my grip as Drake changed direction too fast. *I need to uncloak to save power.*

"Okay." My heart pounded so fast I thought it might escape my chest as the soft blanket of his cloaking magic melted away. I brought my magic to the surface and concentrated on casting banishing intentions. When he dipped toward the demons, I released it.

Drake pushed more of his massive well into the effort. It punched down on the bug looking demons, then spread out and blanketed the ground. Every single one within a two-block radius turned to ash.

Lily threw her hand in the air and whooped, "Meet my sister, bitches!"

Our army cheered and seemed to come alive as Drake brutally attacked a group of Bellicose soldiers with his teeth and claws.

Screams from the direction of the bar raised the hairs on the back of my neck. I twisted around, and my heart jumped in my throat. Several shifters and a couple of demons tore through the back of the crowd, trying to get into the bar to access the gate. "The evacuees are under attack."

Drake didn't even hesitate as he spun and flew in their direction. He also didn't slow down before he opened his mouth, chomped on several shifters, and spit them toward a group of demons. At the same time, he picked several more up with his feet, tore them apart, and threw pieces of them toward the Bellicose leadership.

"That's dramatic," I mumbled as I formed a shield and smashed a group of witches to the ground.

The remaining hybrids cheered. Several of them charged what remained of the shifters with such viciousness, the Bellicose didn't stand a chance.

I squared my shoulders as my chest puffed with pride.

Whomp!

My neck cracked as Drake's massive body jerked sideways. Two demons latched onto his wing and wrenched it backward.

I flung banishing magic toward them.

Drake spun around as I released it and it flew over their heads and smashed into the chest of a third demon.

One of them swung his grotesque, bulbous head toward me. He leaned in so close I could smell his putrid sulfur breath through my spelled scarf.

Drake swept it away with his wing and veered in the other direction.

A memory slammed into me.

I lay on the floor of a cage in a pool of my own blood. My wrists and ankles throbbed and my face was on fire from the claws that dug into it. The burning on my back was almost unbearable. Tears ran down my face and pooled in my matted, bloody hair. I tried not to think about the pain. I didn't dare make a sound.

"My, my, my. What do we have here, Jaques? Of all my sons, you have proven the most useful," a guttural voice said.

"Thank you, Father." The man's boots moved into my field of vision seconds before the cage rattled. "One day, I will gift her to you."

A grating laugh sent a spike of fear through my body. "I highly doubt that. But I appreciate the effort. Let her grow and try not to kill her. Should this prove successful, we shall feast on this realm."

The man cleared his throat. "And my other parents?"
"Kill them. I've discovered some more useful tools."

Reality slammed into me, and I sucked in a breath. "No."

Drake spun in a circle, raised his talon, and stabbed a demon. The other one was gone. I twisted my head toward the Bellicose leaders, my eyes narrowing with determination.

Jenella! No! Drake's voice boomed in my head a second before I flashed to the ground.

"Don't be impulsive. Don't be impulsive. Don't be impulsive." I repeated the phrase as I tried to gather my senses. Instead of flashing, magic bloomed out in a plume around me, coated us, and solidified.

A demon slammed into Drake, inches from my leg.

I yelped and hopped to my feet.

It turned to dust.

Another one bit into Drake's tail and disintegrated.

Did you just coat me in banishing magic?

I lowered myself to his back and hugged my spike. "I think so."

Hold on.

He let out an ear-splitting roar as he barreled toward the massive demon guarding the Bellicose leader.

I wrapped my arms and legs around the spike seconds before we slammed into it.

I jolted so hard, my grip slipped. By the time my bones stopped rattling, Drake was already baring down on two flying demons harassing Bastien.

We slammed into one, and Drake reached out his massive talon and swiped at the wing of another one.

Tracy shouted, but I couldn't make out her words as we plummeted, my stomach flipping with the speed.

He changed direction at the last moment and swept a cluster of demons with his tail.

I craned my neck just in time to see them turn to dust. Several members of our army raised their arms and cheered.

You're such an adrenaline junkie. I used my mind because my mouth was too dry to speak.

It takes one to know one. Amusement laced Drake's voice.

Another human saying?

Hold on.

He swooped over another group and wagged his tail, ready to strike.

Bright light blinded me a second before my eardrums burst. Stabbing pain shot through my head while burning ripped through the left side of my body. Our magic released me, and I bounced off something solid and plummeted. I felt my clothes rip as I hit the ground. My head snapped back as it collided with a hard surface. I had a split second of rational thought before everything went black.

Chapter Thirty-Three

MY HEARING CAME BACK online first. Battle cries and screeches almost blew them out again. I opened my eyes and raised my head. That one rational thought saved my life, I realized, as I struggled to sit up.

I was on the ground in a yard. A solid box formed around me and Drake, who lay a few feet away, still in his dragon form. His body was inside what used to be a house, his head hanging out one side, his tail out the other. "No!"

I tried to sense him through the bond, but got nothing. Tears flooded my eyes as I dragged myself to my feet and limped to his head. My hand stretched out, and I ran it across his cold nose. Silvery magic coated him and I stepped back.

He should have come alive and been restored like everyone else I healed. But nothing happened. He still lay there bleeding from a hole in his scales, unconscious.

Tears trickled down my face, and I threw myself at his nose. "No. You can't leave me! You said you're hard to kill." I touched my forehead to his chin. "You can't die on me!"

I sobbed as I moved to his side and tried to heal him again. When red and yellow magic flared to my right, I gave Drake's snout one last caress and stepped back. My rage flared when I turned toward the source and spotted several Bellicose crowded around my self-imposed cage. I scanned them, my eyes landing on the magic wielder.

Morten stood from his crouch and smirked. "My, my, my. What do we have here? A fallen queen?" He threw his head back and laughed.

Weird, I thought, as I rubbed the lump on the back of my head. Villains were supposed to have maniacal laughs, or at least make a noise that grated on your nerves. But his was a deep, appealing timber that sounded so...normal. I shook out my hands to keep another memory from overtaking me. It was a laugh from my childhood. But it was not the time to relive it.

His magic reached out in a concentrated stream and tried to get underneath my protective bubble. When it didn't work, his face turned to stone. "You can't stay in there forever."

I didn't have to stay forever. I only had to wait until my magic and energy replenished or until backup came. And it would. Drake might have been out of commission, but Mat, Quin, Tracy, and Bastien weren't. Maybe. I wasn't sure what hit us. I only knew I was sore, weak, exhausted, and heartbroken.

Mopping my tears with my shirt, I whispered an apology to Drake and stepped away. I kept my face neutral as I scanned the group surrounding Morten. Gabe and Linda sat on either side of him in their wolf forms, their tongues lulling out at the side. "Are you treating them like dogs?"

I regretted the words when he threw his head back and let out another non-supervillain laugh. "They are mine to do with what I wish."

"If you say so." I examined the other Bellicose in what I hoped was a detached way as I looked for help. A house and a couple of charred trees were in the way, so I couldn't see much. I tested the bond again.

Nothing.

My heart cracked into pieces, the pain stretching deep into my soul and sparking the ball of anger I carried inside. I swallowed the lump in my throat and focused with a new determination.

Linda jumped to her feet and took two steps back.

A loud whistle sounded. I hit the ground as something exploded a few streets over. There went my ears again.

When the sound crept back in, I climbed to my feet. The realization that they took out Drake with a missile hit me and my knees almost buckled. I locked them and squared my shoulders. "Where did you get the explosives?"

Morten waved a dismissive hand. "Humans are no match for our creations."

It took me a second to realize he meant the members of the Bellicose. "They aren't your creations."

Morten's smirk was as ordinary as his laugh. "Oh, but they are. They were merely existing in your world. The bottom of society who no one cared about." He leaned forward and put his palm on my protective bubble. "What you and your mother saw as worthless, I saw as potential. I took them away from their miserable lives and gave them what they'd always craved."

My eyes narrowed. "Did you? And what is it they want?"

"Power and a purpose." He leaned in. "No one cared about them before I came along. They were too weak to be useful. Now, they're empowered. Strong."

"You mean brainless and mind-controlled."

He shrugged. "Po-tay-toe, Po-tah-toe."

My forehead crinkled. "What?"

"Or if you prefer, To-may-toe, To-mah-toe."

I had no idea what that meant. The thought of how I'd ask Drake if it was a human saying fluttered through my mind, followed by soul-deep pain. I shoved it down. I needed to plan an escape. As soon as my strength returned, I could leave Drake inside the protective bubble and flash away. Or I could stay and kill the maniac in front of me. I remembered Alex saying he bought himself time by asking questions. "Where are your siblings?"

"Dead. Apparently, my father was not happy with their life choices." Another too-normal laugh.

"And Cynthia?"

"She's around."

"What do you want, Morten? What is your end-goal here?"

He folded his arms. "Why do you suppose the original queen deleted the other sorcerers?"

I knew why. My grandmother killed them because they went crazy. Ann Marie being the only exception. But I didn't answer, because I needed to keep him talking. "Why don't you tell me?"

"Because they were stronger than your mother. Stronger than your grandmother, even. Which means I am much, much more powerful than you. Smarter." He leaned forward. "Better looking." He threw his head back and let out another deep timber of a laugh.

I fought not to shove my fingers in my ears. That laugh was just wrong. "You think so?"

He was strong, sure. But he wasn't even close to my level. He wasn't even the most powerful hybrid. He may have once been, but he broke his oath to the shifters when he was their alpha. Magic always took its payment for a broken oath. As a result, he was diminished.

I sensed the ruling magic of Ahl surrounding him, but it wasn't something he could internalize or incorporate into his own. It felt more like the natural magic in the air contained by a vortex or something. He could weave spells from it, but not much more. Which made it almost useless for anything other than a short power boost. And I doubted it would replenish itself, so he could only use it a few times. It was a lucky break for our side. Because our apathy and stupid decisions would have handed him the coalition if he had my mother's full power.

Gunshots sounded in the distance from three directions, and he spun toward them. "Find out who that is," he ordered. Several Bellicose ran toward the sounds.

Hope bloomed in my chest. Emine had arrived, and she'd brought backup. I smirked as Gabe and Linda tore off after them. "You're an idiot."

Anger flashed through Morten's eyes a second before magic blasted my bubble and fell harmlessly to the ground.

I glanced back at Drake's still form as I gathered my courage. Then sent love and encouragement through the bond just in case he was still alive. Focusing on Morten, I let my anger swell and flashed out of my bubble.

I landed too close and jabbed my elbow into his throat.

He stumbled backward.

I reached in before he could recover and sucked up my mother's ruling magic, then took massive gulps of his.

Morten screamed. His skin bubbled, and he lowered himself to his knees. Plates formed along his spine, and his legs thickened. His skin turned a bluish color, and his head elongated.

The shift from man to dinosaur took much too long. Or maybe my perception of time was off. I kept my hands loose and at my sides as I waited. He'd be much easier for my allies to recognize in his larger form. When he was almost done, I charged.

I dove for his knees. As soon as my hand made contact, I flashed to the center of the battle.

He flashed us back to the front yard and raised a foot to stomp on me.

I flashed to his neck and back to the battle.

Blue glowing katanas glinted in the corner of my eye as Mat sprinted toward us.

I held on for dear life as Morten charged him. At the last second, he shifted back into his human form and I smashed into the ground with a grunt and rolled across the asphalt.

Mat didn't slow down. He swung his short swords so fast, I barely registered them. Morten tried to block and lost his arm to the whirling blades.

I hurled toward him and didn't slow down as I barreled into the side of his knee.

Mat flashed behind him, his blade swinging toward Morten's neck.

I landed in a crouch and backed out of the way.

Someone slammed into my side, and we hit the ground hard. I latched onto the person and twisted as I fell, dragging them with me.

'Clink.'

My eyes went wide when something snapped around my wrist. I spun around, so I had the leverage. And came face-to-face with the First Cynthia.

She pointed to the side, a tear running down her cheek. "I'm sorry," she whispered in a raspy voice.

I craned my neck to see what she pointed at. Three balloon-headed, stick-bodied demons stood to the side. Their plate-sized eyes unfocused as they swayed. Something on the chest of the middle one glimmered in the light. My eyes trailed the thin chain from them to an equally thin choker around Cynthia's neck. My stomach soured when my eyes trailed another chain from it to the cuff she'd attached to my wrist.

One demon sneezed, and dark sludge oozed out and crept down the chain. The demons must have been the ones who could steal power, I thought as I accessed Gorman's magic. If it were a curse, it was the only way I knew to break it. A small spark of yellow worked its way toward the sludge and fizzled. I was too weak.

The dark oozed closer.

I stared at the chain, my eyes unable to focus on anything else, as a sense of helplessness washed over me. Images of being dragged to a cage by my broken wrists flashed through my mind. Next came my father's blank, dead eyes. Then Mat's rough voice reassuring me everything would be okay.

Another lie.

Everyone said I was impulsive. They warned me to think before I acted. So many people told me to listen better and to think things through.

Screw that.

I sucked in some nasty smoke and death filled air and turned my attention back to Cynthia. And throat punched her.

She grunted and struggled underneath me.

I let her twist away. She wobbled as she climbed to her knees. Just as she started to plant a foot, I lunged. She wasn't far enough away to make much of an impact. But I didn't need to. As soon as I hit, I raised my cuffed arm and wrapped the chain around her neck, and pushed against her back with my foot. I pulled it tight, then when I thought it was tight enough, I pulled it tighter. My power was low, so I reached out and gulped magic from Morten. And sent my tried-and-true shredding magic into the metal.

A wet garble came from her throat as I fell forward, taking her with me. The dark sludge on the shackle touched my skin. The power I'd stolen drained along with my already depleted magic. But I didn't stop. I took three more massive gulps. With one last burst, I shoved shredding magic through the chain.

Cynthia's head rolled away from her body. She fell forward while I landed hard on my ass on the bloody street.

I tried to stand but couldn't as spots danced in front of my eyes. My mind spun as magic drained from me and into the dead woman. I reached out and drank it back down.

Enough energy seeped into me to clear my head before the process started again. The three balloon-headed demons stood still, not acknowledging Cynthia's death or my struggle. "Weird," I croaked.

A grinding sound drowned out the noise of the battle. The gargoyles had arrived. A massive one descended from the sky, as the sound of stones scraping against each other was replaced with a chorus of chants. The three demons turned to ash, the chains clattering onto the road.

A bronze streak darted across the sky, heading straight for me. I stumbled to my feet and blinked the dots away. Deva was still a couple of blocks over when a bright light launched from behind her.

"No!" I screamed as the missile detonated. My head swung toward where Mat fought Morten.

My brother slashed a deep cut into Morten's chest, then flashed to me. "What happened?"

"They killed Drake and Deva."

"To you. What happened to you?"

Tears streamed down my face, and I couldn't clear the black dots. I wobbled. "It's draining me and giving my magic to the dead woman." I pointed at the cuff and gulped my magic again.

The deep timber of Morten's laugh sounded like nails on a chalkboard, and I swung my head his way.

He stood, the picture of health. He pulled a medallion from his neck, using a hand that shouldn't have existed. "You cannot stop me."

"The asshole stole my healing magic."

I thought I'd seen every side of my brother before. His dark side, his light side. His teaching style, and especially his lecturing mode. We laughed together more times than I could count and yelled at each other in anger just as much. I'd seen his healing side and his murderous side. But I'd never seen the kind of rage that exploded from him in that moment.

He took on a golden glow as he drew himself to his full height. Chunks of vegetation and asphalt blew apart, along with everything else in its path as he flashed to Morten. His katanas moved so fast I couldn't track them. He tore into the guy with a ferocity I'd never seen.

I shook myself out of my stupor and turned my attention back to Cynthia's body. The choker collar rested on what was left of her neck. In the center was a pendant with a white rose wrapped in a black vine with six thorns.

My eyes trailed to the cuff around my wrist and noticed the same pattern etched into it. I reached down and wrapped my hand around the choker on Cynthia. When I tugged at it, it resisted. I tried again, but it wouldn't come loose. I put my foot on her shoulder and pulled harder.

"It can't come off unless the creator wills it."

I recognized Linda's voice but ignored it. The black sludge was gone, but the magic on the thing was thick and powerful. The same foreign magic from the pyramid. I didn't have time to work it out, so I left the dead First and dragged myself toward an abandoned blade on the scarred remains of someone's front yard.

Linda trailed behind me. "What are you looking for?"

I shot her a look as I siphoned power from Morten.

She picked up the knife and handed it to me. "You can't cut it off."

"I figured," I said in a conversational tone as I examined the blade. It wasn't ideal, but big enough. I stumbled toward the front steps of the ruined home and collapsed. I sucked more of my power back, but it drained before it could settle inside me. Rising to my knees, I rested my cuffed hand on the concrete step.

Linda gasped. "Are you insane?"

"Possibly." I had to get the angle right.

"You can't do that." Worry laced her voice.

A ragged laugh escaped as I gulped back more of my magic. "I will not only cut off my own hand, but burn the entire coalition to the ground a thousand times before I'll allow that insane fuck to rule for one minute."

"How did I miss your dedication?" Her voice had a slight tremor.

I raised my eyes to meet hers. The former Shifter Alpha was proud and strong just a few weeks before. The woman before me was a thin husk, with gray skin and patches of hair missing. "Don't you have more friends to betray?"

She winced. "It wasn't my idea. Not at first. Gabe convinced me Morten's rule would be better for the coalition." She swallowed. "He's dead. Jonas killed him."

Jonas was doing a great job. His death tally, as far as I knew, was three Bellicose leaders. I craned my neck to where Mat and Morten still fought, then put the knife against my wrist just above the shackle. "I don't give a shit. Not about him, and I sure as hell don't care about you and your guilt."

"That's not..."

I gritted my teeth, raised the large blade, and brought it down on my wrist. I didn't dare make a sound.

Blinding pain shot up my arm and I may have passed out for a few seconds. When I came to, my wrist wasn't quite severed. Blood poured out too fast. I needed to hurry. I raised the blade and hit the same place again.

The cuff rolled down the stairs, along with my hand. I heaved a couple of times as I fought not to cry out against the excruciating pain. It didn't work, so I closed my eyes, focused on Morten, and took enormous gulps of my magic back. Then I took some of his just to irritate him.

My severed wrist quit bleeding, and the wound sort of sealed before the healing stopped. Good enough. I took a second to wonder how long it would take for a new hand to sprout, then drank more magic from Morten. I turned my attention back to Linda. "You were saying?"

The horrified expression on her face matched the brutality of the situation. "How in the hell did you do that without passing out or making a sound?"

"Practice." I stumbled to my feet and shuffled toward the fight. Morten didn't look any worse than before, so I gulped down more of my magic.

"You can't kill him. Your mother tried when she realized Morten was becoming too powerful. He drained her and dumped her in the desert." Linda must have followed me.

"Fuck off." I threw my head back and shouted, "Quin! Ara!" My voice wasn't loud enough. I was still too weak.

A massive cat crashed through a hedge and slammed into Morten.

"Jen!" Lily's voice was muffled.

It took every ounce of energy I had left to turn my head in her direction. "Medallion. Neck."

She disappeared, and appeared in front of Mat, her claws so fast Morten couldn't block. She slammed them into his chest.

"Stop!" The piece of shit used my ruling magic to compel them.

Alex froze, but Lily didn't, nor did Mat. I'd have to remember that.

Mat disappeared and reappeared near Linda. Her head rolled across the ground and came to a rest in front of me.

I chugged the magic faster.

The ground shook, and I fell to my knees as a thirty-foot lumbering mass of muscle came around the corner. The greenish-brown dinosaur swung a spiked tail and wiggled the deep orange plates that ran down the center of its back. He lowered his bulky body and charged. His feet, big as an elephant's, landed on a car. The squealing of metal hadn't even stopped when he kicked it into a group of Bellicose soldiers.

Jonas let out an ear-splitting roar.

I almost peed my pants.

Morten used the distraction to send a burst of magic into Lily.

She flew several feet and smashed into the ground. Her momentum hadn't even stopped before she charged again.

Several vampires melted from the shadows and converged on the fight.

But Morten wasn't there.

Spots danced in front of my eyes as he reappeared so close to Mat that he couldn't react as something came down on his head. My brother slumped to the ground.

Morten swung toward me and raised the object. An axe.

I heaved as the memory of my dead father in front of my cage popped into my head. I tried to flash away but only made it a few feet, landing on my ass. Jonas's massive foot lowered toward me. I rolled out of the way as he veered toward a coven of witches throwing spells at him.

Morten appeared in front of me. I gulped down more of my magic and let it settle into my bones as he raised the axe. "Goodbye, fake queen."

Exhausted, drained, and with only a fraction of my magic, I knew I couldn't escape in time, but I had to try. I stumbled to my feet as the axe came down.

Boom! Boom! Boom! A gun went off so close to us that my ears rang.

A bullet slammed into his side, then the arm holding the axe.

I sprinted in the other direction. Or I tried. It was more like a stumbling walk. Something slammed into my back and I tumbled down the street.

A flash in the corner of my eye caused me to turn just in time to see the axe swinging toward my head. My last thought was that at least I'd be with Drake.

Mat appeared and, with anger and vengeance emanating from him, stabbed a katana into the medallion hanging from Morten's neck.

"No!" I screamed.

A bright orange light exploded from it. Morten's body was engulfed in flames, burning so hot it scorched the ground. I backpedaled when my hair caught on fire.

Mat persisted, raising his other katana and slamming it into the medallion.

The scent of burning hair and flesh clogged my nose as I watched my brother's skin melt off his hands and arms.

The medallion exploded, and I threw my stub of a hand up to protect my face. My magic slammed back into my body, knocking me sideways. I bounced off a tree and slid down, landing on my back, then crawled to my feet.

Blood. Where was the blood? My brain didn't want to acknowledge what my eyes saw. I dropped to my knees beside what was left of Mat. His body was so burned, the only way I recognized him was from one lock of golden hair on the top of his head. "I can fix this. I can..."

"Tell...Emine...love...both...you." His voice was barely a wheeze.

"No!" Tears streamed down my face as I reached out and touched his shoulder. "I can fix this. Use your healing magic, damnit!"

"I... always... knew... die... protecting...."

The light faded from his eyes.

CHAPTER THIRTY-FOUR

MY ENTIRE WORLD SHIFTED. Everything I knew, every moment of safety I'd ever felt. Every ounce of stability was gone in an instant. Stolen from me to satisfy the over-inflated ego of a man who couldn't take responsibility for his failures.

I stood over my dead brother's body and realized how hard he'd fought to keep me from becoming like Morten. Like my mother. How he did everything within his power to keep me grounded and safe and insulated from the horrors of the world. It was his life's purpose, and he was willing to kill or die to achieve it. He fought so hard to save me.

He failed.

A guttural, painful scream came from behind me. Emine.

I climbed to my feet and ignored my wobbling knees as I raised my head.

Jonas stood over Morten's corpse, naked, a blank stare on his face.

"Did you know?" I ground out.

He raised his head, his eyes unfocused. "No. I'd have killed him myself if..." He trailed off.

I inclined my head, then turned and walked away. Ice formed around my heart as I fought to ignore Emine's heart-wrenching sobs as she skidded to her knees beside Mat. Guilt and grief weren't useful emotions. Not when an entire army of brother and match killing Bellicose were still alive.

A thought in the back of my head tried to break through and give me hope. But what little hope I had was an empty, hollowed out husk. It died with the two people I loved most. And I didn't even bother to tell either of them how I felt. I didn't deserve hope, just like I didn't deserve their love.

Because deep down, I wasn't hope and light. Maybe I once was before my innocence got robbed from me. Before I was beaten and abused. Locked in a cage and discarded. Lied to. Underestimated. I'd spent most of my life trying to be hope and light. But deep down, I knew the truth. I was nothing but an immense ball of pain and rage. And I would not pretend anymore.

"Perhaps projecting your pain onto the entire battlefield is not the best idea."

I met Quin's eyes.

They softened, and he inclined his head. "I see."

Except he didn't see. No one could. Because no one knew the vile shit I'd been suppressing my whole life.

"I do," Lily's brother, Alex, said from behind me.

I spun, ready to crush him. How dare he read my most private thoughts.

He raised his hands in a placating gesture. "I had a similar childhood and understand the rage and pain."

A traitorous tear streamed down my face. I swiped it away with my stub of a hand, nodded, and continued to hobble toward Drake, ignoring the paranormals who dropped to their knees as we passed.

"You are not healing." Quin made it sound like a passing comment, rather than concern.

"I don't care."

The battle had gone quiet, and no one said another word as we rounded the corner where I left Drake.

A cluster of dragons created a circle around an intersection. Chunks of house and fence lay scattered in every direction. A gouge in the various lawns stretched down the road. Beneath the cluster of dragons, I spotted a hint of bronze. Deva.

A few houses down, Drake lay in his human form, naked and broken. His side looked like hamburger and his hair was bloody. One arm was twisted the wrong way.

No dragons gathered around him.

I swung my head toward the ones surrounding Deva and opened my mouth to say something, but what was there to say? They'd rejected him his entire life, so why not continue the tradition in death?

More stupid, traitorous tears rolled down my face.

A second later, I realized my mistake in judgment. Glacintial and Bastien uncloaked themselves, along with the purple dragon and the red one Lily befriended. Several others gathered behind them. The First Razazia stood with Gorman a few feet away. My barrier was still intact, so they couldn't get to him.

I dissolved it, and Tracy and I converged on each side of Drake. Her eyes landed on my missing hand and widened before she schooled her face. "I'll give him a healing potion."

I fell to my knees and let tears of relief fall. "He's alive?"

She dumped a potion into his wound, then dribbled some in his mouth. "I mean, yeah. He probably would have lived even without my help, but I can't let him stay like this."

I swiped my sleeve across my face and set my good hand on his. He was so cold and had lost so much blood. I tried to activate healing magic, but it wouldn't work. I wasn't sure what Morten did to it. The urge to kill him all over again almost overwhelmed me.

Lily's hand landed on my shoulder. "It's okay. We'll figure it out."

"Lily's right." Tracy stood. "My dad's around here somewhere and he has stronger potions."

"Shall I get him?" Quin asked.

I realized they were expecting a response from me, so I nodded.

He disappeared.

"What if I lose them both?" I croaked. Though, only a moment earlier, I thought I *had* lost them both. I never once thought about what my life would look like without Mat. Let alone how I'd live with a broken bond. I didn't want to. I couldn't. Because if I did, I'd burn the world to the ground.

"He won't die." Bastien's voice was barely a murmur. "I've seen him with worse injuries and he survived. Back then, he didn't have healing magic or potions."

I stared at the pool of blood. It seemed bad to me. Anyone else would have been dead. Mat was dead. Sharp pain sliced through my chest, and I struggled to breathe. I ejected the thought and shoved the grief into a box. I'd deal with that later. "Okay."

Quin returned, dragging Tracy's dad with him.

Calvin scanned the area, then pulled a bubbling blue vial out of his pocket. "I see what you mean." He nudged me aside and poured the potion into Drake's mouth. Then he poured some into the wound on his side. "Give him a few minutes."

My eyes focused on the healers who raced around the corner towards us.

The God Cavil appeared. He stretched an arm around Lily's back and leaned forward to examine me. "Your power is fried."

"Yeah."

"Why?"

Lily elbowed him in the stomach. "Jen's hurting. Maybe wait until later to interrogate her."

He ran a hand through his perfect hair. "Very well."

"Morten stole it and used it to kill Mat." The words escaped before I could stop them.

"I see."

He didn't. No one could see, except maybe Alex. And only because the little shit wouldn't stay out of my head. I was too weak to make him, and Drake was...unconscious. I hoped.

A roar from across the street blew my eardrums out. Again. I didn't bother turning my head. I knew it was Deva's. Besides, not being able to hear the pity in everyone's voices for a few hours or days was okay with me.

I sat beside Drake for over an hour. After a few minutes, I grew too weak to hold everyone on their knees, so I released them. To say my whole body ached was an understatement. I was in so much pain, both physically and emotionally, that I fought to stay conscious as I lowered myself to my ass, leaned forward, and rested my head on Drake's shoulder.

My hearing hadn't returned, so I didn't have to listen to the fighting or the pity in everyone's voice. I was spiritually, mentally, and physically exhausted, and I couldn't deal with it. I also didn't have enough magic in me to defend myself, so was grateful for the friends and allies surrounding me. It was exactly the situation Mat warned me about when he told me I was too impulsive.

Except he was wrong about how I'd regret it. I was too numb to care.

Movement under my forehead caused me to lift my head.

Drake's eyes were open, and his mouth moving.

I tapped my ears and shook my head.

Tracy shoved a fresh potion into my hands. When I didn't drink it, she crossed her arms and raised an eyebrow.

I eyed the potion and considered throwing it as far and fast as I could. I deserved the pain after the hell I'd given Mat over the last couple of years. Except she'd go get it and shove it down my throat. Then I'd never hear the end of how childish and stupid my actions were. I took two big swigs and closed my eyes.

My hearing came back first, then my cuts and bruises knitted themselves together. The rest of my body still ached and sharp pains shot up my wrist and arm where my hand was missing. My head throbbed. The slicing pain of grief that dug deep into my soul would never heal.

Drake blinked. "I wondered if you'd take that potion."

"Tracy would force it down my throat if I didn't, and I don't want to lose anyone else today."

He pushed himself into a sitting position and winced. "I see."

Except he didn't. I blinked to keep the tears from falling, then stumbled to my feet. Mustering every ounce of power I could, I checked on the fight. Aside from me and my stupid, naïve ideas about taking the crown, the Bellicose were responsible for all the senseless death. And they deserved to die.

I scanned the dragons and members of my inner circle. My eyes landed on Deva. She perched in her dragon form a few feet away, soaked in blood and ash, her bronze eyes boring into me. Quin and Ara stood beside her left foot, their usual bored expressions intact. I refocused on Deva and inclined my head. "Kill them all and banish any demons the gargoyles missed. Then get this mess cleaned up before the humans find it."

She and her dragons launched into the air a second after Quin and Ara disappeared.

The bar with the gateway to the pocket was only a few blocks away, so I dragged myself in that direction, not caring if anyone followed.

Lily linked her arm with mine. "What about Mat?"

Another traitorous tear slid down my cheek. "I need to take him home. Will someone check on Emine and stay with her?"

I sensed a few people peel off seconds before Lily went fluid, dragging me with her toward the bar.

Chapter Thirty-Five

I HATED THE SWEET scent of flowers, I decided, as I sat on the roof of the palace and took a swig of whiskey. Below, a mountain of them in all shapes, sizes, and colors continued accumulating on the lawn just inside the palace gates. Cards containing condolences peeked out of some, while others wilted in the cold sun. Emine ripped the bottle from my newly regenerated hand. We'd been sitting in silence for a couple of hours, watching well-wishers come and go, and drinking.

George and Helen perched behind us in their griffin form, guarding us from harm and ourselves. It made them feel better to watch over us, even though they didn't need to. My healing magic had returned with a vengeance. It injected so much energy into my system, I couldn't even lie around and mope. So I grabbed a bottle and found Emine. Neither of us had said a word as we took turns emptying it.

I took the bottle back and took a gulp. It numbed the pain well enough, but if I didn't keep drinking, the stupid repaired magic would burn it from my system. My only solace was knowing Emine didn't have that problem.

She swiveled her head toward me. "It's not your fault."

A tear slid down my cheek, and I brushed it away. "It is. If I'd pulled my head out of my ass and figured my magic out sooner, I wouldn't have put him in that situation and he'd still be here. Hell, the entire war is my fault."

"Bullshit. He wanted to fight for the coalition. And you didn't tell him to stab that artifact. So get that shit out of your head, right now, chickie. It wasn't your fault."

I didn't speak. I didn't need to. The tears streaming down my face said it all. My stomach felt hollow and my heart hurt so bad it was hard to breathe. I created a handkerchief and mopped my face. I imagined the pain was much worse for Emine and she wasn't a blubbering idiot.

She snatched the bottle out of my hand. "He always knew he'd die protecting you. The jerk told me years ago." A single tear dripped from her face and landed on her arm.

I conjured another handkerchief and handed it to her. "What...." I swallowed the massive lump in my throat. "What are we going to do without him?"

She swiped it across her face and took a drink. "Did he ever tell you how we met?"

"No, but I have a memory of you being one of the assassins."

"No shit? Huh. I shadowed you two for nearly a month after I first saw you. Killed any of those assholes I came across. One night, I hid behind a dumpster in one of those massive human cities. Mat snuck up on me." She closed her eyes. "I didn't even hear him until he had me in his grip and a dagger to my throat."

A ragged laugh escaped me. "You two fell in love trying to kill each other behind a dumpster?" It seemed fitting somehow.

She held up the bottle. "No, no. Not love. It was way too early. But I knew. And he knew that I knew. And I knew that he knew that I knew. He knew too." She shook her head to clear it. "We cut a deal. I'd stay close and be backup. We spent time together when he wasn't busy pampering your sorry ass."

The ache in my heart surged. Mat wasn't pampering me but trying to piece me back together. "I wasn't spoiled back then."

"Coulda fooled me, the way he fawned over you. He *did* fool me. Never said a word about your issues. He wouldn't even tell me where you were going. The shithead. I could have cleared the way and got you here sooner."

"So you just followed us, not knowing why or where we were going?"

"Did you miss the part where I told you I knew he was my match?"

I thought of how Drake followed me around for all that time. "Okay."

"When you came across those two..." She jerked her thumb toward Helen and George. "They insisted I join you in their nest. I never left." Tears flowed down her cheeks. "We were talking about having a family."

I ignored my own tears as I put an arm around her and pulled her close. To my surprise, she rested her head on my shoulder. I pressed my face to the top of her head. "You're still my sister. You don't ever have to leave."

We stayed like that for a long time.

I stared at the steps leading toward the platform built to take us through the streets to Mat's final resting place. My feet wouldn't move toward it. Somehow, it felt like climbing those stairs would make his death so final. I wasn't ready.

"This is some bullshit right here," Lily's voice came from behind me.

"What is?" I didn't take my eyes off the steps.

Ting. Ting. "This!"

I tore my eyes away. If I wasn't so gutted, I would have laughed. Lily wore a long-sleeve black dress that fit her like a glove. The loose jacket over it accentuated the stereotypical vampire look. The only thing out of place was the crown on her head, which I assumed was the reason her eyes glowed and her fangs were out. A large black diamond in the center representing her position as heir to Ara's throne glittered in the sun. Bright purple amethysts running along the sides symbolized the throne of Ahl. "It suits you."

"There isn't a crown in the world that suits me."

I knew exactly how she felt. My own crown felt extra heavy on my head. I wasn't going to pile on, so I went back to staring at the stairs.

A few minutes later, movement behind me tore me out of my thoughts. I turned in time to see Emine's brother, Rayar, escort her down the marble stairs, Drake trailing behind. She wore a black bodysuit and a fur coat. Similar to Lily's, her crown had a white diamond in the center, representing the mages.

Drake wore a silver crown with a single amethyst in the center. It looked out of place against his rugged face.

Jonas rested his hand on Lily's shoulder. "Are you sure about this, Jenella?"

I turned my attention to him. He stood with Ann Marie and Alex. All three wore matching black-on-black suits. "You're Lily's family, so you're mine, too."

Ara and Quin appeared, both wearing solid black, including their crowns. Ara's crown was like Lily's, only bigger and all black, while Quin's was like Drake's, with a black stone.

Deva swept down from the sky, Bastien and Tracy behind her. She shifted as she landed, scanned us, then formed a long black dress. "I do so like the idea of crowns. Though it's rare for dragons to need them." A tall bronze one formed on her head.

Tracy screeched when a smaller one appeared in her hair.

Everyone I considered family was present. My eyes settled on the front floating cart that carried Mat's body. Everyone except the most important person.

I blinked back tears, took Drake's hand, and forced myself to climb the steps.

Sandwiched between Drake and Emine, my spine straight and my eyes dry as we moved through the city, I tried to look strong. A tough task when surrounded by palace guards, enforcers, and griffins. Several platforms floated behind us, carrying the remaining Firsts, the leadership council members, and their families.

Masses of paranormals lined the streets and took to the sky to greet us as we went. The nauseating floral scent filled the air as they tossed flowers in front of the cart carrying Mat. It was a tradition when royalty died. Verity, being the best assistant on the planet and a damn good friend, arranged the funeral but refused to ride with us. Instead, she and Titus went to the final location to make sure everything was perfect.

I appreciated her efforts, but riding on that cart, surrounded by a sea of people, I fought not to vomit. I'd never be able to smell flowers again without thinking of that wretched day.

"It's the Warrior Queen!" someone shouted from the crowd.

"I heard she took on an entire demon army on her own!"

"She saved my dad!"

"She saved us all!"

"No, dummy. The Consort helped."

"The Warrior Queen!"

I closed my eyes and tried to breathe. What a bunch of bullshit. All I did was get people killed, including my own brother.

It seemed to take forever to get to the large meadow as more and more paranormals followed behind our procession. The massive crowd got held back by the army, palace guards, griffins, and enforcers. I scanned it as the platform came to a stop. There were so many. The meadow was overflowing with paranormals. So many that some had to filter into the surrounding forest and perch in the trees.

I reached over and put my hand on Emine's as Bastien stepped onto a large black disc. It raised him above the crowd near where my brother's body rested.

Emine squeezed my hand, her grip so tight it was painful.

"Let me tell you about my friend, Mathias Belnaught Andreas Ahl...."

Bastien's eulogy was amazing and so out of character, it made me uncomfortable. The crowd laughed as he shared stories I'd never heard. When he got to how much Mat loved his family, I squeezed Emine's hand tighter as I fought not to turn into a spineless sobbing puddle.

At some point, Drake wrapped his arm around me, but I was so busy trying to make it through the stupid funeral, I didn't notice.

After Bastien said his last words, one by one, people took the platform and talked about my brother as a friend or boss. Not a single person called him the Bloody Prince, a nickname he hated. After the last speaker finished, a party of elementals moved in.

Emine let out a sob that broke my heart into pieces all over again. I flung my arms around her and pulled her to me. There was no stopping the flood of tears as they lowered the first person who ever cared about me into the ground.

Chapter Thirty-Six

"Jenella." Drake's voice broke me out of a trance.

It had been three weeks since Mat's death, and the pain hadn't eased. I was still so hollow and numb I wondered if I'd ever feel whole again. "Yes?"

His eyes searched my face, then lowered. "We have an update on the Bellicose and hybrids."

I didn't care about the Bellicose or the hybrids. Or about anything, really. Not even the piles of paperwork I'd spent every waking moment going over the last three weeks. Mat handled so much stuff that I hired five new staff members to sort through his projects. I put his assistant, Pablo, in charge of them. He and Verity worked well together but insisted I be aware of every little thing they did. I supposed it was the right way to do things. Or it would be if I could bring myself to care.

My eyes didn't quite meet Drake's. "Oh?"

"Nearly half of the hybrids have migrated to the new pocket."

"That's good."

"Many paranormals we fought weren't with them by choice, so Deva sorted them out and let many live. Ann Marie thinks they can be saved."

"Nice."

His eyes narrowed. "Stop it."

I blinked. "Stop what?"

"You're pretending to hear, but you're not listening."

"Am too."

"Are not."

"Am too."

He was around the desk and had me in his arms so fast I couldn't react. He swept out of my office onto his new balcony before I registered what was happening. I opened my mouth to protest as he launched into the sky.

Icy wind whipped my hair into my face as a talon wrapped around me. I slammed my fist on Drake's toe. Or was it a hand? "Let me go!"

No. His grip shifted so I couldn't fight. *Don't fight me, Jenella. I want to show you something, and you don't have a coat.*

My muscles relaxed. "You could have just told me."

You wouldn't have listened.

I closed my eyes. He was right. I pushed people away every chance I got. Even him. Didn't mean I had to give up without a fight, though. "How long will we be gone? I have work to do."

Moping around and staring at a blank screen for hours isn't working.

"I wasn't staring at a blank screen." Though I had done exactly that many times while trying to work. I struggled without Mat there to guide me. That, the plethora of suppressed memories flooding my head, and the grief made me a little scatterbrained.

Drake squeezed me a little tighter.

My eyes fluttered open when the warmth disappeared. I sat up and stretched. The realization that I had slept for the first time in weeks caused me to pause.

A cup of coffee appeared in front of me. "Drink."

I took it and sipped, then examined our environment. I was on an antique sofa surrounded by a sea of marble. "Where are we?"

"My horde."

I wasn't sure what to expect in a dragon's horde, but what I saw surprised me. The room was average-sized and tastefully decorated with high-end antique furniture and paintings. A chunky corner shelf had some kind of stone tools safely protected behind dragon glass. Several spears hung on the far wall, ranging from primitive to modern. It looked like something an interior decorator came up with. "Oh."

He chuckled. "Don't sound so disappointed."

"I'm not. It's just..." I shrugged. "I expected a massive pile of gold, or maybe a cave packed so tight with stuff I couldn't walk through it."

"Did you?"

"Yeah. A tastefully decorated sitting room never even crossed my mind."

Drake stood and offered a hand. "Come. I'll give you a tour."

By the time we reached the third room, I concluded a dragon horde was merely a second home. Sure, there were priceless items everywhere, even some made of gold and silver. Jewels glittered in every corner, but were so tastefully placed that I wouldn't have noticed them if he hadn't pointed them out. Each room served a purpose. A sitting room, several spare bedrooms, an office, a family room, and a library containing ancient texts and scrolls. My palms itched to dive in and read them.

"There isn't a kitchen," Drake informed me. "There's no reason to have one because the area is so remote I can hunt."

"And conjure food."

"Yes. Though I rarely do unless I have a guest."

I bent down to get a better look at a pile of scrolls. "And how often do you have guests?"

"It's my horde."

"So, never."

"Ah. I see. I have never had a conventional guest here, no. But I have held many priceless hostages within it."

I spun toward him. "What do you mean, priceless hostages?"

Drake's shoulders shook as he laughed. "I don't take part in that practice anymore. But there was a time when it was the logical move when locked in negotiations."

"Human or paranormal?"

He reached up and booped my nose. "Both."

I strolled toward the door to the library and peered out at the stairs. "What's upstairs?"

"Bedrooms and a gigantic pile of gold." He wiggled his eyebrows.

I knew he was trying to distract me from my grief, and I appreciated it. But I couldn't ignore the overwhelming pang of guilt in my chest. It was the only thing that penetrated the crushing grief. I rubbed my temples. "I can't stop feeling awful."

Drake's arms wrapped around me, and he crushed me to his chest for the millionth time since I watched my brother die. He ran a hand down my back. "I didn't bring you here so you could ignore your feelings. You need to feel them so you can work through your issues."

"That's the problem. I feel too much." My voice was barely a croak.

"No, you don't. You suppress, compartmentalize, and then feel guilty when they surface. You need to work through them to heal." He stepped back and rubbed a thumb across my cheek. "I haven't ever lost someone as close to me as you were to Mathias, but I nursed Deva and Bastien through losses. I can do the same for you if you let me."

Because no one had ever bothered getting close to him except his family. Another ache settled in my heart. "I can't. I'm too dangerous."

"You can."

"What makes you think so?"

He tapped my chest. "Because I see what's in here." He tapped my forehead. "And in here. You believe you're broken to the point where all you have left is anger and pain. But you're not. You have love, joy, determination, and a sense of wonder like no one I've ever met."

I shook my head. "See, that's just it. I'm pretty sure I faked all those other emotions."

"You didn't. It only seems that way."

I swallowed the lump in my throat. He wanted to see the best in me. But I knew exactly what I felt, and it wasn't love and joy.

He put a finger under my chin and raised it until I met his eyes. "You've spent a lifetime shoving the anger and pain into any corner of your psyche.

Every blank space in your head is filled with them. Over time, they've festered. Now, the emotions are so big they tower over all the others. You need to release them. Feel them. Work through them. Even acknowledge what caused them. Only after you've cleaned them out can you begin to work through your grief."

The tears I thought dried up trickled down my face. "What if I can't?"

"You can."

"But what if..."

His mouth covered mine.

My whole body lit on fire as my pain and sorrow melted into pure lust. I pulled him closer and fell into the need as I deepened the kiss. I ran my hands up his T-shirt and over his perfectly formed muscles. When they quivered under my touch, I trailed my fingers over his sides and traced a scar on his back.

His hand ran up my side, leaving a trail of fire. He gripped my hip and pulled me closer with the other one.

My world spun out of control with every touch and every caress.

Drake lifted me off the floor, and I wrapped my legs around him. I kissed him down his neck as he walked. A deep groan rumbled through him when I bit the soft spot between his shoulder and neck.

He stumbled up the steps and through a doorway.

We landed on a bed in a tangle of limbs, and his mouth found mine again. My head spun out of control. And for a couple of hours, I forgot about everything.

"Well-played, Sir First," I mumbled into the side of his neck.

He ran a hand up my bare back, then back down, resting it on my hip. "What?"

"Don't pretend you didn't start that to shut me up."

My head bounced when he laughed. "Guilty as charged."

"Damn. Now, I need to figure out how to punish you. Being queen and all."

The rumble of his laughter that echoed through the room made me feel like maybe everything would be okay.

Chapter Thirty-Seven

Everything was not okay, I thought two weeks later as I destroyed yet another boulder with my sheer anger. Sweat trickled down my temple, and between my boobs as I slammed a life-sized dummy I called 'Jaques' onto the floor over and over until it and the rocks Drake dragged into the cave were dust.

A cave where it was impossible to ruin anything, and no one could get to us without wings and the ability to break strong wards. Then, they'd have to navigate some clever traps. Not having to suppress or hide my power felt freeing in a way I'd never known. But it wasn't helping. Not much, anyway.

Drake perched on the ledge above me in what I called his snuffy form. His ear flicked, and his koala-bear-like head turned toward me. After a few heartbeats, he returned to staring over the rugged terrain outside the cave. His horde was on the other side of the volcano, in a massive cave in the human world. The surrounding wards were almost identical to the ones around Mage Mountain, except they hid the volcano from human view and ejected paranormals who came close.

Three days after we disappeared, Tracy and Bastien showed up. Drake went out and talked to them, but I stayed behind. I didn't want to deal with their anger and pity. Apparently, he told Verity and his assistant Charlotte about his plans, but they didn't pass the information on.

I worried about them and thought about Emine often and even sent her a few texts. Her replies were as colorful as ever. It felt good to work out my aggressions where I couldn't hurt anyone. It felt even better to spend time alone with Drake. We talked for hours. Sometimes about ourselves, other times about nothing at all. We showered each other with attention, and he finally got around to courting me. We set aside a couple of hours after I took my aggressions out in the cave to contact Verity to go over business. It wasn't ideal, and I hated leaving her with my work. Again.

I stopped pummeling the Jaques dummy and conjured a towel to mop up the sweat, then moved to the mouth of the cave and lowered myself to the floor to watch the fat snowflakes fall on the other side of the dragon glass. I wasn't there a full minute before the blinding pain I'd spent a lifetime ignoring washed over me.

Drake launched off his perch, shifted into his human form, and sat beside me. He didn't say anything. He didn't need to. His presence was enough.

"It's getting better," I said after I wiped the last tear away. "At least, I think so. It doesn't feel as intense."

"Is it time to talk yet?"

I toyed with the end of my shirt. "Not yet."

He handed me a glass of water and a plate of chocolate. "Take your time."

I thanked him and downed the water before popping a piece of chocolate into my mouth. "We don't have the kind of time I need to heal. When we disappeared, I left a lot of stuff unfinished and in chaos. I need to get back."

He took my hand and kissed it. "Verity has things under control while you pulverize rocks. You have time."

I shook a piece of chocolate at him. "She's okay for now. Eventually, she'll come to her senses and hate me for it."

"I doubt it. She enjoys taking care of things."

I didn't want to talk about work. I knew Verity liked her job, but I still felt guilty for leaving her alone to deal with the mess we left in the human world. "Are you worried about my sanity?" The question popped out before I could stop it.

He threw his head back and laughed. "No. But you are. And that's the problem."

"Oh. I thought you were up there on that perch testing me."

He bent over and clutched his stomach as he laughed some more. "If there is one thing I will never do, it's test you."

I sat there stunned for a few seconds, then burst out laughing. "That was a dumb question." Especially since he could read my mind.

"Yes. But I'll give you a pass since you're working through some things."

I rubbed my stomach. No, Drake would never test me. Mat always did, and I somehow projected that onto Drake. Which gave me the ick. The last thing I needed was for him to take the daddy role in my life. The thought made me want to barf. "I do sometimes think I'm insane."

"You're not."

"But what if I am?"

"I'd tell you."

"What if you're insane, too? They say when you're crazy, you're the last one to know."

The laughter rumbling from him soothed my soul as he took the plate from me and dissipated it. "Go shower. I'm going to hunt."

A few days later, I had a breakthrough.

Instead of pulverizing rocks, I perched on one, opened my mouth, and started talking.

~ "I don't remember much about my parents. But I never got to be a kid."

~ "My mother would slap or shake me whenever I tried to play. Or had too much energy. Or couldn't focus."

~ "I asked Lily about her childhood, and her answer unlocked memories. I suppose I'll never be certain if they're accurate."

~ "Jaques wasn't the only cruel person in Castle Mahri, but he was the worst. He broke my wrists so many times they still ache sometimes, even though they're completely healed."

~ "I pace because I couldn't stand up in my cage. The simple gesture makes me feel free."

And on I went, pouring out all my trauma. When my throat went dry and my voice cut out, I went silent or cried. Then I talked some more. I babbled about how I regretted ever accusing Mat of trying to box me in. How I never even tried to understand him or his motivations until recently. The guilt over how strained our relationship became as I grew up sat heavily on my chest. And I regretted every second I'd been difficult and treated him so awful. How I resented his confidence and competence. I should have tried harder to understand his reasons for all the lies.

Then I cried some more.

Drake stayed perched on the ledge and focused on me the entire time, not making a sound. He didn't move a muscle until the relief from unloading everything turned to exhaustion, and my eyes drooped. Then, he transformed into his human form, carried me to bed, and held me.

The next morning, I found myself both millions of pounds lighter and exhausted. I couldn't stop crying, so I sipped some water and went back to bed.

I did the same the next day.

And the next.

When I woke three days PTD, or Post Trauma Dump, I thought about all the times Mat tried to force me to talk. I'd refused out of fear and shame. It was too late, and I'd never get that chance again. I showered under a natural hot spring running through the cave and dressed in clothes I'd conjured. I was improving at creation but still struggled to use the magic I'd absorbed from others. Except Mat's. My chest tightened as I padded down the hallway to an open door, where I sensed Drake.

I found him sitting on the floor, his back against the wall and his ankles crossed. The room was massive, though I couldn't tell you how big it was because it was packed with gold and jewels. The gold was in the form of bars, coins, nuggets, statues, and every other form. Small aisles ran through the room, wide enough for one person to walk. Massive tubs filled with polished gems were separated by type and filled in an entire row. Behind them, a long line of ancient statues of all different types lined the wall.

"If you came to apologize, don't."

I shuffled toward the barrels, picked up a bright red stone the size of my fist, and held it up to the light. Then set it down. "Wasn't going to." I was totally going to apologize. But with his words, I realized what an insult it would be, considering all he'd done for me. I picked up a small, square sapphire. "Is this how you deal with emotional stuff?"

"I don't remember ever smashing rocks, but yes. This is my safe space. Lissa warded it for me centuries ago and I've enhanced it over the years. It's one of the most secure places in the world."

He'd brought me to the one place where he felt safe. Fighting back tears, I concentrated on the jewels. "I'm gutted and lost and don't know where to go from here." I took a deep breath. "But I'm ready to go back and figure it out."

He climbed to his feet and pulled me into his arms. "Are you sure?"

"Yes. The ball of anger is gone. Or maybe it shrunk. But aside from the crushing grief, I feel better. And I need to check on the coalition."

He lifted my chin, pressed his lips to mine, and stepped back. "Very well." He swiped a hand toward a row of display cases. "Pick a piece of jewelry."

My eyebrows drew together. "No. I have a bunch of jewelry, and it's bad luck to take anything from a dragon's horde."

A small smile ghosted across his face. "Then it's a good thing I am not a dragon."

I crossed my arms. "I'm not falling for that again."

Drake's deep laugh made my stomach flutter. "It's tradition to gift a mate with one thing from our horde the first time they visit."

My eyes trailed down the long line of cabinets. What did I even like? Helen had always chosen my jewelry to match my outfit.

He took my hand and led me down the aisle. "I have an idea, but promise you'll tell me if you don't like it."

"I promise." The magical contract settled over me, and I flinched.

He stopped at a cabinet, swung it open, and scanned the items.

"Do you remember every single thing you have in here?"

"Yes. Dragons never forget our horde. If anyone touches them without my permission, I not only receive a vision of what they touched, but who they are."

My head turned back toward the gems I'd handled.

"You are my mate and, therefore, share the horde. Feel free to touch or take anything."

My head spun with the enormity of the gesture. "I love you." The words slipped out. I shifted my weight from one foot to the other. Not fully understanding dragon bonds, I doubted he cared about the words.

I was wrong.

He froze with his hand inside the cabinet. A tangled mess of emotions blew back at me through the bond. So many I couldn't sort them. Drake extracted a closed fist from the cabinet and stood. His beautiful green eyes searched mine. "Are you sure?"

My face heated. "Yes." My throat was so dry it was barely a whisper.

Pure joy enveloped me, and his face broke into an ear-to-ear smile. He held out his fist. "This came from your grandmother's realm. I brought it here because I was young and stupid and hoped to find a match soon." He shuttered. "It didn't take long to learn how foolish it was." He opened his palm to reveal a ring.

The metal was golden, with red streaks running through it. The ring was inlaid with a gem the precise shade of Drake's eyes. It also emanated a strong and foreign magic that felt like coming home.

I swallowed. "It's beautiful."

"I think the fates ensured I brought it to this realm for you. If you'll have it."

I nodded as a tear dripped down my cheek.

Drake placed the ring on my finger. He used his thumb to wipe the tear away. "I love you, too, Jenella."

Chapter Thirty-Eight

The palace was bustling as we landed near the family entrance. I flashed to the ground and craned my neck to see what had everyone worked up. I couldn't see anything, so I headed toward the door.

It swung open before I reached it, revealing the griffin patriarch in his usual form of a withered old man in a blue dress shirt and black slacks. George grinned from ear to ear. "Welcome home, Jenella."

I returned the smile. "Thanks, George. It's good to be home." It wasn't a lie. And I wondered what it meant as we made our way to our offices.

Verity and Drake's assistant, Charlotte, weren't at their desks. I wondered where they were as I swung open the door to my office. Several heads swung my way from the conference table. "What the hell is this?"

Lily sat at the head of the table, her hands folded, mischief in her eyes, a smirk on her face. "This is what you get for appointing me your heir."

It was Mat who appointed her. And adding her to the line of succession was the one order he had made while cursed that I left in place. I waved a hand. "You're my only living relative. Therefore, the only candidate." I ignored the ache that statement sent through my heart as I rounded the table and lowered myself into an empty chair between Quin and Bastien.

Drake drifted to the wall behind me and leaned against it to loom over everyone.

"So, what are we meeting about?"

"Nope," Verity said from my desk. "You don't get to disappear and then just waltz in and take over our meeting."

"You knew where we were." Drake sauntered around the table to peer over shoulders.

My entire advisory committee was present, along with a few people I never met. All hybrids. I rested an elbow on the table. "And it's my office."

He pointed at me. "Yes. And it's Jenella's office."

Quin sipped from a white bottle and grimaced. "One would think you would spend more time in it."

"Especially following a major battle with an unpredictable outcome," Razazia added. "Though I understand how the throes of passion can override logic."

I tried not to gag at the thought of Razazia's passion. "You're right. I should have been here, but I wasn't." When my mouth opened to explain, I hesitated. I didn't owe them an explanation. "So, who wants to fill me in?"

Quin's head turned in my direction, and he examined me for a long moment before inclining his head and going back into his vampire stupor.

Tracy launched out of her seat from the other side of Bastien, then yanked me out of mine and wrapped me in a hug. "I missed you so much. These people are nuts. I mean, not a single one of them can agree on anything, and the Leadership Council is getting restless. They won't listen to Verity, and it pisses her off. And that's a whole other story." She took a breath. "Are you okay?"

I blinked back tears as I squeezed her. I wondered if they'd ever stop falling. "No, not really. But I'm better. And I missed you, too." I stepped back. "It's time to get back to work." I scanned the faces in the room. "Where's Emine?"

"Gone," Verity said. "She packed up her stuff and disappeared."

Ara waved a hand. "Nonsense, dear. She is at the manor reserved for the mage leadership. She's hurting and needs some time."

I turned my attention to her. Ara hadn't been an advisor before the battle and I wondered why she was there. It didn't matter. I always went to Ara for advice, so it made sense to include her. "You've talked to Emine?"

"Yes. Daily."

I inclined my head and tried to ignore the stab of guilt from leaving her alone. Not that Drake gave me a choice in the matter. I made a mental note to check on her as soon as possible.

When the room stayed silent, I turned my attention to Lily. "So, what's going on?"

She leaned forward and rested her forearms on the table. "We hid most of our activities from the humans, but not all. The neighborhood we fought in is still a mess. Humans being unable to enter is a problem. I caught a cop studying the spell the other day."

The news hit me like a sledgehammer, and I had to remind myself that we planned for that. "How bad is it?"

"Bad," Ann Marie answered. "We hid the battle, but not the dragons, enforcers, and gargoyles who came to back us up. Hundreds of people witnessed them disappearing into our privacy spell and recorded them."

I kept my face neutral. "And our spies within the human government?"

"Silent."

Which meant they were lying low and playing along. It's how Mat trained them. "Then let's wait until their reports roll in before we decide on our next move. What's the status of the hybrid migration to the pockets?"

One of the hybrid leaders, whose name I couldn't remember, crossed his arms. "Only about a third of them have moved. Many think it's a trap."

"What steps have you taken to convince them?"

They shared a look, which said enough.

"I see."

"We're working on it, Your Grace," another hybrid said.

I raised an eyebrow. "Oh?" I stood. "Verity, will you email me the strategic relocation plan filed by the hybrid leadership?"

"Nonexistent," she said in a clipped tone.

"Right." I retook my chair and tapped the table. Legally, I couldn't order the individual leaders to take a course of action unless there was imminent danger. Though manipulating, cajoling, and intimidating were all perfectly fine. "I suppose if you don't mind humans killing and hunting your people, then that's on you. But I highly recommend you reconsider."

The man opened his mouth to argue, but Lily kicked him. Hard.

Jonas cleared his throat. "Right. Moving on. We've tallied our losses. The hybrids lost one thousand twenty-one people, and the pureblood army nearly double that. The Bellicose leadership is dead, and their forces either released from the dark magic or on the run. Roman still has spies on the ground, but they haven't spotted activity."

"Is their magic gone?"

"Yes."

"And the labs?"

"We found a few more, but they weren't active."

I inclined my head. "Activity within the pockets?"

"Exterminated, love." The same sadness that clouded my eyes reflected in Deva's as she spoke.

I scanned the faces at the table and realized it wasn't just us, but everyone. I blinked back more tears. "Bug Magic?" I croaked.

Tracy leaned forward. "The witches are working on it, but my dad says ninety percent is gone."

"What about more curses?"

"None found, but we are also still searching," Gorman the First answered. Another person I never asked to advise me.

"And the owner of that strange new magic?"

"Still unknown," Quin said.

I leaned back and crossed my arms. We needed to find the magic wielder, or we risked the uprising starting over. "Find this person. And don't tip them off. I want to learn what they're doing and why." It would make it easier to play offense should the person become an even bigger problem.

"Leaving stones unturned is not something I do."

I missed Quin. "Great. Update me on the stability of the various crowns."

Everyone exchanged looks, but no one spoke. Mat always handled monitoring the factions behind the scenes, so I didn't expect anyone else to take up the task, but I hoped someone would.

Lily burst out laughing. "Damn! You've changed." She swung toward Drake. "What did you do while you were gone, harvest backbones?"

My cheeks heated. "He helped me work through some stuff." Plus, Mat wasn't there to be the confident, deadly person, so I had to take up that mantle. I hated it.

Thankfully, Ara got the conversation back on track. "I can't speak for others, but my crown is secure."

Deva offered a predatory grin that sent chills down my spine. "As is mine."

"I am very secure in my position, as well," Olwen, the Snow Elf King, said. "Although Razazia is now in charge of the elves."

I turned my focus to Jonas.

He stared back in his calm, reasonable manner. But I could feel the deadly predator that lurked under the surface. After a few seconds, he lowered his gaze. "I am taking over the shifters."

The entire table fell silent.

Except Lily. She slammed a hand down on the table. "How the hell are you going to do that?"

Ann Marie put her hand over Jonas's. "We're moving back to Allure and appointing a new leader to take over the hybrids."

The three hybrid leaders puffed out their chests.

Jonas raised his hand. "Jenella rightly pointed out a power imbalance within the hybrids, so I've asked Dale O'Donnell and Darla Smith to take over."

The hybrid leaders exploded.

I didn't even raise a finger as I placed them back in their chairs and silenced them. A side effect of pounding rocks with my magic. Sort of. I'd practiced control in between the anger explosions because I didn't want Drake to have to clean up my messes. "Excellent choice. Verity, please invite one of them to become my advisor."

"Done." Her tone was icy.

Yeah, she was pissed at me. The next question was going to be tricky. I swallowed back bile and folded my hands on the table. "What are the political consequences of Mat's death?"

Everyone exchanged looks.

I lowered my eyes. "That bad, huh?"

"Mathias was a force," Ara explained. "He kept the coalition together by ensuring no one dared challenge you. Without him, I fear you may have leaders who test your authority."

My mouth went dry. I loved my brother's intimidating magic and knew he used it strategically. "Have there been any signs of these tests?"

"None, yet," Verity answered. "But we need a strategy to handle them."

I nodded. "Try to get a feel for your factions and find out what the consensus is. I need to know what's coming so we can stop being so reactive. Keep me updated on the human situation. Are the tech mages working on burying the story?"

"Yes," Charlotte answered from behind me. "I'm, uh, working on it."

"Great. Keep me posted. Tracy, have you gotten any updates about the status of the witches?"

"They're coming around. It'll take time."

"Perfect." I stood and headed to the door. "Then I'll leave you to your meeting."

I swept out of the room.

Drake shifted his weight, and I slid down his wing, skidded across the frozen pond, and landed with a 'poof' in a snowbank, laughing like a loon all the way.

I sat up and rubbed my stomach. It ached from laughing too hard. "Is this what you do for fun?"

From the other end of the pond, he dove on his belly and spun in wild circles, shifting into his human form right before we collided. He wrapped his arms around me, dragged me with him as he crashed into the snow. "It's winter. Playing in the snow is a requirement."

"It also gives you your adrenaline fix."

"Us. One day, you're going to admit you have the same addiction to danger."

"Nope. Not going to happen."

He smashed a handful of snow on my head. "Liar."

I flashed away, created a snowball, and chucked it at him. It nailed him in the chest.

He charged.

I raced across the pond, slipping and sliding while giggling like a child.

He caught up, tackled me, and somehow spun in mid-air and landed on his back with me on top.

We skidded across the ice, spinning and laughing all the way.

I climbed to my feet, pulled him with me, and tried to brush the snow off us.

He leaned down and gave me a gentle kiss.

I soaked up his warmth and closed my eyes. He was only playing in the snow because of my confession about never playing as a child, but I didn't care. I once worried he'd never find out my most important thing, so he could give it to me in the most dramatic way. A confession of love for dragons. But he had. And then he found a million little ways to give me other things I never knew I wanted or needed.

My heart surged with so much love and appreciation it overshadowed my crushing grief.

A throat cleared behind us. "Your Grace."

I spun to find Dale, the bartender, and new hybrid leader, at the edge of the frozen pond. I latched onto Drake's arm as I skidded in his direction. "It's Jen or Jenella. Either's fine with me."

Drake lifted me off the ice and placed me on the path before joining me.

Dale's hard eyes scanned our bundled-up, snow-covered bodies. "I see you're enjoying the weather."

"Yes. What can I do for you?"

"Your assistant sent me out here to interrupt you. On purpose." He rubbed his chin. "She's pissed at you."

"Yeah. She has been for months. That's what happens when you disappear at a vital time in coalition history and leave an assistant holding the bag."

His mouth opened, then clicked shut. He shook his head. "Right. Is there a place we can talk?"

I scanned the trees. A cloud of pixies huddled together in one, while a group of fairies filled another. A white dragon flew overhead and gazed down at us, followed by six griffins. "Sure."

I evaporated the snow from our clothes before we entered the palace and led Dale to the breakfast nook.

Helen burst through the kitchen door and placed hot chocolates in front of us. She patted me on the shoulder and left.

Dale watched her go. "You keep things awfully casual."

"Yep. Formalities make my teeth ache."

He blinked. "I like you. I didn't expect to. Even though Lily warned me how you had a way of drawing people in."

"Did she?"

A small smile formed on his face. "Among other things."

I waved a hand. "I don't want to know."

"No, you don't." His face grew serious. "Have you heard from your spies within the human government?"

My intuition screamed at me that whatever he planned to drop on us would be awful. "Not a word."

"I'm in contact with several hybrids. They confirmed the U.S. government is ramping up a secret program. They overheard a few things but lacked detail." He took a sip of hot chocolate. "They've known about us for years. My source said they have a program to incorporate us into their military and have actively recruited near some of the smaller pockets. A dragon kidnapping humans in Alabama caused them to alter their program to capture and study."

I closed my eyes and nodded. "Yeah. Not humans. They kidnapped me and my angry assistant. It's how we met. How bad is it?"

"Bad. They have several paranormals working with them who plan to go public."

Drake rested his elbow on the table. "How many?"

"I hoped you had that information. There are federal agents all over Boise. I ordered all hybrids to evacuate, but some went missing before I took charge. They may have moved away, but I doubt it. I'm certain the humans took them. We're monitoring the federal agencies, but it doesn't look like we'll be able to hide much longer."

We asked several more questions. When I couldn't think of anything else, I stood. "Thanks for the update."

He inclined his head.

I raced to my office and stopped at Verity's desk. "I need to talk to you."

She huffed as she stood and followed me. As soon as the door clicked shut, she crossed her arms. "Let me guess. You're leaving again."

"Not even close." I waved a hand. "You have a right to be pissed at me for as long as you want. I can't tell you how sorry I am. But in my defense, if Drake hadn't taken me away and helped me deal with some stuff, I probably would have exploded."

She shook a finger at me. "I understand taking a break from work. But there's no excuse for abandoning your grieving sister-in-law and all your friends without a word."

"Drake said he cleared it with you before we left."

"If you call blowing smoke out of his nose and saying, 'we'll be back when it's sorted,' clearing it with me, then yes. Are you aware how bad your disappearance hurt Emine?"

"No, it didn't. She said, and I quote, 'I can't tell you how relieved I was when you left, chickie. I thought for sure I'd have to put up with your shit at the worst time in my life. No way I had the patience for that.'"

Verity waved a hand. "All bullshit. She missed you."

"If you say so." She missed me, sure. But Emine did better when she could step away from people and reflect. And had I stayed, she'd absolutely have had to kick my ass into gear. "Drake and I had a long talk about how leaving hurt the people we love. It won't happen again."

She crossed her arms. "I'll believe it when I see it."

"Fair enough." I moved toward my desk. "The humans have some of our people and have for a while. They plan to go public."

Her gray eyes examined me for a long time. Then she nodded. "We better get busy."

The end (for now).

One More Thing

Thank you for sticking with this series. I cannot tell you how much I appreciate it.

If you haven't already done so, please take a moment to leave a few stars on Amazon.

Book 3.5, featuring Lily, is expected to be released in February. Book 4, Jenella's final book, should be released in April.

I'm also working on two more series. One features a pet supply shop owner named Addie, who stumbles into a world she didn't know existed and ends up changing it. The other is about a woman in her forties who sets out on a road trip and gets more than she bargained for. Addie's story is further along, so the first book will likely be released in the second half of next year.

Sign up for my newsletter at www.mlconklin.com to stay updated on upcoming releases.

Thank you to everyone who helped me with this book. The editors, proofreaders, beta readers, and ARC readers were all amazing to work with and continue to make me a better writer, one criticism at a time. The cover designers at getcovers.com did a great job bringing the world to the front with little information.

As always, a special thank you to my furry assistants, stress reducers, and the best roommates ever, Callie, Gracie, and Zorro. Without them, I'd get a lot more done, but it wouldn't be as fun.

Most of all, thank you all for the wonderful comments and support. I cannot tell you how much it means.

Cheers.
ML Conklin
Email: mlconklin@mlconklin.com
Here's my socials, if you're interested:
I'm most active on:

- Threads: https://www.threads.com/authormlconklin

- Facebook: https://www.facebook.com/author.mlconklin

- Instagram: https://www.instagram.com/authormlconklin

I also have accounts on:

- Bluesky: https://bsky.app/profile/authormlconklin.bsky.social

- TikTok: https://www.tiktok.com/@authormlconklin

- X (Twitter): https://www.twitter.com/authormlconklin

SERIES INFO